I0583181

GOWGWARTS

GOWGWARTS

and the Powers of the Crystal Stones

GOWGWARTS

and the Powers of the Crystal Stones

M.R. Livly

Text copyright © 2025 by M.R. Livly
Illustration copyright © 2025 by M.R. Livly
All rights reserved. Self-published by M.R. Livly

No part of this publication may be reproduced in whole or in
part, or stored in a retrieval system, or transmitted in any form or
by any means, electronic, mechanical, photocopying, recording, or
otherwise, without the prior written permission of the author. For
information regarding permission, contact:

mrlivly.com
gowgwarts.com
Info@gowgwarts.com

M.R. Livly
Gowgwarts and the Powers of the Crystal Stones by M.R. Livly.
This is a work of fantasy fiction. Emotions fiction. Game fiction.
Crystal stones fiction. Language fiction. Names, characters,
places, are the product of the author's imagination and are used
fictitiously.

Gowgwarts and the Powers of the Crystal Stones names, characters,
settings, fantasy World of the Emotions (Pherríland), Gowgwarts'
Bracelet and all related trademarks and indicia
are ™ and © M.R. Livly. All Rights Reserved.

Printed in the U.S.A.
First published November 3rd, 2025
Series *Gowgwarts*, volume #1
Jacket design and illustration by M.R. Livly

2 0 2 5 9 2 1 6 7 4

Library of Congress Cataloging-in-Publication Data is available.

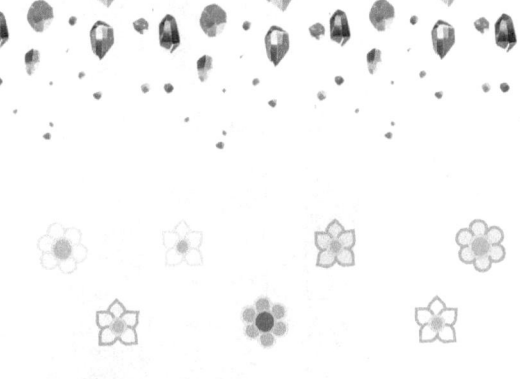

To thee seeking the echo of their own heart.

May the magic of love find its way to thou.

Unto them who dare to feel the storm within.

May thy path be illuminated with resilience in a world full of

possibilities and vivid emotions.

Magical Facts

The Light of the Sun

The Reflection of the Crying Heart

🔴 *The Reflection of the Crying Heart* reflects M.R. Livly's feelings at the time she wrote chapter 1.

⚪ *The Light of the Sun* was painted right after *The reflection of the Crying Heart*—a personal journey of healing for M.R. Livly as she wrote chapter 2.

🔴 Did you know M.R. Livly drew the sketches of the *Reïhng Game* and the *Gowgwarts' Bracelet*?

Reïhng Game Sketch by

M.R. Livly

CONTENTS

GOWGWARTS

and the Powers of the Crystal Stones

ONE

Everyone

"Oh no! A disruption! No, good," Master-Gowgwart-Love says, looking at the big screen in the Gowgwarts' Workshop.

"Who is it? I heard you from my mountïs," Master-Gowgwart-Care asks, after she appears next to Master-Gowgwart-Love in the Gowgwarts' Workshop.

"Oh dear! It's Everyone. I must go. I need to save Everyone," Master-Gowgwart-Love replies with urgency.

"Dear me, dark clouds of heaven. Do you need help?" Master-Gowgwart-Freedom asks, after he heard them speak as he finished teaching a Gowgwart-Freedom class.

"For now, I'll be fine. Everyone is looking for me. I must leave Pherrïland now to appear in the Kingdom of Bloomïeda," Master-Gowgwart-Love replies.

"It's urgent! Very urgent, it seems. Look! The stars are calling you, Master-Gowgwart-Love," Master-Gowgwart-Care says as she's looking at the new image on the screen.

"Uh, yes. I will meet with them soon," Master-Gowgwart-Love says, getting ready to leave.

"This is going to take time, Master-Gowgwart-Love," Master-Gowgwart-Trust says, after he appeared in the workshop—minutes after Master-Gowgwart-Freedom summoned him.

"I must hurry, otherwise, Master-Gowgwart-Pain and Master-Gowgwart-Depression will appear in her life," Master-Gowgwart-Love says.

"Mm, not thrilling. Master-Gowgwart-Depression and Master-Gowgwart-Pain together. My dear! Everyone can end up in Mazeïe Park," Master-Gowgwart-Happiness says, sparkling orange crystals.

"It's urgent. Everyone is looking down. Hurry. I'll take care of the workshop," Master-Gowgwart-Joy says with urgency, after the image of Everyone appeared on the screen again.

"Send us an alert if you need us. I'll be at Gleerwoo House," Master-Gowgwart-Peace says, disappearing from the workshop.

"Okay. I must go now," Master-Gowgwart-Love says.

Sparkling red crystals pop out from Master-Gowgwart-Love's ears and she disappears.

Will Master-Gowgwart-Love arrive on time to save Everyone from her suffering? For that, Everyone must hear the voice of Love, otherwise Master-Gowgwart-Love will not be able to appear in her life. Everyone needs willpower and strength to be brave to survive.

Will she be able to overcome the negative Gowgwarts? I don't know, or maybe . . . I do, but you will have to find out for yourself. I'm only giving you "the tea."

.   .   .

On a shimmering summer day—on an ordinary afternoon—Everyone sits on a red bench across from the lake in Spïeral Park, Brightmieda. Brightmieda is known as the city of the Garden of Joy for its large variety of flowers that bring joy to all who live and visit the Kingdom of Bloomïeda. It's also said that Master-Gowgwart-Joy gave magical powers to the Ūmieda flower—the symbol of the Kingdom of Bloomïeda—that blooms year-round in Brightmieda.

Since then, the Ūmieda flower has held a mysterious secret that only those who are curious enough to figure out the path to Freedom—to receive the reward hidden in the petals of the Ūmieda flower—will discover. This is why Brightmieda is renowned for its colorful magical joy-bringing flowers in the Garden of Joy.

Everyone is delighted enjoying her favorite ice cream—triple chocolate truffle in a waffle cone. Out of the blue, she sees an elderly couple walk by, holding hands, and smiling at each other. She stares at them and smiles, but at the same time, she feels sad. She wonders, "Will I ever be able to find Love?"

After the sun sets and as the moon rises, the stars begin to appear, illuminating the night sky with their bright light.

As Everyone continues to enjoy her ice cream—sitting across from the lake in Spïeral Park—The Big Bright Star appears among the HoneyBee Star Cluster—a beautiful open cluster of thousands of stars born from the same cloud of gas and dust.

All the stars, except for The Big Bright Star and the HoneyBee Star Cluster, begin to make noises that no one can understand.

The HoneyBee Stars ask, "Why does Everyone feel this way?"

The Big Bright Star replies, "She longs to find Love."

The HoneyBee Stars reply, "Love is within herself."

The Big Bright Star says, "For Everyone, romantic love is the only form of love that gives meaning to her life."

The HoneyBee Stars reply, "Love takes different forms."

The Big Bright Star replies, "I know, but that's what true love is to her. She doesn't know anything about self-love. To her love is love and nothing more."

The HoneyBee Stars reply, "Oh my stars! She's so wrong. Love starts with her."

The Big Bright Star replies, "Everyone doesn't know romantic love is only possible if the other person is ready to love too, for that, both must find love within themselves and on their own. And, if it's meant to be, at the right time, self-love will lead them to romantic love in the most unexpected ways they could have ever imagined in their lives, because they are ready to love and to receive love from someone else."

The HoneyBee Star Cluster groups in the shape of a heart with a happy face.

The HoneyBee Stars say, "Once she meets Love, everything will change forever."

.   .   .

Master-Gowgwart-Love appears in Brightmieda.

"Where are you, Everyone?" she asks.

From a not so far distance, Master-Gowgwart-Love sees the HoneyBee Stars giving her a sign, pointing towards Everyone, and immediately she flies to Spïeral Park's Lake.

Master-Gowgwart-Love whispers to Everyone, "I'm here, I've always been by your side. Always! Hear my voice, Everyone. I have come to save you. It's me, Love. Master-Gowgwart-Love."

Everyone continues to eat her melting ice cream; she can't hear the voice of Love . . . She's busy mind-wandering about finding love elsewhere.

"*Why can't I find love?* I want a love like that one," she thinks, as she looks at the elderly couple she saw earlier, fading away from the park. "*I want that kind of love.* A love that lasts a lifetime. Truε lovε."

"What else can I do so Everyone can hear my voice?" Master-Gowgwart-Love wonders.

Sparkling red crystals pop out from Master-Gowgwart-Love's ears and she disappears.

・ ・ ・

Everyone takes off her shoes and places them in the shoe rack that is right next to the entrance of her home. She turns on the lights in her living room and says, "I'm so tired, need to rest." She lets out a yawn, "aaahhh." Then, she walks to her room. She lies down on her back on the bed, completely flat. She begins to look around the room and suddenly sees the portrait above the back of her bed and says, "There, yeo will travel to Neephis, the Kingdom of Neephiun, where fairy tales come true." She sits on the bed crossing her legs. "Why didn't I think of that before?" she thinks. Then, she points to the portrait with her right hand and says, "There! There is where yeo, yeo need to go. I'm most certain, I will find love there. Tagrascïe portrait! You've made my night! I'll finally find love in the Kingdom of Neephiun. Tonight, I'll sleep like a princess of a fairytale storyline. Or like a real one—Princess Everyone."

Everyone begins to plan her trip to Neephis, the Kingdom of Neephiun and a week later, it's the day of the trip.

"I packed my suitcase, my place is clean, and I have my keys. I just have to turn off the lights and take my suitcase outside. Oh, and I have to say adïour to Hïuramïur," she says.

Everyone walks to her room, she says, "There you are. Don't miss me too much. I'll be back soon! Hopefully, I don't return alone. Wish me luck, Hïuramïur, adïour."

Everyone turns off the lights, takes her blue suitcase outside, and closes the door behind her. She says, "See ya! Later, Kingdom of Bloomïeda, I'm gonna find love somewhere else."

She knows the journey to find love isn't easy, but she dreams about it anyway. She's excited for her new adventure to find love.

I wish you luck, Everyone!

. . .

After a four-hour flight to the Kingdom of Neephiun, and a forty-minute drive to her new place in Neephis City, she's arrived to find love, filled with hope and ready for a new adventure.

The Kingdom of Neephiun is ready for you, Everyone.

After settling in, her obsession to find love led her to visit the Neephis Library—the most famous library in The Six Kingdoms—almost every day.

"In my search for love, I've read and read so many books and yet I can't find the answers to what I'm looking for. I've read, really, almost every book about romantic love here, where the prince meets his princess, and they live happily ever after. I want that. In fact, I long for that. I really, really, really do long for that kind of fairytale. That's why yeo traveled all the way from the Kingdom of Bloomïeda to the kingdom where the magic happens. It's what truly makes this kingdom so famous and magical among The Six Kingdoms. That's what this Kingdom is truly known for—its magical enchantment," she thinks, holding a book in her hands in the Neephis Library as she looks in the romance book section on the second floor.

. . .

Everyone opens her eyes to see the image of a couple holding hands. She realizes that she's sitting with a book right in her face and immediately, she removes the book off her face. She speaks, "Ohh, heavens of The Six Kingdoms, I am in the Neephis Library!"

Then, she yawns, "Aaahh." She rubs her eyes with both hands and gets up. She speaks, "I see colors coming from downstairs. I can also hear the song of colors. Hmm? How strange!"

Everyone says, "I'm not alone. Definitely not, because it looks like someone is downstairs. I was so tired that I didn't even realize I fell asleep while reading [looks at the book on her desk], *The Light of Love*. Oh wow, it's so late," she says, checking the time on her phone. "That's absolutely not the librarian. I can't believe he didn't notice me sitting here on the second floor before he went home. He probably locked me in here with who knows—a stranger. I have to be quiet, I don't know who's downstairs. I think, I'd better go check it out."

.   .   .

As she walks down the stairs, the colors intensify, and finally, Everyone can see what they are.

Everyone gasps. "Whoa! Whoa! Ohh . . .! A glowing owl. Ohh, whoa. It's you! The one singing 'Colors.' Am I dreaming? I must be. Is this for real?" she whispers, her voice barely audible.

Everyone pinches her arm to see if she's awake or dreaming. She screams, "OUCH! Guess what? I'm not dreaming. This is real!"

"Heïjour, Everyone, I have been waiting for you," the glowing owl says with a calm voice.

Everyone, scared by the strange glowing owl, takes a few steps back up the stairs. She says, "Don't come near me. Yeo don't know who you are."

In a calm voice, the glowing owl says, "Don't fear, Everyone, I am wisdom, my name is Neephoos."

Everyone says, "Neephoos? I came here seeking knowledge to find love, and instead yeo find wisdom! I guess . . . no matter how many romantic books yeo read; yeo won't find love. Yeo feel empty, sad, lonely, it's like all the characters in the books I read could find love except me. I wonder if there's something wrong with me. You are so colorful and bright. Can you give me the answers I'm looking for?" she asks.

"*Usics*. I'm colorful and bright, but yeo don't have the answers for what you're looking for in the books you're reading here at the Neephis Library. Don't give up. Instead, go back home and spend some time exploring yourself in a deeper way. Nothing is wrong with you; you're just searching for Love in the wrong place; everything you need to know is within you," Neephoos says with a calm voice flying away from the stairs.

Everyone, angry and disappointed, suddenly raises the tone of her voice. "This is so absurd," she says, opening her arms frustrated as she walks down the stairs speaking her mind. "How can you be wisdom, huh? And, how can everything I need to know to find love be within me?" she asks.

Neephoos opens his wings delicately, illuminating the library with his diverse spring colors.

Neephoos says, "My colors can be confusing because of the beauty of their resemblance, yet the answer to find Love is within you and only you, Everyone."

Neephoos flies back to the stairs, stopping at the center of the first red step of the vintage wooden stairs of the Neephis Library.

Everyone walks to the stairs where Neephoos is, she says, "I don't understand why yeo came all the way here for nothing! For a moment, yeo really thought you truly had all the answers. You are wisdom! You're beyond knowledge, yet you can't help me."

"You're here because, maybe, you need to be. Love is more than just romantic love. True love begins with you. It's an individual journey, Everyone. Keep going and you'll find it. And once you do, you'll understand the difference between what you want and what you need. You will see," Neephoos says.

Everyone replies, "Maybe, you're right." She sighs.

Neephoos says, "One thing will lead you to the other. Trust, but first, you'll need to create harmony among the Gowgwarts (your emotions). And then, you will realize that it's not the end but a new beginning. In your search for Love, you must have courage to be strong and brave, to face what lies ahead."

.   .   .

Pherriland, Gowgwarts' Workshop.

"She's in the Neephis Library talking with Neephoos," Master-Gowgwart-Love says.

"Oh, that's good! What are you waiting for Master-Gowgwart-Love? This can be a good time for you to appear before it's too late for Everyone," Master-Gowgwart-Care replies.

"Yes, Neephoos is trying to warn her about negative emotions. The problem is, she doesn't remember that I exist. She thinks he's talking about a different kind of love, not me," Master-Gowgwart-Love replies.

"In that case . . . give her a sign. She might notice you," Master-Gowgwart-Care replies.

"That's a good idea," Master-Gowgwart-Love nods, agreeing.

Sparkling red crystals pop out from Master-Gowgwart-Love's ears, and she disappears.

.   .   .

Neephis Library, Kingdom of Neephiun.

Master-Gowgwart-Love appears.

She spreads her wings around Everyone. "I surround you," she whispers, "I'm in every inch of you. Through and through. Feel me." Master-Gowgwart-Love moves away and blows towards Neephoos and Everyone.

Neephoos sees Master-Gowgwart-Love but pretends he can only feel the wind. He says, "What is this wind yeo feel? Do you feel it, Everyone? Yeo think it's Love."

Everyone says, "I feel something. It's like the breeze of a cherry blossom tree during spring season in Spïeral Park. Like a gentle wind that brings hope. Maybe you're right, Neephoos, and it's love. Yeo guess . . . I'm not gonna find love here. Perhaps, I should go back home. Yeo must be persistent and not abandon my search for love."

In a hurry, Everyone says, "Thanks for sharing your wisdom, Neephoos. *Adïour. Tagrascïe.*"

While fading away, Neephoos says, "Love yourself and then love . . . Adïour, Everyone."

While the sunrise brings light to a new day, Master-Gowgwart-Love flies away.

. . .

After Everyone met with Neephoos, she stopped going to the Neephis Library. Instead, Everyone began to make arrangements to return to the Kingdom of Bloomïeda. A week later, she had finished packing all her belongings into her blue suitcase and was ready to travel back to the city of the Garden of Joy.

Everyone thought a trip to the Kingdom of Neephiun was the right decision to find love, but after meeting with Neephoos in the Neephis Library, she realized that spending time with herself is all she needs and that, maybe . . . Love isn't so far from home.

. . .

Pherrïland, Gowgwarts' Workshop.

Master-Gowgwart-Love says to Master-Gowgwart-Care, "It's already been six months since Everyone returned home from her adventure in the Kingdom of Neephiun." She's looking at the big screen as she speaks.

"Forsooth. We can see it on the screen! Even the leaves have already begun to fall from the trees in the city of the Garden of Joy," Master-Gowgwart-Care replies.

"Something isn't sinking with her emotions . . . And that's not good. I wonder what it is. Hmm? Are you checking her emotions?" Master-Gowgwart-Trust asks.

Master-Gowgwart-Love replies, "Oh dear, you're right. It isn't good." She shakes her head. "I already received two warnings from Master-Gowgwart-Pain and Master-Gowgwart-Depression. She is going to need you."

"I agree with you. Let's hope she remembers me and you too because she needs you," Master-Gowgwart-Trust says.

"And me too," Master-Gowgwart-Care says.

.   .   .

Brightmieda, Kingdom of Bloomïeda.

Everyone untangles herself from the white sheets and blanket, stretching her arms over her head, touching her human-sized plush white stuffed animal, Hïuramïur, next to her on the bed, letting a big yawn escape from between her lips.

"Aaahhh. Everything white . . . White brings me peace, it calms me. Right, Hïuramïur? Heïjour to me and heïjour to you! It's time to weigh myself on the scale, shower, brush my teeth, and look pretty," she says.

Everyone puts on a linen purple dress with satin collar and her favorite shoes—custom white sandals with pink and purple crystals. Then, she looks in the mirror (in her living room) and says, "I love to dress-up. It makes me feel so much better and happier."

Everyone blows a kiss to her reflection in the mirror. "Mwah! Time for ppucceïe and üossant," she says.

Everyone sits on the white couch across from the small table in the living room to have breakfast. "I'm determined to find love," she thinks as she drinks ppucceïe. "Despite my conversation with Neephoos, I believe that if I do as the characters in all the books I read at the Neephis Library did, I'm gonna find love." Everyone drinks ppucceïe again. "I'm gonna get myself out there. I can't stay here waiting for love to find me," she thinks as she eats üossant.

.   .   .

Pherrïland, Gowgwarts' Workshop.

"Oh, no! She doesn't know how to be alone with herself. She needs you to embrace her freedom," Master-Gowgwart-Care says.

Master-Gowgwart-Trust says, "That's not the kind of love she needs. I agree. She must be confident on her own. Ahh, Love."

Master-Gowgwart-Love replies, "I know. In her devotion to find me, she's going to start dating again, and in the end, it will only lead her to the path of Pain."

Master-Gowgwart-Care says, "Instead of continuing to spend time exploring herself profoundly, she's going to do the opposite."

"She doesn't understand that I am free, that what I give is not selfish," Master-Gowgwart-Love replies.

"When two people come together to share their lives, they still want to be themselves, without having to give up the life they had before they met," Master-Gowgwart-Trust says.

"She's confused by the standards she believes society demands for a relationship," Master-Gowgwart-Care says.

Master-Gowgwart-Trust says, "She doesn't know that people don't have to pretend to be someone they're not, just to be loved by the other person, and that it's absolutely okay to like different things and to do things differently, unless they like the same things and do them the same way."

Master-Gowgwart-Love replies, "Surely, if they don't, it's okay too, because when I join two people, it's to embrace them and also to make them better, not the other way around."

"The gist of it is, to love the other person as they are, without trying to change them into the ideal person you think they should be, in order to love them, right?" Master-Gowgwart-Trust says.

Master-Gowgwart-Care replies, "I agree, Trust. She needs to understand who you are, Master-Gowgwart-Love."

"I agree with you. Sometimes, when you don't know me, you can mistake who I am. And that's what's happening to Everyone," Master-Gowgwart-Love replies.

"Forsooth! A person should change because they want to or because it's necessary for their own personal growth. Even if the reason is to live a better life with the person they choose to; not to please others or to be loved by someone else," Master-Gowgwart-Trust replies.

. . .

Six months after in Brightmieda, the city of the Garden of Joy, Kingdom of Bloomïeda.

In her need to feel loved, she has engaged in relationships with guys who are also looking for love; what love can you receive from someone who hasn't met Love yet?

She's single again.

Dawn brings a new day, and Everyone leaves home for a solo walk in Spïeral Park. After a couple of hours of wandering around, walking in the park, lying on the grass and being in her head, she gets up and starts walking back home. As she leaves the park, she sees a food truck. She's hungry, so she stops to order a hot-üossant.

"It's already afternoon; should I wait until I get home to eat, or should I go back inside the park to find a place where I am alone to enjoy this hot-üossant?" she thinks—looking at her surroundings, trying to decide what to do. "Hmmm. I guess I'll go back inside."

. . .

"I can't stop thinking, why? Why didn't things work out in my past relationships? I have done everything, yeo think, I should have done. Yet there wasn't love for me in those relationships. I can't find love," she thinks, sitting on a bench.

Minutes later, grey clouds gathered in the sky, concealing the sun's light. Everyone says, "Oh, no, no. It began to rain." She looks around and says, "I can't find anywhere to shelter from the rain. I'm in the middle of the park, and there are only trees, grass, and rocks. Of course, *excellent choice, Everyone.*" She shakes her head, rolling her eyes.

The rain doesn't last long. The grey clouds disappear, and the sunlight comes out again.

With excitement, Everyone says, "A rainbow! Oh wow, it's the most beautiful rainbow I have ever seen in the city of the Garden of Joy. In the end it was *an excellent choice.*" She believes the rainbow is a sign from love. She forgets how wet she is from the rain and starts walking towards the rainbow.

Master-Gowgwart-Love appears flying in the park.

Hoping Everyone will notice her presence, Master-Gowgwart-Love follows Everyone and then, begins circling around her.

Despite that, Everyone cannot notice the presence of Master-Gowgwart-Love—she is too busy mind-wandering.

"Where is Love?"—Everyone thinks as she's walking towards the rainbow—"I know the rainbow will lead me to Love."

"I am here; I have always been by your side. Hear my voice, Everyone. Open your eyes and you will see me," Master-Gowgwart-Love whispers.

"No—please—don't. The rainbow is gone! Yeo guess . . . I will never find Love," Everyone mutters in disappointment after missing the rainbow.

Master-Gowgwart-Love disappears.

. . .

Everyone finds a flower garden.

Not knowing what is hiding in the garden, she doesn't hesitate to sneak a peek. "Oh whoa! So beautiful! It's astounding!" she says gasping, then smiling.

Everyone enters the garden, then she bends down to greet the flowers. She says, "Daisy wildflowers!"

Amazed by how flawless the daisies seem to her—with their perfect petals—she says, "They're so beautiful and there are so many of them."

Be careful, Everyone, because you're about to meet your feelings.

"I think . . . I see someone, but yeo don't see anyone. What is that glowing and growing thing?" Everyone asks as she stands still staring at a deformed rose in the back of the garden.

"Now it's taking the shape of a giant pink or green roseïey," she thinks, watching the deformed rose shift shape.

"At least, that's what it looks like to me. I can't see the color clearly. What are you? Is it Love? It looks misshapen, not exactly a roseïey. It can't be, *gïocs*, I haven't found Love yet; yeo think . . . Love is different. Also, this green/pink giant thing, whatever it is, has lots of prickles and is missing petals; to me, Love is beautiful, bright, and complete. This is not what I hoped for," she says.

With doubts, she turns around, ready to leave the garden, but before leaving, she hears a voice . . .

"Hello, Everyone, did you think I was Love?"

"Sorry to confuse you but I am Pain. Master-Gowgwart-Pain. Sometimes in your search for Love you can meet . . . me. On various occasions, I may take a different form . . ."

—Any resemblance the misshapen rose had to pink changed completely to green.

Everyone immediately turns around, quickly covering her eyes as the intense green color from Master-Gowgwart-Pain begins to cover the garden.

Master-Gowgwart-Pain's green glow quickly spreads, covering Everyone and the entire garden of daisies with bright, shimmering, sparkly green crystals.

"At first, you can mistake me for Love, but when you realize I am not Love, everything becomes very, really $green$, very green I'd say. Yet, I become the best friend of those who aren't brave enough to keep searching for Love," Master-Gowgwart-Pain says.

"People don't get it; I'm unpleasant with missing petals, ugh, how can anyone think I can be Love? Tell me! How? Argh!!" Master-Gowgwart-Pain's glow briefly intensifies, and his prickles begin to enlarge.

Master-Gowgwart-Pain speaks, "Overestimated at times. Am I not? I am supposed to be temporary—not permanent. Look at my prickles, look at them! Nobody wants me to wound them or to disconnect them from the world while experiencing loss of self. Tell me! Who wants that? Who? But, if you want to stay here, you are welcome in my garden."

He mutters, "I don't have anything good to offer you, really, unless you have the Gowgwarts' Bracelet."

"What?" Everyone asks, "(I couldn't hear the last part)."

Master-Gowgwart-Pain says, "I said that all I have to offer you, really, is sadness, anger (unexpressed), shame, and guilt (anxiety too). You don't have to stay here with me; I already have plenty of guests. Look at all those little daisies."

Her eyes darted to the daisy wildflowers whose yellow center with white petals began to glow after what Master-Gowgwart-Pain said. She thinks, "What are you trying to tell me? Are you trying to warn me about Master-Gowgwart-Pain? I wish to know what you mean. Is it good or is it bad?"

The daisies are trying to warn you that Master-Gowgwart-Pain isn't good unless you can see the goodness in him. I recommend that you leave the garden.

"They were you once and over time they turned into me, but prettier, 'I guess.' I told them the same thing I told you, but they chose to stay," Master-Gowgwart-Pain says.

Everyone cries, "The daisies have stopped glowing! No! Don't let your light go out. Let it shine. Your light is meant to be seen, not hidden. Your light is beautiful, don't dim your brilliance."

"It's already late for them, but not for you. Believe me, there's clarity after I am gone, but first you need to heal. And that will only happen when you meet Master-Gowgwart-Love. Your process will be slow . . . until you no longer remember me," Master-Gowgwart-Pain says with a sharp voice as his green glow begins to dim, and the day turns to night.

She seems confused by what Master-Gowgwart-Pain said. She replies, "There's something about you that makes you so addictive, even though you're not good for me. I wanna leave you but I can't. Maybe it's your color or the way I feel with you. I can't explain it. I am so comfortable here. It feels so good yet so bad. You get me, but you don't. Maybe . . . that's why you have so many guests. You can be easily confused with Love because at first you offer comfort until you reveal your true self."

Master-Gowgwart-Pain replies, "I am what you long for. You love me. I am beautiful, am I not?" He cackles and then says, "You love my unpleasant pain, be my guest."

Master-Gowgwart-Pain sings, "Be My Guest."

Everyone cries, "You tricked me! I fell into your trap! I entered the garden for the beautiful daisy wildflowers, not you. Perhaps . . . it's the way you speak. I guess you're right, you're unpleasant, with prickles and missing petals. Nobody wants to be in pain. I can't stay here. Yeo don't want what you're offering me. I think the only thing you said that's true is that I need to find Love so yeo can heal and forget about you. Adïour, Master-Gowgwart-Pain."

Everyone, without looking back, walks confidently out of the Garden of Pain.

.   .   .

Meanwhile, outside of the Garden of Pain . . .

While Everyone is with Master-Gowgwart-Pain, red and pink crystals pop out in the air and Master-Gowgwart-Love appears with Master-Gowgwart-Care.

"She's finally remembered you," Master-Gowgwart-Care says.

Master-Gowgwart-Love replies, "Yes! She realized that what she needs is me, not romantic love."

"That's good. She'll soon recognize you," Master-Gowgwart-Care says.

Master-Gowgwart-Love replies, "I hope so, I don't want her to end up meeting Master-Gowgwart-Depression."

"Look! She's walking away from the Garden of Pain!" Master-Gowgwart-Care says.

With a glowing smile, Master-Gowgwart-Love watches her say goodbye to Master-Gowgwart-Pain and then, she fades away with Master-Gowgwart-Care.

.   .   .

A few weeks later . . . after meeting Master-Gowgwart-Pain, as part of her daily routine, Everyone runs in Spïeral Park.

Master-Gowgwart-Love appears in the park.

Hoping this time she feels her presence, Master-Gowgwart-Love blows towards Everyone.

Everyone says, "Oh, it's very windy this morning. It must be the new season."

Master-Gowgwart-Love wonders, "How can I make Everyone aware of my presence? Oh, I know."

Master-Gowgwart-Love not just blows a gentle breeze, but this time the breeze also carries cherry blossoms towards Everyone.

Everyone feels the gentle breeze hugging her, as she sees the cherry blossoms pass by.

Everyone stops to wonder. "What is this gentle wind yeo feel? Is it Love sending me a sign? *Giöcs*, it can't be. Cherry blossoms? Deepïery thögh! It's springtime, of course! So beautiful! It must be Love."

She begins to see and feel the signs of Master-Gowgwart-Love. *So close, yet so far from finding Love.*

.   .   .

Cheerfully, Everyone says, "It's Summer Hïuramïur! I am so excited to meet my friends later today at the Kosmïes concert—my favorite band. Just what I need to escape from Pain. I am trying to forget, but it's not easy. What do you think about this outfit? Right! You can't talk, but yeo know you like it too. I wish you could talk. You're, like, my absolute best friend. The bestest of all my friends. My white plushie Hïuramïur."

Hïuramïur sits on the white couch of her living room.

Everyone says, "Don't miss me too much, Hïuramïur. Okay? Here, this necklace looks good on you. I wish I could bring you too. If only you were alive . . . Oh, the things that I wish for. I only wish."

.   .   .

Everyone arrives at the concert around 6:15 p.m. It's loud and crowded, but she doesn't care. She's ready to have a blast singing and dancing all her favorite songs with her friends, Maiephis, Luseïe, Ufaïa, Rayïq, and Geossuth.

Everyone says, "Heïjour, 'forees!' Look who's here. I am so excited for the concert." A wide grin on her face.

Luseïe says, "We've been waiting for you. The band is about to start performing soon."

Ufaïa says, "Heïjour! Heïjour! Let's have fun tonight."

Rayïq says, "The sweetest of all, always looking pretty."

Geossuth says, "Deepïery thögh, you made it right on time. The band is about to start."

Maiephis says, "Cheers! What matters is that you're here. Let's have fun."

Excited, Everyone screams, "Whoo hoo! It's Kosmïes! I can't believe it. I love you, Kosmïes! I love you!" She claps while Kosmïes is on stage and then begins to sing with her friends and the echo of the crowd in the Phoenïx Stadium.

At around 10:00 p.m., the concert is over, and as her friends,

Maiephis, Luseïe, Ufaïa, Rayïq, and Geossuth say goodbye to her, she waves goodbye to them.

While they go in different directions, she walks back home.

. . .

Everyone looks at the full moon. Distracted, she trips over a stick, landing with a dull thud. "Aaaah!" she shrieks. As she tries to get up, she sees a mirror leaning against a one-hundred-year-old tree. "Ooh, a mirror! How strange," she says.

Everyone starts to look at herself in the mirror, not liking what she sees. She cries softly staring at her reflection, then starts talking, drying her tears with her hands. "This is awful," she mutters with a thick voice, complaining. She pauses and looks at her surroundings. The street is empty, and the park is in full solitude. It's only her and the old tree.

Everyone continues, "I can't do this anymore. This journey is so tiring. Every time, I think I found Love; I come to realize that Love is not Love. I don't know what Love is anymore. I don't want to keep going. It's a waste of time. An illusion that only exists in my mind. How can Neephoos say that Love is free? Love isn't for me. I'm trying to forget about Pain, but instead, yeo can't stop thinking about it. I feel trapped in a dark room with black walls where there's no exit. Life has no meaning anymore. I am a disappointment. How did I get here? How? What happened to me? Why can't I feel joyous and happy? Where is the light and why can't it reach me?" She looks around. She says, "It's getting even darker. Why are the branches of this tree spreading out around me? Wait, stop! What are you doing? Who's doing this? Why are you surrounding me?" she asks.

"Hello, Everyone. Do you feel trapped, unable to find Love? Aww!" he says sarcastically. "Do you feel like it's the end, and you cannot see beyond Pain? Stay here with me. Why keep going? I can give you what you need. With me, there are no rainbows, butterflies, or sunshine, but you won't be disappointed again. Don't believe in a fantasy of true love. It doesn't exist. You say you are tired, so rest here with me. In your search for Love, you have found wisdom, and it has served you no good, only bringing you Pain. Mwah ha ha!" His maliciously laughter echoed in the old tree.

Everyone, looking around, confused by the voice and the evil laughter, asks in fear, "Who? Who are you? And why? Why are you surrounding me?"

"Pain is supposed to be temporary, not permanent. But if you cannot forget him, I appear in your life. I am Depression. Master-Gowgwart-Depression!"

—Pause!

Prior to Everyone tripping over the stick, Master-Gowgwart-Depression took the form of the old tree. As a distraction to confuse Everyone, he also added the mirror and while Everyone cried and talked to her reflection, he spread his branches to surround her, just before he began to whisper.

—Go on.

"Depression!" Everyone gasps, a cold dread clawed her throat, her eyes widened.

"Yes! It's hard to find a way out unless you can see the sunlight that comes with the dawn and for that you must hear the voice of Master-Gowgwart-Love. And where is Love? WHERE IS LOVE? She abandoned you; there is no light for you. Don't you see I'm surrounding you? Love gave-up on you. Take what I give you. Stay here forever. Isn't it easier? Think about it. I'll make Pain go away. Like magic, there will be no more suffering, disappointment, and sadness. Make me part of you and I'll free you from Pain," he says.

Desperate, Everyone says, "Wait! There's so much uncertainty in everything you're saying. How could you, possibly, make Pain go away? You're lying. You're here, and I still feel the same. If you had come to free me from Pain, I shouldn't be feeling this way. Without strength to go on, as if everything weighed me down. You're only making me feel worse. Increasing my suffering. Since you arrived, I haven't had any strength. And it's not that I'm in physical pain; it's all in my mind. That's where I can't rest. It's like something beyond my control it's keeping me from going on. I'm feeling sad, mad, and disappointed because I can't find Love. I want to give-up, but yeo refuse to believe that Love gave-up on me. What about the signs? The wind and the cherry blossom petals? Neephoos believed the wind was a sign from Love. And so, do I. You don't want me to find Love. Do you? This must be a trap too. You're not good Master-Gowgwart-Depression. I refuse to accept what you're offering me. No matter how tired I am, I will keep going. I know Love is worth it. I feel it in me. I must find the courage and strength within me to be brave and strong to leave you."

"Yeah, yeah, yeah. You're right about one thing, I'm not good, not like this. I am good, I mean it," Master-Gowgwart-Depression replies.

"How can you be good?" Everyone asks.

"You'll only find out if you manage to escape me, so for now, thanks to your obsession with Pain, here I am. Now face me. No running!" Master-Gowgwart-Depression replies.

"But how? I only wanted to forget about Pain, not find you," Everyone replies.

After what Everyone said, Master-Gowgwart-Depression gets upset.

He groans, and then growling, he says, "Yet, you couldn't let him go, instead you gave me life. Now, you wonder how I can make Pain disappear." Master-Gowgwart-Depression pauses, takes a deep breath trying to calm himself. He sighs and then says, "Simple, I give people eternal rest. Do you remember the daisies planted in the Garden of Pain?" Master-Gowgwart-Depression asks.

"Uh-huh," Everyone, fearfully, replies.

Master-Gowgwart-Depression says, "It was me, Depression. I gave them eternal rest. I laid them to rest, and I intend to do just the same with you." He laughs mischievously.

Everyone replies, "You are bad. You are evil. You are trying to make me feel small and inferior, unable to leave you."

"Who cares? They loved Pain so much that I turned them into Pain. You are weak, you don't have the courage and the strength to escape. You love Pain. Admit it. You know you love Pain." Master-Gowgwart-Depression cackles.

"I don't love Pain! I don't! Enough! That's enough! AAAH!" She screams as she tries to untangle herself from the branches of the old tree. "I AM TIRED OF EVERYTHING!!! AAAAAH!!!" she screams from the depths of her being.

"Your suffering, and everything that comes with Pain, are the reason we met. You cannot even move. Look at you, this is where you belong. You're depressed . . . Try to escape if you can." Master-Gowgwart-Depression cackles.

Everyone needs a push. She doesn't know how to take the first step to leave Master-Gowgwart-Depression behind, so she faints.

Only with the power of Love, Everyone can break free from her reality.

Master-Gowgwart-Love appears around the branches of the old tree. She whispers, "Do not give up, Everyone. Everything you need is within you. Find strength and courage, because you, and only you, have the power to light the flame within your heart. It's the only way to hear my voice to give life to my powers."

Desperate because she is running out of time, while Everyone is weakening surrounded by Master-Gowgwart-Depression, Master-Gowgwart-Love shouts, "Don't give up, Everyone! Not now! Please wake up, Everyone! Stop searching. Open your eyes and look at me. I am here with you and for you. Look at the light of dawn that brings a new day. Hear my voice. I bring a new beginning for you. Like the sunset between day and night. Remember everything that makes you happy. Be brave, Everyone! Have courage! Be strong to start again. Once the darkness passes through, the sun will rise, and you will see the light of the sun embracing you as you are."

Slowly, she begins to hear the echo of the voice of Love—an ethereal whisper carrying a dreamy breeze.

Meanwhile, the mirror, and the old tree—Depression—begin to disappear, and the sunlight from the sunrise comes to Everyone.

—Pause!

While Master-Gowgwart-Love is still trying to save Everyone, Master-Gowgwart-Depression hides, upset with Master-Gowgwart-Love, because she appeared, right ere he was about to turn Everyone into a little daisy wildflower. And it became worse for him, when he noticed that Everyone was beginning to hear the voice of Master-Gowgwart-Love. All the little daisy wildflowers Master-Gowgwart-Depression planted in the Garden of Pain began to make noises in his mind, asking him to leave Everyone alone, until he couldn't take it anymore and vanished, as if by magic.

—Go on.

As Everyone lies on the ground, she wakes up, feeling the glare of the dawn sunlight directly on her face. She at once tries to cover her eyes because the sunlight is too bright. As she tries to get up, she realizes the mirror and the old tree are not there anymore. Then, she says, "It was a trap set by Depression! I don't know. Oh yes, Master-Gowgwart-Depression."

"Ugh."

"I knew it."

"I was right."

"I'm glad I didn't listen," Everyone says, standing up.

.   .   .

Everyone starts walking towards her house.

As she's passing by the park that's right before her place, she thinks, "Mmm. I should sit on that swing for a moment to process everything that's happened to me."

Everyone swings for a little bit while watching people passing by going in different directions and then stops to go home; suddenly, she notices the presence of a beautiful shiny white Gowgwart, with a sparkling purple amethyst star on her heart, red sparkling crystal feather wings and shiny red sparkling crystal ears where Everyone's feelings are cherished.

Master-Gowgwart-Love notices that she's hesitant to approach her, so with a gentle voice, she says, "Don't be frightened, it's me, Love. Master-Gowgwart-Love."

With wide-eyes and full of surprise, Everyone stares at Master-Gowgwart-Love flying in front of her. She can't hold back her tears and with overwhelming sobs, she says, "I see you and hear you Love.

Please forgive me for not hearing you before. I was blinded by the beliefs as a child my family taught me, the absence of my father, the rejections of my siblings; all of it combined got me where I am today. I always wanted to feel loved, included, and accepted by others. You know? I wanted to belong and in between, I forgot about me. Who I am as a person and what love truly is."

In a sweet, gentle voice, Master-Gowgwart-Love replies, "My dearest Everyone, no one can decide how you feel but you. I'll help you rediscover your inner power to help you heal. With me, you will find yourself again. Remember that love and acceptance begin with you and only you. Embrace yourself and remember that your true self is hidden within you."

Everyone replies, "Thank you for showing up. In my search for you, yeo lost clarity about what yeo was truly looking for. Now, I understand, I don't need any of that. I must forgive myself for not loving me before. It's never too late to start again."

Master-Gowgwart-Love replies, "Always remember, that I am part of you. With me, you also have—Joy, Care, Trust, Happiness, Peace, and Freedom. I am free, light, and peace. Remember, after the sun sets and as the moon rises, the stars will begin to appear in the sky, illuminating the night with their light, and I'll be there with you. I AM WORTH IT."

. . .

A year later, after meeting Master-Gowgwart-Love.

Master-Gowgwart-Love appears in Everyone's living room. She says, "Hello, Everyone!"

Everyone says, "Master-Gowgwart-Love! Joureïe!"

Master-Gowgwart-Love smiles and says, "There's someone I want you to meet. It's Master-Gowgwart-Care."

Everyone replies, "Aaah. Care . . .? Paccürs."

Sparkling pink crystals sparkle everywhere.

Master-Gowgwart-Care appears flying in the air.

"Hello, Master-Gowgwart-Care. You're so pink. Very pink, I'd say," she says, "(oh, a pink Gowgwart with sparkling pink crystal feather wings and shiny pink crystal ears)."

Master-Gowgwart-Care replies, "Hello Everyone, I have come to teach you how to take care of yourself in ways that will help you reconnect with your inner self, allowing you to consciously choose how to respond to negative emotions when they appear in your life. With me, you are also going to laugh, dance, practice gratitude, find a relaxing hobby, ask for help when need it, and connect with others. I'll teach you how to protect your energy and practice self-love. As we spend time together, we will get to know each other better every day."

Everyone replies, "Welcome, Master-Gowgwart-Care. Thanks! I will embrace you. I didn't like how I felt before with them, Master-Gowgwart-Pain and everything that came with Master-Gowgwart-Depression, when they both appeared in my life. Probably, I felt fear and anger too, who knows. All I know is, I love who I am now and can't wait to see who I become as we get to spend time together."

Master-Gowgwart-Care replies, "Thank you. This is where the journey to healing truly begins."

Master-Gowgwart-Love says, "I also want you to meet Master-Gowgwart-Trust."

Everyone replies, "*Deepïery thögh!* Sure. I'd love to meet Master-Gowgwart-Trust."

Shiny, starry-night-blue crystals sparkle in the air, and Master-Gowgwart-Trust appears in the living room.

Master-Gowgwart-Love replies, "Terrific! Because he's here. I warn you—he might be scary at first, but once you open-up to him, you will discover the wonders of his magical powers."

Master-Gowgwart-Trust emerging from behind the single grey couch where Everyone sits, sprouts sparkling crystals.

Master-Gowgwart-Care introduces Master-Gowgwart-Trust.

"Please meet Master-Gowgwart-Trust; you need him," Master-Gowgwart-Care says.

With a smile, Everyone says, "Aww. You look . . . so serious. Can't wait to get to know you."

Master-Gowgwart-Trust replies, "Hello. I won't get too close to you yet. It takes time and patience to let me be part of you. I warn you that fear may come between us, so please be careful, Everyone. I'll help you regain your confidence. Be brave; healing may take time, but it's worth it."

Master-Gowgwart-Love says, "We are emotions disguised as Gowgwarts, with different colors and magical powers that allow us to help people in different ways. When we appear, our shiny crystal ears will glow depending on how strong our spirit is in you. At times, we may take different forms based on the needs of others. We are consciously and unconsciously present in humans' lives because not all are aware of us. While the reason is unknown, some people live a life of denial, pushing us away and ignoring us, whether positive or negative it doesn't matter which side we stand for. The energy, the spirit, and soul, through which humans view life stands for us (emotions disguised as Gowgwarts) and it will vary from person to person, giving authenticity to everyone's life in The Six Kingdoms. Over time, you'll learn about the magic of our distinct powers when we—the positive and negative emotions—are in harmony with each other. Go and spend time with Master-Gowgwart-Trust."

Sparkling pink and red crystals begin to appear everywhere;

Master-Gowgwart-Care and Master-Gowgwart-Love disappear.

.   .   .

Everyone goes for a long walk with Master-Gowgwart-Trust.

"Master-Gowgwart-Trust, I understand that it will take time for me to be comfortable around you, and I am really excited to know how it will be to live my life with everything you stand for as part of me. I've heard a lot about you, but I never thought this day would come. I am curious to know, how can you help me regain my confidence? And why are you so important in my life?" Everyone asks.

Master-Gowgwart-Trust replies, "If you make me part of you, I will encourage you to reach your dreams and hold on to them. No matter what life throws at you, you'll know that at the end of the day it will be okay, and everything will work out in your favor because you have me. Without me, you'll live in fear; Master-Gowgwart-Fear is very strong and can destroy you by stopping you from doing the things you dream of and that are good for you. Master-Gowgwart-Fear brings darkness, negative thoughts, confusion, and separates you from you. You become a different person with him and unless you know how to embrace the positivity in him, you might end up destroying yourself. You need me for balance. With me, you will feel that everything is possible. I make you stronger and also give you that extra little push you need to be alone and not feel lonely to help you be comfortable with yourself and Master-Gowgwart-Love. With me, you won't care if things go wrong, because I'm part of you. I stand by you and no matter what happens, I will always be there to help you grow in confidence to see the bright side on everything. You will be safe with me. I will teach you how to live a positive life."

"Thanks, Master-Gowgwart-Trust. Even though I am afraid,

today, I freely choose to make you part of my life. Yeo want to wake up every day knowing that I am safe with you. I don't want to worry about the future or feel sorry about my past; yeo want to enjoy the present, go with the flow and be positive about my life," Everyone replies.

Master-Gowgwart-Trust says, "Trust, Everyone. Be confident in yourself. I won't disappoint you."

Two

Huïumi

"I'm so tired of all the emotions I met today, that all I want to do is relax," Everyone says while lying on the grey couch in the living room.

"Oh, the delivery of sweet and spicy sheets is here. Yes! *Qomïen!* Please leave it at the door. *Tagrascïe!*" Everyone says after she hears the delivery guy knocking on her door. She waits until the delivery guy leaves, and then she opens the door to take the delivery.

After closing the door, she says, "Mmm, so yummy. Smells so good, right Hïuramïur?" she asks.

"Usïcs," Hïuramïur answers, staying still.

"Mmm? What was that? No. It's impossible. You're my plushie unless my wish has truly come true. But I don't think so. Come, let's watch two episodes of my favorite baking show, *'Flower or Flowerless?'* Aaah, I truly love this show. Don't you, Hïuramïur? Do you think that they'll be able to guess, if the desserts are baked with flowers or not?" Everyone asks.

"Mm, yes. Maybe. It was hard to guess last time," Hïuramïur replies.

Gasping, Everyone says, "Aaah! You are talking. It's real. My wish came true. No way."

"Ah, yeah," Hïuramïur says, nodding.

Amazed, Everyone says, "Oh whoa. It is real. You are alive!"

"Usïcs! You're my best friend. We love this show," Hïuramïur says, jumping off the sofa to hug Everyone.

"Aww. A mutual hug. You're so fluffy. This is what I needed— a hug," Everyone says, squeezing Hïuramïur.

"Same," he replies, his voice muffled and his face buried in her shoulders.

.   .   .

Master-Gowgwart-Love says, "The sky is pale blue, the white clouds move, and I see thee."

Everyone enters a colorful tulip garden following a beautiful— blue, purple, pink, white, and lilac butterfly that leads her to Master-Gowgwart-Love. As soon as she sees Master-Gowgwart-Love, she shouts, "Love! Love! Here! Please turn around, it's me, Everyone. May we talk, please?"

Master-Gowgwart-Love turns around to see Everyone, and the butterfly disappears. She smiles at Everyone, flying in her direction.

"Hello, Everyone! Of course, dear. What is it about?" Master-Gowgwart-Love asks.

"The butterfly is gone . . ." Everyone says.

"Oh, dear. That's Morphïea, my friend from home," Master-Gowgwart-Love says.

"Oh, okay. Hmmm. It's . . . what I wanna talk about. I want to understand what's happened to me after yeo met you because I've changed. I'm different now. I feel like a brand-new person. Since the day I met you, I've never felt alone again. It's like you're within me. I feel you, Love. A different kind of love I have never experienced before. I've never thought you could feel this way. While before, nothing made sense, and everything was sunless, since I found you again, I feel like you've given me a new life. It's like a re-birth, you know. Eh, a second chance to live the life I've always wanted to live but didn't know how. I didn't know what it was, but now that I am here with you, I am most certain it's you. A feeling growing stronger within me every day," Everyone says.

Master-Gowgwart-Love asks, "It felt, and it feels like a flame that had been put out for a long time and suddenly lit by a force beyond your grasp, right?"

Nodding, Everyone replies, "Yes! That's exactly what I meant. How do you know?" she asks.

Master-Gowgwart-Love responds, "Because that's my power."

Everyone asks, "Your power?"

Master-Gowgwart-Love responds, "Mm-hmm. Your battle is in your mind, and I'm the healing for your suffering. As if by magic, you can call it transformation; with the powers of my red sparkling crystals, I can make Pain, Depression, Anger, Fear, Guilt, Sadness, and Shame disappear but only if you wish it."

Promptly, Everyone asks, "How is that? I mean the part where you say if if I want you to . . ."

"My healing only works when you bring my powers to life. To do so, you must hear my voice to welcome me into your life. That's why you feel different. You're beginning to feel my powers because your healing has begun," Master-Gowgwart-Love replies.

Enthusiastically, Everyone says, "You're right. You're so much more than I thought . . . How lucky I am."

"That is certain. I am much more than what it seems. I am a fountain of new life. An opportunity for a new beginning. A second chance to live a positive life with purpose and a sense of belonging in The Six Kingdoms. I make everything new again. Think of it as a brand-new vase that looks like it had never broken before, but the truth is, it shattered in pieces, with zero chances that it could ever be salvaged and made brand new again," Master-Gowgwart-Love replies.

Listening, Everyone nods, "Mm-hmm."

"What would you do with a broken vase that's beyond repair?" Master-Gowgwart-Love asks.

Everyone replies, "Aah. I'd pick-up the pieces and put it in the garbage (it's already broken and there's nothing I can do with it) or I'd pick-up the pieces and try to amend them, however, it will never look the same again."

Master-Gowgwart-Love says, "Exactly. But that's not how it is with me. I show up and pick-up the pieces, put them back together and make the vase brand new again."

Everyone asks, "Like if it had never broken before?"

Master-Gowgwart-Love responds, "I never give-up on people. I'm always there watching and waiting to be discovered, and yes."

Everyone replies, "I wonder what happens to those who don't hear your voice."

Master-Gowgwart-Love replies, "They never find me."

"Why?" Everyone asks.

"They lack courage, hope, and strength because their spirit is dying, and their soul is frail. They're not aware of us and even though we're present in their lives they ignore us. In other cases, those who hear my voice end up pushing me away, because what I offer them is strange. Alas, I must leave them. You cannot help someone unless they want your help," Master-Gowgwart-Love responds.

"Can you give me an example of someone who did?" Everyone asks.

Master-Gowgwart-Love responds, "Of course, my dear. That happens all the time."

Everyone asks, "How?"

Master-Gowgwart-Love responds, "Well, some people choose to be with Master-Gowgwart-Pain, others choose to remain trapped with Master-Gowgwart-Depression, others make room for Master-Gowgwart-Fear, and others submerge deep with Master-Gowgwart-Anger, becoming their best friends. And when you summon the Master Gowgwarts: Fear, Pain, Anger, Depression, Sadness, Shame, and Guilt in your life; the chances of losing yourself in your suffering increases, and when that happens, it makes you completely unable to hear my voice, until you lose yourself completely."

Everyone says, "That's catastrophic!"

Master-Gowgwart-Love replies, "No matter what I do to reach you, my presence is lost on you. You are resting in your suffering. Therefore, you no longer want to be part of this world. You want to join death. Your goal is to escape these emotions. At this point, you forget about me and my friends—Master Gowgwarts—Happiness, Freedom, Trust, Care, Joy, and Peace, and when you meet death, it's over."

"Over?" Everyone asks.

"Yes! Your existence in this world has come to an end. You become a memory. A little daisy wildflower planted in the Garden of Pain," Master-Gowgwart-Love responds.

"That's what was about to happen to me when you saved me," Everyone says.

Master-Gowgwart-Love replies, "Yes, but you heard my voice right on time when you were tangled-up with Master-Gowgwart-Depression."

Everyone says, "Yes, lucky me. If not, I'd be a memory today, planted in the Garden of Pain with all the other little pretty . . . little daisy wildflowers."

Master-Gowgwart-Love replies, "But your willpower and hope to find me, gave you the strength to still hear my voice and opened your eyes in your darkest time."

Everyone says, "I wonder if you and your friends ever fought with negative emotions to save someone, even when their ultimate goal was to find death . . . I mean, for me it was different, because I didn't want to find death; I was simply . . . with 𝔇epression."

Master-Gowgwart-Love says, "Oh dear, that's not our job. We don't fight; we balance each other to create a harmonious state."

Everyone asks, "How do you do that?"

Master-Gowgwart-Love replies, "You'll find out soon enough. But for now, since you want to know what happens when someone pushes me away, I will show you."

Everyone asks, "You will do . . . what?"

Master-Gowgwart-Love turns around; with her right hand she presses the purple star on her heart. Then, she says, "Star sparkle, purple sparkles, come out with your charming glamour."

The Star of the Universe appears in the garden sparkling purple amethyst everywhere, wearing a crown of shimmering and sparkling purple amethyst with white jade and dressed in sparkles of silver and white crystals.

The Star of the Universe says, "Oh, oh, Tulips." She giggles.

Everyone gasps and says, "Whoa, you are so glamorous and beautifully enchanting."

The Star of the Universe speaks, "Aww! So many tulips and Everyone."

"Meet, The Star of the Universe . . . In her eyes, you can see beyond The Six Kingdoms. She will transport us to an old memory," Master-Gowgwart-Love says.

Everyone replies, "Uh-huh. Cool. So exciting."

Master-Gowgwart-Love says, "I warn you, this isn't going to be thrilling, but don't be sad, this can happen to anyone."

The Star of the Universe says, "She's right, Everyone." Then, she looks at Master-Gowgwart-Love and says, "Master-Gowgwart-Love, I wasn't expecting you to call me. You pulled me out of a party where I was having a fantastic time with Master-Gowgwart-Joy and Master-Gowgwart-Happiness and all of their Gowgwarts."

"Oh dear, it will be quick, I promise. I need you to transport us to one of those old memories you keep in the purple star on the palm of your hands, where the healing journey was disrupted by the negative emotions, prithee," Master-Gowgwart-Love commands to The Star of the Universe.

The Star of the Universe replies, "As you command, let's show Everyone."

The Star of the Universe extends her arms, opens her hands, and shows Everyone old memories from Master-Gowgwart-Love. Meanwhile, as different memories from person to person in The Six Kingdoms shift, Master-Gowgwart-Love promptly shouts, "Pause! That one! There! Take us there!"

Sparkling purple amethyst crystals transport Everyone, Master-Gowgwart-Love, and The Star of the Universe to a memory from fourteen years ago.

. . .

Looking everywhere, Everyone gasps. "Whoa. Punta Ablanc, Pearl Islands, so many fun memories in this kingdom. It's so windy, sunny, and the water feels warm. Yeo missed this weather and the crystal-clear water. I almost forgot how gorgeous this beach is," she thinks as the water caresses her feet.

Excited, Master-Gowgwart-Love says, "We're here, Everyone,

at Luneïe Hotel!"

"Kingdom of Zūlear—oops. I think that woman who passed by heard me," Everyone replies, covering her mouth with her hands.

The Star of the Universe replies, "Don't worry. So you can speak freely and not interfere with the past while you're here, I made you invisible and inaudible to others. You're like a superhuman."

"Really? Aah! Hi there! Nice hat! Hahaha. Phew, I want some of that food," Everyone says, joking around.

The Star of the Universe giggles. "Don't be silly!" she says.

Master-Gowgwart-Love says, "The Star of the Universe has a special place in my heart." A smile on her face.

Holding a lïanda drink—a frozen coconut cookūn drink, The Star of the Universe says, "Your heart is my home."

"Uh-huh, I agree with you," Everyone says, "(I saw it with my own eyes)."

"Now that you're here, I will return to join Master-Gowgwart-Joy and Master-Gowgwart-Happiness; they're waiting for me," The Star of the Universe says.

Everyone asks, "Where did you get the lïanda drink?"

The Star of the Universe replies, "Oh, ah, my magical sparkles. Would you like some?"

Everyone replies, "Deepïery thögh!"

In seconds, a lïanda drink appears in Everyone's right hand. "I wasn't expecting that. Tagrascïe!" Everyone says, chuckling.

After The Star of the Universe covers Everyone with sparkling purple amethyst crystals, she says, "I hope you like your beach outfit, Everyone. When you're ready to return, say the magic words." She winks with a smile and then goes back inside the star on Master-Gowgwart-Love's heart.

·   ·   ·

Excitedly, Everyone says, "I remember this place as if it was yesterday! I have so many fun memories here! The main entrance of Luneïe Hotel and Resorts, ah, the palm trees all the way to the main lobby where all guests are welcome with a beverage of their choice (so yummy) and a tray of sweet and salty snacks (I love it). They truly know how to make us feel at home (in paradise). The coconut trees, flowers, tropical animals, and the warmth of their staff . . . Can you believe they greet you with a smile? All the time."

Master-Gowgwart-Love replies, "That's charming."

Everyone replies, "I know."

Master-Gowgwart-Love says, "Well, let's find a place where we can talk. Later tonight, we'll see a show with a performance featuring Loreïe."

"Is Loreïe the reason we are in this memory? Did Loreïe push you away from his/her life?" Everyone asks.

"Mm, yes." Master-Gowgwart-Love nods as she looks around trying to find a place to talk with Everyone. "Look! There are two hammocks on that side, by the VIP area, next to a coconut tree."

Everyone asks, "Where?"

"There! Look! Where the white cabanas are with the sign—'*Do not enter, area reserved. Platinum members only*,'" Master-Gowgwart-Love replies.

Everyone says, "Aah, I see it."

Master-Gowgwart-Love replies, "Good. Let's sit there so we can talk quietly."

.   .   .

"Tell me, Master-Gowgwart-Love, what happened to Loreïe?" Everyone asks.

Purple amethyst crystals sparkling in the air.

Everyone gasps. "Just what I need, another lïanda drink. Look, she even left us sunscreen to protect our skin from the sun. She definitely thinks about everything . . . I love, love, love The Star of the Universe. She's so thoughtful," she says, holding the drink.

Master-Gowgwart-Love replies, "She's part of me."

Everyone replies, "I know . . . Not even in my wildest dreams, would I have imagined that someone like her could be part of you, in a good way of course."

"Thanks, Everyone," Master-Gowgwart-Love says.

Everyone asks, "So, what happened to Loreïe?"

"Oh, yes. About that, I want you to understand that I face a wall in people's minds that prevents them from doing the things they want to do. Let me be more specific, people begin to see everything as a threat and danger. In between, there is no room for my friends, Master Gowgwarts—Trust, Peace, Care, Happiness, Freedom, and Joy, instead, they invite Master-Gowgwart-Fear and friends, Master Gowgwarts—Pain, Guilt, Shame, Anger, Sadness, and Depression, to join them. Master-Gowgwart-Fear's friends don't join people at the same time—only in rare occasions. For example, in this memory, Loreïe, who pushed me out and then welcomed Master-Gowgwart-Fear, allowed Master Gowgwarts Shame, Sadness, and Depression, suppress my voice, pushing me and my friends completely away," Master-Gowgwart-Love replies.

Everyone says, "Oh, that's awful."

Master-Gowgwart-Love replies, "Oh dear, I know. Loreïe was a dancer; he was part of the entertainment show for all the tourists traveling from around The Six Kingdoms, including the local ones who enjoy a vacation, here, at Luneïe Hotel."

Everyone asks, "Really, like for real?"

Master-Gowgwart-Love says, "Forsooth, dear. He performed

in the hotel show three times a week."

Everyone says, "Oh, whoa, a dancer."

"And a singer too. Before Master-Gowgwart-Fear entered to Loreïe's life, he had a dream; Loreïe wanted to be a famous StarLight show performer. Back then my friends and I were part of his life; he was joyful, happy, caring, and nothing could stand in his way because he had trust, until he started to welcome Master-Gowgwart-Shame into his life," Master-Gowgwart-Love replies.

Everyone asks, "But, how?"

"In Loreïe's mind, his friends were living a better life than him; he had no appreciation for all the good things he had. He only cared about what others had achieved until he became lonely and later on found the Garden of Pain," Master-Gowgwart-Love responds.

Everyone says, "Oh, that's not good."

"After that, there wasn't room for us anymore. And it didn't stop there. Loreïe then gave life to Master-Gowgwart-Sadness, and as time passed, Loreïe stopped hearing my voice until he no longer remembered me," Master-Gowgwart-Love says with a profound sad voice.

"No! He did what?" Everyone asks.

"Uh-huh. It was then that Master-Gowgwart-Fear and Master-Gowgwart-Depression became his permanent companions. Loreïe began to change, and nothing made him happy anymore. He isolated himself and began to cry almost every day, all day. His mind filled with negative thoughts, and then he began to call death . . ." Master-Gowgwart-Love responds.

Gasping, Everyone says, "Death . . ."

Master-Gowgwart-Love says, "We're here to help you, but you must save yourself by allowing us to enter into your life to restore the broken pieces and Loreïe did the complete opposite."

Everyone asks, "Wasn't any other way to help him?"

Master-Gowgwart-Love responds, "We give signs, like those we gave you before you met us, but Loreïe was in a state where he couldn't see the signs anymore. Although we tried, he decided to focus on the negative side of the negative Gowgwarts. I didn't give up on him; things happened so fast that we—Master Gowgwarts—couldn't help him complete his training to embrace the positive side of all Gowgwarts."

"That doesn't sound good. Clearly you didn't give up on him. That's so sad. If only he had been a little strong and hopeful, things would have been different for him and maybe he'd still be around," Everyone replies.

"Yes. If only Loreïe had chosen to be positive, he would have had completed his training with us. He simply failed to embrace our powers," Master-Gowgwart-Love replies.

Everyone says, "I want to complete my training, I don't want that to happen to me."

"Are you ready to create harmony among your emotions to embrace the positivity in all of them?" Master-Gowgwart-Love asks.

Everyone replies, "Yes! Deepïery thögh! I'm ready for that and everything else that may come after that too."

"In due time, when your emotions are in harmony with each other and the time is right, we'll decide if you're ready to receive the Gowgwarts' Bracelet," Master-Gowgwart-Love replies.

Everyone lets out a gasp. "Aaahhh. The bracelet everyone talks about, but no one says the name . . ." she says, her eyes widened, her chin down, her mouth open.

"Yes, dear. It's time you knew that in life, there's a Gowgwarts' Bracelet—two bracelets that connect to each other to create balance, a positive and negative Gowgwarts' Bracelet. And it is you who hold the power to balance these bracelets—when you click one with the other—until they become one," Master-Gowgwart-Love replies.

"What's the secret to balancing the bracelets?" Everyone asks.

Master-Gowgwart-Love responds, "The secret is within you."

"Me? What is it?" Everyone asks.

"It is awareness and that is the inner power you hold," Master-Gowgwart-Love responds.

"I think I'm starting to understand it a little. But what you say still sounds puzzling," Everyone says, after drinking her lïanda drink.

"Of course, my dear. I understand that it can sound puzzling because I just started to explain it to you. That's okay. Let me explain further . . . What happens with us is that if you don't make time to get to know yourself deeply to understand and be familiar with your emotions, when we appear in your life as Gowgwarts, you won't be able to recognize us or to differentiate one from the other because we are unknown to you. And, therefore, you might confuse negative Gowgwarts with positive ones. But, for now, don't worry about that, it's part of your training and through our teachings, you will develop awareness," Master-Gowgwart-Love replies.

"Deepïery thögh! You'll teach me how to develop awareness, and everything else I need to complete my training. Cool!" Everyone says hopefully.

Master-Gowgwart-Love replies, "You must believe in what's beyond your reach. I have yet to reveal to you what the powers of the crystal stones in the Gowgwarts' Bracelet are."

Everyone gasps. "The powers of the crystal stones. Yes!" she says excitedly.

Master-Gowgwart-Love replies, "In time, you will discover our magical powers, which are beyond anything you could imagine."

Everyone replies, "Paccürs!"

Master-Gowgwart-Love gasps. "Aaah. The sunset has already passed; I almost forgot that it's getting late to go see the show on the other side. Let's go, Everyone," she says.

Everyone asks, "What? To see Loreïe while we're here?"

Master-Gowgwart-Love replies, "Yes. Let's go, it's getting late; we don't want to miss it."

. . .

Everyone says, "Yay! We made it right on time for the opening of the show."

Excited to see Loreïe, Master-Gowgwart-Love says, "There he is. Look! That's him! That's Loreïe! He's about to perform a solo act singing 'Sparkles'—a song about me."

"Oh, that's him. What happens after that?" Everyone asks.

Master-Gowgwart-Love replies, "Then, everyone who is part of the show, joins him for a big opening with a choreographed dance about the culture of the Kingdom of Zūlear. But I will not tell you more so you can enjoy it."

Everyone replies, "Paccürs."

. . .

The show lasted like two hours with performances about The Six Kingdoms' cultures. Master-Gowgwart-Love and Everyone had a blast with the show. They were clapping, dancing, and singing with the rest of the audience.

Everyone says, "It was definitely . . . fun. Luneïe Hotel knows how to put a show together."

"Forsooth, a wonderful show. Also, it was Loreïe's last show. A terrible loss," Master-Gowgwart-Love replies.

"Mm-hmm. I agree. So talented," Everyone replies, nodding.

"I guess it's time to go back to the tulip garden. What do you think?" Master-Gowgwart-Love asks.

Everyone responds, "Mm, yeah."

Master-Gowgwart-Love says, "Already. I'll call The Star of the Universe to return us in time."

She presses the purple star on her heart, and says, "Star sparkle, purple sparkles, come out with your charming glamour."

The Star of the Universe appears and blows sparkling purple amethyst crystals to return Master-Gowgwart-Love and Everyone back in time.

In between, Everyone says, smiling, "Thanks for the outfit, the lïanda drinks, and the sunscreen. It hit the spot. On point."

The Star of the Universe smiles back at Everyone.

.   .   .

Everyone hears thunder and lightning, waking her up. She says, "Ugh, it's still nighttime."

She looks outside through the windows of her room to see it's pouring. "Ooh! I should go back to bed to try to sleep. Maybe I meet with Master-Gowgwart-Love again," Everyone says.

The sound of the storm is so loud, it keeps her awake. "I can't sleep," Everyone says while lying in her bed, staring at the ceiling.

Sparkling red crystals appear in the air and Master-Gowgwart-Love appears.

Everyone says, "Master-Gowgwart-Love! You're here!"

"Dear, now that you have learned about my powers and know about the Gowgwarts' Bracelet, I've personally brought you a gift," Master-Gowgwart-Love says.

Everyone asks, "A gift?"

"Mm, yes. This gift box has the positive Gowgwarts' Bracelet with the Gowgwarts—Love, Trust, Freedom, Joy, Care, Happiness, and Peace crystal stones' magical powers," Master-Gowgwart-Love responds handing the gift box to Everyone.

Everyone asks, "How does it work?" she looks at the box with a smile on her face.

Master-Gowgwart-Love responds, "To bring the spirit of the positive Gowgwarts to life in the crystal stones of the bracelet, press the golden stars that seal the bracelet and call upon the name of the Gowgwart you want to appear. Oh, I forgot you must say, 'Sparkles, sparkles, red crystal sparkles, Gowgwart-Love, I summon you . . .!' Once the spirit of the Gowgwart is released from the crystal stone in the bracelet, in the ears, you will see a reflection of how intense the spirit of the Gowgwart is inside of you, the more intense is the glow, the stronger is the presence within you."

Everyone replies, "Ooh, just like when I first met you."

Master-Gowgwart-Love replies, "Yes, now reflected in your emotions. I recommend you, to spend some time with Gowgwart-Care. She has the wisdom of Master-Gowgwart-Care and with her magical powers, she will strengthen you with self-care, meditation, mindfulness, and exercise. With her, you will also discover the things you are good at but didn't know, because you never took time to figure them out."

"No wonder why almost everyone in The Six Kingdoms talks about this bracelet with magical crystal stones . . . whose name is— Gowgwarts' Bracelet," Everyone says.

Master-Gowgwart-Love replies, "There's more to know about the Gowgwarts' Bracelet. For now, spend time with all the positive Gowgwarts in your bracelet. You'll continue to develop awareness."

"Tagrascïe, Master-Gowgwart-Love," Everyone says, with the positive Gowgwarts' Bracelet on her right hand.

"You're doing good. Now, I'll return to Pherriland," she says.

In a hurry, Everyone shouts, "Wait, Master-Gowgwart-Love! What about the negative Gowgwarts' Bracelet?"

"Slow Everyone, you need to go back in time. You will see. Be patient. Trust that everything will happen at the right time," Master-Gowgwart-Love responds.

Sparkling red crystals appear in the air and Master-Gowgwart-Love disappears.

"Wait, Master-Gowgwart-Love, please," Everyone says, "(yeo have more questions about . . . Okay, I guess it's too late)."

.   .   .

"I wonder where Pherriland is . . ." Everyone says, placing the positive Gowgwarts' Bracelet on the nightstand, on the right-hand side of her bed.

Everyone is trying to go back to sleep, but she can't. "Why do I have to go back in time? How is it even possible? Unless The Star of the Universe takes me back in time with her magical powers. But I wouldn't know where to start. Where in time should yeo go back? Childhood? Is it my teenage years? I need help figuring this out. I don't understand. How can going back in time help me to heal in present time? This is all confusing. Master-Gowgwart-Love said that everything will happen at the right time. I don't even know what that means. When is the right time? How does Master-Gowgwart-Love know when the right time is? I guess, it's gonna be a long night for me," Everyone says.

Hïuramïur comes out from under the bed. "Or not. Be patient. Master-Gowgwart-Love knows what she's doing," he says.

"Hïuramïur you're just what I need. I guess, yeo will be patient and go to sleep. Tomorrow will be a new day and who knows what it will bring," Everyone says, and then hugs Hïuramïur.

.   .   .

—In the meantime, while Everyone waits for the right time to find the negative Gowgwarts' Bracelet . . .

A year passed, and during that time, Everyone and Gowgwart-Care spent time together doing the things Master-Gowgwart-Love recommended. Everyone learned how to bake different breads and pastries, swim, dance, knit, drawing, and even practiced mindfulness every other day.

Exercise has become a habit for her, and to be consistent and disciplined with her routine, she even started to track her workouts in the monthly calendar she keeps in her kitchen. For every day of the week she works out, she draws a heart (how sweet). At the end of every month, she counts how many workouts she completed and challenges herself to do better the next month—or at least, to keep the same pace from the earlier one.

Everyone is so busy learning new things and forgetting about her suffering, that the right time to learn more about the Gowgwarts' Bracelet has come. And the time is now.

Will Everyone be able to find the negative Gowgwarts' Bracelet?

.   .   .

On a regular day, Everyone wakes up as usual . . . to follow her normal routine. "Heïjour Hïuramïur!" she says with her eyes closed touching her blanket looking for Hïuramïur. "Hïuramïur?" she asks, opening her eyes. "Taccgrah! Where am I? This isn't my room! How did I get here? Hïuramïur!!" she cries.

She gets out of bed, walks to the mirror and looks at herself. She is so shocked by how young she looks and how long her hair is that she says, "Who am I? I look like I did when I was fourteen years old!" She takes a deep breath and says to her reflection in the mirror, "I'm dreaming, the Gowgwarts aren't here, and I don't remember seeing The Star of the Universe. Take a deep breath. Stay calm. It's just a dream," Everyone says.

Everyone glances around the room, trying to familiarize herself with the surroundings to know where exactly she is. She stares at an old picture frame of herself in a red dress and golden sparkling slide-on sandals, hanging between two pink dolls on the wall next to her bed. "I remember those golden sparkling slide-on sandals were my favorite ones when I was eight years old," she says, then gasps. "This is my old room."

All her shoes are lined up on the floor beside the closet set into the wall across from her bed—the way she likes. Her bed's frame is made of white wood. The room has pink Ūmieda flowers wallpaper halfway up the walls, and the mirror she's currently standing in front of—located right by the entrance of her room—is made of white wood covered with pink cherry blossoms.

"Yeo remember my favorite part of this room was the veranda, where I used to spend idle hours, time wandering around looking at the ocean, singing songs, and reading novels my dad gifted me every time he returned home from a trip. My dad always encouraged me to read and dream big. I love my dad," Everyone says.

"All my childhood memories are coming back. This can't be a dream. It must be real. That's just how it was. I remember (almost) everything now," Everyone says.

"Deepïery thögh, there they are, Master-Gowgwart-Love and Master-Gowgwart-Care, ha! Looking at the ocean directly from my room's veranda. How nice. That means I'm not dreaming or maybe . . . I am," Everyone says.

Master-Gowgwart-Care hears her speaking and promptly says, "Master-Gowgwart-Love, I hear Everyone. She finally woke up; let's go inside."

Master Gowgwarts Love and Care entering the room.

Master-Gowgwart-Love says, "Hello Everyone. Right on time. We were waiting for you to wake up. You are in a dream."

"I knew it! Was it The Star of the Universe?" Everyone asks.

Master-Gowgwart-Love responds, "Yes! She brought us here. How do you know? This is a memory from eighteen years ago. We're in your childhood home, Punta Blereuzule, Pearl Islands."

"I feel outside my hula hoop today. Eighteen years ago . . . That explains why I look so young," Everyone replies.

Master-Gowgwart-Love says, "Many days ago in our home, I came up with a wonderful idea of bringing you back to your teenage years. Right Master-Gowgwart-Care?"

"Mm-hmm, we want to help you remember how it started with the negative Gowgwarts," Master-Gowgwart-Care replies.

"The only thing not planned was you being fourteen years old. Mmm. How did that happen? Something must have gone wrong," Master-Gowgwart-Love says.

Briefly touching her hair, Everyone says, "That's great. Look at me now with long hair. I miss my short hair. I'm not complaining, really, it looks good, but what if I stay looking like this forever and I can't go back to the real me? I look so young . . . What happened, Master-Gowgwart-Love? Do you think The Star of the Universe has anything to do with this? She likes to be funny. Don't get me wrong. It's just that all yeo can think of is how am I supposed to return to the real me? What if something goes wrong again?"

"Don't worry about it," Master-Gowgwart-Care responds.

"Oh, dear. You're stressing over nothing. Embrace this change and then we figure out how to fix it. Trust, I'm sure The Star of the Universe will take care of it. Remember, this is a memory," Master-Gowgwart-Love says.

"But . . . How can you say that? Hmm, a memory. So, I guess in this dream, me being fourteen years old is just temporary. Right? Can you please double check? Can you please, please, summon The Star of the Universe? I need to hear it from her. Was it a mistake or not?" Everyone asks.

"Okay," Master-Gowgwart-Love says, nodding.

She presses the purple star on her heart and says, "Star sparkle, purple sparkles, come out with your charming glamour."

Amethyst crystal sparkles everywhere . . . covering Everyone's hair and giving it a fresh look.

The Star of the Universe appears behind Everyone. She says, "Oh, hello Everyone."

Everyone turns and says, "Hi glamorous!"

Master-Gowgwart-Care says to Everyone, "I like your new . . . hair. Cool and bright."

Everyone replies, "Hmmm, why do you say that? It's longer, but you already know that."

Master-Gowgwart-Care replies, "Hmm, not just longer. Look at yourself in the mirror."

The Star of the Universe asks, "Do you like the purple crystal sparkles?"

Looking at her reflection in the mirror, Everyone says, "Aaahh. Definitely . . . not complaining about that. I love the purple crystals in my hair."

Everyone smiles, and so do Master-Gowgwart-Love, Master-

Gowgwart-Care, and The Star of the Universe.

"I nailed that! So, why am I here, Master-Gowgwart-Love or should I say, Everyone?" The Star of The Universe asks.

Master-Gowgwart-Love responds, "We don't know what went wrong with Everyone. She wasn't supposed to be fourteen years old in this memory."

Everyone says, "I want reassurance that this is temporary."

The Star of the Universe giggles. "Oh, that! I wanted to add a little sparkle to Everyone's adventure. What's wrong with your sense of humor? Enjoy it while it lasts. Aren't you loving it? Because I do! You look fabulous, Everyone," she says.

Looking in the mirror, Everyone says, "Well, at first, it wasn't so funny, but now it is. I do love it." She turns, saying, "Shouldn't you have at least warned me before traveling back in time? Huh? I wouldn't have had so many questions."

"It was a silly joke, Everyone. Besides, it wouldn't have worked if you had known," The Star of the Universe replies.

Master-Gowgwart-Love says, "It was a marvelous idea. I love it!"

"I am into it. A sparkle of fun is always welcome. You certainly make us feel closer to Master-Gowgwart-Joy," Master-Gowgwart-Care says.

"You're all welcome! Good luck, Everyone," The Star of the Universe says, "(what they don't know is that I didn't do anything wrong. I wanted Everyone to remember how it feels to be fourteen years old, again, and why not add a bit of amethyst crystal sparkles to Everyone's hair to make it fun)." She winks and amethyst crystal sparkles cover her while she goes inside the purple star on Master-Gowgwart-Love's heart.

Master-Gowgwart-Love says, "That went well."

Everyone says, "Uh-huh." Then, she turns and asks, "What? Why are you laughing, Master-Gowgwart-Care?"

Master-Gowgwart-Care responds, "I think . . . you look prettier with purple hair. It suits you. It's better when you see the bright side on everything. You feel better when you have a positive attitude."

"You're right. I stopped complaining and instead embraced the change and at once, I started to feel better," Everyone says.

"Well, dear, now that you know things will go back to normal, how does it feel to be fourteen years old again?" Master-Gowgwart-Love asks.

"Hmm. I remember many things. I was a bright student in high school. I had many dreams. I dreamed about being a singer, dancer, actor, model, architect, economist, writer, work for the government, travel to every kingdom, be a businessperson, work on tv. Oh, whoa! I wanted to do it all. I deeply loved entertainment, exercise, history, and math. My truest dream was to be a creative writer. I wanted to inspire people and to contribute to a better world. I can't believe yeo wanted to do so many things. I forgot about all that. I guess I forgot about me," Everyone replies.

Master-Gowgwart-Love says, "It's surprising how throughout time you've forgotten all the things that you once dreamed about. Being here will help you reconnect with who you truly are, your true self."

In that instant, Everyone hears someone arriving to the room. She looks at Master-Gowgwart-Love and Master-Gowgwart-Care, wondering what to do.

. . .

"Mmm? What's that noise?" Everyone asks.

Master-Gowgwart-Love replies, "It's you, from this memory."

Everyone replies, "Me!"

Master-Gowgwart-Care says, "Yes! You! And she's coming."

Everyone asks, "To the room?"

Master-Gowgwart-Love replies, "Yes! Don't worry, she cannot see you; she can only hear you. I only asked The Star of the Universe to make you invisible."

Everyone asks, "Why didn't you ask her to make me inaudible too?"

"Hmm. That's a good question," Master-Gowgwart-Care says.

"I know, sorry. Please try not to make any sounds while she's in the room, Everyone. Don't worry about us, we're shielded by our powers," Master-Gowgwart-Love says.

Everyone replies, "Okay. Silent as a stone."

Everyone freezes when (the real) Everyone enters the room.

She opens the door and walks straight to her inflatable green-hue single sofa chair that looks like a bean bag chair, but is more like a lazy chair . . ., located right by her natural wood desk with midnight blue, red, pink and yellow shelves, near the floor-to-ceiling windows that exit to the veranda to pick-up her pink backpack for school. She wears a white polo shirt with the school logo, brown trousers, black belt, black shoes, black socks, and her jewelry accessories—featuring the famous Gowgwarts' Bracelet, a small pair of gold earrings with diamonds, a thin gold chain with a daisy flower, and a gold ring with a butterfly and white diamonds. Quickly, she styles her long chestnut brown hair—which has layers and waves. Before leaving the room, she picks up her cherry-colored lipstick (a must have) and applies it while gazing in the mirror one last time. As she finishes applying her cherry-colored lipstick, she hears a noise. At once, she looks around to locate the source of the sound but realizes it's nothing. She turns off the lights, closes the door, and leaves.

Everyone takes a deep breath. "Whew! That was close. I don't understand, why did you choose this memory? I looked so happy," she says.

Master-Gowgwart-Care responds, "Everyone, you are here to reconnect with your younger self. Uh, and let's not forget, you are also here to find the negative Gowgwarts' Bracelet. Remember, you need to create balance among the Gowgwarts, and for that you must combine both bracelets."

As Everyone turns the lights back on, she replies, "Yeah, yeah, I know. I guess I forgot how happy I was . . . Before."

"It's okay. What's important is that you're remembering. That's exactly why we're here. Did you notice that the real you, was wearing the Gowgwarts' Bracelet?" Master-Gowgwart-Care asks.

"Oh, my . . . Taccgrah! Yes!! I completely forgot what it looked like. It's been ages since . . . that's why it's different from the one, Master-Gowgwart-Love gave me. Of course, you just said it, Master-Gowgwart-Care."

Master-Gowgwart-Care asks, "What?"

Everyone replies, "*She was wearing the Gowgwarts' Bracelet, and I am*—" Master-Gowgwart-Love interrupts, "missing the other half (the real) you, was wearing a few minutes ago, when she was here."

In a soft tone, Everyone replies, "Yes, that's the—" Master-Gowgwart-Care interrupts, "negative Gowgwarts' Bracelet."

Everyone replies, "Yes! How come I didn't remember any of this?"

"Oh, dear, you lost the positive Gowgwarts' Bracelet. And for a while, you only wore the negative Gowgwarts' Bracelet. Then, you lost that one too. That's when you lost awareness of your emotions, and eventually forgot them, and no longer recognized them. All the people around you were able to acknowledge the emotions in you, except you. Awareness is key to keeping your emotions checked and you forgot about it. Can you imagine living a life not knowing what direction you're going and at the same time, being governed by your emotions?" Master-Gowgwart-Love asks.

"Gïocs. No, no," Everyone replies.

"That was you . . . Then, you started to forget everything that made you happy and started looking for Gowgwart-Love elsewhere, until you no longer remembered yourself. Luckily . . . things changed for you when you found me again," Master-Gowgwart-Love says.

"That's why you chose this memory, to show me how it was before my emotions got out of control. That's why I looked happy and glowing," Everyone says.

"In this memory, your emotions were in harmony with each other, and you were the master of them. We want you to experience that again, to help you remember yourself. Your true self," Master-Gowgwart-Care replies.

"I get it now," Everyone says with confidence.

"You are so clever," Master-Gowgwart-Love says with a sweet voice.

"How am I going to find the negative Gowgwarts' Bracelet in this memory?" Everyone asks.

"Well, we have a plan. First, you are going to observe (the real) Everyone for a week to remember how you behaved when you were emotionally balanced. In addition to that, at the end of each day you will write down three things you discovered about all the things that you did differently, that made you happy. Then, Master-Gowgwart-Love will take possession of the negative Gowgwarts' Bracelet, from (the real) Everyone for you, and then you'll click it with the positive Gowgwarts' Bracelet. Thereafter, your emotions will be in harmony with each other and The Star of the Universe will take us back home.

The end!" Master-Gowgwart-Care replies.

"Isn't that going to unbalance me in present time? That doesn't sound right," Everyone says.

"Yes, I agree. That's not entirely what's going to happen except for the first part. Master-Gowgwart-Care is playing around with you. Master-Gowgwart-Care, this is serious; please be mindful with what you say to Everyone," Master-Gowgwart-Love replies.

Master-Gowgwart-Care looks down and says, "I am sorry. It was an innocent joke. I thought it would make you laugh. Seriously, Master-Gowgwart-Love is telling you the truth. It's not entirely true. My bad."

So, for the next week, Everyone observed herself, and at the end of each day, she shared three things about herself, with Master Gowgwarts Love and Care.

Doing simple things like, singing, dancing, and playing board games with her siblings. All the fun times spent with all her friends in school. How much she loved eating cake and listening to music. Her love for acting, modeling and how she always made room for exercise. It was priceless for her to relive those memories where she used to spend time with her family, eating a meal she prepared for them and how proud she made her parents by being a responsible student with good grades. The time and effort she put every day into keeping the house clean, and how hard she worked on weekends at her mother's clothing store—whenever she had free time. And also, not to forget, that every Sunday morning she attended the church's biblical school. How kind and compassionate she was, and the level of emotional awareness she had! Seeing herself write a letter to her father to apologize because she raised her voice at him. Whoa, all these little genuine gestures really touched Everyone. She loved how generous she was with those in need and her sense of fashion, which showed that she had always loved dressing up. And of course, her deep fondness of reading, that she definitely . . . got from her father. It was unquestionably a week of rediscovery for Everyone.

.   .   .

Everyone wakes up from the dream. Hïuramïur jumps all over her. She says, "Hïuramïur! I missed you!" She giggles.

"Same," Hïuramïur replies, getting under the blanket.

Everyone says, "Guess what?"

"What?" Hïuramïur asks.

Everyone replies, "I traveled back in time! I can't believe how much I had forgotten about myself and everything that truly made me happy. I realized I had entirely forgotten who I was. Going back in time to remember this important part of my life has truly changed an entire part inside me forever."

"Oh, really?" Hïuramïur asks.

Everyone replies, "Mm-hmm. We often think that diving into our past life experiences can only bring pain, but sometimes it can remind us of happy times that can help us find ourselves again."

"Mm-right!" Hïuramïur says.

"Oh, no way!" Everyone says.

"What happened?" Hïuramïur asks.

"I just realized, I'm still only wearing one bracelet," Everyone replies.

"Is that bad?" Hïuramïur asks.

"Mm-hmm. I need the negative Gowgwarts' Bracelet. It's okay Hïuramïur, I guess I'll go to sleep for now. Night!" Everyone replies.

"Night!" Hïuramïur says.

.   .   .

A new day has blossomed in the Kingdom of Bloomïeda and Everyone still doesn't have the negative Gowgwarts' Bracelet.

Everyone thinking, "It took me so long to finally grasp it, but now yeo understand everything. As I grew older and went through different life experiences, I simply let those experiences change me. I forgot who I am and the things that truly bring contentment to my life. Now yeo realize that those experiences were an opportunity for my personal growth—to embrace who I am—not meant to change myself in a bad way, but to rebuild myself in a new one, allowing me to preserve my essence, keeping my authentic self-unchanged, only elevating and refreshing my outlook on life."

Hïuramïur asks, "What are you doing lying down on the couch staring at the ceiling so early?"

"Reflecting on memories from my past years," she replies.

Hïuramïur says, "And thinking about the bracelet?"

Everyone replies, "Mm-hmmm. Maybe my emotions can help me. Tagrascïe, Hïuramïur."

Everyone presses the golden stars and says, "Sparkles, sparkles, starry-night-blue crystal sparkles, Gowgwart-Trust, I summon you!"

Sparkling crystals burst from the starry-night-blue crystal stone of the positive Gowgwarts' Bracelet. Gowgwart-Trust appears.

"Hi Everyone," Gowgwart-Trust says.

"Heïjour, Gowgwart-Trust," Everyone replies.

"Everything okay?" Gowgwart-Trust asks.

"No. Not really," Everyone replies.

"You seem sad," Gowgwart-Trust says.

"Yes. I'm a little bit overwhelmed because I still don't have the negative Gowgwarts' Bracelet. Can you please help me?" she asks.

"Yes. I'm here to help you boost your confidence," Gowgwart-Trust says.

Everyone says, "Thanks, Gowgwart-Trust. How can I find my missing bracelet?"

"You're not so far from finding it. Trust yourself. You will find it at the right time," Gowgwart-Trust replies.

"How?" Everyone asks.

Gowgwart-Trust responds, "Don't focus your energy thinking why you don't have it; rather think you will find it soon. Of all the things you have remembered from your past, focus on how it feels to have your emotions in balance. Be positive. Remember the good from your past and enjoy your present. Have hope that the future will bring good things into your life and soon you'll find the bracelet. Dress-up, do your make-up, go for a walk, and smell the flowers. It is springtime. Enjoy it. It will bring happiness." Slowly, Gowgwart-Trust turns into crystal sparkles, disappearing into the starry-night-blue crystal stone of the positive Gowgwarts' Bracelet.

. . .

After listening to Gowgwart-Trust, Everyone goes for a walk in Spïeral Park. She sees a rainbow of flowers—reddish roses, purple sweet pea, blue and green hydrangeas, yellow and orange tulips, and as Gowgwart-Trust said, Everyone begins to feel happy and joyful. And when she hears them singing "Harmony in Emotions"—a song of wonders—she smiles and starts singing with them, letting all the worries she has about the lost bracelet disappear.

—Pause!

Once upon a time, when Everyone was a teenager, she lost the negative Gowgwarts' Bracelet. Do you remember that part?? Well, I will remind you. It was then that she lost her identity and became known as Everyone. You might wonder when exactly this happened.

A long time ago, she had her heart broken by her first love. She was fourteen years old. Now you remember? Even though her emotions were in perfect balance, she wasn't ready to welcome romantic love in her life. Therefore, she began to ignore her emotions, unbalancing them, until her emotions became unknown to her, and she no longer remembered them, forgetting her true self, including her name.

—Go on.

.   .   .

Pherriland, Gowgwarts' Workshop.

Master-Gowgwart-Freedom says, "Come! Everyone has found the rainbow of flowers."

"What? That only means one thing, Master-Gowgwart-Love," Master-Gowgwart-Peace says.

"She is ready," Master-Gowgwart-Love replies.

"It is time to wrap up the missing bracelet in the Gowgwarts' gift box! Yay! Graduation time!" Master-Gowgwart-Joy says.

"We're ready," Master-Gowgwart-Depression says.

"That means you met with all the negative Master Gowgwarts, right?" Master-Gowgwart-Love asks.

"Uh-huh. Her negative emotions are already inside the crystal stones," Master-Gowgwart-Depression responds.

"That means you already had a graduation. So, I guess it's time, Master-Gowgwart-Love," Master-Gowgwart-Happiness says.

"Oh no! I missed the graduation. Where was I? Oh, I was gone teaching a class," Master-Gowgwart-Joy says.

"She is really ready to be herself again. Aww. This is exciting," Master-Gowgwart-Care says.

Master-Gowgwart-Love says, "Well, in that case, I will handle the delivery of the negative Gowgwarts' Bracelet, but before, I will introduce someone to Everyone."

"Are you going to show her the part of herself she is missing?" Master-Gowgwart-Care asks.

Master-Gowgwart-Love replies, "Yes. The time has come. She is ready."

.   .   .

While Everyone is singing joyfully free in Spïeral Park, Master-Gowgwart-Love appears.

From behind a large cherry tree, floating in the air to Everyone, Master-Gowgwart-Love blows cherry blossom petals.

Everyone sees the cherry blossom petals forming an identical reflection of herself.

She gasps and says, "Aaah, cherry blossom petals . . . I see my reflection. It's me! I see me. I remember. I remember my name. I'm not Everyone. My name is Huïumi."

Huïumi can see Master-Gowgwart-Love behind her reflection. She thinks, "It was Master-Gowgwart-Love and Master-Gowgwart-Care. They were reminding me of my identity. The wind, the cherry blossoms, Neephoos, all the signs that led to finding myself. Master-Gowgwart-Love has never abandoned me. Even before yeo met her, she was there with me. Always!"

Huïumi says, "Master-Gowgwart-Love! It's you. I see you. All this time you have been sending me signs with the cherry blossoms. You wanted me to remember who I truly am. My true self. My name. Me! All these years I have been known as Everyone because I forgot my true identity. It was always there inside me; I simply buried it. I lost myself in my suffering. So focused on everything else except me. Thank you, Master-Gowgwart-Love!"

"This is you, Huïumi. You're not Everyone. It was always there inside you. I knew you'd remember," Master-Gowgwart-Love says.

"My old self has left me, I am no longer Everyone, I have been renewed. From now on, I will be known by my true name, Huïumi. This is who I am. This is me and I will embrace it," Huïumi says.

Huïumi hugs the cherry blossom's petals, becoming one. "This is the real feeling of freedom, joy, happiness, and peace. It's a bliss once you learn to be free. Thank you for real!" Huïumi says.

—She left Everyone behind to be herself.

Well done, Huïumi.

.   .   .

The Master Gowgwarts—Freedom, Peace, Happiness, and Joy appear in the park, sparkling their crystal colors everywhere.

"What's happening?" Huïumi asks.

"Master-Gowgwart-Freedom here. Hello Huïumi."

"And Master Gowgwarts Joy, Happiness, and Peace," Master-Gowgwart-Love adds.

"Oh, whoa. Joureïe to you all!" Huïumi says with a smile.

"Now you know why it was so important to go back in time to remember all the things that once made you so happy and balanced," Master-Gowgwart-Love says.

"Mm-hmm," Huïumi nods, agreeing.

"It is wise, from time to time, to reference your past to keep your essence in present time. Is it not? Right?" Master-Gowgwart-Peace asks, reflecting bright glow in her ears.

"Mm, I agree," Huïumi replies.

"Now you know what true love really is," Master-Gowgwart-Joy says, opening her yellow sparkling wings.

"Uh-huh. It's self-love," Huïumi replies, nodding.

"A kind of love fostered by you," Master-Gowgwart-Freedom

says, sparkling purple amethyst everywhere.

"A love that blooms, flourishes, and blossoms in me," Huïumi says, opening her arms and looking at the blue clear sky.

. . .

"Hïuramïur! What? What is it?" Huïumi asks.

"She was here," Hïuramïur says.

"Who?" Huïumi asks.

"Master-Gowgwart-Love," Hïuramïur whispers.

"Why are you whispering? Why was she here?" Huïumi asks.

"She told me your name is Huïumi, not Everyone and she left that for you," he says, pointing out the small table in the living room.

"Finally, after a long wait, it happened. Oh, there's a clear vase with starry-night-blue hydrangeas. Mmm. I don't remember buying hydrangeas. Oh, there's a note from Master-Gowgwart-Love." She smiles, smells the hydrangeas, and reads the note aloud:

"Dear Huïumi,

Now that you have remembered your identity, we will no longer call you Everyone. You are ready to wear the missing negative Gowgwarts' Bracelet. Yay! Open the Gowgwarts' gift box, click both bracelets, and wear your emotions with pride. We believe in you. You can keep your emotions balanced but remember to always be calm. And don't summon the negative Gowgwarts yet. Wait until you learn about the powers of the crystal stones in the Gowgwarts' Bracelet.

Rejoice Huïumi, you will soon know how to embrace the goodness in all Gowgwarts—your emotions.

Oh, and enjoy the hydrangeas.

—From Love and friends."

Huïumi opened the Gowgwarts' gift box and there it was . . .

the bracelet she longed for.

Huïumi cries with joy as she clicks on the positive and negative Gowgwarts' Bracelets. "Whoo hoo! Finally! It's happening! I did it! I created harmony among my emotions, and it feels so, so good."

"That's the negative Gowgwarts' Bracelet," Hïuramïur says.

"I can't believe I am wearing the Gowgwarts' Bracelet. I mean, finally! I have become the master of my emotions. And everything happened when I least expected. This is the greatest surprise ever!" Huïumi says, full of joy and excitement.

"Whoo hoo!" Hïuramïur says.

"Thank you! Thank you!" Huïumi says with joy.

. . .

Pressing both golden stars on the bracelet, she says, "Sparkles, sparkles, yellow, purple crystal sparkles, Gowgwart-Joy, Gowgwart-Freedom, I summon you!" She releases them from the yellow and purple crystal stones in the Gowgwarts' Bracelet.

Gowgwart-Joy says, "Finally!! I thought this day would never come."

Gowgwart-Freedom opens his mouth to speak to Huïumi, and a butterfly comes out. "Ohh. Same here. I see the light. It's so bright in here . . . I like it." He pauses, gazing around at the surroundings of her apartment. "Pink and purple flowers everywhere surrounding me," he says.

While Gowgwart-Freedom speaks, Huïumi laughs. Then, she says, "You mean sweet peïe? Where do you see the pink and purple flowers, Gowgwart-Freedom? The ones in here are starry-night-blue from Master-Gowgwart-Love." She looks at the hydrangeas.

"Yes! Sweet pea flowers everywhere . . . Close your eyes and open them again. See beyond your reality and use your imagination,"

Gowgwart-Freedom says.

Huïumi closes her eyes briefly and the sweet pea flowers begin to appear. "Oh. Wow! How did you do it? These sweet peïe flowers are so beautiful," Huïumi says.

Gowgwart-Freedom replies, "Sweet pea flowers bring joy and happiness to everyone in the room."

Huïumi says, "Unexpected and beautiful. Thanks, Gowgwart-Freedom."

Gowgwart-Freedom replies, "I can see beyond your eyes. The places you want to go to, where you cannot be yourself and still want to be you. I can take you there. I can show you the things you never knew existed, like all the sweet pea flowers in this room."

Meanwhile, Gowgwart-Joy is walking around sniffing. "I smell. Mmm. Hold on, I smell ppucceïe," she says.

"Ppucceïe? Sure, help yourself. Yeo bought it on my way here. I didn't even try it, but the ppucceïe from that place, it's really, really yummy," Huïumi replies, smiling at Gowgwart-Joy.

Gowgwart-Joy drinks the whole cup in one shot.

"Wait, Gowgwart-Joy. You are supposed to drink it slowly, not in one shot," Huïumi says with an alarming tone.

"Oops. I guess . . . it's too late. It's delicious. How can they make a delicious drink like this?" Gowgwart-Joy says.

Huïumi couldn't stop laughing.

Gowgwart-Freedom magically brings out canvas, oil paint, and brushes.

Huïumi curiously asks, "What's that for, Gowgwart-Freedom? Paint? Canvas? Brushes? Is it for me?"

"Yes, for you. Express yourself and create something new and different," Gowgwart-Freedom replies.

"But I don't paint. I've never done it before," Huïumi replies.

Gowgwart-Freedom insists. "Try it and you'll see what you are capable of. You will be amazed at your talent. Besides, how can you know whether you can paint or not if you don't try it? And, if you cannot, try something new," he says.

Gowgwart-Joy adds, "Gowgwart-Freedom is right about that. It's a healthy way to express your feelings. You will be surprised how ordinary things can help you boost your well-being. Engaging with art can foster a deep and positive connection with yourself. It gives you a sense of satisfaction and accomplishment. A feeling of peace and mental clarity."

"Paccürs. I'll try it. You have convinced me. Now it's time for both of you to return inside your crystal stones on the Gowgwarts' Bracelet," Huïumi replies, pressing the golden stars on the bracelet. Gowgwart-Joy and Gowgwart-Freedom turn into sparkling crystals inside their crystal stones.

.   .   .

Huïumi immediately began painting, and within a few hours, she had already completed *The Reflection of the Crying Heart* and *The Light of the Sun.*" Without realizing, she also felt better, calmer, more relaxed, and happier, experiencing a freedom, she had never before experienced, and a joy filled of accomplishment and vibrant energy. She was amazed with what she painted by allowing herself to freely illustrate what was in her mind.

Master-Gowgwart-Love appears in the room.

"Master-Gowgwart-Love, glad you're here. Look! *The reflection of the crying heart* and *The light of the sun.* I painted those today," Huïumi says while pointing at the wall of her living room.

"Oh, wow," Master-Gowgwart-Love replies with a smile.

"I summoned Gowgwart-Freedom and Gowgwart-Joy earlier

today, and Gowgwart-Freedom suggested I try something new and different," Huïumi adds.

"I am not surprised by your talent. I guess . . . things are going better than I thought," Master-Gowgwart-Love says.

"Yes, I'm experiencing freedom in a unique way. For example, in this painting, *The light of the sun,* through the sunlight, I illustrated clarity and a new mindset that allows me to see the bright side of all things and reminds me to be positive in my present and future, while the open ocean stands for freedom," Huïumi replies.

"Mm, I see. It's a confirmation that you're no longer in pain," Master-Gowgwart-Love says.

"Yes, I don't feel pain anymore. Those days are gone. Now yeo feel joyful, happy, free, and at peace. I'm embracing everything I am and everything I didn't know I was . . . I am open to welcoming all the positive energy the universe has to offer me, and I am also letting go everything that holds me down," Huïumi replies.

"Oh, sweet. Let's take a closer look to *The reflection of the crying heart,*" Master-Gowgwart-Love says.

"In *The reflection of the crying heart*—which yeo painted before *The light of the sun,* I see the suffering yeo was hiding, which at times was greater than what I portrayed on the surface. It was my intention to illustrate what's inside me, but not like that. Maybe yeo needed to let it out. I guess after I did, I was able to bring out a brighter image of my inner self to light," Huïumi says.

"That's okay, dear. At times you won't be able to recognize the distinct stages of your suffering and your healing. It's like if you are inside a glass bottle trying to see outside of it, but the view isn't clear enough through the glass. The same goes for those who try to see what's inside the glass bottle from the outside but cannot clearly see what's inside because of the glass. The paintings are subjective, and what really matters is that you have completed your training. So go ahead and enjoy life. Things will start to make sense now," Master-Gowgwart-Love says, fading away.

.   .   .

Now that Huïumi has the Gowgwarts' Bracelet, she decided to focus more on her well-being doing the things that make her happy. She's no longer worried about finding romantic love; she's happy on her own. And while she spends time alone with Gowgwart-Freedom and Gowgwart-Peace, she's learned the difference between now and then.

Now she's embracing all her emotions.
She's learned to love herself.
She's happy.
She's free.
She's at peace.
She's calm and stable.
She's who she is meant to be . . .

Three

Lucky Girl

The moon says goodbye with the starry sparkles that illuminate the night, and the sun brings its light with the distinct colors of dawn ascending to the sky.

At Haiokïto's home, it's 5:00 a.m., all the lights are off, and he doesn't want to wake-up. "Ugh, the alarm keeps going off," he says, reaching across the nightstand near the right side of his bed to turn it off. "Thirty more minutes please," he says, setting a new alarm for 5:30 a.m.

Thirty minutes later, Haiokïto hears the alarm. "Ugh, no way, the alarm is ringing again. It's already been thirty minutes. Please, I just wanna stay in bed a little longer," he says.

Haiokïto is trying to stop the alarm, and accidentally he presses the button that opens the bedroom curtains on the multi-functional remote sitting at the nightstand, which controls the security, power, and sound systems, as well as the cameras in his home.

"What did I just do?" Haiokïto asks.

The white and silver curtains in his room opened, allowing the natural light from the pink, orange, and yellow sun's rays to flood the entire space. As the sun's rays trailed across the sky, covering the entire city, through the floor-to-ceiling glass windows, Haiokïto had a unique, privileged view and an exquisite feel of Spïeral Park, from his multi-level penthouse on the eighty-eighth floor in Spïeral Park Tower, named after the park.

At once, he covered his eyes from the sunlight, then he opened them and enjoyed the view. "It was an accident, and it turned out to be one of the most beautiful sunrises I've ever seen in my entire life. There's absolutely no way I would have missed this serendipitous sunrise. Oh, deepïery thögh, it's the second week of June! It was the earliest sunrise of the year that comes around a week before the summer's solstice," he says.

A few minutes after the sun had risen, Haiokïto began to make his bed.

.   .   .

Pherrïland, Gowgwarts' Workshop.

Master-Gowgwart-Love says, "He doesn't know yet, but today he's finally going to understand everything . . ."

Master-Gowgwart-Care replies, "Look at him making his bed, how adorable."

Master-Gowgwart-Love asks Master-Gowgwart-Joy, "Did you take care of my request?"

"Oh, yes. I made sure there's ice cream ads everywhere in the mall . . ." Master-Gowgwart-Joy replies.

Master-Gowgwart-Freedom says, "They are destined to meet. It's fate, they don't need us to interfere."

Master-Gowgwart-Trust says, "Forsooth! Master-Gowgwart-Freedom is surely right, Master-Gowgwart-Love, let it flow like the river, naturally."

"You are right. Master-Gowgwart-Joy, please remove the extra ads and let it be destiny. If they're meant to be, they will be," Master-Gowgwart-Love says.

"As you command," Master-Gowgwart-Joy replies.

Master-Gowgwart-Happiness says, "Oohh! The universe will bring them together. Look at them. Aww, they're so perfect for each other."

Master-Gowgwart-Joy replies, "She's getting ready to leave the house. She's going to the mall!"

"She's down-to-earth," Master-Gowgwart-Depression says.

"They are embracing growth," Master-Gowgwart-Pain says.

"Yes, they are ready," Master-Gowgwart-Peace replies.

Master-Gowgwart-Love replies, "Forsooth! She is ready, and today she will understand everything. Almost everything . . ."

.　　.　　.

As Haiokïto makes his bed with a white three-hundred-thread count king size bed sheet set that includes four king size pillowcases and a king size white blanket, he listens to music. After he finishes, he goes to the bathroom to brush his teeth with his orange Ūmieda toothbrush and whitening fresh-mint toothpaste, rinsing his mouth with alcohol-free mouthwash pomegranate-mint flavor. Afterwards, Haiokïto washes his face with Ūmieda essential anti-aging skincare products, and before getting ready for work, he walks to the closet right next to the bathroom to change clothes for a thirty-minute on the treadmill routine while watching the news and enjoying the view of Spïeral Park straight from his room.

After finishing his workout, he showers with Ūmieda Royal scent bath oil, puts on light clothes, and makes a sugar free ppucceïe drink—made with espresso, steamed milk, and a layer of foam— and a cceïebbu—sunny side-up eggs over Bree cheese with sprinkles of honey on toasted bread. Then, he takes his laptop from the coffee table in his living room to catch up with work.

. . .

Pherriland, Gowgwarts' Workshop.

"He is at the mall!" Master-Gowgwart-Freedom says.

"Nice outfit," Master-Gowgwart-Care says.

"Ooh! A white polo shirt and white trousers with red sneakers. Nicely done!" Master-Gowgwart-Joy says.

"Those red sneakers are *Light of Masseïel*—a limited edition in my honor," Master-Gowgwart-Love replies.

"She is on her way to the mall. Yay!" Master-Gowgwart-Care says excitedly.

"It's happening, I am confident they will meet today," Master-Gowgwart-Trust says.

"A disruption! A disruption!" Master-Gowgwart-Love says.

Master-Gowgwart-Care guffaws. "Hahahaha."

"Master-Gowgwart-Care, stop joking around. It's not funny," Master-Gowgwart-Love says.

"Oh, he's walking to the elevator. He's looking at the ice cream ads from the ice cream shop on the third floor, inside the mall. And I have nothing to do with it," Master-Gowgwart-Joy says.

"Enticed by the ice cream ads, he's going to get some," Master-Gowgwart-Happiness says.

. . .

Haiokïto is taking the elevator down to the third floor and also checking his email on his phone. After reading an urgent email from his company, he changed his mind. He pressed the lobby button to go home to complete an evaluation of a new jewelry franchise store scheduled to open in six months in the city of the Garden of Joy, at The Sparkmieda Labyrinth Fantasy World.

Haiokïto walks outside the mall, stops, and then looks up the sky. "Why not stop worrying about work for a day and simply enjoy some ice cream on this beautiful weather. After all, it's a sunny day, and everything else can wait," he thinks.

.   .   .

Huïumi arrived at the Bluemieda Mall to meet with her friends, Ufaïa, Maiephis, Luseïe, Rayïq, and Geossuth, at the ice cream shop on the third floor.

—Pause!

Huïumi's friends are unique, in their own ways, with different life experiences that strengthen their friendship. All her friends have the Gowgwarts' Bracelet, but not all of them know about it. Once everyone knows they have that in common, they'll be able to speak openly about their own personal journey to finding Love.

—Go on.

Before going up to the third floor, since she arrived at the mall fifteen minutes earlier than the time scheduled with her friends, she stops at the entrance to check her phone. While she is outside, she sees a tall, handsome guy with reddish hair wearing a white polo shirt and white trousers with red shoes. She thinks, "Why is he standing outside the mall looking up at the sky? He is so handsome. I hope I see him again, while still at the mall today."

.   .   .

"It's already 3:00 p.m. and my friends are not here yet," Huïumi thinks.

She takes her phone out of her *Roseïey Vūm Ūmieda purse* to send a text in the group chat—the six forces, to confirm if they're still meeting with her at the ice cream shop.

Sending text in group chat: **"The six forces."**

Huïumi: I am at the ice cream shop on the third floor at the Bluemieda Mall. Are you still coming?

Ufaïa: Heïjour, 'forces' . . . Gïocs qomïen.

Maie: On a date . . .

Luseïe: In a meeting. Gïocs qomïen.

Rayïq: Sorry, 'forces' on a date.

Geossuth: Don't wait for me. Get some ice cream.

Huïumi: Paccūrs.

"Since I'm already at the ice cream shop, I'm gonna get some ice cream anyway," she thinks.

She gets in the line to order ice cream.

Minutes later, it's Huïumi's turn to order.

"Next please!" the employee at the register says, calling to the next customer. Distracted on her phone, Huïumi doesn't hear him.

The employee at the register notices she's busy on her phone, so he calls again, louder, "Next customer please!"

Huïumi hears the employee behind the register and says, "Hey. Heïjour, sorry about that. A triple chocolate truffle in a waffle cone, please. Tagrascïe!" She grins.

After paying for her ice cream, she walks away from the register to wait for her order. Meanwhile, she opens her phone again.

The employee who prepares the orders at the ice cream shop says, "One triple chocolate truffle ice cream in a waffle cone coming right up."

While Huïumi puts away her phone, she hears that her order is ready—or at least, she thinks it's hers and at once she says, "Here!"

The employee who prepares the orders at the ice cream shop asks, "Triple chocolate truffle ice cream in a waffle cone?"

She, at once, grabs the ice cream. "Tagrascïe!" she says, "(that was fast)."

She tasted it and savored it, not helping to murmur, "Mmm, yummy, it's so delicious."

Meanwhile, Haiokïto looks at her confused. "She took my ice cream. I'm sure it's mine. I remember ordering the same ice cream as her right before her. Literally, she was on her phone when it was her turn to order," he thinks. He approaches her and says, "Heïjour! Apologies, I believe that's my ice cream."

Huïumi staring at him dumbfounded. "It's him! The same tall handsome guy with reddish hair I saw outside the mall earlier today after I arrived. I can't believe he's here standing there right in front of me. Speechless. Flabbergasted, I don't know how to put it. Yeo hoped to see him today while still at the mall and my wish came true. But why is he saying that my ice cream is his ice cream? This is what I ordered. Aww, snap! Maybe he ordered the same ice cream before me, and I accidentally took his order. Is it possible that all this time, while I was distracted on my phone, he was just standing in the line right in front of me? How is it possible for two people to like the same ice cream and order it back-to-back from the same ice cream shop? Maybe it's fate, and it's meant to be that we meet today. Oh, he is so handsome. I'm glad I grabbed his ice cream," she thinks.

Haiokïto asks, "Did you hear me? It's okay. I will check at the register."

Promptly, Huïumi responds, "No! Wait! Sorry, I ordered triple chocolate truffle ice cream in a waffle cone. Did you order the same exact ice cream as me, right before me?"

"I see what happened, we both ordered the same, and you've

mistaken your order for mine," Haiokïto says with a smile.

She, at once, sees a sparkle in his white teeth and thinks, "Oh, whoa. What a beautiful smile he has . . ." Then, she smiles back.

Huïumi cannot stop smiling as she speaks. She says, "Ooh boy. So sorry. I already tried the ice cream thinking it was mine. I'm only thinking about swapping orders right now."

For some reason, Haiokïto feels the same way and cannot stop smiling.

Haiokïto replies, "Deepïery thögh! That's fine. Tagrascïe."

"You're welcome . . ." Huïumi replies, a smile on her face.

"Aaah, Yeo . . . Yeo forgot to say my name. Is Haiokïto. And your name is?" he asks, blushing.

"Deepïery thögh! I am Huïumi. How wonderful to meet you, Haiokïto," she responds, touching her chest with her left hand.

"It's so nice to meet you, Huïumi," Haiokïto replies.

"Hmm. I saw you earlier today when yeo arrived at the mall," Huïumi says.

"Really?" Haiokïto asks.

"Mm, yes. You were standing outside the mall, looking up the sky and then you walked inside the mall and went straight up the stairs," Huïumi responds.

"Oh, wow. That explains the look on your face when you saw me," Haiokïto smiles.

"Mm-hmm," Huïumi nods, looking down at the floor.

"Yes. Earlier today, I was trying to decide if I should go home or get some ice cream. I was so tempted by the ice cream ads all over the mall," Haiokïto says.

"Tell me about it," Huïumi replies.

"The ice cream ads looked so delicious, I had to get ice cream," Haiokïto says.

"Are you visiting the city? Perhaps with relatives or friends. I don't know. Maybe . . . you can tell me," Huïumi chuckles.

"I am definitely a local. And you?" Haiokïto asks.

"Usïcs. Yeo live here," Huïumi responds.

Haiokïto says, "Can't wait for my order to be ready, haha. So jealous."

"This is the absolute best ice cream in the city. It's so hard to resist. So delicious," Huïumi says.

Haiokïto replies, "What a coincidence, we both like the same ice cream and we happen to order consecutively from the same ice cream shop."

"That's what I thought," Huïumi says.

They both laugh smugly.

The employee who prepares the orders at the ice cream shop says, "Triple chocolate truffle ice cream in a waffle cone is ready for pickup."

"That order surely is mine," Haiokïto says.

"Yes, hurry," Huïumi says with a smile as he walks away to pick up his order.

The employee who prepares the orders says, "Here's your ice cream. Have a nice day."

"Tagrascïe," Haiokïto replies, taking his ice cream and walking back to Huïumi.

Haiokïto says, "Such a small world, Huïumi."

"I know, Haiokïto," Huïumi replies.

Then, Haiokïto asks, "Do you have any plans? I mean, are you expecting to meet someone?"

"Usïcs. I mean gïocs. I was supposed to meet with my friends, but they cancelled earlier today right before I ordered my ice cream. Probably . . . that's why I didn't hear you ordering. I was so distracted on my phone that I mistakenly took your order. My bad. Sorry. What about you?" Huïumi asks.

Haiokïto responds, "All is good. I had a business lunch earlier today at the Glittmieda Restaurant on the tenth floor, but now my schedule is clear."

"Cool," Huïumi says.

They both made a brief pause waiting for the other to speak.

Haiokïto thinks, "I don't want to miss this opportunity. I will invite her out for a walk."

"Would you like to go for a walk in Stripes Park? It's not that far from here . . . We can finish eating our ice creams there, and why not share a little bit about each other. Of course, if that's okay with you," Haiokïto says.

"The Stripes Park? I love that park! It's a real gemmïe. I can't get enough of it; it's one of my top picks in the city . . . Yeo love its colorful stripes. Yeo love going there, especially on weekends for its movies and concerts. It's such a beautiful day to go for a walk there," Huïumi says, beaming, "(he asked me out)!"

"I don't have much free time to go to concerts and movies on the weekends because of work, but it sounds fun. So, is that a yes?" Haiokïto asks.

"Deepïery thögh! I don't have plans at all. I will be the happiest to join you. Thanks for asking," Huïumi says, "(infinitely, yes, yes, yes, oh, yes)!"

. . .

Smiling at each other, they began walking to Stripes Park. They couldn't take their eyes off each other. It's love at first sight. They, at once, connected as if they'd known each other for a long time.

With uncertainty, Huïumi says, "For some reason, you look a

little bit familiar." She shifts her tone to playful and says, "Hmm. I don't know; I believe I've seen you before. This is so weird, I feel like we have met. It feels like a *déjà vu.*"

"Really? I don't remember seeing you before," Haiokïto says.

"Strange. Maybe, it's just the connection between us," Huïumi says. Then, with a surprise tone, she says, "Oohh, I remember now. *Deepïery thögh!* It was a long time ago, when yeo traveled to Neephis, Kingdom of Neephiun, and frequented the Neephis Library to read romance books almost every day."

"Oh, really?" Haiokïto asks with a serious tone.

"Uh-huh. Do you—like reading?" Huïumi asks.

"Hmm. I . . ." Haiokïto says.

Huïumi says, "I remember seeing someone in the library who looked a lot like you. Seriously!"

Haiokïto looks at Huïumi and uncertainly asks, "Are you sure? In the Neephis Library?"

"Uh-huh. Why? Have you been to Neephis Library?" Huïumi asks as they continue walking to the park.

"Behold the Neephis Library, enchanted with romantic stories that only exist in the magical Kingdom of Neephiun, was more than honored to have the presence of this distinguished gentleman," he replies with humor.

Huïumi laughs, a soft whimsical sound escaping her lips. "You are full of whimsy."

"Sometimes," Haiokïto replies.

"What a small world," Huïumi says.

"Maybe you're right, and we surely crossed paths," he says.

"Mm-hmm. Eh, so when did you travel to Neephis?" she asks.

"Hmmm. Years ago . . ." Haiokïto answers.

"If it's not private to share, why did you travel there?" she asks.

"It's okay, I can answer that," Haiokïto responds.

"Oh, paccürs," Huïumi says.

"To find Love," Haiokïto says.

"Me too!" Huïumi replies.

"To be honest, yeo spent a good amount of time in the magical Neephis Library, where—" Huïumi interrupts, "ꜰairꜱ talᴇs coмᴇ truᴇ . . ."

Haiokïto laughs. He says, "You know it." He winks at Huïumi.

Blushing, Huïumi says, "Paccürs."

"To clear up doubts. How long ago was it?" Huïumi asks.

"We're talking about ten years ago, almost eleven years ago to be exact," Haiokïto replies.

"And I was there almost six years ago. I think, I must have seen someone else who looked a lot like you," she says.

He says, "Say no more, I assure you, we definitely didn't cross paths."

"Mm-hmm. And did you find Love there?" Huïumi asks.

"No, I met Neephoos," Haiokïto answers.

"Oh! You met Neephoos!" Huïumi says surprised.

"Usïcs!" Haiokïto replies.

"How was it?" Huïumi asks.

Haiokïto responds, "I remember on the night I met him, I went into the library after it was closed."

"Ooh, so mysterious, huh?" Huïumi says with a playful tone.

"Usïcs. I wanted privacy hoping Love will appear while I was alone, but instead it was Neephoos who showed up," Haiokïto says.

"And did he encourage you not to give up? What did he say?" Huïumi asks.

Haiokïto responds, "Uh-huh. I remember I was looking at the section of romantic books on the second floor when he said . . ."

. . .

Long ago, in Neephis Library, Kingdom of Neephiun.

Neephoos says, "Let me guess. You're looking for . . ."

"Huh? Shadows of the past and future!" he says, surprised to see Neephoos.

Neephoos asks, "How many books have you read looking for Love?"

"How many—books have I read?" Haiokïto asks.

"I don't have what you need or want, except a romantic story, hidden here," Neephoos says.

"And that means . . . What?" Haiokïto asks.

"You'll know soon enough," Neephoos answers.

"Is this a game of riddles?" Haiokïto asks.

"Trust again. . ." Neephoos says calmly.

"I'm not understanding anything," Haiokïto replies.

"The book you're holding in your hands, *Flameless*, is a tragedy romance. Love is beautiful and peaceful. Love is light and cheerful," Neephoos says.

"Who says?" Haiokïto asks.

"These books might be entertaining, but perhaps, if you think about it, Haiokïto, what you really need could be somewhere else," Neephoos replies.

"Where?" Haiokïto asks.

Neephoos replies, "Hidden in the bookshelves of this library."

Haiokïto asks, "Is that what you meant? When you said earlier, 'except a romantic story, hidden here.'"

"Don't lose hope and stay true to yourself. That's when you'll receive the Gowgwarts' Bracelet," Neephoos replies.

. . .

Master-Gowgwart-Love appears in the library.

"What's that?" Haiokïto asks.

"Did you see that?" Neephoos asks.

"The sparkling red crystals? Yes, I saw it," Haiokïto replies.

"That's good," Neephoos says.

"Isn't it strange? Oh, I see it again. A whole lot of red sparkling crystals," Haiokïto says.

"I think it's a sign from Love," Neephoos says.

"Do you think so? It's so magical and bright," Haiokïto replies.

Neephoos replies, "Forsooth, I am sure it is. She is magical."

"Maybe you're right, and it's a sign from Love. Wait, you didn't say your name when I asked, who says?" He pauses. "Also, I never told you my name. How do you know—my name?" Haiokïto asks.

"I am wisdom."

"My name is Neephoos."

"I hold information that only Love has."

"Call me, Wisdom, if you want."

"I can see the unseen and most desirable thoughts in people's minds. I'm never expected and rarely found. I can be colorful, black and white, just like the day and night. I am a sign that Love is not so far from being found," Neephoos replies.

"That makes sense. Still, it's strange. Where is Love?" Haiokïto asks.

"Love is everywhere . . . I'm part of Love, yet you only see me. We're together, but we're not," Neephoos answers.

"Hmmm? More riddles. Paccürs, paccürs," Haiokïto says.

Neephoos asks, "Have you wondered why you haven't found Love yet?"

"Gïocs! Not even a thought. Mm. Maybe . . ." Haiokïto replies.

Neephoos says, "Some answers are only within yourself."

"You're right, Neephoos; I've been here for six months now and nothing has changed. Yeo think it's best to change directions," Haiokïto replies.

"To the Kingdom of Gemmïes . . ." Neephoos says.

Haiokïto says, "Truly, your words cast sincerity. That's where I am going."

Neephoos says, "Be careful there, young man; things might not be what you expect."

"Huh?" Haiokïto asks.

Neephoos replies, "Let your heart guide you to find Love."

"Why do you say that?" Haiokïto asks.

"You'll need Love to see things as they are because they might be in disguise," Neephoos answers.

"In disguise?" Haiokïto asks.

"Have hope in Love," Neephoos replies.

"Paccürs," Haiokïto says.

"Adïour, Haiokïto," Neephoos says.

"Adïour, Neephoos," Haiokïto says.

.   .   .

Present time, at Stripes Park.

Haiokïto says, "Neephoos is wise and mysterious."

"He is a colorful lining, and he definitely appears in a sparkle of hope. That's how it happened with me. I'm glad to have met him. Also, he's very colorful and bright, not sure why he told you that he can also be black and white," Huïumi says.

"Hmmm." Haiokïto sighs.

Huïumi asks, "I'm curious, what happened next? Did you go to the Kingdom of Gemmïes?"

"Usïcs. Have you been to the Kingdom of Gemmïes?" he asks.

Huïumi shakes her head. "I read, it's a very wealthy kingdom, because of the variety of precious stones found in their mountïs. I don't really know much about it and never had the opportunity to go there. But I'm glad you did, so you can tell me everything about it," she replies.

"Oh, deepïery thögh! Count on that," Haiokïto replies.

"Did you follow Neephoos's advice?" Huïumi asks.

"Back then, I was so blinded by my obsession to find Love that yeo completely ignored what he said," Haiokïto answers.

"Don't we all do," Huïumi says, making a funny face.

Haiokïto replies, "I suspect that's why Neephoos said he could be black and white; not everyone can see his colors and brightness. And, at that time, I wasn't receptive to his wisdom. All I had in my mind was what I wanted to believe about Love, until I met her."

Huïumi says, "That makes sense. Tell me more. What did you do after Neephoos disappeared? Did you immediately travel to the Kingdom of Gemmïes?"

Haiokïto responds, "After I met Neephoos, I read a love story I found on the second floor, at the Neephis Library, where the king exiled his firstborn son from his kingdom."

Gasping, Huïumi asks, "Aaah! Why?"

"Because he fell in love with a girl who people said was half human and half spirit," Haiokïto answers.

"The king exiled his own son because of that?! Huïumi says.

"The king believed her powers would be catastrophic for their kingdom," Haiokïto replies.

"But why?" Huïumi asks.

"Because he feared the girl's powers, everyone was gossiping about her in court. He thought her powers were going to destroy his son the same way they almost destroyed him," Haiokïto replies.

"Ooh, I see," Huïumi says.

Haiokïto replies, "Yeah. But the truth is, she was only human, and her powers were the ones from the stones she wore in a bracelet that allowed her to balance her emotions. The king was aware of it, but he didn't want anyone to know it. So, when his son shared his good intentions to marry her, he opposed, doing everything possible to separate them."

"Oh, wow," Huïumi says.

Haiokïto replies, "Yeah, I know. But the crown prince of the Kingdom of Neephiun was so in love with her that he confronted his father."

"Aaah, is that the old famous story everyone talks about in The Six Kingdoms?" Huïumi asks.

"Uh-huh. This is the one," Haiokïto replies, nodding.

Huïumi replies, "No way! Really? I've always wanted to know this story."

With curiosity, Haiokïto asks, "What did you hear about it that made you so interested?"

"The romance. So charming," Huïumi replies.

"Of course, romanticize it! It's a true story that happened long ago, full of love," he says.

"I know. Isn't it awesome? Aww, tell me more! What happened next?" Huïumi asks.

"Oh, sure," he answers. "Out of anger, the king exiled him and the girl from his Kingdom and swore to never welcome them again."

Huïumi asks, "And what did the crown prince and the girl do next? Where did they go?"

"After being exiled from his own kingdom, the crown prince and the girl left the Kingdom of Neephiun, to move to the Kingdom of Gemmïes. There, they had a normal life until their time came to reign in the Kingdom of Neephiun," Haiokïto answers.

Huïumi says, "Oh, wow. That must have been really hard for them, especially the crown prince."

"I can't imagine being in his shoes," Haiokïto replies.

"And did the crown prince ever know why his father opposed to his marriage with the girl?" Huïumi asks.

"No. He never knew why the king disliked everything he loved about her so much," Haiokïto replies.

"So, what happened next?" Huïumi asks.

"With discontent and deepest sorrow in their hearts, after they left the Kingdom of Neephiun, they never saw King Neephis the Great again," Haiokïto replies.

Huïumi says, "How shocking. Why didn't the king give her a chance?"

"Good question," Haiokïto says.

Huïumi says, "I don't get it. I mean, the crown prince was very brave, and I am glad he stood up to his father, but he didn't get to see him again and that's very sad."

Haiokïto says, "King Neephis the Great was very judgmental, and he supported his decision of not accepting their marriage based on his personal experience with the stones; he feared what the stones could do to his son, so he remained firm in his decision."

Huïumi says, "But you can't judge other people based on your own individual experiences."

Haiokïto says, "I follow you, but remember that not everyone shares your perspective."

Huïumi replies, "I get it. But still, everyone's journey in life is different."

Haiokïto says, "That's valid, but for King Neephis, the stones in the bracelet she wore were a threat to his kingdom, and nothing was gonna change his mind about it."

"Definitely, completely different times and mentality," Huïumi replies.

"We're talking about centuries ago . . ." Haiokïto says.

"Makes sense," Huïumi replies, "(how come, I didn't find this book in the Neephis Library)?"

Haiokïto says, "Hmmm. It was . . ."

. . .

Long ago, in Neephis Library, Kingdom of Neephiun.

With a slight gasp and tilt of head, Haiokïto says, "Aaah. What on earth? So much dust." He takes the book and dusts it off.

Morphïea responds, "That's for sure the romance story you are looking for."

With wide eyes, raised eyebrows, and dropped jaw, Haiokïto says, "No way!"

Morphïea replies, "Two souls find each other, embrace change and grow together."

"This is the one! The one Neephoos was talking about. I found it!" Haiokïto says excitedly.

Morphïea replies, "With Love life begins. That's the one."

"Tagrascïe! You didn't introduce yourself, what's your name?" Haiokïto asks.

She responds, "I am Morphïea. The power of Love," Morphïea disappears.

"No! Wait! Morphïea!" Haiokïto shouts. "Oh snap. She's gone. And it was so fast, I couldn't ask her, where is Love?" he says.

. . .

Present time, at Stripes Park.

"I met Morphïea too, but briefly," Huïumi says.

"Really?" Haiokïto asks.

Huïumi nods. "Mm-hmm. Very brief. Really brief. Minutes. So, what happened next?" she asks.

"In the book?" Haiokïto asks.

"Yeah. Don't leave me hanging! Tell me the full story! I'm all ears," Huïumi responds.

Haiokïto replies, "You can imagine throughout the years, some pages could have gotten lost."

"What are you trying to say? The book is incomplete?" Huïumi asks, her voice held a hint of disappointment.

He nods. "Mm-hmm. But the good thing is that we don't need the missing pages," Haiokïto responds.

"Huh? I'm not following. How come?" Huïumi asks.

"My grandma knew this romantic story, and it was after I read the book in the Neephis Library, I concluded the story my grandma used to tell me when I was a teenager was the same one," Haiokïto replies.

"Really?" Huïumi asks.

He nods. "Mm-hmm. But then, I realized part of the story my grandma told me wasn't in the book, which confused me a lot, and for a moment, even though it was very similar, I doubted that it was the same story," Haiokïto replies.

"And how did you end up confirming it was the same story?" Huïumi asks.

Haiokïto replies, "It was then, when I met Master-Gowgwart-Love in the Kingdom of Gemmïes. In her special place, she told me everything else about the crown prince and the girl, which covered everything my grandma told me about the story."

"I can't believe what you just told me. Which leads me to think that maybe . . . she took the missing pages of the book," Huïumi says.

"Hmm, you might be right," Haiokïto says.

"Yes, give it some thought, Haiokïto," Huïumi replies.

"Hmm, the missing pages," Haiokïto says.

Huïumi nods. "Mm-hmmm. The things she told you that were part of the story but weren't in the book and that later on Master-Gowgwart-Love shared with you," she says.

He says, "Taccgrah! I never thought of it because why would my grandma do that?"

"It finally rings?" Huïumi asks.

"Yeah! You're right! The things my grandma told me about the stones in the bracelet—which are the same that Master-Gowgwart-Love shared with me in the Kingdom of Gemmïes—are just what's missing in the romance book I read in the Neephis Library," he says.

"We've solved the puzzle!" Huïumi says excitedly.

"Mm, yeah," Haiokïto replies, "(I wonder where those pages are)."

Huïumi says, "And now, I want to know absolutely everything about this fairy tale, Haiokïto. Including what you know about the stones in the bracelet."

"I won't be able to tell you everything about the stones today, but I can tell you the names of these magical stones in the bracelet," Haiokïto replies.

"Deepïery thögh! I'm okay with that," Huïumi says.

Haiokïto says, "Paccürs, the precious stones on the bracelet are ruby, pink sapphire, starry-night-blue sapphire, white jade, purple amethyst, yellow sapphire, and orange sapphire."

Huïumi looks at her Gowgwarts' Bracelet. She gasps. "Aaah! The bracelet that everyone talks about, but they can't say the name.

That's the positive Gowgwarts' Bracelet. I mean, not for nothing, but she wore a bracelet with these stones, and you just said that they balanced her emotions, representing her powers," Huïumi says.

He replies, "That's a great observation; indeed, it is."

"I knew it!" Huïumi says certain.

"And the stones of the negative Gowgwarts' Bracelet she wore are emerald, lavender tanzanite, blue topaz, peach sapphire, brown tourmaline, blue aquamarine, and white sapphire," Haiokïto says.

"I still need to learn about the magical powers of the negative emotions," Huïumi says.

"Leave that to me. I have the answers you need," he replies.

"Really?" Huïumi asks.

"Uh-ho! The negative emotions are also good for us," he says.

"Good for us?" Huïumi asks, her brows furrowed.

"Yeah. But only if you embrace its positive powers," Haiokïto says.

"Oh, I get it," Huïumi says, "(I don't know how yet)."

Haiokïto replies, "There's so much more to tell you about the Gowgwarts' Bracelet."

Huïumi says, "I can't believe this goes back to ancient times."

Haiokïto says, "The Gowgwarts' Bracelet is far more powerful than you think. It's a true gift from Master-Gowgwart-Love."

"We are so lucky to have it," Huïumi says with a smile.

.   .   .

"Hmm. I remember what Master-Gowgwart-Love said to me some time ago," Huïumi says with a cheerful tone.

"What did she say?" Haiokïto asks.

"'We're emotions with magical crystal stones that allow us to help people in different ways.'"

"'At times, we may take different forms, based on the needs of others. We are knowledge, spirit, and soul, transformed into energy, through which human beings perceive us.'"

"She also said, 'When we appear in your life, our shiny crystal ears will glow depending on how strong our spirit is within you. With time . . . With . . .' Phew, I don't remember the rest. Sorry, Haiokïto. This is all I remember right now," Huïumi says.

"That's alright, Huïumi. You remember many of the things she shared with you. I am impressed," Haiokïto replies.

"Tagrascïe. Love works in ways we can't imagine are possible," Huïumi says.

Haiokïto says, "Love gives you purpose and direction to live a life worth living, where one's life makes sense."

"That's true, nothing made sense to me until I met Love and received the Gowgwarts' Bracelet," Huïumi replies.

"Thus, it was for Crown Prince Phiuphos until Masseïel . . ." Haiokïto says.

Huïumi asks, "Can I add something?"

"Paccürs," Haiokïto answers.

"But before, can you tell me if Masseïel is the name of the girl?" Huïumi asks excitedly.

"Mm, yes. The name of the manuscript is *Masseïel & Phiuphos: A Tale of Love*," Haiokïto responds.

"I thought the name of the story was *A Tale of Love*, I didn't know the full name," Huïumi says.

"Why are you so excited about her name?" he asks.

Huïumi replies, "Because I know the meaning. And I love how magical it is."

"What is the meaning of her name?" Haiokïto asks.

Huïumi replies, "It's the star that shines among them all. Aww.

It's so magical. Right?" she asks.

"Yeah. Do you know the meaning of Phiuphos too?" Haiokïto asks.

"Usïcs, his name means dawn light," Huïumi replies.

"How refreshing. And what does your name mean?" Haiokïto asks.

"My name means so many things. It means to shine, glow, give out love, and it means the moon, but to me, it means flower and happiness. I will tell you a secret about my name. Before I was born, my mom used to do hameïeo every spring—to celebrate the beauty of new beginnings and life. And there is where she met my dad," Huïumi says.

"Hmm. Charming or should I say romantic?" Haiokïto says.

"Hahaha. Maybe both. Do you do hameïeo?" Huïumi asks.

Haiokïto shakes his head. He says, "No. But I know it means flower viewing, where people do picnics under a blossoming tree. Specifically cherry blossom flowers."

Huïumi replies, "Uh-huh. In fact, that's why my mom named me Huïumi. Because Huïumi means flower, and she says, I brought happiness to her life. So, of all the meanings of my name, flower and happiness mean the most to me."

"How nice," Haiokïto replies.

"And what does—your name mean?" Huïumi asks.

"I know the answer to that. My name means precious jewel," Haiokïto says with a smile.

"You're a precious jewel just like the stones of the Gowgwarts' Bracelet," Huïumi says.

Haiokïto blushed with Huïumi's comment.

Huïumi sees his cheeks turning reddish and asks, "What? Did I say something wrong? Sorry. I didn't mean that."

"No, I actually . . . liked it. I . . . I wasn't expecting it," Haiokïto replies.

"Phew. I feel better. Sometimes, hmm, I say what I think," she says embarrassed for what she said earlier.

"I like that," Haiokïto says with a shy smile.

"Tagrascïe. What were you going to say before we talked about the meaning of our names and so? Sorry I cut you off," Huïumi says.

Haiokïto replies, "Oh, that! You remember! I was about to say that they were lucky enough to have each other and the Gowgwarts' Bracelet."

Huïumi replies, "Aaah. Yes. Are you sure? I thought you were gonna say something else. And yes! They were very ʟᴜᴄᴋʎ, indeed."

.   .   .

"The Gowgwarts' Bracelet is the reason I went to the Kingdom of Gemmïes to find Love," Haiokïto says.

"The Gowgwarts' Bracelet?" Huïumi asks as she savors the last spoonful of ice cream.

Haiokïto replies, "Yes. Remember what we were talking about earlier?"

She responds, "The fairy tale your grandmother told you when you were a teenager, the book you found in the Neephis Library, the missing pages, and so on."

He replies, "You're spot on! It was the night I met Neephoos that his comment about the Gowgwarts' Bracelet reminded me of the story my grandma told me. At once, I thought, 'That book has to be here, hidden somewhere, and I will find it.'"

"*Smarty-brainy-genius*, I tell you," Huïumi says.

"You're exaggerating . . ." He laughs smugly. "Anyway, after Neephoos disappeared, yeo searched through all the bookshelves on both floors of the Neephis Library, until I finally found the romance story—the manuscript Morphïea said, 'That's surely the romance story you're looking for.' I looked closely at the name, *Masseïel & Phiuphos: A Tale of Love*, and immediately thought, 'This is the one,'" Haiokïto says.

"In one night?" Huïumi asks surprised.

"Gïocs! Silly. It took me a week to find it," Haiokïto replies.

"Now we're talking, I was lost in the sauce," Huïumi says.

"Laugh or laugh. No cap," Haiokïto says with a smile.

Huïumi says, "I'm listening." She smiles.

"That's when I came to realize that it was the same story, but after reading it, I wasn't entirely sure because of the missing pages. Anyway, I started searching for the full manuscript in other libraries in the city," Haiokïto says.

"And I guess . . . You were not lucky ducky," Huïumi says.

"Not the kind of *lucky ducky* guy back then, so one night after I got home, I decided to change direction and started packing my suitcase to move to the Kingdom of Gemmïes," Haiokïto replies.

She says, "So that's how you ended up moving to the Kingdom of Gemmïes. Huh?"

He nods. "Mm-hmmm. I thought, If I found the Gowgwarts' Bracelet, I was going to find Love. In the end, it was the complete opposite—I needed to find Love so I could find the Gowgwarts' Bracelet. And it wasn't that easy, but Master-Gowgwart-Love made it possible," Haiokïto replies.

"That's why Neephoos told you, you would need Love to see things for what they are, because he knew the reason you were going to the Kingdom of Gemmïes," Huïumi says.

"Mm-hmmm, and there's more . . ." Haiokïto replies.

"About how your grandmother met Master-Gowgwart-Love?"

Huïumi asks, "(does he knows how)?"

Haiokïto replies, "No, I don't know how it happened for her. And she's no longer with us . . . is sad to think about."

"Sorry, Haiokïto," Huïumi replies.

"It's alright," Haiokïto says.

She asks, "Is it about the Kingdom of Gemmïes? Maybe the emotions you met?"

Haiokïto responds, "There's so much to tell you. Anyway, it's a long story, and it's getting late. If I didn't have to travel tomorrow, I'd stay a little longer. I really want to see you again."

Huïumi replies, "Paccürs. I'll be happy to see you again."

Haiokïto says, "I had a wonderful time talking with you today, Huïumi."

Huïumi replies, "Me too. It was a wonderful time spent with you."

"Can I have—your number?" Haiokïto asks.

"Oh, deepïery thögh," Huïumi says with a smile.

Huïumi thinks, "How are we going to see each other again if we don't have each other's number."

"Great!" Haiokïto replies with a cool voice.

"Save my number and text me to save yours," she says.

"I'll send you a message so we can schedule sometime to meet again," Haiokïto says.

"Sounds cool," Huïumi replies.

"I promise, as soon as I return from my travels, I'll tell you all about the Gowgwarts' Bracelet," Haiokïto says.

"Fantastic!" Huïumi replies with an exciting voice.

"I'd also like to know more about you . . ." he says.

She blushes, scratches her forehead, and with a smile she says, "Uh-huh, I'll confirm my availability once I hear back from you."

He replies, "So exciting. It was a pleasure to meet you."

"Can't wait to see you again," Huïumi says with a smile.

"I am glad I decided to get ice cream today," he says.

"Likewise. Safe travels and until next time," she replies.

"Adïour and see you soon, Huïumi," Haiokïto says.

"Adïour, Haiokïto," Huïumi says, waving goodbye.

As he walks away, she begins to think, "If he just knew that my story ended up being much more than I ever wanted or wished for. I am indeed a very . . . Lucky girl."

.　　.　　.

After saying goodbye to each other, the night fell, and the stars began to appear in the sky.

The Big Bright Star says, "I know all of you are excited about what just happened."

"Uh-huh. She's the girl who was looking for true love in the wrong places," the HoneyBee Stars reply.

"She found truest love first—self-love, and then she found her true love, and it happened right when she wasn't looking for it," The Big Bright Star says.

In a sweet voice, the HoneyBee Stars say, "Aaah. So romantic."

"Two people with diverse backgrounds met on a random day to give life to romantic true love," The Big Bright Star replies.

The HoneyBee Stars separate to form multiple heart shapes.

Master-Gowgwart-Love joins the HoneyBee Stars and The Big Bright Star in the sky.

"As they were still eating their ice creams and talking in Stripes Park, people passing by wouldn't stop looking at them. Everyone could notice the connection between them. It was like for her there was only him and for him there was only her and nothing else. That was magically enchanting," Master-Gowgwart-Love says.

The Big Bright Star replies, "They focused on themselves until they were ready, and the universe finally brought them together."

"Aaah, even more romantic. I love, Love," the HoneyBee Stars say in a sweet voice, as they begin to form a big bright happy face, shining as much as The Big Bright Star.

Thereupon, Love becomes light merging with The Big Bright Star as it disappears into the sky.

Four

The Fall and Rising of Haiokïto

After a few weeks of watching the day and night pass by, a new day begins in The Six Kingdoms, giving hope to all the things that can only be possible with Love.

"Today is the day, Hïuramïur! The day of the picnic has finally arrived," Huïumi says excitedly.

"Usïcs! You're overly excited. What time? You're ready and it's not even noon yet. Mm? You woke up early today," Hïuramïur says.

"That's because Haiokïto asked me to meet him around noon today," Huïumi replies.

"You are running out of time," Hïuramïur says, looking at the time in the living room.

Huïumi replies, "Hmm, but first let's make sure all items of my list are checked off. I don't want to forget anything."

Huïumi reads, "Freshly baked üossant, ham, and cheese?"

Hïuramïur looks inside the floral-lined Ūmieda picnic basket, adorned with vibrant colored flowers. "In here," Hïuramïur replies.

Huïumi continues reading, "Raspberry jammeïe, peanut butter, and utensils?"

Hïuramïur replies, "In here. Is that all you need for the picnic? I don't see anything else."

She nods. "Mm-hmm. I am finally ready to go. Yay! Wish me

luck. Do I look pretty?" she asks.

Hïuramïur says, "Uh-huh. You do! I wish thou hast a magical date with thy heart's winner."

"Adïour, Hïuramïur! Don't rest too much. I will be back soon," Huïumi says, waving goodbye.

She steps outside her one-bedroom apartment on the second floor of a brown two-hundred-year-old townhouse, which has been her home for the past five years.

. . .

Pherrïland, Gowgwarts' Workshop.

Master-Gowgwart-Joy says, "Yes! She's arriving to Spïeral Park Tower."

Master-Gowgwart-Care replies, "Nooo! The picnic is today. I forgot! Let me see."

"Come! Come see. Look. He's there. He's standing outside his building waiting for her to arrive," Master-Gowgwart-Love says.

"He's the one!" Master-Gowgwart-Trust says.

"Yes! Forsooth," Master-Gowgwart-Love says.

"Oh, I feel it too! Stars sparkling with purple sparkles," Master-Gowgwart-Freedom says.

The Star of the Universe appears.

"Aaah! Freedom!" The Star of the Universe gasps.

"I was referring to my sparkles. Welcome, glamorous," Master-Gowgwart-Freedom replies.

Master-Gowgwart-Love says, "Master-Gowgwart-Freedom is very much excited because Huïumi and Haiokïto are having a picnic today."

"When the sunlight is gone, and the moon lost; the moon will cover the sun that illuminates the earth, until the moon finds its way to the night again. Thereupon, while the moon meets with the stars as it brings light to the night, the sun will move around the earth to bring light to the day," The Star of the Universe says, sparkling shiny purple amethyst everywhere.

.   .   .

Haiokïto turns his face to the left and sees Huïumi is arriving, wearing a two-toned pink Ūmieda linen dress. At once, he blushes feeling nervous. And when Huïumi sees him standing outside with a fresh haircut and wearing white linen pants, a plain white t-shirt with a red short-sleeved jacket and red shoes, she blushes too.

They both seem nervous and can't find the right words to greet each other.

"Heïjour! Eh. Yeo. Aah," Haiokïto says, "(what did I just say)?"

"Heïjour! Joureïe!" Huïumi says, "(what was that)?"

They hug each other.

"I love your braids! Nicely done! Did you do them yourself?" he asks.

"Usïcs! Tagrascïe! Nice haircut!" Huïumi replies with a smile.

"What's that?" Haiokïto asks, looking at her picnic basket.

"Oh! The Ūmieda basket?" Huïumi asks.

Haiokïto nods. "Mm-hmmm. For lunch?" he asks.

"Uh-huh! How you guess? *Smarty-brainy-genius*," Huïumi says.

"Oh! The picnic basket!" Haiokïto smiles.

"Deepïery thögh!" Huïumi smiles.

"Let's walk to Spïeral Park. I know of a peaceful haven secret garden I used to frequent a lot that only a few people know. It's like a gemmïe, you know? A lesser-known city escape hidden in a plain sight from all the locals that enjoy picnic at the park," Haiokïto says.

"Ohh. Paccürs!" Huïumi replies.

.   .   .

Hïuramïur followed Huïumi to Spïeral Park, sat near the secret garden from a not-so-distant place, from where he could see them from afar.

Hïuramïur thinks, "Huïumi thought I'd stay home and let her go to the picnic alone. Gïocs! No way! I'm her protector. She doesn't need to know. I'll stay here until she's ready to go home."

"Heïjour! Joureïe, pretty flower," Hïuramïur says . . .?

.   .   .

"Between the day and night, there is a thin line defined by you," Haiokïto says.

"How so?" Huïumi asks.

"You'll find out soon, as I tell you my story," Haiokïto replies.

"Mm, paccürs," Huïumi says.

"When yeo got to the Kingdom of Gemmïes in search of Love, I met a girl with long brown hair. I remember when I first arrived at the building I was moving into, she was wearing an *ablanc* long dress with black sandals and she was sitting in the lobby right next to the entrance of the building. I was amazed by her beauty and couldn't stop staring at her emerald, green eyes," Haiokïto says.

"And?" Huïumi asks.

"Well, she saw me arriving with my big, square, yellow Ūmieda suitcase—filled with all my personal belongings—and immediately introduced herself," Haiokïto says with a casual tone.

.   .   .

Ten years ago, city of Mountïs, Kingdom of Gemmïes.

"Joureïe, nice suitcase," Lïesia says as she puts away her phone.

"Tagrascïe," Haiokïto says a little bit shy.

"Are you moving into the building?" Lïesia asks.

"Yes. Just arrived in the city. Heïjour! My name is Haiokïto."

Lïesia replies, "Pretty name, Haiokïto. Welcome to the city of Mountïs. My name is Apple just like the fruit."

Haiokïto says, "I like apples. They're sweet and healthy. Catchy name, Apple. Short and sweet." He smiles.

"It might be weird, but apples are my favorite fruit too," Lïesia chuckles.

"I don't think it's weird, I think it's sweet," he replies.

"Mm, Tagrascïe! Are you going to be my new neighbor?" Lïesia asks.

"Huh?" He looks at her, confused by her question.

"There's an empty apartment on my floor, silly," Lïesia says.

"Aaahh. My apartment is on the last floor. Is that your floor?" Haiokïto asks.

Lïesia smiles. "Uh-ho! You're on my floor, new neighbor," she says.

"Cool. Neighbor," Haiokïto says with a smile.

"Welcome! Welcome, Haiokïto," Lïesia says.

"Tagrascïe! See you around, Apple," Haiokïto replies.

.   .   .

After settling into his apartment, in search of clues to find the Gowgwarts' Bracelet, Haiokïto begins to research about the stones.

Master-Gowgwart-Love appears.

She blows warm wind towards Haiokïto to give him a sign and then disappears.

Haiokïto feels the warm wind. He thinks, "I have to close these windows. Wait, I don't remember opening them. Hmm. Maybe the windows were open before I moved in. Hmm, I'll check just to be sure." He gets up and walks towards the windows. "The windows aren't open. Mmm. How strange? Where's the wind coming from?" he thinks.

Haiokïto returns to his desk.

"How can the windows be closed? It doesn't make sense. I felt a warm breeze, blowing into my room. A soft sighing sound. Maybe it's nothing or who knows. I'll let it pass and focus on my research," he thinks.

"After reading some articles about the mountïs, I still haven't found any clues about the Gowgwarts' Bracelet . . . Nothing leading me on to finding Love; instead, I've found a mountïs that's not far from here," Haiokïto thinks.

He says, "Yeo don't know if it's true, but this website says that Love has appeared on that mountïs before. What's the name of the mountïs?"

Haiokïto reads, "The Tanzanite Mountïs, the mountïs of the lavender tanzanite stone."

"I'd better plan to go there," Haiokïto says.

Before going to sleep, Haiokïto set his alarm to wake-up at 5:45 a.m. and then saved the directions to go to the mountain the next day.

. . .

As the moon continues its journey around The Six Kingdoms, dawn brings light to a new day. Meanwhile . . .

"Ohh snaps! I missed my alarm! It's almost 6:00 a.m. I need to get ready to go to the mountïs. I won't even have time for a ppucceïe and my favorite—a cceïebbu," Haiokïto says.

. . .

On his way out, he sees Lïesia two doors down walking outside her apartment.

"Heïjour, Apple. Joureïe? Apple? That's your name, right?" he asks.

Lïesia turns and says, "Joureïe, new neighbor! Sorry, I'm a little sleepy."

"I know the feeling . . . I missed my alarm this morning. Where are you going?" Haiokïto asks.

"On my way to work," Lïesia answers.

"Where do you work?" Haiokïto asks.

"You woke up with a lot of energy today. Huh? What's with all these questions?" Lïesia asks.

"Can you tell?" Haiokïto chuckles.

"It's the most successful jewelry store in town right before the Tanzanite Mountïs," Lïesia replies.

"How nice. I'm actually going there this morning," he says.

"To Masseïel's Jewels?" Lïesia asks.

"No. I'm going to the mountïs," Haiokïto responds.

Lïesia chuckles. "Yeo was gonna say, are you following me?"

"How? Yeo didn't even know the name of the jewelry store," Haiokïto replies.

"How can you not know the name?" Lïesia asks.

"Just moved in, capïcsh?" Haiokïto replies.

"Mm, right. My bad," Lïesia says.

"It's alright," he says as they walk towards the elevator.

Lïesia replies, "No! My bad, really. Okay. I'll tell you about the store. Masseïel's Jewels store owes its name to the ancient love story of Crown Prince Phiuphos and Masseïel, who later on became King Phiuphos I and Queen Masseïel of the Kingdom of Neephiun."

Entering the elevator, he says, "How funny, I just traveled here from the Kingdom of Neephiun."

"Really?" Lïesia asks.

"Mm-hmm. In fact, I read the manuscript, *Masseïel & Phiuphos: A Tale of Love* by Masseïel, back in the Neephis Library in the city of Neephis," Haiokïto responds.

Lïesia gasps. "Aaah! I've always wanted to go there," she says.

"That means you didn't read their story in the Neephis Library. Did you?" Haiokïto asks as they step outside of the elevator to leave the building.

Lïesia replies, "Gïocs! All employees of Masseïel's Jewels must read their story. It's part of our onboarding process. Yeo wish. Not joking."

"That's impressive. I believe you," Haiokïto says.

"Well, it's not that impressive . . . What's impressive is that you read the original manuscript in the Neephis Library. I only got to read the synopsis. That's why I wanted to travel to the Kingdom of Neephiun to visit the Neephis Library. I wanted to read the whole story, and I've also heard that magical things happen there," Lïesia replies as they continue walking to catch the bus.

Haiokïto replies, "Yeah, that's why I went there. But yeo didn't find what I was looking for. Anyway, I ended up moving here, where yeo hope I can find it."

With a romantic tone, Lïesia says, "I think you already found it." She smiles.

"Hmm? Not sure what you mean," Haiokïto replies with a dry tone.

Speaking with an extremely muffled voice, Lïesia says, "Ugh. He doesn't get it."

Haiokïto asks, "Huh? did you say something?"

Lïesia replies, "I'm saying, yes!"

"Aaah. Isn't it the same way to get to the mountïs?" he asks as he is looking at the bus sign.

"What? On the bus?" Lïesia asks.

"Mm-hmmm. Can I take the bus with you?" he asks.

Lïesia replies, "Paccürs, that's fine. It's the same bus."

"Great! I'd love to have you as my tour guide while we travel together by bus. You seem, like, you know a lot about the city of Mountïs," Haiokïto says.

"Deepïery thögh! I can share some local knowledge with you," Lïesia says.

The bus arrives; they pay the fare and sit in the back until they reach their destination.

.   .   .

Haiokïto is on his way to get his mail, and there's Lïesia in the mailroom. "Joureïe, Apple," he says.

Lïesia sees Haiokïto. "Hey! joureïe, how was your day?" Lïesia asks, cheerfully.

"I'm just picking up my mail," Haiokïto says, casually.

Lïesia asks, "How was the mountïs? Did you get any precious jewels? Perhaps . . . a lavender tanzanite bracelet in their shops?"

Haiokïto replies, "No, not really. It was closed for extractions. It wasn't my lucky day to buy jewelry or to discover the secrets of the mountïs."

"Oopsy-daisy! I forgot what day it's today. They do extractions the day before they open for tourists. I'm sorry, I forgot about it this morning," Lïesia says.

"You're forgetting a lot of things. It's fine. I should've looked at their schedule last night. I guess . . . I was too tired and sleepy from travels. I'll go back another day," Haiokïto says.

"I don't work on weekends. Do you want to go to the mountïs with me? We could also go to the movies and, I don't know, go to the mountïs another day. What do you think? Would you accept my invitation? I can be your tour guide for a day," Lïesia says, "(I hope he says yes, I really like him)."

Haiokïto chuckles. "Why not? Let's go to the movies, and I'll go to the mountïs later," he says.

"That's a date. See you tomorrow, neighbor," she says.

"Paccürs. See you tomorrow, Apple," he says, waving goodbye.

"Oh, about that. My real name is Lïesia," she says.

"Wait, what?" Haiokïto asks, surprised.

"Yeah! It was a silly joke. Don't be mad," Lïesia replies.

"It's okay. Why would I be mad? Both names suit you, Lïesia," Haiokïto says.

"Aww. Tagrascïe, Haiokïto. See you tomorrow. Night," Lïesia says.

"Night, Apple. Sorry, Lïesia," Haiokïto says.

Lïesia chuckles. "Paccürs!" she says.

So, from that night on, Haiokïto and Lïesia spent most of their time together, at a point that he forgot about finding the Gowgwarts' Bracelet, which was the main reason he had traveled to the Kingdom of Gemmïes.

.   .   .

A year after moving to the Kingdom of Gemmïes.

Haiokïto sends a text to Lïesia.

Haiokïto: Happy anniversary, love.

Haiokïto: Dinner at my place tonight?

Haiokïto: 7:00 p.m. good? Yeo have a surprise.

Lïesia: Happy anniversary!

Lïesia: Paccürs, see you at 7:00 p.m.

Lïesia: Tagrascïe!

Haiokïto: Love u!

"Perfect! She's coming tonight. Now, it's time to prepare everything for the surprise," Haiokïto thinks as he jumps out of bed.

.   .   .

Lïesia knocks on the door. "Qomïen," Haiokïto says.

"Everything is perfect. The cheesy macceïe is on the table and the candles are lit," Haiokïto thinks.

Haiokïto opens the door. "You arrived on time," he says.

"Usïcs! It's our anniversary," Lïesia replies.

"Happy anniversary!" Haiokïto says.

They hug and briefly kiss each other.

Lïesia gasps and says, "Aaah, this is so romantic. Aww, I love the candles. You also ordered my favorite, cheesy macceïe meatballs with a glaze of spicy honey. So thoughtful."

Haiokïto says, "Tagrascïe! I wanted tonight to be extra special."

Lïesia with a tender voice says, "I love you."

"I love you too," Haiokïto replies.

"Shall we eat now? I'm so hungry," Lïesia says.

"Deepïery thögh!" Haiokïto replies.

.   .   .

Moments later, while eating macceïe.

"I have something important I want to ask you tonight. This is a big step in our relationship, and yeo want to use this occasion for that," Haiokïto says.

"Oopsy-daisy! He's going to propose," Lïesia thinks. "Same! I also have something important to say," she says.

"After you," Haiokïto says.

"This isn't the best time to share this with you and believe me, I had to process it myself but here it goes. I suspect you're going to ask me to marry you . . . and before you say anything, I want to give you the opportunity to choose. Recently, I received a diagnosis with a terminal illness," Lïesia says.

A moment of silence.

He holds her hands. "Please don't do this, Lïesia," he says.

With a gloomy voice, Lïesia says, "I don't have much time. I'm grateful for the time we've spent together, and yeo hope that, after I'm gone, you'll find love again."

Haiokïto cries, upset, "Taccgrah! Why?"

Lïesia says, "This has come to me as a surprise too. I know it's the worst timing. I love you and that's why I had the urge to tell you. You deserve it all . . . Everything in The Six Kingdoms. You're my greatest gift, Haiokïto."

"Yeah, but this was supposed to be a happy celebration of a new beginning over macceïe and laughter to start building our lives together, and instead, turned out to be the opposite," Haiokïto says, "(since my grandma passed away, this is the hardest thing in a long-time yeo had to deal with. I'm gonna propose anyway)."

"Marry me! I want you to be my wife for as long as you live," Haiokïto says with a comforting voice.

"Are you sure?" Lïesia asks with a serious voice.

"Usïcs! Completely sure. With all my heart. I only want you," Haiokïto says with a gleeful voice.

Lïesia nods. "Paccürs. I will marry you. I love you," she says.

Both cried with joy and sadness.

. . .

Present time, Spïeral Park.

Haiokïto says, "Three months later, we got married. It was a simple wedding with our closest friends in the city of Mountïs."

"Yeo don't know what to say," Huïumi says.

"I did absolutely everything you can possibly imagine, making each day less painful and more joyful for her, until there was nothing left to do to keep her alive. It was really hard," Haiokïto says.

Huïumi says, "You loved her. Only you know how much you had to overcome."

"Seeing her suffer and being unable to do anything to ease her pain, turned me into a different person. After her passing, I struggled to cope with the negative emotions," he says.

.   .   .

City of Mountïs, Kingdom of Gemmïes. Two years after Lïesia passed away.

"Lïesia? Lïesia, is that you?" Haiokïto asks.

Lïesia says, "Come! Come! Come to Raef Mountïs! Come to the mountïs where the lavender tanzanite stone is found."

Haiokïto replies, "I can't go there. Sorry! You're at the top of the hill."

"I am waiting for you. Remember you wanted to come here. Don't forget that's the real reason why you came to the Kingdom of Gemmïes before you met me," Lïesia says.

Haiokïto wakes up. He gasps. "Aaah! It was a dream," he says.

"I continue having the same dream. I'm going to cancel all my meetings for the week. I am going to Raef Mountïs, the mountïs of the lavender tanzanite stone," Haiokïto says.

.   .   .

The next day, he arrives at the mountain early in the morning and when he's at the top of the hill, he hears a voice calling his name, "Haiokïto, Haiokïto, Haiokïto."

Haiokïto thinks, "Who's calling my name? Who? Whose voice is that?"

He hears the voice again. "Haiokïto, I am waiting for you, keep walking and you will find me; follow my voice," says the voice.

Haiokïto follows the voice until he finds a cave.

Haiokïto thinks, "I am here, but all I can see is a cave that looks as if it's empty. I am confused; I think . . . I'm in the wrong place."

As Haiokïto turns to leave, he hears the voice again. "You are only seeing the surface, don't leave yet. I am here. Turn around and you will see me," says the voice.

Haiokïto does as told by the voice.

"A shiny lavender tanzanite stone is what I see inside the cave," Haiokïto replies.

"I'm more than just a lavender tanzanite stone," says the voice.

Confused, Haiokïto says, "A lavender tanzanite stone is all I can see. How can a lavender tanzanite stone talk? Or is this voice only in my head? Am I going insane?"

"I could be many things; I'm certainly not what you're looking for," says the voice.

"Who are you then? I want to know. Is this a riddle? I have no idea who or what you are, nor do I know what you mean by saying that you could be many things," Haiokïto replies.

"I'm odd. When you decided to isolate yourself from everyone, you brought my spirit to life. Lïesia wouldn't have wanted you to live afraid of everything . . . Scared to fall in love again because you believe it will end the same way. You have to take risks. No matter how it might be, you have to embrace the unknown. How can you know how it's going to end if you don't try or at least are open to give yourself a chance?" asks the voice.

With a wrathful voice, Haiokïto replies, "That's not true. Stop talking as if you know me. You're lying. How can you know anything about Lïesia? Who are you to tell me what to do? You know nothing about my pain. This is the only way that yeo can protect myself from hurting again."

Emerging from the cave, with a grand voice, "All the time you have invested in building walls to protect yourself from the outer world has brought you here . . . I am Fear. Master-Gowgwart-Fear."

Haiokïto gasps and says, "Aaah. It was your glowing ears that illuminated the cave."

Master-Gowgwart-Fear replies, "You are not channeling your pain the right way, and your obsession with me is driving you insane. How can I make you see that right now, I'm not good for you, and that here with me, you're going to end on the edge of the hill?"

"The edge of the hill?" Haiokïto asks, looking back.

Master-Gowgwart-Fear says, "You are trapped here with me. There's no way out of this hill. Love isn't here to save you."

Haiokïto is thinking as Master-Gowgwart-Fear finishes talking, "Only with the power of Love I can break free from Fear."

Master-Gowgwart-Fear continues, "Without Love, you won't be able to survive." He cackles.

Frightened by Master-Gowgwart-Fear, he falls to the ground.

"Yeo came here looking for Love. You're a monster. A big liar. Don't get closer to me! Stay away and go back to your cave. That's where you belong. Your words have zero power over me, and your beautiful lavender tanzanite glow will soon disappear. Watch how I undo all these walls. I don't need them anymore. And yes, it's true, you're driving me insane, but I want to be free from you," he says.

Haiokïto crawls backwards towards the edge of the hill.

"Yes! I am a liar, but it was you who created these stone walls, not me," Master-Gowgwart-Fear replies with a firm voice showing the walls to Haiokïto.

Elevating his voice, Haiokïto replies, "I don't know what I see anymore. You won't destroy me. I'll have hope until my last breath. I know Love will appear anytime. Love will save me. This is not the end of me. Not now, not like this, not today."

Master-Gowgwart-Fear sings, "Stone Walls." With his powers, he shows Haiokïto all the images of everything he built to push Love away and never fall in love again.

Master-Gowgwart-Fear says, "See? Can you see now? I'm but a reflection of what's in your mind. These walls brought you to Raef Mountïs, not me. You have come to the wrong place to find Love. This is my mountïs, not Love."

"You tricked me! Yeo followed your voice," Haiokïto says.

"Did you really think all these walls were protecting you? Huh? Burying yourself in your pain and increasing your suffering instead of facing it and focusing on what to do to neutralize me. Don't you get it? I have fooled you! My name is backwards; this is Mountïs of Fear where not everyone survives." Master-Gowgwart-Fear cackles.

Haiokïto gasps. "Raef is Fear. You're right. I am in the wrong place. I have made a mistake," he says.

Master-Gowgwart-Fear says, firmly, "A healthy boundary is all you needed, not these walls you see. Have you heard anything about balance? . . . All extremes are dangerous. Hmmm? How can I put it? Approaching life understanding that everything is temporary and that experiences are unique to each individual, can foster a sense of trust."

"Trust? Trusting only led me to pain," Haiokïto replies.

"Don't use your past experiences to punish yourself. If so, it will lead to a toxic behavior, and you'll end up hurting other people including you. Your past experiences are there to give you wisdom, not to drag you over the edge," Master-Gowgwart-Fear says.

Looking back, Haiokïto says, "Oh snaps! I am getting closer to the edge."

"Now, it's too late for you. Your time is about to end," Master-Gowgwart-Fear says, with a grand voice, cackling.

. . .

Master-Gowgwart-Love appears flying around the top of the Mountain of Fear.

Hoping he hears her voice, Master-Gowgwart-Love says, "Stay strong and have hope! Look up! I am here! I have come to rescue you from Master-Gowgwart-Fear. It's me, Love! Haiokïto, I give you willpower so you can hear my voice."

Sparkling red crystals form a blanket surrounding the edge of the mountain.

. . .

Master-Gowgwart-Fear walks two steps closer to Haiokïto and Haiokïto walks two steps back, getting even closer to the edge of the hill.

"One more step back, and you'll be finished. It will be quick, and you won't have to worry about building walls to protect yourself from pain anymore," Master-Gowgwart-Fear says.

With a desperate voice, Haiokïto says, "Love! Where are you? I believe in you, please save me. Sorry for ignoring your signs and even forgetting you. I need you. Please!"

In a lively voice, Master-Gowgwart-Love replies, "Here I am!

Hear my voice, it's the only way I can save you."

Master-Gowgwart-Fear is growing bigger as he gets closer to Haiokïto to push him to the edge.

Meanwhile, Haiokïto looks back.

Haiokïto says, "Taccgrah! There's no more room. I'm getting closer to the edge. This is the end . . . Oh snaps! Master-Gowgwart-Fear is so huge, I don't have a choice. I'm gonna trust-fall." Without a thought, he gives his last step back, falling onto the red crystals' blanket.

As Haiokïto falls, he says, "The red crystals! It's Love! Love didn't abandon me! Love saved me!"

His hope to find Love allowed him to hear her voice, enabling her powers to save him when he fell from the top of the cliff of the Mountain of Fear.

Master-Gowgwart-Love carries Haiokïto in her wings, to a safe place made only for Love.

. . .

The sunlight enters through the shining rubies surrounding the couch, waking-up Haiokïto from the traumatizing fall from the top of the cliff of the Mountain of Fear. He lies on a ruby-stone couch.

Haiokïto thinks, "Where am I? Is this heaven? Why are there so many rubies everywhere?"

"You're finally awake," Master-Gowgwart-Love says.

Confused, Haiokïto sees Master-Gowgwart-Love. "Huh? An angel! I am truly in heaven," he says.

Master-Gowgwart-Love chuckles. She says, "Oh, dear. It's me Love. Master-Gowgwart-Love. I saved you when you were falling from the Mountïs of Fear."

Haiokïto takes a deep breath. "Yeo remember, the red crystals' blanket. What a relief. I can't believe it's you," he says.

"Oh dear, you're safe now," Master-Gowgwart-Love says with a hopeful voice.

"I went to Raef Mountïs looking for you and instead I found Master-Gowgwart-Fear. It was the dream. Yeo kept dreaming about going there," Haiokïto says.

Master-Gowgwart-Love says, "Sometimes in hope of finding something that you long for, you can find something else."

"I don't understand . . . Thinking it would lead me to you, yeo travelled here to look for the Gowgwarts' Bracelet. Then, I read that you appeared on that mountïs before and that's why I went there. Everything I read about Raef Mountïs is a lie. In the end, I did find you, but it didn't happen the way I thought it would be," Haiokïto says.

"Only through me can you receive the Gowgwarts' Bracelet. Oh, my dear, you read about the Tanzanite Mountïs, the mountïs of the lavender tanzanite stone. Sometimes, things aren't the way you may think they are," Master-Gowgwart-Love replies.

"No kidding, I dreamed about Raef Mountïs. It was the dream. That's how Master-Gowgwart-Fear tricked me. He confused me!" Haiokïto shakes his head.

Master-Gowgwart-Love replies, "In the past, I only appeared in that mountïs to save others who, like you, went there looking for me. Yet not everyone was able to survive Master-Gowgwart-Fear, because they didn't believe in me the way you did. Your hope in me, kept my memory alive in you, allowing you to bring my spirit to life."

"How did Master-Gowgwart-Fear grow so strong?" Haiokïto asks.

Master-Gowgwart-Love replies, "Unconsciously, you began to feel Fear and little by little you began to build walls that separated you from everyone."

Haiokïto says, "Master-Gowgwart-Fear showed me the stone walls yeo thought were protecting me but instead were destroying me."

"These walls turned you into a person with a negative outlook on life. You were blinded by Pain and there was no room for Trust in your life anymore," Master-Gowgwart-Love replies.

"I felt like I was going insane. I perceived everything as a threat and I couldn't trust anyone until I faced Master-Gowgwart-Fear and realized I was wrong," Haiokïto says.

"All extremes are dangerous, dear. It's important to remember awareness of your emotions and to recognize that being emotionally balanced is your responsibility," Master-Gowgwart-Love replies.

"I didn't know it until I faced Master-Gowgwart-Fear. Perhaps it was my ignorance that led me to Raef Mountïs," Haiokïto says.

"You ignored Fear and really put yourself in danger," Master-Gowgwart-Love replies.

Haiokïto says, "I must admit that my lack of awareness almost destroyed me at the top of the mountïs. Yeo look back now and see how lonely I was and how much yeo kept myself from loving again. To the point where I began to see flaws in everyone and started to push everyone away."

Master-Gowgwart-Love says, "Being aware of your emotions is key to create emotional balance. See it from the bright side. It can really help you avoid extreme behaviors, that can cause an emotional disconnection with yourself."

"Now I understand, I must change. I can't keep living like this. Yeo must find a way to open myself to all the good things that await me. I must do it for myself," he says.

"Not letting your past experiences interfere, is a good way to begin embracing all the good things in life with an open and positive mindset, creating more fulfilling and joyful experiences. Think of it as a fresh start," Master-Gowgwart-Love replies.

"Hmm, I guess . . . that's why I didn't notice how Fear grew stronger in me," Haiokïto says.

"To protect yourself from repeating past experiences, all you need are healthy boundaries that can still allow you to be emotionally stable, engaged, and effective with those around you; not walls that'll completely block your mind from seeing things for what they are, at a point that you have zero trust in other people. That can create a disruption in the harmonious state of your emotions, where you go up and down," Master-Gowgwart-Love says.

"It sounds like a rollercoaster of emotions," he says.

Master-Gowgwart-Love replies, "Yes. It's a rollercoaster of emotions. That's why it's so important for you to try to keep your mind calm, even when things are hard, so you can avoid sending the wrong messages to your mind."

"I must regain confidence that there's always a bright side in everything yeo go through in life," Haiokïto says.

"We, my friends and I (Master Gowgwarts), will show you how to become the master of your emotions," Master-Gowgwart-Love says.

Haiokïto gasps. "The master of my emotions. I like the sound of that," he says.

"First, thou must find thyself again, thereupon, thou wilt have risen from thy pain. Trust that thy light wilt find thee again and thou wilt shine brighter than all the stars in the sky, when the moon rises, and the sun sets," Master-Gowgwart-Love says.

.   .   .

Haiokïto looks around. "Like the light filling this place through the sparkling rubies," he says.

"Mm-hmm. My place. Mountïs of Love, my workplace, and the home of the ruby stones," Master-Gowgwart-Love replies.

He says, "Oh, that's cool! You have a mountïs all to yourself."

"We are in Pherrïland, our world—an enchanting realm where there are hidden wonders that echo your emotions. You are in the Gowgwarts' Workshop, where there's also a Mountïs of Joy, full of yellow sapphires," Master-Gowgwart-Love says.

"Whoa," Haiokïto says, looking around the mountïs.

"There's even more," Master-Gowgwart-Love says.

"I see the colors. No way!" Haiokïto says excitedly.

"Yes! That one is Mountïs of Happiness with orange sapphires; Mountïs of Care with pink sapphires; and if you want starry-night-blue sapphires, you have Mountïs of Trust over there. And finally, there is Mountïs of Peace with white jade and of course, Mountïs of Freedom with the purple amethyst," Master-Gowgwart-Love replies showing the positive mountïs to Haiokïto.

"Oh, whoa! I love this place," Haiokïto says excitedly.

"You'll be surprised with all the wisdom you'll have after you return to the city of Mountïs in the Kingdom of Gemmïes," Master-Gowgwart-Love says.

"Mmm. How will I return?" Haiokïto asks.

"Through our portals," Master-Gowgwart-Love responds.

"This is cool! Seven mountïs with precious stones and magical powers," Haiokïto says with a gleeful voice.

"These are the mountïs of the positive Gowgwarts. Our world is magical, very positive, but it's also dangerous," Master-Gowgwart-Love says.

"Why is it dangerous?" Haiokïto asks.

Master-Gowgwart-Love responds, "Because the powers of the crystal stones of the seven negative Gowgwarts' mountïs can also be destructive if you don't know how to embrace their positive powers. These crystal stones hold our spirits and every single one of us has different magical powers."

"Seven positive mountïs and seven negative mountïs. That's fourteen mountïs! Just like in the city of Mountïs," Haiokïto says.

Master-Gowgwart-Love says, "Mmm. The mountïs of the city of Mountïs are connected with the mountïs of our workshop, but with different names."

"Different names?" Haiokïto asks.

Master-Gowgwart-Love responds, "In the city of Mountïs, the mountïs are known by the names of their crystal stones and here, our mountïs are known by our names."

"Is that how I ended up in Raef Mountïs, the Mountïs of Fear when I went to the Tanzanite Mountïs, the mountïs of the lavender tanzanite stone?" Haiokïto asks.

Master-Gowgwart-Love replies, "Yes, dear. You took a Pherrï to our world. Our mountïs are magical and special, because each one of them has a portal that connects them with the mountïs from the city of Mountïs in the Kingdom of Gemmïes."

"That's why when I followed the voice of Master-Gowgwart-Fear, I entered, Pherrïland," Haiokïto says.

Master-Gowgwart-Love replies, "Yes, dear. Besides, we have always been here, even if sometimes we are not seeing nor found."

"Whoa. Who knew," Haiokïto says.

"Here, you will visit the seven positive mountïs, where you will learn how to embrace our powers to catalyze your healing," Master-Gowgwart-Love says.

"All seven positive mountïs?" Haiokïto asks.

She nods. "Mm-hmmm. As you visit them, you will meet with the Master Gowgwart of each mountïs. With them, you will receive wisdom as a reflection of the powers of the crystal stones. All Master Gowgwarts are going to help you transform your suffering into great strength," Master-Gowgwart-Love replies.

"What are their powers?" Haiokïto asks.

"The powers of the crystal stones in the positive Gowgwarts' mountïs are:

- Ruby; willpower, strength, leadership, Love.
- Pink sapphire; cheerfulness, compassion, friendship, Care.
- Starry-night-blue sapphire; stability, loyalty, confidence, Trust.

  White jade; purity, safety, calmness, Peace.

- Purple amethyst; wisdom, creativity, royalty, Freedom.
- Yellow sapphire; positivity, warmth, hope, Joy.
- Orange sapphire; Optimism, enthusiasm, youthful, Happiness.

To inspire and empower everyone to live a better life, a positive life," Master-Gowgwart-Love replies.

"A life worth living," he says with an effusive voice.

Master-Gowgwart-Love replies, "That's exactly what we want. Our goal is to improve everyone's life in every way possible."

Haiokïto says, "Tell me about the others. What are the names of the negative mountïs and what makes the powers of the crystal stones so dangerous?"

Master-Gowgwart-Love replies, "For centuries—I mean, since the creation of The Six Kingdoms—you have been the ones making the powers of the crystal stones seem dangerous. We can be good and bad; it depends on the belief you have."

"Good and bad?" Haiokïto asks.

Master-Gowgwart-Love responds, "Yes, my dear. The stones hold the spirits that create energy to give life to your emotions. You are responsible for caring for them to maintain balance, even when there's a disruption. This is also beneficial for your personal growth and well-being. That is why it's so important that you learn how to embrace their positive side; otherwise, they could be bad and lead to your destruction."

Haiokïto says, "Aaah. It's about how I use their powers for my personal development."

"Mm-hmmm," Master-Gowgwart-Love agrees.

"Brilliant!" Haiokïto says.

"I will tell you the names of the negative Gowgwarts' mountïs, but before you should know that the names are backwards, just like the Mountïs of Fear," Master-Gowgwart-Love says.

"Capïcsh!" Haiokïto replies.

Master-Gowgwart-Love says, "Backwards for the names of the negative Master Gowgwarts—Pain, Shame, Anger, Guilt, Sadness, Depression, and Fear."

"Aaah, capïcsh." Haiokïto nods.

Master-Gowgwart-Love asks, "Ready?"

"Mm-hmmm," Haiokïto agrees.

"Niap Mountïs, Emahs Mountïs, Raef Mountïs, Noisserped Mountïs, Regna Mountïs, Tliug Mountïs, and Ssendas Mountïs," she says.

"Question. Why are the names backwards?" Haiokïto asks.

"Mmm, it's all connected with the ancient love story you read at the Neephis Library; however, you don't know the whole story," Master-Gowgwart-Love says.

Haiokïto gasps and says, "Aaah, you know about Masseïel and

Phiuphos. Today is my lucky day."

"Yes, dear," Master-Gowgwart-Love says.

"No way! I'd better get comfortable," Haiokïto replies.

Master-Gowgwart-Love says, "Very well. When Crown Prince Phiuphos moved to the Kingdom of Gemmïes with Masseïel, they lived here with me in the Gleerwoo House."

"You mean here, in Pherrïland?" Haiokïto asks unsure.

"Yes! You might wonder how that happened. Right?" Master-Gowgwart-Love asks.

"Uh-huh! I am all ears . . ." Haiokïto nods.

"Long ago, Masseïel appeared in this mountïs as a newborn. I knew it before it happened. I saw her lying on a brown picnic basket covered with burgundy blankets, and a simple white and blue knitted hat. Masseïel smiled at me, and with her charming eyes, she blinked. Immediately, I took her in and gave her shelter and a name. She was a fallen diamond from the stars to us, so we named her Masseïel. I raised her here in Pherrïland, and as she grew, she spent most of her time in the mountïs with Master Gowgwarts—Joy, Happiness, Care, Freedom, Peace, and Trust," Master-Gowgwart-Love says.

"Whoa. With all of you? You gave her the bracelet?" he asks.

"Yes. When she turned thirteen, we gifted her the Gowgwarts' Bracelet and taught her the importance of each stone and how to use their powers. Later on, as she continued to spend time with the spirits of the stones, her confidence with their powers strengthened more and more. And at eighteen years old, she received energy from the spirits of the stones, which gifted her special powers, wherefore set her apart from all other human beings. At a point, she couldn't hide it from them and so rumors began to spread everywhere in the city of Mountïs, where she had a normal life . . ." Master-Gowgwart-Love replies.

"What rumors? What were they saying?" Haiokïto asks.

"They were saying she was half-human half-spirit, so to protect her, we decided it was best for her to move to Neephis City, where she fell in love with Crown Prince Phiuphos . . ." Master-Gowgwart-Love replies.

"Oh, so that's where they met," Haiokïto says.

"Yes. By then, rumors had already reached King Neephis the Great of the Kingdom of Neephiun, and as you already read in the manuscript back at the Neephis Library, both were exiled from the Kingdom of Neephiun," Master-Gowgwart-Love replies.

"I was wondering, but now yeo understand," he says.

"And that's how they ended up living here in Pherrïland. It was not easy for Crown Prince Phiuphos to adjust to his new life here, away from his kingdom and everything he ever knew before he fell in love with Masseïel. He struggled with the spirits in the negative Gowgwarts' Mountïs—Depression, Anger, Guilt, Shame, Sadness, Pain, and Fear," Master-Gowgwart-Love replies.

Haiokïto asks, "Is he the reason why the names of the negative mountïs are backwards?"

"Crown Prince Phiuphos is the reason, yes, forsooth," Master-Gowgwart-Love replies.

"Why?" Haiokïto asks.

Master-Gowgwart-Love replies, "Masseïel decided to rename the mountïs backwards—rearranging the spirits of the stones—to give them positive powers that neutralize their negative powers, so every time Crown Prince Phiuphos passed by the mountïs, he could see the goodness in them without letting the negative powers of the crystal stones in the mountïs overpower him."

"How did she do that?" Haiokïto asks.

"This is how she did it:

- Emerald; comfort, growth, renewal, life, neutralizing Pain.
- Lavender tanzanite; uplifting, optimism, calmness, serenity, neutralizing Fear.
- Blue topaz; trustworthiness, relaxation, calmness, security, neutralizing Shame.
- Peach sapphire; contentment, warmth, optimism, comfort, neutralizing Sadness.
- Brown tourmaline; resilience, security, down-to-earth, safety, neutralizing Depression.
- Blue aquamarine; patience, weightlessness, peacefulness, calmness, neutralizing Anger.

  White sapphire; forgiveness, honesty, protection, healing, neutralizing Guilt.

These are also the powers Masseïel got from the spirits of the crystal stones that set her apart from the rest, which she decided to share with The Six Kingdoms to help those who, like Crown Prince Phiuphos, struggle with negative emotions," she replies.

"Impressive!" Haiokïto says.

"Very keen girl with a kind heart," she says.

"Mm, I agree," Haiokïto says.

"Thereupon, all of Master Gowgwarts in Pherrïland activated the positive powers of the spirits inside the Mountïs—Pain, Shame, Sadness, Fear, Depression, Anger, and Guilt—assigning them the stones chosen by Masseïel and renaming them backwards. After it, we began sharing an updated version of the Gowgwarts' Bracelet— a refreshed version that includes the positive powers of the negative emotions—with everyone who has completed their training with us. Even with Masseïel who wore the updated version of the bracelet until her last day as Queen Masseïel of the Kingdom of Neephiun,"

Master-Gowgwart-Love says.

"Masseïel loved Crown Prince Phiuphos and truly cared for the people of The Six Kingdoms. I am eternally grateful for her kindness towards us," Haiokïto replies.

"Forsooth. Masseïel loved Crown Prince Phiuphos immensely, so much that she did everything she could to protect him," Master-Gowgwart-Love says.

"That's what you do when you love someone . . . This is a true love story full of emotions. Whoa. Their love was in truth stronger than anything that stood between them," Haiokïto says.

"A resilient love," Master-Gowgwart-Love says.

"A rare kind of love," Haiokïto replies.

"Thereupon, we taught him the positive powers of the spirits of the crystal stones in the different mountïs. And as he completed his training with us—to become the master of his emotions—I grew closer to him and then gave him the Gowgwarts' Bracelet, which he then used to remember the powers of the crystal stones whenever he struggled with his emotions. Later, it was time for Crown Prince Phiuphos and Masseïel to rule the Kingdom of Neephiun, so they returned to Neephis, the city that King Neephis the Great renamed after himself when he became the King of Neephiun," she says.

"Aaah, now that you say that I remember there's one thing I'd like to ask you," Haiokïto says.

"And what is that?" Master-Gowgwart-Love asks.

"Not a big deal, really. It's curiosity. When I was in the Neephis Library, I read that King Neephis the Great feared what the powers of the crystal stones would do to Crown Prince Phiuphos," Haiokïto says.

Master-Gowgwart-Love asks, "Are you referring to the powers of the crystal stones on the Gowgwarts' Bracelet?"

Haiokïto nods. "Mm-hmmm. Were you unknown to him?" he asks.

Master-Gowgwart-Love responds, "Aaah that . . . No. He had the Gowgwarts' Bracelet."

"Mmm. Really?" Haiokïto asks.

Master-Gowgwart-Love replies, "Forsooth. That's why he was so afraid of the detrimental effects the spirits residing in the negative crystal stones of the Gowgwarts' Bracelet could have done to Prince Phiuphos—heir apparent to the imperial throne."

"I'm not really understanding," Haiokïto replies.

"King Neephis the Great was once in love and happy; he loved himself deeply and experienced the most profound way of balance in life. He was so good at keeping his mind calm. He was the master of his emotions until his wife died giving birth to his third child . . . After that, he broke his Gowgwarts' Bracelet and blamed us for her death. He swore while he was still king of Neephiun, we would never again be welcome in his home," Master-Gowgwart-Love says.

"That explains why when Masseïel arrived in Neephis City and fell in love with Phiuphos, King Neephis the Great tried to separate them," Haiokïto says.

"When Crown Prince Phiuphos decided to introduce Masseïel to his father—over dinner at his castle—he immediately recognized the Gowgwarts' Bracelet Masseïel was wearing," she says.

Haiokïto replies, "Now I understand why he exiled them from his kingdom. Did Crown Prince Phiuphos ever discover the truth?"

"I never told him why King Neephis the Great was against his relationship with Masseïel. Instead, I focused on helping him create harmony among his emotions so he could achieve a sense of inner peace," Master-Gowgwart-Love replies.

"Life is not perfect, and I'm witness to that," Haiokïto says.

"Yes. But it is possible to be happy if you are positive. Lïesia would have wanted you to fall in love again and to have the family you couldn't have with her because she loved you as much as you loved her," Master-Gowgwart-Love replies.

Haiokïto says, "I know, I buried myself in Fear, trying to avoid falling in love again and it only led me to the top of the Mountïs of Fear, where I almost lost myself. Now I realize, life is about taking risk and not losing hope. No matter how hard we fall, it's important to always be hopeful, optimistic, and persistent to rise up again, and even after, always remembering that we hold the power to change the outlook of how we perceive the events we face in our lives."

Master-Gowgwart-Love nods. "Forsooth!" she says.

"We only live once, and this life is a gift. We must find a way to embrace it to the fullest, even when we find ourselves drowning in a sea of Pain, Sadness, Fear, Guilt, Depression, Shame, and Anger; because nothing lasts forever and sometimes hardships come to our lives to make us better and to gift us wisdom," Haiokïto says.

"It's hard to let go of someone who you loved deeply, but who are you while you are alive if you are not living the life you were born to live?" Master-Gowgwart-Love asks.

"I never asked myself that question," Haiokïto says.

"Never let your flame die, because if you do, your spirit dies too. That's why we give the Gowgwarts' Bracelet to all those who complete their training with us—to help them maintain balance of their emotions—so they can embrace their inner light, living with truth, passion, and purpose. Rest assured that with the Gowgwarts' Bracelet, you will remember our existence. The color of the crystal stones will remind you of our powers, and so too of our presence in everything you do and are," Master-Gowgwart-Love says.

"After Lïesia died, my emotions were a mess, all over the place.

Unconsciously, I started to forget them. I gave up the power I had over them and instead let them overpower me. I am so glad I never lost hope in you. I must say, tagrascïe! Thank you for saving me and for sharing the story and the powers of the crystal stones. It's time for a change. I will live as if I were alive, by allowing myself to trust and to fall in love again," Haiokïto says.

Master-Gowgwart-Love replies, "You have survived the worst part of your journey to find me, my dear. Now it's time to heal. Go ahead and visit Mountïs—Joy, Happiness, Care, Trust, Peace, and Freedom. And for now, don't visit the negative Gowgwarts' mountïs until you have completed your training with us."

"Paccürs," he says.

Sparkling red crystals pop, and a map appears.

Haiokïto asks, "What is that for?"

"This is a map of the Gowgwarts' Workshop. Take it with you, it will tell you which mountïs to visit first and which ones to avoid. Also, it will give you instructions on how to cross from one mountïs to another. Don't forget that the names of the negative Gowgwarts' mountïs are backwards," Master-Gowgwart-Love responds.

"Tagrascïe! I won't, Master-Gowgwart-Love," Haiokïto says.

"Follow this map, and if you have any questions, the map will answer them. But not all of them. I have designed the map to only answer what I want you to know," Master-Gowgwart-Love says.

"Paccürs. I'll do what the map says, first Mountïs of Trust, then Mountïs of Care, followed by Mountïs of Joy and Happiness, with my last stop at Mountïs of Peace and Freedom," Haiokïto replies.

"Go and rise, Haiokïto. I will appear again when you need me," Master-Gowgwart-Love says.

So, for the next six months, he spent time on all the mountains except the ones Master-Gowgwart-Love told him not to visit.

Present time, Spïeral Park.

Huïumi asks, "And did you try to visit the negative mountïs?"

"Uh-huh. But the map gave me an error," Haiokïto replies.

She says, "She wasn't playing. And do you remember anything from your visit to the positive mountïs?"

"Deepïery thögh! Master-Gowgwart-Trust said, 'While they are hugged by patience, I'll appear to embrace them. The light of the sun will show them Love and Love will give them hope.' Then, yeo visited Master-Gowgwart-Care, and before I left her mountïs, she said, 'As Love reaches the sky, merging with the stars, a dream will come true redirecting them in the path they once dreamed of and wished to one day see; that only with the power of Love it would be,'" Haiokïto replies.

"Aww. Everything is so dreamy," Huïumi says.

"Master-Gowgwart-Joy is my favorite, I remember as if it were today that she said, 'While I shower them with moments of fun and laughter, giving them memories that will last a lifetime, I will remind them of the power they have, to keep their Love alive. It is hope that brings Love and the power of Love that brings Joy,'" Haiokïto says.

"I love Joy!" Huïumi says.

"Me too! Then, I followed the map to Mountïs of Happiness, and I remember she said, 'I'm here to spark their joy, warmth, and fun. With me they'll sing songs of light that will embrace their inner light, to shine bright like the stars of the starry-night-sky,'" he replies.

Huïumi says, "Aww."

Haiokïto replies, "But what I loved most of everything that I can remember is what Master-Gowgwart-Peace said."

"What did she say?" Huïumi asks.

"'There will be no storm in the mint-green waters of the ocean, and everything will look clear from above the hills of the mountïs, because I'll be there hugging them both and Love will be protecting them from above,'" Haiokïto replies.

"That's so sweet," Huïumi says.

Haiokïto nods. "Uh-huh. But wait until I tell you what Master-Gowgwart-Freedom said," he says.

"Spill the tea, don't make me wait," Huïumi says.

"'As they approach me, time will move slowly in the direction of their needs. And on a random day, when they are hugging each other, they will see the solar eclipse, because Love is free,'" he says.

Huïumi says, "Aww, I have no words to express how touching everything they shared with you is . . . Why did they speak in plural?"

Haiokïto replies, "For a long time I wondered the same thing, but now I understand why . . ."

.   .   .

Past time, city of Mountïs, Kingdom of Gemmïes.

Haiokïto thinks while looking out of the windows in his room, "The only way that yeo can rebuild myself is by facing the negative Gowgwarts in the mountïs that Master-Gowgwart-Love told me to avoid. I will use the powers of the crystal stones to neutralize them. It's time to step outside my comfort zone to embrace them. I just need to figure out how."

Sparkling red crystals appear, Master-Gowgwart-Love appears.

Master-Gowgwart-Love says, "Clever boy! I came to help you figure out how to neutralize them. Forsooth, the key isn't to ignore the negative Gowgwarts in the forbidden mountïs, it's to hug them so you can use their positive powers to rebuild yourself. Remember, their positive powers will allow you to neutralize them."

"How?" Haiokïto asks.

Master-Gowgwart-Love replies, "Remember the powers of the crystal stones, Haiokïto."

.   .   .

Present time, in Spïeral Park.

Haiokïto says, "Master-Gowgwart-Love taught me how to use the powers of the crystal stones in the different mountïs to shift my mindset into a positive one. She also taught me why it's important to have awareness of emotions and encouraged me to always focus on the bright side of everything, but most importantly, I completed my training and finally healed. I transformed into a new person. This time I found myself at the top of the Mountïs of Love, ready to shine bright like all the precious jewels of the Kingdom of Gemmïes," he says effusively.

Huïumi chuckles. She says, "The way you say it, so theatrical. It transports me to the top of the Mountïs of Love. I can see myself shining bright next to you."

Haiokïto laughs. "I can see it too. Mmm, how do you like the sound of this one?" he says, "I chose to use the powers of the crystal stones to rebuild myself, rising like The Phoenïx of Bloomïeda's Reïhng Team when winning the Quartz-Stars Reïhng Bracelet of The Six Kingdoms' Quartz-Stars Championship."

"You have a whimsical sense of humor . . . And clearly a big fan of reïhng," Huïumi says, laughing.

Haiokïto says, "A huge fan of reïhng. No, but seriously that's just how it was. With Master-Gowgwart-Love I also learned about the power of hugs . . . And everything combined, helped me create harmony among my emotions."

"The power of hugs?" Huïumi asks.

Haiokïto nods. "Everything is interconnected. A hug sends a positive sign to your brain, releasing endorphins and hormones like serotonin and oxytocin that changes the state of your mind into a happier one."

Huïumi gasps and says, "Aaah, that's why we smile every time we hug someone."

"Deepïery thögh! Hugs foster trust, joy, and happiness. They also help reduce anxiety, depression, and stress," he says.

"Is that why hugging the negative Gowgwarts allowed you to neutralize them?" Huïumi asks.

"Mm-hmmm . . . By hugging them, I remembered the powers of the crystal stones, and it made it easier for me to neutralize them," Haiokïto answers.

"Aaah. A simple hug changed everything. Unexpected, huh?" Huïumi says.

"Yeah. Look at your Gowgwarts' Bracelet," he says.

"Mmm, why?" Huïumi asks.

"How are the crystal stones positioned?" he asks.

"Now that I look at the Gowgwarts' Bracelet, the positive and negative Gowgwarts are hugging each other. I see your point," she responds.

"That's why when we look at the Gowgwarts' Bracelet, we feel happier—because of the positive sign a hug sends to our brain," he says.

"Capïcsh!" Huïumi replies.

He says, "That's why after Crown Prince Phiuphos received the Gowgwarts' Bracelet, he always looked at it every time he passed by the negative mountïs; because a hug fosters harmony among the Gowgwarts, reminding us of their powers."

"Ooh." Huïumi nods.

"Usïcs. Remember, before learning about the positive powers of the negative Gowgwarts, and the power of hugs, we didn't know how to neutralize them and therefore, they weren't good for us," Haiokïto says.

"That's why Master-Gowgwart-Love told me not to summon the negative Gowgwarts until I've learned the powers of the crystal stones," Huïumi replies.

Haiokïto says, "She was trying to protect you because, the state of our emotions strongly influences our well-being. Therefore, when our emotions are in harmony with each other, we find ourselves in a state of calm."

"Yeo think that she didn't want me to cause a disruption in my emotions. I must say that the powers of the crystal stones are truly magical," Huïumi says.

"Deepïery thögh," Haiokïto says.

"The secrets of Love hide between the lines," Huïumi says.

. . .

Past time, city of Mountïs, Kingdom of Gemmïes.

Haiokïto is ready to move on with his life. In the end, he has nothing left in the Kingdom of Gemmïes, so he decides to return to Brightmieda, the city of the Garden of Joy, Kingdom of Bloomïeda. And for a fresh start, he's also moving the headquarters of Masseïel's Jewels.

You should know that, to honor Lïesia, Haiokïto saved enough money to become the owner of Masseïel's Jewels, becoming a very wealthy young man who swore to never fall in love again. Of course, that was before he met Master-Gowgwart-Love.

. . .

Fifteen months later. Brightmieda, the city of the Garden of Joy, Kingdom of Bloomïeda.

On a very late night, Haiokïto arrives at his penthouse on the eighty eighth floor in Spïeral Park Tower. He enters his room and sees a note from Love and friends on top of his bed. Haiokïto smiles and reads the note.

"Dear Haiokïto,

If you're reading this note, it's because you're ready to wear the Gowgwarts' Bracelet. Look for the Gowgwarts' gift box on top of your nightstand on the right side of your bed and open it. Remember the powers of the fourteen crystal stones and everything you've learned about the power of hugs to improve your overall well-being to foster a positive mindset. And now that you've rebuilt yourself and are ready, I can return the emerald crystal stone to you, lost when you fell off the cliff of the Mountïs of Fear. Look inside the gift box and you'll find it.

—From Love and friends."

He walks to the nightstand to see the Gowgwarts' gift box. He opens the gift box and then smiles. "I can't believe I have risen from my pain," Haiokïto says.

Haiokïto puts on the Gowgwarts' Bracelet.

"Where's the emerald I used to propose to Lïesia? Oh, here it is," Haiokïto says. He takes the emerald crystal stone he turned to a necklace after Lïesia passed away and smiles.

That night, Haiokïto realized he no longer needed to keep the emerald with him to honor Lïesia, so he decided to put it up for sale at Masseïel's jewels.

· · ·

Present time, Spïeral Park.

"For a long time, I wondered what Master-Gowgwart-Love meant in the note where she wrote that I am ready," Haiokïto says.

"Yes, ready for what?" Huïumi asks.

"Sometimes Master-Gowgwart-Love can be a bit mysterious, but now that I see you, I believe she meant I am ready for you . . ." he says with a romantic voice.

A shy smile graced Huïumi's lips as Haiokïto leaned in gently for their first brief, genuine kiss.

.   .   .

Hïuramïur gasps. "Aaah! They're kissing. *Pop-lips-smoochers!* I didn't expect that. Yeo better go back home. Adïour, pretty flower . . ." Hïuramïur says, taking a deep breath.

Five

The Clear Rock Crystal House

Moons after the picnic at Spïeral Park when the moon was in full bloom.

Huïumi hears her phone buzzing several times on the coffee table next to her. She sees multiple texts coming into the group chat:

"The six forces."

Ufaïa: Joureïe, forces! What are you up to?

Maie: Eating dinner. Greequose salad. Lol.

Luseïe: Finishing a one-thousand-puzzle I started this week.

Rayïq: Just got home from a reïhng game.

Geossuth: Heading out to give a private concert.

Ufaïa: And have you heard about Huïumi lately?

Maie: No.

Geossuth: Gïocs signs of her since last week.

Luseïe: Gïocs!

Rayïq: Same.

Ufaïa: Where is she? Last time yeo spoke with her she was very enchanted.

Luseïe: She probably met someone.

Geossuth: Adïour. Out of the conversation. Yeo have arrived at the venue.

Ufaïa: Paccürs. Good luck!

Rayïq: Fun times.

Maie: I think Huïumi has a mystery-man.

Luseïe: She's definitely happier. That's the glow you can only get from love.

Ufaïa: I haven't seen Huïumi so enchanted since moons ago.

Huïumi says, "I am not replying to them. Obviously, they have started noticing my feelings for Haiokïto. Yeo guess I can't hide him from them anymore."

Hïuramïur asks, "What are you going to do?"

Huïumi replies, "I'm going to turn off notifications and finish watching our favorite baking show, '*Flower or Flowerless?*'"

Hïuramïur says, "The connection between you and the winner of thy heart has grown rapidly. Your friends have started to notice a change in you; they're suspicious it's love, and they're not wrong. If not, you can ask me."

"Huh? Hïuramïur!" Huïumi says.

"What? I'm telling the truth. It's clear that you're falling in love with the winner of thy heart," Hïuramïur replies.

"I think I've found *true love*," Huïumi says.

.   .   .

Weeks later, over dinner at Huïumi's apartment.

Huïumi's friends are sitting on the floor, around the solid wood square table in the living room, eating cheese macceïe baked by her.

"Mmm. This is so yummy, Huïumi," Luseïe says.

Agreeing, Maiephis says, "Delicious!"

Geossuth nods. Mouth full, he says, "Uh-huh."

Huïumi replies, "Tagrascïe, forces!"

Ufaïa asks, "And . . . Are you finally going to reveal who's the mystery-man?"

"I was waiting for that question to pop," Huïumi replies.

"Me too!" Hïuramïur says.

"Hïuramïur! I thought you were in the room," Huïumi says.

"Paccürs, but first I want to eat some of your cheese macceïe," Hïuramïur says.

Everyone laughs.

"You can't hide it from us anymore. It's obvious that you're in love with the mуstery-man," Luseïe says.

"Please spill the tea. C'mon," Maiephis says.

"Paccürs. I will tell you. It all happened at the ice cream shop on the third floor of the Bluemieda Mall Center on the day we were supposed to have ice cream together. But since you all were *so busy* and cancelled at the last minute and yeo was already at the ice cream shop, I decided to get ice cream anyway. And that's when . . ."

.   .   .

"Aww. I am in awe of such good news," Maiephis says happily.

Ufaïa says, "You have to thank us for not joining you that day."

"Usïcs! Is he handsome?" Luseïe asks.

Huïumi blushes and says, "*Usïcs* . . . very handsome and funny. Yeo really like him. Mmm. He's everything yeo ever dreamed of."

"Aww. You must introduce him to us. Please!" Maiephis says excitedly.

"I already like him," Luseïe says with a smile.

"Yes! What about a game? Invite him to a reïhng game. Right Rayïq?" Ufaïa asks.

"Sure, why not? I am cool with it," Rayïq replies.

Geossuth says, "If you want, you can invite him to one of my concerts."

Huïumi replies, "Tagrascïe, 'forces.' You're so supportive. I'll discuss it with him, and then I'll let you know what we've decided."

.   .   .

Hours later, after Huïumi's friends left.

Huïumi says, "I am feeling the pressure to introduce Haiokïto to my friends."

"Why?" Hïuramïur asks.

Huïumi responds, "Because they want to meet Haiokïto and at the same time, I want Haiokïto to meet them too, but I'm so nervous . . . Yeo don't know if Haiokïto wants the same."

"Call him. What are you waiting for?" Hïuramïur asks.

Minutes later, on a phone call with Haiokïto . . . Huïumi shares her friends' interest in meeting him. For her surprise, Haiokïto also shows interest in meeting her friends. In fact, Haiokïto wants to host a get together with them . . .

After the phone call, a text comes through.

"It's Haiokïto!" Huïumi says with a surprised smile.

Hïuramïur sighs. "The winner of thy heart . . ." he says.

Haiokïto: Joureïe darling, haven't I told you that yeo own a house nestled on the shores of Lake Flurmieda?

Huïumi: Joureïe babe! No.

Haiokïto: It's near the Flurmieda River, you know, just a few hours away from the city of the Garden of Joy.

Haiokïto: Since it's big enough to host everyone and not so far from the city, I think it would be a great idea to offer it to spend . . . Eh. I don't know. A weekend there?

Haiokïto: What are your thoughts?

Huïumi: Oh dear . . .

Huïumi: Isn't that too much for you?

Huïumi: I don't wanna trouble you.

Haiokïto: Absolutely not!

Haiokïto: I'd be honored to host everyone.

Haiokïto: It'd be great to spend some time with your friends at my estate.

Huïumi says, "Hïuramïur! Guess what?"

Hïuramïur asks, "What?"

Huïumi responds, "Haiokïto is inviting my friends to visit his estate in Flurmieda. And I think it's a great idea for everyone to have enough time to get to know each other. Right?"

Hïuramïur replies, "Mm, yes."

"I think it's a much more comfortable environment to ease the tension among everyone. He knows how important it is for me to make a good impression on my friends . . . Especially now that he's my boyfriend," Huïumi says.

Hïuramïur says, "He certainly knows how to get to thy heart."

"I am going to say yes," Huïumi replies.

Huïumi: I think it's a terrific idea. Tagrascïe, dear!

Haiokïto: You're welcome, darling. I will prepare everything for that weekend.

Haiokïto: I just need to know the date for a three-night weekend in August.

Huïumi: Paccürs. I'll confirm with my friends.

Haiokïto: Wonderful, dear.

Huïumi: As soon as yeo confirm the date with them, I will message you about it.

Huïumi: Love you.

Haiokïto: Great! Love you too.

Huïumi is over the moon with the idea of spending an entire weekend at Haiokïto's lake house.

"My friends are nature lovers, and it is summer, which makes it perfect for an outdoor fun time. They're going to love this idea, Hïuramïur," Huïumi says.

Hïuramïur replies, "The winner of thy heart is a clever one."
She sends a text in the group chat: **"The six forces."**

Huïumi: Hey, 'forces.'

Huïumi: Yeo have good news! Guess what?

Luseïe: Why are you up so late? It's the middle of the night!

Maie: Yes! You woke me up. I thought it was my alarm clock.

Huïumi: Sorry. Maybe . . . it can wait.

Ufaïa: Oh, gïocs. I am awake now.

Maie: Yes. Please tell the news.

Rayïq: What's going on?

Luseïe: Huïumi has some news to share.

Huïumi: Paccürs. Get ready to pack your suitcases for a three-night stay at Haiokïto's lake house in August.

Huïumi: Let me know what weekend works for you.

Huïumi: He is hosting.

Ufaïa: Seriously?

Luseïe: I told you I like him.

Maie: That's good news.

Rayïq: He is cool. Where's his lake house?

Huïumi: On the shores of Lake Flurmieda.

Maie: Oh, nice!

Geossuth: Did I miss something?

Ufaïa: Catch-up.

Luseïe: We're going to meet Huïumi's mystery-man.

Maie: Yes! Next month.

Geossuth: Paccürs!

Huïumi: He is good-natured.

After several text messages, they finally agreed to meet for the second weekend of August, which suits everyone.

· · ·

Huïumi's friends are on their way to meet Haiokïto for the first time. Haiokïto and Huïumi are standing outside—at the entrance of the estate—waiting for them to arrive.

Huïumi says, "They'll be here shortly. Nervous?"

"Usïcs. A little bit. Perhaps, you can tell me a little more about your friends. I want to be prepared," Haiokïto says.

"Deepïery thögh," Huïumi replies.

"Geossuth isn't an outgoing person. He's a bit timid, but he's also funny. You will like him once you meet him. He loves food and can be considered a simple guy who doesn't ask for much. Most of the time he prefers to be alone unless he's with us. He *loves* classical music. It's his passion. He told us it calms him and at the same time makes him feel free and relaxed. He told us that's why he became a classical music producer. Entertaining others is his way of sharing the freedom he gets from music, with them," she says.

"He seems interesting," Haiokïto replies.

She smiles. "Maie is a writer. She's a very . . . private person. She doesn't like the spotlight and she's originally from Neephis, the Kingdom of Neephiun. She understands Ūlïe language, but the truth is she doesn't speak Ūlïe at all. I don't really have much to say about her. But don't worry, she's cool," Huïumi says.

"Private. Nice!" Haiokïto replies.

She nods. "Usïcs. My other friend Rayïq is from the Kingdom of Greequose, and he loves reïhng. He's also an outgoing person and an incredibly good friend. He doesn't speak Ūlïe fluently, but he can cook a nice Greequose meal," Huïumi says.

"He likes cooking, huh? How nice," Haiokïto replies.

Huïumi nods. "Yeah, really delicious food. Now let me tell you about my friend, Luseïe. She is, uh, unique. She grew up in the same neighborhood as me, Punta Blereuzule in Pearl Islands. What else?

She's the smartest one among us and when I say always, I mean she always has an answer for you. I mean the correct answer. She's our brainy-genius-encyclopedia," she says.

Haiokïto chortles at her funny comment and then says, "You are funny."

Huïumi says, "And Ufaïa . . . She moved to Punta Blereuzule from Punta Roseïey, Pearl Islands, when she was six years old and we met at school, where we became best friends."

"Punta Roseïey is beautiful. I cannot wait to go back," he says.

"Oh, I see them. They're here!" Huïumi says excitedly.

.　　.　　.

After Huïumi welcomes and presents her friends to Haiokïto, her friends proceed to leave their suitcases with the service attendant staff standing right at the entrance of the house.

Huïumi and Haiokïto give a brief tour of the house and show everyone to their rooms.

After Huïumi's friends arrive at their rooms, they find a note from Haiokïto and Huïumi.

"This is much needed," Luseïe says as she lies back in bed.

"Oh, a note," Luseïe says, looking to her left. She picks up the note and reads it aloud.

"Welcome Luseïe!

Huïumi and I invite you to enjoy a barbecue on the picturesque shore of Lake Flurmieda at the Clear Rock Crystal House at 3:00 p.m. We're excited to spend this weekend in your company and look forward to a weekend filled with sunshine, delicious food, and great drinks.

Instructions for the Clear Rock Crystal House are on the back of the envelope.

See you at 3:00 p.m.
—Huïumi and Haiokïto."

Group chat: **"The six forces."**
Luseïe: Tagrascïe! Yeo love the note! See you at 3!
Rayïq: What note?
Luseïe: On your bed . . . There's a note from Huïumi and Haiokïto inviting us to a barbecue at the Clear Rock Crystal House at 3:00 p.m. Check your bed!
Rayïq: Cool, I see it. See you later. Thanks, Huïumi.
Maie: I got the note, too. Thanks, Huïumi!
Ufaïa: Just saw mine. See you at 3:00 p.m. forces. You made my day, Huïumi.
Geossuth: I'll be the first one to arrive. Thx Huïumi.
Huïumi: Aww . . . Tagrascïe, 'forces' so exciting. Don't be late!

. . .

Huïumi and Haiokïto are first to arrive at Clear Rock Crystal House, followed by Huïumi's friends who then begin to arrive one by one.

"We're so lucky to have such great weather for this weekend," Huïumi says to everyone at Clear Rock Crystal House.

"I'm excited to meet you all," Haiokïto adds.

"Thanks for inviting us. Delighted to be here to finally meet you," Maiephis says.

"So great to be here. Though, I wasn't expecting a clear rock crystal house," Ufaïa says.

"Is that good or bad?" Haiokïto asks.

"Good, of course," Ufaïa replies.

"Phew. Good thing it's good," Haiokïto says with a smile.

"Are you nervous?" Rayïq asks.

Haiokïto responds, "Not much. Very eager to connect with all of you." He rubs his hands together.

"You'll be fine in a few hours. We're thrilled to be here meeting you," Rayïq says.

"Yes, trust we are," Luseïe adds.

"You're right. I just have to relax a bit," Haiokïto says.

"Usïcs, babe. It's gonna be fun," Huïumi says.

Haiokïto presses the button that opens the removable ceiling, which is on the wall next to him, allowing sunlight and fresh air into the house.

"Oh, that's nice," Geossuth says.

Ufaïa whispers to Maiephis, "He's so nervous."

Maiephis replies, "Yes. Oh, dear."

"What crystal rock did you use to build this house?" Geossuth asks.

"Oh, I know. For the look of it, it sure is clear quartz crystals. Am I right?" Luseïe asks.

Haiokïto looks awestruck with her prompt answer. "Oh, whoa, impressive. Yes, this crystal house is of clear quartz crystals," he says.

Luseïe smiles. She says, "I was correct! I knew it! A crystal that appears clear, glassy, and transparent, it's for sure clear quartz."

Haiokïto says, "The idea was to create a closer connection with nature to reflect a sense of tranquility and relaxation for the mind, while having the choice to still be indoors in case of an unpleasant weather." He gestured expansively.

"Very clever," Luseïe says.

Huïumi taps him on the arm and whispers, "I told you so."

Haiokïto smiles, nodding.

.   .   .

After Huïumi finishes serving snacks to Haiokïto, she says, "I hope that while we're here, we create memories that last a lifetime."

"That's the goal," Luseïe replies.

"Yes! Right Ufaïa?" Rayïq asks.

"Mm-hmmm, yes. Sorry. Looking at the dahleïea garden. Is so beautiful. The best view from inside the Clear Rock Crystal House," Ufaïa says.

"You noticed the dahlia garden . . ." Maiephis says.

"*Deepïery thögh!* From the moment I arrived. Having a direct view of the dahleïea garden was a brilliant idea," Ufaïa replies.

Haiokïto says, "Tagrascïe. The dahleïeas started to bloom last week."

"So lucky to be here in time to see them blossoming," Huïumi says as she also looks at the dahlia garden.

"This place reminds me of my home," Maiephis says.

"The view of the lake reminds me of my hometown . . ." Rayïq adds.

"And . . . these snacks are so good, I cannot stop eating them," Geossuth says.

Everyone burst out laughing.

"Seriously. Who prepared them?" Geossuth asks.

"It was my idea," Huïumi responds.

Haiokïto adds, "I hired a chef for this weekend, so we can have extra time to get to know each other. But Huïumi is very persistent, she insisted on preparing some snacks ahead of the food."

"You are a genuine fountain of creativity," Geossuth whispers to Huïumi."

"Haha, you're silly," Huïumi replies in a voice murmured with amusement.

Haiokïto says, "We hope you enjoy the snacks. Right dear?"

"Oh, that's the idea," Huïumi says, settling in next to Haiokïto.

"The snacks look so appetizing. Thanks for organizing this get together," Maiephis says.

"Yeah. Thanks for hosting us this weekend, Haiokïto," Rayïq says.

"Of course, I hope everyone feels like home," Haiokïto replies, "(everything is going well)."

"Thank you everyone for being here today. It means a lot to me," Huïumi says.

Huïumi whispers to Haiokïto, "Thanks for organizing, hosting us this weekend. Everything is perfect."

Haiokïto replies, "I know meeting your friends means a lot to you, and I wanted to make it a little extra special."

.   .   .

Rayïq asks Ufaïa, "Is everything alright? I noticed you're not yourself since you started looking at the dahleïeas."

Ufaïa replies, "Is it that obvious?"

"Mm, yes," Rayïq replies.

"I guess, I got distracted by the dahleïea garden," Ufaïa says.

"Well, maybe you can ask Haiokïto about the garden," Rayïq says.

"That's a great idea, Rayïq. Tagrascïe," Ufaïa replies.

"Come, let's have some snacks," Rayïq says to Ufaïa.

"Paccürs," Ufaïa replies.

Geossuth asks, "Hey Rayïq, could you please bring me some more snacks?"

"Sure," Rayïq answers.

Ufaïa finishes getting some snacks with Rayïq, and then she takes a seat next to Luseïe. Rayïq, who is right behind her, hands a plate of snacks to Geossuth and then takes a seat next to Ufaïa.

Rayïq whispers, "Ask him now, Ufaïa." Ufaïa nods and then asks, "What inspired you to plant the dahleïea garden, Haiokïto?"

Haiokïto responds, "Oh, well, the dahleïeas remind me of my grandma. Every summer, here at the lake, she would replant them exactly where you see them."

Ufaïa says, "Oh, this is your grandmother's estate."

Haiokïto replies, "I inherited this estate when she passed away many years ago. Later, I hired a construction company to design and build this clear rock house with clear quartz crystals, which later on I named Clear Rock Crystal House."

"Ingenious!" Ufaïa says.

"So clever! You've got yourself a clever one, Huïumi," Luseïe says.

Huïumi chuckles at Luseïe's comment.

"You were saying, Haiokïto?" Ufaïa asks.

He replies, "I wanted to have an unobstructed view of the lake, especially of the dahleïeas during summer which is when yeo spend most of my time here. Also, the clear quartz crystal rock has such a positive vibe that transfers peace and good energy to those around. I have so many fond memories of my grandma from all my teenage years here, that having the dahleïea garden makes me feel closer to her every time I visit the estate, and being here inside this clear rock crystal house turns it into a sanctuary."

Geossuth says, "No wonder why I feel so relaxed and at peace here."

"So thoughtful," Rayïq says.

"I can't stop staring at the dahleïeas. I wanna know more . . ." Ufaïa says.

"Hmm. What else can I say? My grandma used to frequent the

dahleïea garden very often when they were in full bloom. And most of the time we spent here, she used to tell me love stories—fairy tales that ended happy. Those were fun times. Honestly, this is my way of honoring her," Haiokïto replies.

"Why did she love dahleïeas so much?" Huïumi asks.

Haiokïto responds, "I wish I know the answer. I asked myself the same question."

"I do know that dahlias symbolize beauty, inner strength, and kindness. And sometimes depending on the flower colour and the culture, they can stand for eternal love—strength and resilience in love to be exact—especially when they are in full bloom. And from the colours of the dahlia garden—pink, purple, and red—I can tell that that your grandmother was a romantic who believed in Love," Maiephis says.

"She definitely . . . believed in Love," Haiokïto replies.

"I guess there's more to know about the dahleïeas than what I thought," Ufaïa says.

"Sometimes you plant flowers because they are pretty, but who knows, to Haiokïto's grandmother dahlias meant much more than that," Maiephis says.

Haiokïto says, "I think you're right, Maie. My grandma never told me anything about the meaning of dahleïea flowers to her. But I must admit, she was special in her own way."

"Hmm. Your grandmother . . . The one who knew about the Gowgwarts' Bracelet? Remember? The one you told me about in Stripes Park when we met," Huïumi says.

Haiokïto replies, "Yes, that's she."

.   .   .

Huïumi and Haiokïto forgot Huïumi's friends have no clue that they know about the Gowgwarts' Bracelet . . .

Ufaïa gasps. "Aaahh! Are you kidding? Do you know about the bracelet everyone talks about, but no one says the name? Did I hear that right?" Ufaïa asks with a vibrant voice.

Suddenly there is a brief silence, everyone looks at each other, hiding the hand on which they are wearing the Gowgwarts' Bracelet, pretending that they don't hear what Ufaïa, Huïumi, and Haiokïto have said.

Ufaïa says, "Yeo guess I'm the only one who isn't afraid to talk about the bracelet that everyone talks about, but no one says the name—the Gowgwarts' Bracelet."

Rayïq gasping, says, "Aaahh, you said the name!"

Ufaïa replies, "Huïumi said it first. His grandmother had the Gowgwarts' Bracelet."

"I said she knew about the bracelet," Huïumi says.

Haiokïto whispers to Huïumi, "Babe, you're just making things worse, not better."

Huïumi whispers to Haiokïto, "I'm sorry. You're right."

"Tagrascïe, Huïumi," Ufaïa says.

Haiokïto whispers to Huïumi, "Or maybe . . . Not."

Luseïe raises her right arm, moving her hand from side to side, to show them that she has the Gowgwarts' Bracelet.

—Pause!

Until that moment, not everyone had shared with each other that each one had the bracelet everyone talks about, but no one says the name, the enchanting Gowgwarts' Bracelet. So, after Luseïe did, everyone proudly began to show their Gowgwarts' Bracelet.

—Go on.

"It seems like we all have it. How so? We've spent a lot of time together, and I never realized we all have the Gowgwarts' Bracelet," Huïumi replies, surprised.

Rayïq says, "I got my bracelet fifteen years ago, back home in the Kingdom of Greequose."

Huïumi replies, "Fifteen years ago . . ."

"I tried to hide it for as long as I could, until I started to notice everyone was wearing it, so I decided to wear it too," Rayïq says.

Luseïe says, "I knew you had it, Rayïq, but I didn't wanna tell you about mine yet. I've been hiding it for a while. Or at least that's what I thought."

Rayïq replies, "Well, Luseïe, a few years ago, I saw you wearing it at the Kosmïes's concert, when they were on tour for the launch of their new album, *Fly Away*. You must have forgotten to leave it at home that day before meeting us at the concert."

Luseïe replies, "Really? Aaah. Paccürs. I guess, we were both wearing it that day. Though, I do remember seeing you putting your Gowgwarts' Bracelet away in your *Ablanc Ūmieda* backpack. That's when I remembered I was wearing mine too, so I decided to put it away inside my purse. I didn't want anyone to notice but I guess it was too late."

"You mean, your *Roseïey Vūm Ūmieda purse*," Rayïq says.

"Yeah, yeah, that one," Luseïe replies.

"Yeo have it in *purple*," Huïumi says.

"And, I have it in *yellow*," Maiephis says.

"Did I say yeo got a new one in *red*," Ufaïa says.

"You did!" Luseïe replies excitedly.

"Nice. Yeo want a red one, too. Anyway, I still hadn't met Love back at the Kosmïes concert," Huïumi says.

Rayïq replies, "That means you wouldn't have recognized the

Gowgwarts' Bracelet."

"Right," Luseïe says.

"That's correct!" Huïumi adds.

"Taccgrah! I don't remember," Ufaïa says, shaking her head.

Luseïe says, "Dinguï!"

"I must have been singing and dancing because I missed it. The concert was a lot of fun," Ufaïa replies.

"Well. Later, after yeo got mine, Luseïe told me she had it too, but until now, yeo didn't know about the rest of you," Huïumi says.

Geossuth thinking, "Mmm? The rest of us? Are they talking about them? Because I don't have the . . ." He looks at his right hand and realizes that he's also wearing the Gowgwarts' Bracelet, and then he says, "Ooh, you're talking about this bracelet." Geossuth shows the bracelet to everyone.

"Usïcs," Huïumi replies.

"You didn't know that you're wearing the Gowgwarts' Bracelet . . ." Rayïq says.

"I'm as surprised as you are," Geossuth says.

Rayïq asks, "What? I'm confused. How can you be wearing the Gowgwarts' Bracelet? It doesn't make sense . . . Have you even met Master-Gowgwart-Love yet?"

"That's a very good question," Geossuth replies.

"Really? Geossuth, are you kidding?" Ufaïa asks.

"Why do I need to lie? Yeo haven't met . . ." Geossuth says.

"Ufaïa and Rayïq are right. That's strange," Luseïe says.

"There has to be an explanation," Huïumi says.

"I totally agree with all of you," Haiokïto says.

"Me too. Yeo didn't know I had to meet . . . to get this bracelet. I thought it was a nice accessory," Geossuth says.

"How did you get the bracelet?" Luseïe asks.

"It was a long time ago when I was ten years old, back at home. To be honest, I don't remember much. I . . . It was in a trash can," Geossuth replies.

"In a trash can?" Ufaïa asks.

"Really?" Luseïe asks, surprised.

"That's so strange, Geossuth. Luseïe is right," Huïumi says.

"I would say very very strange," Rayïq says.

Geossuth replies, "I know. Until now I didn't even know the name of the bracelet. How was I supposed to know?"

"Sorry, Geossuth. We didn't know you were unaware of the existence of the bracelet. It's simply so unexpectedly strange to us. The only way to receive the bracelet is through Master-Gowgwart-Love and friends. At least that's what we thought," Rayïq replies.

Haiokïto says, "Your friends are correct, but yeo guess it was different for you, Geossuth."

Geossuth says, "I suppose, among us, I'm the only one who hasn't met Master-Gowgwart-Love yet. Am I right?"

They all nodded in agreement with Geossuth.

Geossuth asks, "Since I'm the only one here who hasn't met Master-Gowgwart-Love, I'd like to know, how was your experience like?"

Huïumi replies, "That's a great idea."

"Usïcs. I'd like to know too," Haiokïto says.

"Who wants to go first?" Huïumi asks.

"Rayïq!" Ufaïa exclaimed.

"Me? What about Luseïe or you?" Rayïq asks.

"Usïcs, Rayïq. Go on, don't be shy," Luseïe replies.

"Okay. Fine," Rayïq says with a serious voice.

. . .

Chef Glüedo served them barbecued asparagus, jïocs, rib-eye steak, sirloin steak, salmon, chicken, carrots, yïecs, and potatoes.

And while Rayïq is nervous about telling his story, everyone is delighted with the food, especially Geossuth, who loves to eat.

After everyone finished their meal, Chef Glüedo served them miniature berry chocolate cakes with vanilla ice cream and a mocktail that was garnished with edible bubbles and fruits for dessert.

.   .   .

Rayïq isn't ready to tell his story yet, so after everyone finishes eating dessert, he decides to ask Haiokïto about his grandmother.

"Hmm? A distraction to pushback on telling my story . . . how clever," he thinks, "Why not start with the host of the house?" Rayïq smiles.

Huïumi looks at Rayïq and asks, "Why are you smiling, Rayïq?"

"Me? I'm not smiling. In fact, I'd like to ask Haiokïto if he can tell us a little bit about how his grandmother met Master-Gowgwart-Love," Rayïq replies.

Huïumi dislikes what Rayïq said and right away jumps in the conversation. She says, "I don't think that's a proper question to ask Haiokïto."

"That's okay dear, I don't have much to say. Rayïq, if I had an idea of how my grandma met Master-Gowgwart-Love, I wouldn't oppose to answer your question . . . Honestly, that's a question for Master-Gowgwart-Love. All I know from the stories my grandma used to tell me when I was younger—in which she mentioned the Gowgwarts' Bracelet—is that she knew about Master-Gowgwart-Love. If you're curious about her, we have lots of photos of her all over the family's private hall in the main house. Feel free to look in the hallway adjacent to your room," Haiokïto says.

As soon as Huïumi hears Haiokïto saying that there are photos of his grandmother in the family's private hall in the main house, she gets impatient. "Hmm. Think, Huïumi. I need an excuse to go back to the main house to see photos of his grandmother. Uh, like, right now," she thinks.

Huïumi says, "If you'll excuse me, please. I must step aside for a moment. I forgot something in my room. I'll be right back."

Haiokïto replies, "Everything okay, dear? Do you want me to come with you?"

"Oh, gïocs. It's nothing. Tagrascïe, darling. I'll be right back," Huïumi replies.

.　.　.

After Huïumi arrives at the main house, she at once begins to look for the family's private hall and eventually encounters portraits of Haiokïto's family.

"Hmm? How strange? Haiokïto's grandmother isn't wearing the Gowgwarts' Bracelet in any of these portraits. Assuming this is her, of course. Uh, I wonder if she only knew about the Gowgwarts' Bracelet because of the story she read at the Neephis Library. Still, it's strange that she isn't wearing the bracelet in any of the portraits I've seen so far. This must be her. It has to be her, because there are many portraits of her here. I can guarantee it's her."

"Hmm? Still, I don't understand it. Why isn't she wearing the Gowgwarts' Bracelet? Huh! I'm starting to get frustrated. Maybe she didn't meet Master-Gowgwart-Love. Aaahh. That could be the why. Hmm? Huïumi, wait. Haiokïto's grandmother used to tell him the story about Masseïel and Phiuphos when he was a teenager, which means it was more than twenty years ago. I remember he said that his grandmother passed away fifteen years ago; therefore, she must have met Master-Gowgwart-Love. And if she did, it must have been as an elderly person. That could explain why she isn't wearing the Gowgwarts' Bracelet in any of these portraits. She's a young adult in all of them. Of course, if it's her," Huïumi thinks.

.   .   .

While Huïumi is looking through the portraits—trying to find a portrait of Haiokïto's grandmother as an elderly person—Haiokïto walks into the family's private hall to surprise her.

"Joureïe, dear. Are you lost?" Haiokïto asks.

Huïumi cries out in fright, "Aaahhh! Oh, it's you! You scared me. Sorry for screaming."

"Gïocs. It's okay, honey. I knew I'd find you here . . . You are inquisitive," Haiokïto says.

Huïumi replies, "I guess that's my superpower—Oh, are those your grandparents?"

He nods. "Mm-hmm. That was their last photo together before my grandfather passed away," Haiokïto replies.

"Really? That explains it. Compared to all the other portraits here, your grandmother looks much older in that one," Huïumi says, "(I knew it was his grandmother)."

"Are you here because of what I said earlier at the Clear Rock Crystal House?" Haiokïto asks.

"Gïocs, not really. *Though* I was curious. Don't blame me," she replies.

"I knew it," Haiokïto says.

Huïumi asks, "Why doesn't she have the Gowgwarts' Bracelet on in any of the portraits I've seen so far? Not even in the last photo she took with your grandfather before he passed away."

"Good observation," Haiokïto replies.

"Don't you think it's weird?" Huïumi asks.

"I think so," Haiokïto replies.

"Perhaps she met Master-Gowgwart-Love as a senior and that is why she is not wearing the Gowgwarts' Bracelet in any of the portraits in here," Huïumi says.

"You can certainly be right," Haiokïto replies.

"I know," Huïumi says.

"There's something I wanna show you. Something that I've never been able to open since she passed away. I wasn't ready before . . . but now—with you by my side, I have the courage I need to do it. Do you mind coming to my room for a moment?" Haiokïto asks.

"Not at all," Huïumi replies.

"Great! Come. It's this way. You first. I'll close the door behind you," Haiokïto says.

. . .

Huïumi walked with Haiokïto to his room, where he showed her a sturdy 12 x 12 x 4 1/2 gift box, wrapped in a white satin lace and sealed with an old-fashioned lock that only Haiokïto had the key to open.

Joyfully, Huïumi says, "Oh, Haiokïto! It's beautiful! I love the *ablanc* satin fabric lace in which she wrapped it."

Haiokïto replies, "I must confess my grandma had a good taste for fabrics."

Huïumi wonders what could be inside the box. "What's inside the box, honey?" she asks.

"Let's find out," Haiokïto replies.

He reaches into the right front pocket of his shorts to retrieve his red Ūmieda wallet, where he keeps the small golden key to the gift box. He pulls out the key and unlocks the box.

In a surprised tone, after opening the gift box, Haiokïto says, "Loose papers!"

"That looks like a letter," Huïumi says.

"Yes, it's a letter," he replies, holding the loose papers.

"Mmm? Why would your grandmother write you a letter and keep it in a locked gift box?" Huïumi asks.

"I don't know," Haiokïto answers.

"Do you wanna read it when you're alone? Maybe you prefer privacy," Huïumi says.

"My love, I don't need privacy from you. I don't want secrets between us," Haiokïto replies.

Huïumi smiles. "Paccürs," she says.

"Let's see what the letter says," he says.

Huïumi nods, agreeing.

At once Haiokïto begins to read the letter aloud.

"Dear Haio,

My sweet grandchild."

Haiokïto pauses as his eyes water. He continues.

"Today, I've decided to write this letter to you, because I believe my time on earth is ending. I've lived a wonderful life, full of laughter and warmth from those around me. I must say, there have been tears too, but that's what life is about. I have embraced everything that life has thrown at me, except for one thing that I regret I did not embrace earlier on—my love for writing.

When I joined your grandfather in matrimony, I put my dream aside to help him raise our beautiful family and support him in every way I could. I must say, everything comes with a price, and for me, it was my dream. I don't regret my decision entirely, but after he passed away, a lot has happened. I once thought I knew what love was, but recently I learned I was far from knowing its true meaning.

As I spent the past twelve years trying to find meaning in life again, with all the freedom your grandfather left me with, I traveled to many places. It was during that time that I learned the story I used to tell you about Masseïel and Phiuphos. And it was in the most magical place in The Six Kingdoms, Neephis Library, in Neephis, Kingdom of Neephiun, where I discovered this ancient story about Love. Since then, I became obsessed with finding the Gowgwarts' Bracelet, until I finally met her—Master-Gowgwart-Love. Before that, I went to a jewelry store to order a custom-made version of the Gowgwarts' Bracelet, which Masseïel describes in the manuscript—but with a minor adjustment to remind me of my commitment to Love.

It was in this estate where I met Master-Gowgwart-Love and her friends in the dahleïea garden. With her, I learned that it's never too late to dream again. With the help of The Star of the Universe, I also remembered my love for writing. Until not so long ago, I had no voice, but now with the power of Love, I have one. This time, I won't keep it to myself. I have done that for a long time. I want to share my story of transformation with the world, and I want you to help me do that. I might not be in this world to see it with my own eyes, but I trust you will publish my story. In this gift box, you will find the manuscript I have written. I hope I am light for those who may think it's too late to make their dreams come true.

I love you, Haio.
—Your granny, Leïea."

Haiokïto puts the letter on the bed. After that, he dries his tears with his hands. Huïumi hugs him as he sits on the bed, and then she waits for him to say something to her.

Haiokïto says, "It took me fifteen years to open this gift box. I don't understand. Why me?"

"Sometimes the responsibility falls upon those who can fulfill the task. You can still make her dream come true," Huïumi says.

"You're right. Let's look inside the box," Haiokïto says.

He looks inside the box once more. Then, he reaches in, takes the manuscript, and reads the title. He says, *"The Game of Emotions: A Tale of Dahleïeas,* by Dahleïea."

Huïumi asks, "Dahleïea? Was that her name?"

Haiokïto replies, "I always called her granny, Leïea. I guess her real name was Dahleïea. Perhaps that's why she planted the dahleïea garden."

Huïumi says, "I guess it makes perfect sense. Also, that's where she said she met Master-Gowgwart-Love and friends."

"I guess . . ." Haiokïto says.

"Let's see how many pages she wrote," Huïumi says.

Haiokïto scrolls to the last page of the manuscript. Surprised, he says, "Almost three hundred pages! Whoa!" He pauses, looking over at Huïumi. "Can you believe it, Huïumi? As soon as I get back to the city, I will take this manuscript to get it published. If she has entrusted me with this task, I will make sure to fulfill her wish."

.   .   .

"Wait, I see something else inside the gift box. It's all the way inside, like, way at the bottom of it," Huïumi says.

Huïumi finds a small burgundy gift box, wrapped inside a plum velvet and pastel pink satin mini bag. Immediately, she hands it to Haiokïto and puts away the mini bag where it was.

Haiokïto opens it. He gasps. "It's the customized Gowgwarts' Bracelet she mentioned in her letter. The one she had customized before she met Master-Gowgwart-Love. I cannot believe she wants me to have it," he says, surprised.

Excitedly, Huïumi says, "Oh, whoa! Look! She added an ablanc diamond in the center of each of the stars that seal the bracelets. Did you know that ablanc diamonds symbolize endurance, elegance, and commitment?"

Haiokïto says, "I guess she was committed to creating balance among her emotions." He hands the bracelet to Huïumi.

Huïumi turns it over, admiring its beauty. With a surprise tone, she says, "Oh, whoa! She also engraved a message in the back of it that says, 'The power of Love is in you,'" she reads, her fingers tracing the message engraved in the back of the bracelet.

"It sure is . . ." Haiokïto replies.

"That's beautiful, Haiokïto. What are you going to do with the bracelet?" Huïumi asks, handing the bracelet back to him.

"I'm sure it will look beautiful on you," Haiokïto replies.

"Are you serious? It belonged to your grandmother," Huïumi says.

"I'm sure about how I feel about you, my dear, and I want you to have it. I love you. You're my moon and I see myself spending the rest of my life with you," Haiokïto replies.

"I love you too, babe. I've never loved anyone the way I love you. You're more than anything I could have ever dreamed of. You are my sun," Huïumi says.

They embrace each other, lost in a moment of tender warmth.

.   .   .

As Haiokïto is putting the letter and the manuscript back inside the gift box, he sees the missing pages of the manuscript, *Masseïel & Phiuphos: A tale of Love.*

"There it is!" Haiokïto says, surprised.

"What?" Huïumi asks.

"The missing pages of the manuscript yeo read in the Neephis Library . . ." Haiokïto responds.

"Gïocs! For real? What?" Huïumi asks, touching her head with her left hand.

"Usïcs! Look!" Haiokïto says.

"We were right!" Huïumi says.

Haiokïto replies, "This is what she used to have the bracelet custom made."

"Are you gonna return it?" Huïumi asks.

Haiokïto nods. "Mm-hmmm. These pages should be with the original manuscript," he says.

"Yeo agree with you," Huïumi says.

Haiokïto says, "I will arrange to return them when I get back to the city of the Garden of Joy."

Huïumi replies, "That's a great idea. Oh dear, we forgot about my friends. Should we head to the Clear Rock Crystal House? We left my friends alone for quite a long time."

"Alright. Let me put this back where it was," Haiokïto replies.

"Paccürs!" Huïumi replies.

. . .

Minutes later, Haiokïto and Huïumi arrive at the Clear Rock Crystal House.

"Guys, where have you been? We're debating who's gonna tell their story first," Rayïq says.

"While you were gone, Chef Glüedo prepared these delicious marshmallows. They're so so good," Geossuth says, pointing at the marshmallows.

Haiokïto replies, "Well, that's exactly what we need."

"Paccürs, let's have some marshmallows," Huïumi says as she takes one. "Have you decided who's gonna tell their story first?" she asks.

Maiephis answers, "I've decided I'll be first. Are you ready?"

—I don't know if you are ready . . . But I'm ready to hear some truth.

Six

Gowgwarts' Doll's House

"It all happened when I was a teenager just before I moved to this kingdom to study English Literature at Brightmieda University. I remember that I wasn't happy at home and all I wanted to do was to go away from my family to start fresh. Also, my emotions were a zigzag after what I had discovered. I didn't know what direction to take back then. All I knew is that I wanted to escape from reality and go somewhere where I could simply be me, Maie."

—Haven't we all gone through a zigzag of emotions? I have.

"And as many of you know, when I was a young child there was a time that I didn't speak for five years—most likely until I was fourteen. I also have something to confess, but before I say it, I must say that I have my reasons for keeping this from all of you until now, so please don't be upset at me for not saying anything sooner—I am a princess . . . The Princess of Neephiun, daughter of King Neessaph III," Maiephis says.

—Pause!

You may think Maiephis is asking for too much. I know, she's lucky to have good friends . . . Even though the news of being part of the House of Pharranes in the Kingdom of Neephiun has been unexpected for her friends, Maiephis will always be their best friend.

—Go on!

"A princess?" Huïumi asks with a surprised voice.

"Why did you wait until now to say that you are part of the House of Pharranes?" Ufaïa asks.

"Did you think we were gonna treat you differently because you're a princess?" Luseïe asks.

"No! Why would I think that? I just love how it feels to simply be myself around you and not Maiephis, The Princess of Neephiun. Since we are all in here together and I am sharing my story with you, I've decided to finally be completely open and transparent with all," Maiephis replies.

Luseïe replies, "We've been friends for so long that we didn't expect you to be a princess overnight."

"Usïcs. We understand. Don't worry, we're not gonna judge you. It's all good," Huïumi says.

"Really?" Maiephis asks with a hopeful voice.

Everyone in synchrony says, "Usïcs! Yes! Paccürs!" Except for Ufaïa, who says, "Gïocs!"

Maiephis asks, "Why Ufaïa?"

Ufaïa responds, "I'm kidding. We're best friends."

Maiephis says, "Thank you for understanding me, forces. As I was saying, because I couldn't speak when I was a young child, I was home schooled and kept away from the media. And as the youngest child of ten children, no one outside the castle noticed my existence. There were a lot of stories said about me in the news, (everywhere) even that I had died a year after I was born . . . (that was shocking to me). I guess, I always found a way to hide from the media (trying to go unnoticed). However, in celebration of my sixteenth birthday, the castle released a new photo of me to commemorate the occasion and to introduce me to society. So, after all the newspaper articles in honor of my special birthday, a lot of speculation followed because of my absence from the media. Therefore, my papa ordered that no new recent photos of me be published until my twenty-first birthday, and if anyone wanted to publish recent photos of me, they'd need my approval first. That's why on my twenty-first birthday, our office of engagements had no choice but to release an old, never-before-seen photo, and, of course, a letter congratulating me in the occasion of my milestone birthday. Then, I was already attending Brightmieda University, and I didn't want any of you—my best friends—to know what I just revealed to you: that I'm the daughter of my father, King Neessaph III of Neephiun. So, I refused to give them my approval. Thanks to that, I was able to keep a low profile with all of you. That's why sometimes I act a little weird around you, and also, I don't give interviews or like to take photos with people that I don't know. It's also the reason why I never told you about my royal lineage. In the end, my family wasn't the reason I came to Brightmieda University, it was Love."

Everyone is looking at each other as Maiephis continues to tell her story. They don't want her to stop, but rather they want to know more.

Maiephis continues, "The truth is, I wasn't looking for Love when I found it. As a child, I had a happy upbringing and was deeply loved by my family—until one day everything changed. I wasn't as happy anymore, and not because my family stopped loving me, but because of what I discovered when I looked out the window while I was playing with my dolls in my room located on the east wing of the castle."

Everyone is listening attentively to Maiephis.

"When I was a child, my papa was everything to me. I admired his connection with the people in general and how he always put his family first, especially the way he was with my mama: kind, gentle, patient, and sweet. So, when from the window facing the courtyard of my room, I saw my Nana kissing my papa in the balcony of his room—on the west wing of the castle across from the back of my room—I was crushed. I couldn't speak for the next five years." She pauses briefly, then continues. "The day my voice stopped making sound, I stopped believing in Love and had no interest in finding it. But Love is persistent and surely wanted to find me. Anyway, before it happened, during the time that I couldn't speak, I devoted myself to taking care of my mama, who, at the time, suffered from a tumor in her head. I remember back then, I couldn't understand how my papa could have done this to my beloved mama, when she needed him the most," Maiephis says.

"I'm sorry, girlfriend. It must have been extremely difficult for you to endure so much pain at such an early age," Ufaïa says with a compassionate voice.

"I cannot imagine how painful that was for you," Rayïq adds.

Maiephis replies, "Thanks, forces."

In support of Maiephis, Huïumi makes the love sign with her hands.

Maiephis continues, "I remember the last words of my mama, 'When the sun sets and the moon rises, look up to the sky and wait to see the stars. I will be there among them, watching you from the sky.' The day she passed away was the hardest day of my life, and I don't know whether to say, happily or sadly, that's when my voice returned." Maiephis pauses briefly.

"Everyone around me was sad because my mama had died, yet they had joy because my voice had returned. But all I could think of was her last words. From that day on, no matter where I am, I always try not to miss the sunset; because I know my mama is among the stars somewhere in the sky and I want her to know that I remember her last words," Maiephis says.

"Sorry for your loss, Maie. I know what it's like to lose a loved one. My late wife, Lïesia, passed away six years ago at the Kingdom of Gemmïes, where we met and also where I met Master-Gowgwart-Love," he says, his gaze already wandering. "I'm not sure if I should ask you this, but since you are a Pharranes, I wonder if you know, who founded the Neephis Library?" Haiokïto asks.

"Thanks, Haiokïto. I can definitely answer that. The founder was the second king of Neephiun, King Phiuphos I. He founded the Neephis Library to honor his papa, King Neephis the Great, and to celebrate his wife and truest love, Queen Masseïel, who profoundly cherished books. Later on, after his death, Queen Masseïel decided to write a manuscript about them, *Masseïel & Phiuphos: A tale of Love,* to share their love story with The Six Kingdoms. For centuries, since then their love story has attracted many tourists seeking answers to finding Love at the Neephis Library," Maiephis replies.

Geossuth says, "I should pay a visit to Neephis Library. Who knows—I might find Love there."

Maiephis replies, "Yes. Maybe you get lucky . . . Anyway, I am sure Love will appear in your life when you least expect it."

"Maie is right, that's exactly how it happened for me. Haiokïto, like me, traveled to Neephis City looking for Love, where we ended up in the Neephis Library. But instead, we found wisdom in an owl called Neephoos, a sign that Love isn't so far from us," Huïumi says.

Haiokïto nods, agreeing. "Mm-hmm. Meeting Love is different for everyone, Geossuth," he says.

"You're very brave for opening up to us, Maie," Luseïe says.

Ufaïa says, "Trust that we will keep everything you have shared with us confidential, right guys?"

Everyone nods, agreeing with Ufaïa.

Maiephis smiles. "Thanks, forces," she says.

"The years after my mama's death were really tough for me. A zigzag of emotions . . ." Maiephis says.

"A big transition between events?" Luseïe asks.

"The zigzag of emotions it's actually a thing," Maiephis replies.

"No way. Really?" Luseïe asks.

Gasps erupted around the room. All eyes were on Maiephis.

"Yes! It can be described as the line between facing Anger or any other negative emotion," Maiephis replies.

"Ooh. It's like a border line," Luseïe says.

"Yes! Exactly. If you get the zigzag line, you have been given a chance to recover before it's too late for you. You just need to get to the finish line," Maiephis replies.

"Capïcsh!" Luseïe says.

Everyone with a smile, nodding in agreement.

Maiephis continues, "My papa married my Nana, now Queen Cleirphi of Neephiun. Can you imagine how hard that was for me? She was my Nana and also, like, a mama to me until that day I told you about. I felt stuck. I had no friends other than my nine siblings, and I wasn't going to talk to them about my feelings. I must say that it was fun and stressful to grow up in a large family. Honestly, to me it was a blessing; I never felt alone because I had all of them—six elder brothers and three elder sisters. Ooh. I miss them so much but having your friendship now means a lot to me too."

.   .   .

Pharranes Castle, Neephis City, Kingdom of Neephiun.

Shaphnee, looking for Maiephis in the outdoors of Pharranes

Castle, shouts, "Maie! Maie! Maie! Where are you? We're too old to play hide and seek. I know you're hiding in the Garden of Hope. It was mama's favorite place. It's your sixteenth birthday. C'mon, I'm your eldest sister; you must obey me. Hahaha. Got you! Come here little sis. I have a gift for you from our dear mama. Here, open it."

Maiephis giggles. She replies, "You cannot give me a morning alone in mama's favorite garden on my birthday." She stops giggling. "Let me see what you have there for me. Aww. These were mama's favorite pearls; she only wore them for special occasions."

Shaphnee replies, "Mm-hmm. This is a special occasion, little sis. Aren't they marvelous? She wanted you to have them on your sixteenth birthday."

Maiephis says, "Gosh, I miss mama."

Shaphnee says, "I know. Me too. She said, since you were born in June, your birth stone is pearl. You should wear it tonight. Aaah, also, in the occasion of your birthday, our dearest papa has a special announcement during dinner, tonight."

Maiephis's facial expressions changed from happy to serious; she isn't too happy about her sister's comment.

Maiephis replies, "Sure. I wonder what it is?"

.   .   .

It's already 6:00 p.m. in Neephis, Kingdom of Neephiun and the banquet in the royal blue hall is ready to welcome the attendees. As directed, the staff have decorated the table with five center pieces and candles. Each center piece has ten white roses, six white tulips and four blue daisies. All attendees are dressed in white—black-tie attire—to honor Maiephis's sixteenth birthday. Maiephis is dressed in a royal blue dress with the pearl necklace gifted by her late mother. The ten siblings, the king, and queen of the Kingdom of Neephiun are sitting at the table. The king raises his glass to make a toast in honor of Maiephis's birthday. Immediately, the staff brings her gift to the king. The king presents the gift to Maiephis.

King Neessaph III gives a short speech.

"Today, our family is gathered to celebrate our beloved, sweet Maiephis. She's turning sixteen years old, and on this special dinner, I'd like to present her this stunning twenty-carat white sapphire, that once upon a time belonged to my great, great, grandmother, Queen Pheephesa of the Kingdom of Neephiun. Not only has this unique, twenty-carat white sapphire been in our family for generations but it also symbolizes forgiveness, honesty, protection, and healing. May one day you can forgive me, my darling. Cheers!" he says.

Everyone raises their glass and says, "Cheers."

Soon after, Maiephis hears Shaphnee whispering, "Put on the white sapphire, Maie." Maiephis rolls her eyes at her sister and then proceeds to wear the white sapphire brooch on her dress. Maiephis couldn't wait for dinner to be over; overwhelmed by her emotions, she looks sad. Her big sister Shaphnee, sitting next to her, notices it. Right before dinner is over, knowing that Maiephis isn't happy with the gift her father had presented her, Shaphnee decides to cheer her up. She plays the piano and sings her sister's favorite song, "Today Tilting Blue."

. . .

After dinner is over, Maiephis goes back to her room and the first thing she does is to remove the white sapphire from her dress. Then, out of frustration, she talks to herself.

"Forgiveness? Really? I cannot believe he said that in front of everyone on my birthday. HAAA. A white sapphire to ease his guilt for what he did to my mama. I need to find a way to leave this place.

I don't want this white sapphire; it reminds me of the reason why I cannot forgive him," she says, upset.

Master-Gowgwart-Love appears in Maiephis's room.

Master-Gowgwart-Love says, "Leave this place? Why dear? I mean you can, but not like this. Your father is trying to help you. You cannot undo the past, but you can forgive and move forward."

Maiephis, with her eyes wide open, looks around, trying to find the voice. "Who is that? What do you know about forgiveness? You have no idea what I went through! It took me five years to speak again because of what he did to my mama, only to see my mama die in my arms so I could speak again. Nope! I cannot forgive him! He hurt me!" Maiephis says, not knowing who she's speaking to.

"Oh, dear. You have a good heart, don't let the wounds from your past change you. My precious girl, don't be so hard on yourself. Whatever you feel that's hurting you now, it will go away once you decide to forgive and let go. I'm Love. Master-Gowgwart-Love. The flame in your heart that can transform your sadness into happiness. Look down here by the window in the dollhouse."

Maiephis asks, "What window? I don't see you. I'm looking at the front window. Also, I don't want to forgive him."

"Oh, sweet dear, do you want me to help you heal?" Master-Gowgwart-Love asks.

Maiephis asks, "How can you help me do that? Whatever that means."

Master-Gowgwart-Love replies, "With my powers. Your good heart has enabled them."

Maiephis asks, "What powers? I know I have a good heart, but I'm tired of being good."

Master-Gowgwart-Love replies, "You must never get tired of being good. That's your strength. My powers bring healing to you. I give you strength and willpower. I have come to help you close the wounds that ache inside you." Red crystal sparkles all over Maiephis.

. . .

Present time, Clear Rock Crystal House.

"'I'm a Gowgwart,' Master-Gowgwart-Love said. I asked her, 'What's a Gowgwart?' and she replied, 'We are emotions,'" Maiephis says.

"That's what she said to me," Luseïe says.

"Maybe, she says that to everyone," Maiephis replies.

"Because that's what they are: emotions in disguise," Huïumi adds.

"Did she say that to all of you except Geossuth?" Ufaïa asks.

All eyes on Ufaïa. Everyone nods in agreement.

"Me too," Chef Glüedo winks while he's setting up a table with snacks for everyone.

Everyone looks at Chef Glüedo, their eyes wide with surprise.

"Wait, chef. Do you know Master-Gowgwart-Love?" Haiokïto asks.

Chef Glüedo responds, "Yes, sir. I know Master-Gowgwart-Love. But don't mind me. I'm just the chef."

Maiephis says, "I better go on telling my story."

Everyone is listening.

"I have a doll's house that belonged to my great, great, great, grandma . . . Once upon a time, my doll's house was customized by her when she was thirteen years old. My great, great, great, grandma was the youngest child of Neephiun's then-monarch, who, after her father and brother passed away, became Queen of Neephiun. Since her passing, it has been a tradition to pass on the doll's house to the youngest daughter or youngest granddaughter (if no daughter alive) of the reigning monarch of Neephiun. So, on my fifth birthday my mama gave me the doll's house whose façade is of the distinct colors of the crystal stones on the Gowgwarts' Bracelet—which I came to realize after I received my Gowgwarts' Bracelet."

Huïumi gasps. "She probably met Master-Gowgwart-Love."

Maiephis replies, "Oh, I did ask Master-Gowgwart-Love, and she confirmed that, yes, truly it did. She also told me that the doll's house is where she appeared in her life before she had it customized. So that's kind of how it happened for me. When Master-Gowgwart-Love appeared in my life, she did it from inside my doll's house."

"No!" Ufaïa says.

"It sounds like a precious magical dollhouse covered with the Gowgwarts' Bracelet crystal stones," Luseïe says.

Huïumi says, "Woo! With the crystal stones of the Gowgwarts' Bracelet, I can picture it sparkling."

Maiephis nods, agreeing. "Mm-hmmm. Imagine it full of them. A beautiful sparkling doll's house. So dreamy. I must admit that even before knowing of the connection between the Gowgwarts' Bracelet and the doll's house, I named it—Gowgwarts' Doll's House. Can you believe it? I know, that's so me. I remember seeing the sparkles of Master-Gowgwart-Love through the living room window . . ."

.   .   .

Maiephis's room, Pharranes Castle, Neephis.

"Look at me down here inside the dollhouse. Bend so you can see me," Master-Gowgwart-Love says.

"Where? I cannot see you," Maiephis replies.

"By the windows of the living room, dear. Where you saw the red crystal sparkles. Right here," Master-Gowgwart-Love replies.

Red crystals sprout from Master-Gowgwart-Love's ears.

Maiephis sees the red sparkling crystals. "Aaah, there you are. You're so tiny. Who are those next to you?" she asks.

"They are Master Gowgwarts like me. Let me introduce you to them, Master Gowgwarts—Care, Trust, Happiness, Peace, Joy, and Freedom," Master-Gowgwart-Love replies.

. . .

Present time, Clear Rock Crystal House.

"You met all of them at once?" Huïumi asks.

Maiephis replies, "Yes. Why? Didn't you?"

Huïumi responds, "Gïocs, I met Master-Gowgwart-Love first and then she introduced the rest of them slowly . . . My process of healing was very slow. It took me a long time to forget about Pain."

"I guess everyone's story is different. The Master Gowgwarts appear in unusual ways in people's lives, and each person's path to healing varies depending on their level of suffering. We all have very unique experiences," Maiephis replies.

Ufaïa says, "You will be surprised . . . Through their teachings, Master Gowgwarts help us transform our suffering into something beautiful and unexpectedly unique. I call it the power of embracing a positive mindset, where you shift negative thoughts into positive ones, which allows you to live a happier life."

. . .

Maiephis's room, Pharranes Castle, Neephis.

"Everyone knows of our existence, but not everyone is aware of our presence . . . That's why it's so important for you to develop awareness to create a harmonious state among your emotions, which will allow you to experience a greater well-being. We will help you accept and embrace our positive side," Master-Gowgwart-Love says from inside the Gowgwarts' Doll's House.

Master-Gowgwart-Peace says, "Even though you have never seen me before, I have always been here with you . . . I noticed that you started spending more time in the Garden of Hope almost every day, just like your mother did before she passed away. Immediately, it raised my concern that you could find Anger there, especially after you received the white sapphire from your father at the banquet today. So, I shared my concern with Master-Gowgwart-Love and asked her to appear in your life before it was too late, and Master-Gowgwart-Anger could find you there. There's something you don't know about your mother. Four years ago, when you were twelve, your mother met Master-Gowgwart-Anger at the Garden of Hope."

"My mama? Are you sure? . . . She loved the Garden of Hope. How is that possible?" Maiephis asks.

"When your mother found out about her tumor, she decided to create the Garden of Hope with blue forget-me-not flowers that symbolize true love and respect. These are the flowers your father gave her when they met, as a symbol of fidelity and faithfulness. It is a promise he was supposed to always remember and keep in his thoughts, but he didn't. As soon as she found out about your father's relationship with your Nana, she ordered the Garden of Hope to be closed. Shortly after, she learned that her tumor was in the last stage, so she changed her mind and instead decided to keep the garden to torture him," Master-Gowgwart-Peace replies.

"To torture him? She wasn't like that," Maiephis says.

"Your mother wanted to remind your father of the promise he made to her here—the day of their engagement—thirty years ago. As a result of his infidelity, she got so, so angry at him that she began to frequent the Garden of Hope almost every day—until one day Master-Gowgwart-Anger received a sign from her Anger, and then she found herself with Master-Gowgwart-Anger inside the Garden of Hope, where he consumed her slowly. Until the day she died she couldn't forgive your father," Master-Gowgwart-Peace replies.

"Why didn't you help her?" Maiephis asks.

"There was nothing we could do to save her. Not even Master-Gowgwart-Love was able to light her flame. We don't want that to happen to you, too. You're young, with a beautiful life ahead of you. Genuinely accept the white sapphire brooch you father gave you. It is a symbol of hope and forgiveness that will empower you to leave behind everything preventing you from moving beyond the past," Master-Gowgwart-Peace replies.

"Set yourself free by allowing yourself to forgive your past so you can enjoy your present and have a happier life. Holding a grudge only holds you back, but if you forgive, you will be free," Master-Gowgwart-Freedom says.

Master-Gowgwart-Happiness says, "Then, I'll appear in your life, again."

Master-Gowgwart-Joy says, "Beyond happiness, you will feel great and content—a long-lasting state of harmony."

Maiephis replies, "I will need time to process it. It's not that easy. A lot has happened, and I'm not prepared to do what you ask of me."

Master-Gowgwart-Freedom says, "I can help you with that. Perhaps, exploring writing and painting can help you channel your feelings in a positive way that helps you calm Anger."

Master-Gowgwart-Care adds, "That's what you need to create balance in a healthy and constructive way, which in turn leads to freedom and a greater well-being."

Maiephis says, "I like to paint, and it does relax me a lot, but I don't write. I am not good at it. What else can I do to calm Anger?"

"Try to pursue a new goal that's linked with your skills. Even if it's sports. There's so much to explore. Set a moment apart each day to give thanks to attract positive energy into your life," Master-Gowgwart-Care replies, sparkling pink crystals everywhere.

"Believe in yourself. Feel comfortable expressing your talents. Be confident without fear of judgement. Close your eyes and let your imagination transport you to a fantasy world . . ." Master-Gowgwart-Trust says.

In a chorus, the seven positive Master Gowgwarts sing, "Your Imagination is your North."

After they finish singing, Master-Gowgwart-Love says, "We'll give you time so you can explore new hobbies."

.   .   .

Five months after.

Maiephis is planning to move the Gowgwarts' Doll's House to the west wing of the Pharranes Castle—where all the donations for distribution to the various charities in the Kingdom of Neephiun are stored in addition to all unused items—to forget the Gowgwarts.

Maiephis says, "I hope to never see Master Gowgwarts again. I have always pleased everyone. I don't need to know what others think I should do to forget and forgive what my father has done to me. I've had enough."

Meanwhile, from inside the Gowgwarts' Doll's House, Master-Gowgwart-Love says, "Maiephis, dear. What are you doing? Are you trying to bury your emotions? You are going to bury yourself. You cannot get rid of us so easily; we're part of you."

Maiephis says, "There you are again." She begins to fade away. "AHHHH!!" Maiephis screams as she realizes she's fading.

.   .   .

"Where am I? Master-Gowgwart-Love? Oh no! I am trapped in a white box where there's only a thin line to a golden door," she says.

Morphïea says, "You're seeing through. You would need to climb up and then slide down until you get to the exit." The thin line shakes Maiephis as Morphïea speaks. The colors of the thin golden line (the colors of the positive and negative Gowgwarts) change as it moves. Maiephis is standing on the green side of the thin line.

"So, what do I do? I don't see the steps to move up," Maiephis asks Morphïea.

Morphïea replies, "They will appear when you're in control of Pain."

"Pain?" Maiephis asks, sitting, not knowing what Morphïea is trying to say. "What if I don't need the steps? I'm going to build my own steps," she says. Suddenly, yellow steps appear and Maiephis climbs up. She feels joyful, but that feeling doesn't last long. As soon as she is relaxed, she slides all the way down the baby-blue side.

"Ugh!! I am all the way down again. The golden door is all the way up. It's not going to be an easy path to reach it. Especially now that I'm so close," Maiephis says, upset.

Morphïea says, "Don't give up. You can do it. No matter how hard it might seem, it is possible. Be persistent and don't look back."

"Who are you? Why do I move every time you speak? Are you under the thin line?" Maiephis asks.

"I am Morphïea, a friend of Master-Gowgwart-Love. You are about to bring Master-Gowgwart-Anger to life. Your Anger brought you here. Master-Gowgwart-Love sent me to help you reach the exit of the Zigzag of Emotions. It's a thin line between your world and ours. You move up and down until you reach the golden exit or else you enter our world to face Master-Gowgwart-Anger—Master of all

Gowgwarts-Anger."

Maiephis sighs. "Please help me! I don't want that to happen."

Morphïea surrounds Maiephis with her wings. "I need you to close your eyes and trust yourself to find Peace. It's the only way up to the golden exit," Morphïea says.

. . .

Master-Gowgwart-Love says, "She moved up the line. Yes! I should see her soon. Oh! There you are. I am glad I sent Morphïea to help you. Do you still want to get rid of us?"

"Master-Gowgwart-Love! I'm back! Thank you! No! You will stay here with me," Maiephis replies.

"Are you spending time with Master-Gowgwart-Freedom?"

Maiephis replies, "Not exactly. I did what he suggested me. I painted, which I love, but it's the writing part. It's not working for me. I'm not good at it. I tried but it didn't work. I told you I am not good at that."

Master-Gowgwart-Love replies, "My dear, I know that trying something new is hard, but it is possible. You should spend time with Master-Gowgwart-Trust. Don't lose hope. Keep trying. You can do it."

"I tried to write, but I cannot. Writing is hard; it is not easy," Maiephis says with dissatisfaction.

"Oh, dear, that's all right. I know what you need—the magical sparkles drink," Master-Gowgwart-Love replies.

Purple amethyst crystals sprinkle from the purple star on her heart, and a cup of gardenia tea with magical sparkles appears.

"Magic drink is this gardenia tea; drink the sparkles, Maiephis, and you'll see," Master-Gowgwart-Love says.

Maiephis drinks the magical sparkles and at once falls asleep.

. . .

Maiephis wakes up to realize that she's a doll-sized person lying on the bed of the master bedroom in the Gowgwarts' Doll's House.

Looking around her, she says, "This isn't my room. Where am I? I recognize this place. I'm inside the Gowgwarts' Doll's House." She gasps. "That means I'm the size of a doll. How did this happen? It must have been the gardenia tea—the magical sparkles . . . That's the last thing I remember before falling asleep."

She quickly gets out of bed, and the first thing she does is call Master Gowgwarts, but no one replies. So, she quickly walks to the front porch of the Gowgwarts' Doll's House looking for Master-Gowgwart-Love.

. . .

"Dost thou remember me, Maiephis?"

"YOU? Nope. I don't think so. Or maybe I do. Hmm? I think I remember you. I haven't seen you since . . ." Maiephis says.

"Since thou wast eight years old, here in thy room."

"I remember you from the night I saw my Nana kissing my papa, with a smile, you shushed me. Then, covered me in sparkling purple amethyst crystals, disappearing from the doll's house. That wasn't pleasant. After that day, I couldn't speak for five years. It was you! You're the reason I couldn't speak, not my papa. All these years I was wrong to blame him for what happened to me back then," Maiephis says.

"Please forgive me. As difficult as it may seem, turning a blind eye on certain things is the right thing to do. Thou wast too young to understand back then. Believe me, I did what was right to protect thee and thy mother. She had just received a brain tumor diagnosis and was devastated. Understand that not everyone knows how to deal with physical illnesses, above all, when they have everything anyone could have asked for in life and thy mother had it all."

"You're simply justifying your actions," Maiephis replies.

"No, please let me explain."

Maiephis sits on the white rocking chair next to her. "Okay, go on," she replies.

"When your mother received the news of her illness, she kept it to herself . . . During the time she kept her illness from your father, she ignored him and unconsciously made him feel unloved. So, not knowing the real reason behind her behavior was the tumor in her brain, his judgment clouded his mind, and he began to put distance between them. Since then, there were no more garden walks, meals together and as a result, they began to attend social events separately. Your father stopped loving her and soon after found love again with your Nana. One day things got out of hand; your mother fainted, so she had no choice, but to be honest with all. Sometimes things can get out of control, and the easiest way to ease guilt is to blame others. Few are those brave enough to admit wrongdoing. What happened before had absolutely nothing to do with thee. If I kept thee silent for five years, it's because I didn't want thee to live with the burden of having to tell thy mother about thy Nana. Before thy Nana and father started seeing each other, thy parents had already separated, with no chances of getting back together."

Maiephis says, "Yes, but she found out anyway when I was ten years old, and she was so sad that I couldn't resist blaming him for causing her so much pain."

"Thanks to me, thou art not responsible for revealing the truth to thy mother. It was better the way it happened. I'm telling thee all this, so thou canst forgive and leave the past behind. Give thyself an opportunity to try something new. Don't give up writing and finish thy book. Travel to other kingdoms, eat different foods, meet new people, and fall in love . . . Thou livest in a beautiful world full of possibilities, where thou canst be anything thou wishest to be. Allow thyself to dream big and remember to have fun. Everything is better when thee hast Joy and Happiness."

"You're right, I should try it. Wait a second!" Maiephis says, standing and leaning forward. "You never said your name."

"I am The Star of the Universe."

"Thank you for showing up to clear things up with me and for freeing me from the emotions that didn't allow me to forgive my papa. With the truth revealed, I'm sure it's the beginning of a much brighter future for us," Maiephis says, sincerely.

The Star of the Universe says, "That is the purpose of my visit. Forget not to genuinely accept the sapphire thy father gave thee on thy sixteenth birthday. Turn it into a necklace if thou wantest. Show him thou hast forgiven him by wearing the white sapphire."

"I will do as you say. Thank you," Maiephis replies.

"Farewell, Maiephis," The Star of the Universe replies. Purple amethyst crystals begin to appear, and she begins to disappear.

.   .   .

The light of the sun brings a bright new day. Maiephis wakes up to see breakfast is already served and the windows already open. She says, "The staff already came. I overslept. What time is it? Oh, it's only 10:00 a.m., I had a long night with . . . Hmm? What was her name? I cannot remember it. She reminds me of the painting in the hallway. Now that I think about it, they're identical. Let me check, it has to be her."

Maiephis rises from bed, slips into her slippers, and goes into the hallway that connects both wings of the Pharranes Castle.

. . .

Maiephis looks at the painting. She murmurs, "Wow, they look identical. They must be the same person. What was her name?"

Maiephis pauses a few seconds, then remembers and shouts, "I remember, you're The Star of The Universe!"

. . .

Cleirphi is walking towards Maiephis's room to bring her tea. She sees Maiephis standing in front of the painting, when Maiephis shouts, 'The Star of the Universe.' She gets so, so nervous that she drops the tea tray she holds in her hands, making a loud, crashing sound followed by the clinking of the tray.

Maiephis looks to the right. She sees her Nana and immediately rushes to help her.

"Nana? Are you okay? Please let me help you clean that up," Maiephis says. She begins to pick up the teapot, teacup, teaspoon, and honey pot, placing them on the tray.

Meanwhile Cleirphi wipes the floor with the linen napkin she held in her left hand before she dropped the tea tray.

With tears, Cleirphi says, "Sweet Maie. After almost ten years, you finally called me Nana again."

"I forgive you, Nana. Why did you drop the tea? Did I scare you? Is something wrong? Are you okay?" Maiephis asks.

Cleirphi wipes away her tears. She says, "Aww. Thanks, dear. That makes me so happy. The tea . . . The staff forgot to bring you tea, so I offered myself to bring it to you. Then, while I was walking to your room, I heard you say, 'The Star of the Universe.' Why did you call her The Star of the Universe? Do you know who she is?"

"Not really. She has a strong resemblance to The Star of the Universe—the woman from my dream. I could say they're twins, if not sisters because they're identical. She's exceptionally beautiful. It has to be her . . ." Maiephis says.

"She's late Queen Masseïel. Do you know her story?" Cleirphi asks.

Maiephis replies, "Yes, but she looks different in this painting compared to the others in the castle and in the city. Are you sure that she's late Queen Masseïel? In this one, she looks like The Star of the Universe."

"I think so," Cleirphi replies, unsure.

"Aaah," Maiephis says.

"Long ago . . . when I was a child, my mama who then worked in this castle, told me your late grandpa, King Neessaph II, painted this portrait. After many years of wondering who the woman of the painting was, because of the resemblance to other paintings we have of the late Queen Masseïel, we just assumed it was her. Since then, no one ever spoke about this painting again," Cleirphi says.

"It makes sense. I'd say they are the same person, if not twins," Maiephis says.

"I have something to confess . . . Years ago, when my mama used to work here, I asked her to bring me so I could eat my favorite dessert, chocolate crème brûlée [chuckles]. I remember that, just like today, during that time, the fridge was stocked with chocolate crème brûlée every day—because it's also your papa's favorite. That day in the afternoon, while I was sitting in the kitchen enjoying chocolate crème brûlée, I overheard the staff whispering among themselves that your grandpa was in his last hours . . . Soon after, I finished the dessert, and as quickly as I could, I headed to his room in a discreet way. Don't tell anyone, but I know of a secret door between the room next to his and the library—where he used to receive all guests to address matters of the state. From that room, I entered his and hid behind the thick blue curtain on the door between the rooms. From there, I heard him say, repeatedly, 'Bring me The Star of the Universe.' I also heard the people in the room replying back, 'We don't have it.' They whispered to each other, 'He's delirious. He's passing away,'" Cleirphi says.

"Is that why you dropped the tea tray when you heard me say her name?" Maiephis asks.

Cleirphi replies, "Yes. Over the years, no one paid attention to this painting. Now, after hearing you say the name, The Star of the Universe, while you looked at the painting, I was stunned. Everyone who was in his room that day was wrong. He was asking for this painting. The Star of the Universe is real. It's been here—hanging on this wall—for a long time."

"She is the same woman from my dream. I am certain. He must have met her here in the castle. Or maybe in one of his dreams. It's definitely her," Maiephis says.

"She looks a lot like late Queen Masseïel . . . I wonder if they're related . . . But right now, the priority is to inform your papa so we can rename this painting with its righteous name, The Star of the Universe. I must hurry. I will see you later, Maiephis. Thanks, dear," Cleirphi says.

"You're welcome, Nana," Maiephis replies.

.   .   .

Maiephis is returning to her room, thinking, "I guess, The Star of the Universe likes to spend time with my family, huh? First my grandpa and now me. I wonder if she and late Queen Masseïel are the same person."

Maiephis enters her room. She hears voices from inside the Gowgwarts' Doll's House.

"Anyone here? Master-Gowgwart-Love?" she asks.

"Dear, it's Master-Gowgwart-Love! Look down here on the porch of the dollhouse." Pink, purple, and white crystals sparkle in the air outside the Gowgwarts' Doll's House.

"Master-Gowgwart-Love! With the magic drink, I had a dream where The Star of the Universe told me everything. It isn't my papa's fault. I was so wrong . . . The Star of the Universe used her powers to protect my emotions," Maiephis says.

Master-Gowgwart-Love replies, "I'm glad you and The Star of the Universe spent time together."

"That means you do know The Star of the Universe," Maiephis says.

"Yes, Maiephis," Master-Gowgwart-Love replies.

"Great! Can you tell me if late Queen Masseïel and The Star of the Universe are the same person?" Maiephis asks.

"Of course, my dear," Master-Gowgwart-Love replies.

.   .   .

Present time, Clear Rock Crystal House.

"'There's a secret I will tell you. Upon the death of late Queen Masseïel, wife and only love of late King Phiuphos I of Neephiun— son of the greatest conqueror known in The Six Kingdoms, King Neephis the Great.' I interrupted Master-Gowgwart-Love, 'We can skip that part Master-Gowgwart-Love, I'm daughter of the king of Neephiun,' I said. Then, Master-Gowgwart-Love said, 'Oops, that's right, dear. I was about to say that her spirit became The Star of the Universe, and since then, I made room for her in my heart.' Master-Gowgwart-Love pointed to the purple star on her heart," Maiephis says.

"Maiephis! No way, girlfriend! Queen Masseïel is The Star of the Universe? I can't believe it," Huïumi says with excitement.

"Did you also meet The Star of the Universe? What a surprise!" Maiephis says, looking at Huïumi.

"Mm-hmm. She also appeared in my dreams," Huïumi replies.

"Wow, for you too. I mean, she's part of Master-Gowgwart-Love," Maiephis says. "Let me tell you, that's not all. She . . ."

.   .   .

Maiephis's room, Pharranes Castle, Neephis.

"When your grandfather, King Neessaph II, was alive, he met The Star of the Universe and was so impressed with her beauty that he painted her and kept her painting hidden in his painting room. Years later, after his death, your father found the painting, and he was so impressed by how your grandfather used his imagination to illustrate a portrait he thought belonged to late Queen Masseïel that he decided to honor the art by placing it in the center of the hallway right outside your room, which connects both wings of the castle," Master-Gowgwart-Love says.

"What he didn't know is that she's indeed late Queen Masseïel, but with a new identity—The Star of the Universe," Maiephis says.

"That's right. Since they are both the same person, and your father didn't know, he assumed she was the late Queen Masseïel. It was today, when your Nana heard you say the name of The Star of the Universe, that the true identity of the art was revealed," Master-Gowgwart-Love says.

"For them, only half the truth, because they don't know she's also The Star of the Universe," Maiephis says.

"Forsooth. Only half the truth," Master-Gowgwart-Love says.

"Thanks, Master-Gowgwart-Love. Mmm, smells so good. I'm so hungry," Maiephis says.

Master-Gowgwart-Love replies, "That's the breakfast, dear, it's getting cold. You might want to eat it while it's still warm."

Maiephis says, "But first, one more question. Please. Can you please tell me one last thing about The Star of the Universe?"

"What would that be?" Master-Gowgwart-Love asks.

Maiephis asks, "How did Queen Masseïel become The Star of the Universe after she died?"

"Her connection with me was so deep that when she died, her spirit turned into sparkles of light, creating purple amethyst crystals that attached to my heart, making room for her until it created this purple star that became her home for all time," Master-Gowgwart-Love replies.

"That's truly emotional and magical," Maiephis says.

Master-Gowgwart-Love says, "Once she became The Star of the Universe, she gained a new identity that gave her a new purpose and magical powers."

Maiephis says, "Thanks, Master-Gowgwart-Love. This is more than I expected."

Smiling, Master-Gowgwart-Love turns into red shiny sparkles of light, disappearing from the Gowgwarts' Doll's House.

.　.　.

Maiephis has finished her breakfast.

She looks at her mother's painting hanging next to her bed and in the blink of an eye, she hears movements coming from inside the Gowgwarts' Doll's House.

"Master-Gowgwart-Love, are you still there?" Maiephis asks.

"I am here."

"That isn't Master-Gowgwart-Love. I recognize your voice. It is Master-Gowgwart-Freedom," Maiephis says.

Master-Gowgwart-Freedom replies, "Yes, it's me."

"I knew it!" Maiephis says, moving closer to the dollhouse.

Master-Gowgwart-Freedom says, "I sense a different energy in you. Have you been able to express yourself in ways that allow you to channel your Anger in a positive way?"

Maiephis replies, "Even better . . . I have spent time with The Star of the Universe and Master-Gowgwart-Love. I learned the truth about what was holding me back from forgiving my papa. They have changed my life."

"That explains the change. What happened with your writing?" Master-Gowgwart-Freedom asks.

"I tried writing, but it didn't work, so I quit. I want to try again. I know if I try harder, I will be able to unlock my imagination in new ways I never thought I could," Maiephis replies.

"In your writing, you will travel to places that only exist in your imagination," Master-Gowgwart-Freedom says.

"It's everything I need and want, Freedom. I will try one more time," Maiephis says.

Master-Gowgwart-Freedom smiles. "Follow your imagination. All you need to do is unlock it," he says.

"Aaah, like in the song, I'll follow my imagination to create my own fantasy world . . . A different kind of world where I can express myself in my own words," she says.

"Mm-hmm. I don't see you wearing the white sapphire. What did you do with it?" Master-Gowgwart-Freedom asks.

"The white sapphire? I will wear it in a necklace, and when my papa sees me, he will know I have forgiven him," Maiephis replies.

Master-Gowgwart-Freedom says, "Well done, Maiephis. That

will truly show him you have a good heart."

. . .

Nine months later.

After tirelessly drafting her book, Maiephis finally finished it. The updated version of the white sapphire (a necklace) has arrived, and she has started wearing it all the time.

On a random night, while Maiephis was deeply asleep, Master-Gowgwart-Peace read her novel, *The Two Faces of the Spirit*. As soon as Master-Gowgwart-Peace finished reading it, she returned to the Gowgwarts' Workshop.

. . .

Pherriland, Gowgwarts' Workshop.

"Maiephis sent me a sign . . . she brought my spirit to life. She's calm and content with herself. So, I appeared in her room and found her book and read every page. She has no emotional conflict. She's ready to wear her Gowgwarts' Bracelet! Isn't that excellent news?" Master-Gowgwart-Peace asks Master-Gowgwart-Love.

"Alright we must get her Gowgwarts' Bracelet wrapped up and delivered," Master-Gowgwart-Love replies.

. . .

Maiephis's room, Pharranes Castle, Neephis.

It's a bright new day for Maiephis. She wakes up to realize the Gowgwarts' gift box is on her white wooden vanity desk with a note on top that reads:

"Dear Maiephis,
Not a doll, this is the Gowgwarts' Bracelet. A gift from us to you, so that

you remember your responsibility to always create harmony among your emotions. Do not forget the importance of being aware of their presence. Congratulations, dear! You have become the master of your emotions. Inside the gift box, under the bracelet, lies a note with the description of the powers of the crystal stones, and how you can use them to your advantage every time you find yourself facing them or lost. Safe travels!

—From Love and friends."

Maiephis's excitement after reading the notes brought the spirit of Master-Gowgwart-Joy to life.

"Maiephis! You're so overjoyed and delighted today," Master-Gowgwart-Joy says.

"Master-Gowgwart-Joy! That's right! I feel so much joy right now that I am going to start changing things around here, starting with creating a homage in the Garden of Hope to honor my mama," Maiephis replies.

"Yes! That's a great idea, Maiephis. The power to make things better is in you," Master-Gowgwart-Joy says.

"I'm learning! Thank you for making my life better," Maiephis says. Master-Gowgwart-Joy pops yellow crystals disappearing in the Gowgwarts' Doll's House.

.　　.　　.

The homage Maiephis created for her mother reads:

"*Welcome to the Garden of Hope.*

In honor of late Queen Maiesaphe of Neephiun, our beloved mother who used to enjoy visiting this garden. A new flower, daffodil, blossoms with the forget-me-not flowers. Her children, who love her infinitely, will forever remember the true meaning of this garden: peacefulness, weightlessness, calmness, and patience.

May everyone be embraced by the special meaning of this garden in your everyday, from dawn to dusk and from dusk to dawn. In between, may you be hugged by the light of love that surrounds us all, giving us hope.

—With Love, always."

The four words describing the meaning of the Garden of Hope Maiephis used in the homage—patience, calmness, weightlessness, peacefulness—neutralize Anger. Maiephis decided to include them to help others, who, unlike her mother, still have the opportunity to escape Anger to live a peaceful life with Joy and Happiness.

.　.　.

Present time, Clear Rock Crystal House.

"Next to do? I packed my pink Ūmieda suitcase and moved to this kingdom to study English Literature and . . . voilà, I met Huïumi in writing class. Since then, we became best friends," Maiephis says.

"*Aww.* Best friends forever . . ." Huïumi says, blowing a kiss at her as a gesture of affection.

Geossuth says, "Yes, bestie! Hahaha."

Guffaws filled the room.

"Master-Gowgwart-Love sounds interesting. She clearly works her magic around people. I wanna know more about her," Geossuth says.

"And you will," Rayïq replies.

—This time is about not giving up . . .

Seven

Gleerwoo House

"Okay, let's do this. Where should I start? Uh, I didn't meet The Star of the Universe, although I wish I had and hope to meet her one day. What are the odds? Anyway, my healing process was about finding strength in my pain to open new doors which later on helped me reinvent myself. Briefly, Master-Gowgwart-Love met me, then I met her. Although I met Master-Gowgwart-Love fifteen years ago, I still remember how I felt the day I entered The World of the Gowgwarts. There, I found new meaning for my life. All the things that caused me pain, suddenly brought joy and happiness, shaping me into who I am today, changing me forever." Rayïq pauses briefly.

Surprised, Huïumi whispers to Haiokïto, "I think he's been to the Gowgwarts' Workshop. Has he?"

Haiokïto shakes his head and whispers, "I don't know. I don't think so. Let's see."

Ufaïa says, "I went to The World of the Gowgwarts, where did the emotions take you?"

With wide eyes, Huïumi looks at Haiokïto, like she did too.

"C'mon, Ufaïa, let Rayïq tell the story," Geossuth says.

"Taccgrah! I wanted to know if we went to the same place. Sheesh. Go on, Rayïq," Ufaïa replies, annoyed.

Rayïq says, "Easy guys, I will get to that part. Okay?"

All faces on Rayïq, nodding. Rayïq continues.

"I was young when I was introduced to reïhng. To be specific, I was nine years old. Oh, and how it happened . . . I got a ticket inside the birthday card my dad gave me on my ninth birthday. I said, 'reïhng game championship?' Then, I researched it and was like, 'No way! I can't believe it!' It was my first time ever attending a reïhng game, I was so young, can you imagine how excited I was when my dad told me that we were going to The Six Kingdoms' Quartz-Stars Reïhng Championship? I was so, so thrilled, I couldn't sleep. I told all my friends about it in school and only talked about reïhng until it was the day of the championship."

"We were both getting ready to leave the house to go to the championship, when my dad—who back then was a huge fan of the Greequose Reïhng Team of the Greequose Kingdom, who, that year were competing in the finals against the Ūlïe Reïhng Team of the Ūlïe Kingdom—explained the game. I remember him saying, 'Rayïq, come. Let me explain you how the game works before we arrive at the stadium to see the championship. In the reïhng game, each team has six players and one defender. The defender is the most valuable player on the team. The defender prevents the opposing team's rim from scoring in the defensive area of the team, although without the other six players the team cannot win the game. Which means that all players are important to winning the game. The game begins with the defender throwing the reïhng from his position—on his team's side of the court—toward the center line of the court to expand the reïhng to start the game. If the reïhng doesn't expand on the second throw, the other team's defender gets the chance to throw the reïhng to start the game. After the game has started, each team will try to score reïhng goals by throwing the reïhng ball from the other team's side of the court through the opponent's reïhng. If any team shoots the reïhng ball through their side of the reïhng, the other team gets a point and if the defender moves outside of the defender's area, the other team gets a point. The game last ninety minutes with a fifteen-minute halftime break occurring after the first forty-five minutes of play, in between the two halves of the game. The team that scores the most reïhng balls through the reïhng on the opposite side of the court, wins the game. Capïcsh?' he asked. I said, 'Yes!' Since then, I became so fascinated with reïhng, above all, after attending my first reïhng championship and seeing our kingdom win the Quartz-Stars Reïhng Bracelet. From then on, all I wanted was to become a reïhng defender player. I told my dad, I wanted to join my school's reïhng varsity team, Qreïeze."

"Thus, that's how my dream to become the number one reïhng defender player in The Six Kingdoms was born. Though, since then, I also dreamed of playing with the Greequose Reïhng team in The Six Kingdoms' Quartz-Stars Reïhng Championship."

"I bet your dad was thrilled," Haiokïto says.

"You have no idea . . . he told everyone about it," Rayïq replies.

Geossuth says, "Proud dad."

Rayïq replies, "My parents were huge supporters of my dream, even with our limitations, they always did everything they could to support me. They took me to all my training sessions and absolutely never missed a single game. They also took me to watch other school teams in our neighboring kingdoms, so I could learn from them and thus be the best version of myself at playing reïhng."

．　．　．

Fifteen years ago, Kingdom of Greequose.

The Kingdom of Greequose, characterized by its clear waters and long coastline, boasts the largest maritime trade with the most impressive architecture in The Six Kingdoms, rich in renaissance, gothic, and baroque structures. Also, it is well known for its delicious traditional cuisine, including rooqūo, macceïe, and yëorh.

Aside from being a major connecting hub for maritime trade among The Six Kingdoms, its proximity to the ocean brings a cooler breeze to the kingdom, making it the only kingdom with the coolest temperatures year-round.

· · ·

It's pouring rain . . . another day lost for Rayïq to play reïhng outside.

A new day, a gloomy one, thus Rayïq has decided to stay home. At around noon, he sees incoming messages from his closest friends, Dovïq and Lennïq.

> **Dovïq: Lennïq and I are going for a horse ride by the beach. Do you wanna join us?**
> **Lennïq: Hey, bruh! It will be fun! Come, join us.**
> **Rayïq: Hey! Hold on. Let me check.**

Because of the weather, Rayïq is debating whether he should join his friends or not. Perhaps suggest them to stay home until the weather is nicer outside. Meanwhile, while waiting for the weather to improve, Rayïq takes his time to reply.

> **Rayïq: Okay, I'll join you.**
> **Lennïq: Cool bruh!**
> **Rayïq: Meet me outside my house in thirty minutes.**
> **Dovïq: Sure. Later bruh.**

· · ·

After heading to his room for a change of clothes to get ready to join his friends, he wears waterproof riding black trousers with black waterproof brush protector chaps and a blue rain jacket with his black riding boots and gloves. After that, he heads straight to the stables to find his horse, Rooqï. Rooqï isn't feeling well, but Rayïq excited to meet with his friends doesn't pay attention. He thinks that Rooqï is in a bad mood, so he rubs his face against Rooqï's neck to calm and comfort him and then takes him out of the stables to wait for his friends to arrive outside.

While Rayïq is waiting outside, he tries to cheer Rooqï up. This time Rayïq rubs his hands against Rooqï's face and says, "Everything is going to be okay, big fella. The weather outside isn't so bad. We're gonna have a lot of fun with my friends. Look! They're arriving."

Rayïq joins his friends, ignoring the signs that Rooqï is unwell.

As they're riding their horses to the beach, Lennïq says, "Guys, let's race the horses against each other to see which one is faster."

Rayïq, realizing that they don't have good weather, immediately replies, "No. That's not a good idea."

On the other hand, Dovïq, who also wants to race the horses against each other, says, "Come on, Rayïq, join us."

Rayïq—pressured by his friends—replies, "Okay, but a short race. Okay?"

Lennïq replies, "Cool, bruh, are you ready? Let's go!"

In the middle of the race, Rayïq's horse collapses, landing on his knees and on top of Rayïq's legs. At once, his friends hear the loud scream coming from afar and immediately turn around to help Rayïq. They cannot move Rooqï, so they try to pull Rayïq out from the side of Rooqï, until Rayïq is completely out. Instantly, Rayïq tries to get up, but he cannot move his legs. Both of his friends get really scared and promptly carry him to one of their horses to take him to the hospital, leaving Rooqï in pain and behind at the beach.

. . .

Several hours later.

Nurses and doctors are coming in and out of Rayïq's room in the hospital. His friends and family are in the waiting room waiting for news. Meanwhile, Rooqï has passed. Rayïq finally wakes up from the anesthesia and realizes the doctors had put casts on his legs. His friends and family are able to see him briefly, breaking the sad news of Rooqï's passing at the beach.

Rayïq finds himself alone with a mix of feelings he had not felt before. A busy night at the hospital, Rayïq's nurse approaches him and says, "Rayïq, a new patient will join you tonight. A staff member will bring a new bed shortly. Please try to rest. You'll be fine soon."

Rayïq replies, "Okay, thank you."

Rayïq is not in a good mood. He isn't having a good night, the last thing he wants is company in his room, so when the new patient joins him, he ignores him—pretending he cannot hear a word.

"Heïjour, my name is Qarloüs. What's your name?"

Rayïq thinks, "I don't wanna talk. I'm feeling a lot of pain right now. I just wanna forget about today."

Qarloüs insists, "Joureïe! It's only us here. Don't ignore me. Yeo know you can hear me."

"Alright, yes, I can hear you. Hi Qarloüs. My name is Rayïq."

Qarloüs replies, "Rei is all yeo wanna be."

"Hmm??" Rayïq looks at him confused.

Qarloüs says, "Usïcs. *Yeo quesseux vo ut rei.*"

Rayïq replies, "Sorry, *yeo giocs pharqluo Ūlïe.*"

"I said, 'I want to be a king.' Just like you, Rei," Qarloüs replies.

Rayïq replies, "I am not a king, that's just my name, Qarloüs— with an *ayïq* not an *ei.*"

Qarloüs replies, "Aaah, sorry. I am from the Kingdom of Ūlïe, and the sound of the names are very similar. Yeo thought your name spelled like in our language. For a moment, I thought you spoke our language too. You are very lucky!"

Rayïq says, "I am not an Ūlïe. I'm a Greeqïes. And, yes, pretty . . . lucky, I guess."

Qarloüs says, "Yeo wanna be like you, but yeo guess that will never happen."

Rayïq says, "Ohh don't be sad, Qarloüs. Why do you say that?"

Qarloüs replies, "Unlike you, I won't live. I'm very ill. You may not be a king in their eyes, but everyone calls you, Rayïq. Certainly, that makes you a king."

Rayïq, compassionately, says, "Very sorry to hear that, Qarloüs. You know what?"

Qarloüs asks, "What?"

Rayïq replies, "I have an idea."

Qarloüs asks, "Really? What is it?"

Rayïq responds, "For tonight, you're going to be a king, King Qarloüs. If you pass me that piece of paper, I'll make you a crown; certainly, that will also make you a king."

Qarloüs replies, "That's a great idea, Rayïq. Tagrascïe! I will be the king for tonight. I'm glad yeo got to meet you. You've made my night so much better."

He smiles at Qarloüs, and Qarloüs returns the smile, full of joy.

That night, Rayïq made a crown for Qarloüs, and they played and pretended Qarloüs was the king of kings in The Six Kingdoms, until they both fell asleep.

The sunlight enters through the windows, waking up Rayïq. As the nurse prepares him for discharge, Rayïq notices Qarloüs isn't in the room. Immediately, Rayïq asks, "What happened to Qarloüs?" A cold dread slowly settles in his gut. He asks, "Why isn't he in the room?"

The nurse responds, "Qarloüs passed away this morning while holding a crown that said, 'King Qarloüs.'"

Qarloüs was only eleven years old. Rayïq was shocked with the news and didn't say another word to the nurse. After the nurse left, Rayïq was ready to leave the hospital, so he waited for his parents to pick him up.

·   ·   ·

A week after the accident, Rayïq had a follow-up appointment. The doctor told him that he needed to spend the next three months in bed before they could give him a final diagnosis on his knees. The news threw him off. Rayïq was anxious to know his chances to play reïhng again, but first, the doctors needed to remove the casts from his legs.

As time went by, Rayïq found it difficult to adapt to the casts, but the hardest thing for him was the wait. Finally, after ninety days and ninety nights, the wait was over, and it was the date for his next doctor's appointment. He was informed, sad to say, that his knees were not as good as before and therefore he wouldn't be able to play reïhng again.

From then on, for the next four weeks, Rayïq isolated himself in his room. During that time, he refused to see his friends, rebuffing their calls. His parents struggled to get him to eat some food—every meal left untouched—causing him to lose weight. He knew that he couldn't go on like this, but he didn't have the mental strength to go on with his life. He felt like nothing had meaning to him anymore. His reality had gone grey, drained of all colors. Rayïq felt destroyed. His world had crumbled and all he had left was dust. He didn't know how to begin to find meaning and purpose for his life again.

·   ·   ·

On a foggy night, Rayïq hears noises against the windows. "Is there someone throwing pebbles against the windows? Hmm, how strange. *Trespassing*," he thinks, "I should look out the windows, just to make sure that there isn't anything or anyone out here."

"Aaahh, I don't see anyone outside," he says, his voice muffled by the glass. "It's probably strong wind." He opens the windows to check if it's just wind and at once feels a gentle, chilly wind hugging him—a stark contrast to his initial concern.

"A drastic change in the weather. It's summer, and the wind is as cold as a winter night. This is strange, I better close the windows. I don't wanna catch a cold. I need to get out of this room. I can't go on like this. Nah-uh. I'm sad, and I feel so guilty about the accident and Rooqi's death. It's my fault that I can't play reïhng anymore. If I had just stayed home the day of the accident, but instead I joined my friends for a horse ride, and even though I knew better than to let the horses race against each other (ignoring the weather and signs that Rooqï wasn't feeling well), I still did it. I should have paid more attention to Rooqï. If I had done things differently, I would still be playing reïhng, and Rooqï would still be alive today. I lost my knees, I lost my horse, and I lost my dream. It is my fault," he thinks.

Rayïq closes the windows, returns to bed, and falls asleep right away.

. . .

After the moon sets and the night passes, the sun rises—a new day blossoms with its hidden hope for those who believe in Love.

Rayïq looks out the windows and says, "It's a bright sunny day, perfect for a walk along the shoreline to clear my head."

He takes a shower, brushes his teeth, and walks to the kitchen to eat something quick. When his mother sees him, she hugs him tightly, crying with joy. "Rayïq! My dear! My sunshine," she says.

Rayïq replies, "Mom, I'm fine and hungry. Is there anything for breakfast? I'm going out for a walk, and I'd like to put something on my stomach first."

She replies, "Of course, darling."

His mother is so happy to see him out of his room and hungry that she begins preparing his favorite breakfast: Greequose egg salad sandwich with bacon and sausages, and a plain yogurt bowl, topped with honey mixed berries. After she finishes serving him breakfast, he eats everything, leaving a clean, empty bowl.

As Rayïq gets ready to leave the house, he kisses his mother on the forehead, thanking her for such a wonderful meal.

.   .   .

Rayïq headed to Quozereis Beach, a ten-minute walk from his house (where the accident occurred).

He arrives at the beach, takes off his shoes, and walks barefoot. While enjoying the calming sound of the ocean waves, zoned out on the beauty of the sea, he hears a voice saying, "Rayïq, do it! It's your fault! Walk in the waters of the Quozereis Beach. Join me. You have lost everything."

Rayïq stops, looking around, trying to find the source of the voice. For a moment, he thinks about drowning in the waters of the Quozereis Beach, but an inner voice stops him.

He continues walking along the shoreline. Then, unexpectedly, he sees a giant wave rising—a pure white glow radiating from within the ocean through the huge wave.

Rayïq thinks, "What's that thing coming out of that huge wave? Big waves are rarely seen on this beach . . ."

As the wave clears, he sees sparkling crystals shining brightly.

Rayïq gasps. "Aaah! What's that?" he asks.

"Hello, Rayïq. Cannot stop thinking about your losses? Do you want to swim with me in the ocean? The waters will calm your pain. You won't remember everything you lost through your actions that day you went horseback riding with your friends. Remember? Is this beach familiar?"

Rayïq asks, "Who are you?"

"You don't recognize me? I am what you have been drowning in since your accident," says the voice.

Rayïq asks, "How do you know about all that and my pain?"

"I am a Gowgwart—the spirit of the emotion, Guilt—Master-Gowgwart-Guilt."

"Who? What? Rayïq asks, "(I think I have spent too much time locked away in my room. I am hallucinating)."

Master-Gowgwart-Guilt replies, "You've awakened my spirit, so I have come to join you, Master-Gowgwart-Sadness and Master-Gowgwart-Pain."

"Huh? There's more Master Gowgwarts? But I only see you," Rayïq says uncertain.

Master-Gowgwart-Guilt replies, "It seems like all you've been feeling is us lately."

Master-Gowgwart-Guilt rises from the water showing his glow as he gets closer to Rayïq. Rayïq stares at him, stunned. He cannot resist the brightness of his ears, and at the same time, overwhelmed by his words, his subconscious tells him to run. In between, he looks back, his heart beating fast, he sees Master-Gowgwart-Sadness and Master-Gowgwart-Pain coming after him. Rayïq runs as fast as he can from them. Although as he's running, he hears a different voice calling his name, he doesn't look back. He's afraid thinking it could be from Master-Gowgwart-Sadness or Master-Gowgwart-Pain.

Rayïq doesn't understand what is happening. Frightened and confused, after running almost two miles non-stop, without shoes, he faints.

.   .   .

Rayïq enters Pherrïland. He opens his eyes and realizes he is lying on a purple bench with golden legs and freaks out.

Rayïq cries out, "Aaahh!"

"Hello Rayïq. You are finally awake."

Rayïq cries, "Aaah! You spoke! Who are you?" he asks.

"Calm down, Rayïq, I will not harm you."

Rayïq gets up. He asks, "So, what do you want from me? I am trying to escape from Master Gowgwarts—Guilt, Sadness, and Pain. You are a bench talking to me. How can you ask me to calm down? I am scared!"

"Oops, I just wanted you to be comfortable."

Master-Gowgwart-Freedom returns to his Gowgwart form.

"You're a Gowgwart too!" Rayïq says, wide-eyed. "You're very comfortable. Maybe I should go back to sleep to return to reality."

Master-Gowgwart-Freedom replies, "Yes, I am an emotion in disguise, with magical powers—a Gowgwart."

"Shiny and purple with bright golden feathers except that your ears are not glowing," Rayïq says.

"I am Freedom, Master-Gowgwart-Freedom. The reason why my ears don't glow is because you surely don't feel any freedom right now," he says.

Rayïq replies, "Freedom? Freedom is what I need from Guilt, Sadness, and Pain." He looks around confused and asks, "Where am I? This is not the Quozereis Beach."

"Welcome to Pherrïland—our world—a fantastical Pherrï full

of magic and emotions on the other side of your world, where a day in your kingdom is a minute. Master-Gowgwart-Love has brought you here," Master-Gowgwart-Freedom replies.

Sparkling red crystals begin to sprout from Master-Gowgwart-Love's ears—towards them—after she appears.

"Master-Gowgwart-Love? Time runs so fast compared to my kingdom. How can a minute in my kingdom be a day here? Why it's so cold? It's summer in my kingdom, but here it feels like autumn transitioning to winter. It feels just like the wind I felt in my room after I opened the windows last night. Was it you?" he asks. "Ooh, it also brings sparkling red crystals. Pherriland is filled with magic," Rayïq says, watching the red crystals pass by.

Master-Gowgwart-Freedom replies, "I am afraid it is Master-Gowgwart-Love—the master of all Gowgwarts. In Pherriland, we have different seasons that differ from your kingdom. Look behind you and you'll see where the sparkling red crystals are coming from. There she is waving at us."

Rayïq turns and sees Master-Gowgwart-Love flying outside a seven-story house. He says, "Master-Gowgwart-Love! I see your red crystal ears."

Master-Gowgwart-Love replies, "Hi Rayïq. Come! We've been waiting for you."

Master-Gowgwart-Freedom flies and Rayïq walks to the house. Master-Gowgwart-Love opens the door with her magical crystals. "Welcome to Gleerwoo House, our home," she says.

.   .   .

Present time, Clear Rock Crystal House.

Luseïe asks, "Hold on, Rayïq, if Master-Gowgwart-Love was the one who brought you to Pherriland, why wasn't she with you instead of Master-Gowgwart-Freedom when you woke up?"

"Hmmm. When I ran away from Master Gowgwarts (Guilt, Sadness, and Pain), Master-Gowgwart-Love appeared on Quozereis Beach and rescued me. In fact, the voice I heard—that I didn't know who it was from—was from Master-Gowgwart-Love. That's when I took a Pherrï to Pherrïland, where I met him, Master-Gowgwart-Freedom," Rayïq replies.

"Why wasn't she with you when you woke up?" Luseïe asks.

Rayïq replies, "Mmmm, that. The reason is because she didn't wanna leave me unattended while she prepared their house for my arrival, so she asked Master-Gowgwart-Freedom to watch over me while I woke up. That's why I met Master-Gowgwart-Freedom first and not Master-Gowgwart-Love."

"Aaah, that makes sense. How lucky! You had the opportunity to visit Pherrïland. I didn't," Luseïe says.

Huïumi says, "Me neither."

Geossuth, playfully, says, "Neither did I." Everyone looks at him, funny smiling.

Luseïe says, "Question, Rayïq."

Rayïq replies, "Yes."

"How is it there, Pherrïland and Gleerwoo House?" she asks.

"Where can I start?" Rayïq looks around, a glimmer of awe in his eyes. "Aside from the sparkling magical crystals, the time change, the weather, and the greenwood, Gleerwoo House is an out-of-this-world, enchanting, colorful place in a forest, where only Pherrïland exists."

"The façade of the house is of greenwood in the most refined way. Seriously, the most refined. The windows are mirrors, can you imagine mirrors, where—technically—you can see the reflection of everything surrounding the house," Rayïq replies.

Huïumi asks Rayïq, "Everything?"

Rayïq responds, "Yeah. Absolutely, everything. You don't even have to enter the house to know how big the interior is."

"Really?" Geossuth asks.

Rayïq responds, "Yeah, bruh. And the front door, that one got me . . ."

"Why?" Geossuth asks Rayïq.

"Bruh, it's a red door with a shiny purple star-shaped knobby," Rayïq replies.

"What?" Geossuth asks.

"Yeah. I remember like today my reaction when I first entered the house, and everything was so red . . ."

.　　.　　.

Back to Pherrïland, Gleerwoo House.

Master-Gowgwart-Freedom returns to the last floor, his floor. Master-Gowgwart-Love gives Rayïq a tour of the house to introduce the other positive Master Gowgwarts—Care, Joy, Happiness, Trust, and Peace. Then, Rayïq and Master-Gowgwart-Love return to the first floor—the red floor.

.　　.　　.

Present time, Clear Rock Crystal House.

"Is that all you have to say? No details? What happened in the tour?" Luseïe asks.

Geossuth says, "Yeah. Don't skip that. I want to know too."

"Me too. I think we all want to know," Maiephis says.

Rayïq replies, "I forgot to say that part. No worries. I got you. The house has one floor for each Master Gowgwart."

Luseïe says, "There's a shift in emotion from floor to floor."

Rayïq replies, "That's right. Master-Gowgwart-Love is on the first floor, where everything is red, and as soon as you enter, you feel her willpower and strength. On the second floor, where everything is pink and friendly, with Master-Gowgwart-Care you begin to feel cheerfulness. Right after, when you move up to Master-Gowgwart-Trust, on the third floor, where everything is starry-night-blue, you feel confidence blooming within you. Thereafter, when you are on the fourth floor with Master-Gowgwart-Peace, you feel and breathe calmness in every inch of your skin. Then, on the fifth floor, you're surrounded by a lighting yellow with Master-Gowgwart-Joy, feeling positivity bathing you. On the sixth floor, with Master-Gowgwart-Happiness, everything hums a sweet orange—a bright and glowing orange softened with a hint of yellow light—that sparks enthusiasm within you. Finally, on the last floor—the seventh floor, my favorite, where everything is purple—with Master-Gowgwart-Freedom, you feel a deep sense of wisdom settling in you."

"So uplifting and magical. How lucky!" Luseïe says.

Rayïq replies, "Yeah, very lucky. Yeah. My favorite part of the house, I have to say, is the spiral staircase, because of the sparkling crystals covering it, changing color as it connects all the floors within the house."

"It's my favorite part and I haven't been in the house." Huïumi chuckles.

Rayïq replies, "I tell you; it was magical to see the color of the crystals on the spiral staircase changing to the color of each Master Gowgwart as I advanced to the next floor."

.   .   .

Back to Pherrïland, Gleerwoo House.

Rayïq asks Master-Gowgwart-Love, "Why am I here?"

"I have brought you here to offer you an opportunity to find meaning and purpose for your life," she replies.

Rayïq says, "I am going through a difficult time and you wanna help me. Why?"

Master-Gowgwart-Love responds, "Yes. We want to help you create harmony among your emotions so you can live a happier life. You don't have to stay here; you're free to leave whenever you want. It's a choice you're free to make. But if you accept our help, with us you will find forgiveness for all your losses."

"Master-Gowgwart-Guilt said something like that," he replies.

"Like us, there are seven negative Master Gowgwarts in our world; the ones you met, Guilt along with Sadness and Pain, are part of them," Master-Gowgwart-Love says.

Rayïq asks, "Why were all those emotions coming after me?"

"Those emotions grew so strong within you that you brought their spirits to life on Quozereis Beach, where they chased you until you heard my voice and then appeared here, in Pherrïland," Master-Gowgwart-Love replies.

"I remember that I was, desperately, running away from them. I thought I wasn't gonna make it," Rayïq replies.

Master-Gowgwart-Love says, "In perfect time, you heard my voice, and I was able to bring you here."

"Thanks to you, look at me now, I am here in your world where I will meet the other positive Master Gowgwarts. I hope I can find forgiveness, meaning, and purpose for my life," Rayïq says.

Master-Gowgwart-Love replies, "You are certainly right, you'll meet with Master Gowgwarts—Care, Trust, Peace, Joy, Happiness, and Freedom, one by one, here this week."

"What about the seven negative Master Gowgwarts?" he asks.

"Aah, they are Master Gowgwarts: Pain, Fear, Shame, Sadness,

Depression, Anger, and Guilt. You cannot escape those emotions, but you can learn how to face them to transition away from them as fast as you can, without losing control of yourself," she responds.

Rayïq replies, "Tell me about it. I already met three of them."

Master-Gowgwart-Love says, "It's vital that you know positive and negative emotions are equally important in your life. The worst thing to do is avoid negative emotions because they aren't positive. It's essential to continuously create balance among your emotions by accepting that negative emotions will appear from time to time—and that's okay—because you know how to embrace the positivity in them. The effect emotions have on your life will depend on how long you let them affect you and also, the way you choose to express them. Thusly, the more you entertain them, the greater the impact in your life."

"That's why I was trying to escape from them," Rayïq says.

"With us, you'll learn everything you need to know to create balance among your emotions," Master-Gowgwart-Love says.

Rayïq replies, "That doesn't sound too easy."

"It's a game of emotions and if you don't know how to play it, you can get lost. You will be trained. During that time, you will learn about our powers and how to harness them, and when you are ready, you will receive your Gowgwarts' Bracelet with your emotions in the crystal stones," Master-Gowgwart-Love says.

Rayïq replies, "The most famous and desirable bracelet in The Six Kingdoms—the Gowgwarts' Bracelet! Oh, I can't believe I said the name . . . I like that very much."

Master-Gowgwart-Love says, "The Gowgwarts' Bracelet will remind you that you have greater power over your emotions. Also, it is your responsibility to stay calm when things go wrong."

While Master-Gowgwart-Love speaks, Rayïq muffles, "Oof, I

need that very much."

Master-Gowgwart-Love says, "Everything I am saying is new to you and good for you. After you complete your training with us you will feel different—brand new."

Rayïq replies, "Totally new. Can't wait until I'm ready."

Master-Gowgwart-Love says, "The reason you must wait until you're ready to receive your Gowgwarts' Bracelet is because you will command your emotions. That's a great responsibility, dear. It's like a graduation, where you receive a diploma for the degree you have earned, proving you're ready to go out and apply everything you've learned. That's why you will spend time with each one of us. You'll learn how to balance your emotions and why emotional awareness is key to maintaining a harmonious state among all emotions."

"Why is emotional awareness important?" Rayïq asks.

Master-Gowgwart-Love responds, "Emotional awareness is a necessity. It gives you the ability to understand and acknowledge us when we're present by identifying the signals that trigger us, enabling you to respond to us effectively. The way you react to us is strongly influenced by your thoughts. If those thoughts are not positive, your reaction to us, when we are present, can be detrimental to your well-being. Without emotional awareness, your response, when you are experiencing us can lead to a state of anxiety and depression. That's why emotional awareness is essential to living a positive life, allowing your emotions to coexist in harmony without significant conflict. It's a power that comes with responsibility; if misused, it might lead to your destruction. In this process, we hope you find forgiveness for your losses, so that you can experience a sense of gratitude and inner calm."

"I didn't realize a positive life is crucial for emotional harmony. How important emotional awareness is, the impact it has on living a positive life, where I have the power to create harmony among my emotions to find a state of inner calm, and the responsibility I hold. Thank you, Master-Gowgwart-Love," Rayïq says.

Master-Gowgwart-Love smiles. "We want to empower you to take back your power. Remember that the only power we have over you is the power you give us. Changing your mindset to a positive one will clear your way to a brighter future full of possibilities. This time, you will lead us to win the game of the mind. Just like the coach of a reïhng team leads the team to win the game, it is teamwork and each of us has a role to play to win the game. We will help you reach a harmonious state where you feel emotionally calmed, present, and stable," she says.

Rayïq replies, "That's what I want."

"Excellent, Rayïq. Additionally, you'll learn the powers of the negative emotions as a strength," Master-Gowgwart-Love says.

Rayïq asks, "As a strength? How?"

"Well, you met Master-Gowgwart-Guilt at Quozereis Beach— and it could have ended badly—but you ran away from him because you felt his negativity and didn't have the knowledge to embrace his positivity. Deep down you knew it wasn't right to stay there. Am I right?" Master-Gowgwart-Love asks.

"You're right. I see you're trying to get to the point," he replies.

Master-Gowgwart-Love says, "Let me explain. I know you feel guilty for your losses, thinking that things could have been different if you had made better choices. What if you shift your view to think about your past experiences as a source of strength to embrace other areas of your life?"

Rayïq asks, "Change my approach to what happened? How?"

"There is always a positive approach in your daily life," Master-Gowgwart-Love responds.

"I am learning," Rayïq replies.

"The question for you is how can you still make your dream come true even if you cannot play reïhng anymore? Are you going to give up? Have you thought of other ways to embrace your dream? If you can have an answer to these questions by the time you finish the tour of the house, on your last day, you will be ready to receive your Gowgwarts' Bracelet. You will be here seven days, and you will spend a day with each Master Gowgwart on their respective floors. As the days pass by, you will ascend until you reach the last floor, which is the floor of Master-Gowgwart-Freedom. Then, we'll meet again," Master-Gowgwart-Love says.

"That wasn't the answer to my question," Rayïq says.

"You have seven days to think about the answer you'll give me. Then, I'll give you the answer to your question," Master-Gowgwart-Love replies.

"Seven days!? Such a short time!" Rayïq scratches his head.

"Mm, yes. That's seven minutes in your kingdom . . ." Master-Gowgwart-Love replies.

"Even less time in my kingdom . . . I forgot that time runs fast here compared to time there. Ha! Better start to think," Rayïq says.

"It's time to explore possibilities," she says.

"I never thought of it this way . . . Before I met you, I couldn't think outside of my Pain and Sadness. I felt Shame, Anger and for a moment, I submerged into Depression. But now, you've given me hope to explore a different world full of possibilities where I can see that there is an opportunity for me to shift my mindset to a positive one. The truth is my knees will never be the same again and I will never be able to play reïhng. I will think about how to reframe my perspective towards the door that has closed for me, and I hope that at the end of these seven days, I have an answer for you," he replies.

"Very good. I like hearing you talk positively, Rayïq," Master-Gowgwart-Love says.

Rayïq says, "It's all thanks to you. Also, I want the Gowgwarts' Bracelet and I wanna master my emotions."

Master-Gowgwart-Love says, "Very well, dear, let's talk about that."

"Sure," Rayïq replies.

"The Gowgwarts' Bracelet is the combination of the positive and negative Gowgwarts' Bracelets—linked by the stars in each of them. Understanding what the colors of the crystal stones in each bracelet represent will remind you of their powers. Especially the negative Gowgwarts—they are a source of strength, not weakness. Knowing the true meaning of each color chosen for the negative Gowgwarts is neutralize their negative powers, will allow you to face them with a positive outlook in any given situation where you may find yourself in the edge of crossing to the borderline of the negative emotions," Master-Gowgwart-Love says.

"Can you explain that? I lost you. What is the edge of crossing to the borderline of the negative emotions?" Rayïq asks.

"I am happy to clarify. It's like crossing the traffic lights, where the edge is represented by the yellow light, a state of caution. At this level, you still have awareness of your emotions—a key moment of introspection to choose a mindful path forward before the negative emotions take over. When you cross having the red light, you have crossed to the borderline. You are putting yourself in danger, now experiencing an extreme emotional behavior, where you have lost emotional control to negative emotions, like Anger, Fear, etc. In this stage you may experience ups and downs, Teeter-Totter of negative emotions, where the emotions have taken control," she replies.

"I get it! It's a progression of intensity, where I experience ups and downs with the negative emotions. Is Tᴇᴇᴛᴇʀ-Totter a thing here?" he asks.

"Yes, dear. You are lucky to be here. That's where the negative emotions were going to take you," Master-Gowgwart-Love replies.

Rayïq gasps. "No way!" he says.

"Don't worry, dear. We are going to teach you how to embrace the goodness in all emotions. Through their colors . . . you will see," Master-Gowgwart-Love replies.

"Aaahh, that means their different colors are gonna help me embrace their powers in a positive way," he says, "(she is answering my question)."

"Mm-hmm. The baby blue crystal stone calms Anger. The pure white crystal stone reminds you of forgiveness removing the feelings of Guilt. The brown crystal stone reminds you of your power to be resilient when you are feeling Depression. The purpose is to remind you the power you have over these emotions. So, if you feel Sadness, you look at the peach crystal stone and remember to feel happy and optimistic. When you are feeling Shame, the blue crystal stone will remind you that you are trustworthy. The same goes for Pain; with the green crystal stone, you will feel comforted. The lavender crystal stone will calm your Fear, making you feel uplifted instead of small," Master-Gowgwart-Love replies.

"So unexpected. I'd never thought of it that way. Typically, we don't wanna acknowledge those emotions. But after you explained how they can also be good for me, I don't fear acknowledging them. I am beginning to understand the importance of embracing all of them and I can't wait to meet you again at the end of my tour of the house, on this floor," Rayïq says.

"That's my answer to your question. I changed my mind, why wait until the end? Now is the right time," Master-Gowgwart-Love replies.

Rayïq replies, "I agree. Your answer will help me a lot. Thanks for changing your mind."

"Officially, I welcome you to Gleerwoo House."

Master-Gowgwart-Love sings, "Gleerwoo."

"Your first day is about to end. Soon you'll meet with Master-Gowgwart-Care. Rest before dawn, I must go," Master-Gowgwart-Love says.

.   .   .

Present time, Clear Rock Crystal House.

Geossuth asks, "What happened next?"

Rayïq responds, "Every time I advanced to a new floor to meet a Master Gowgwart—a step closer to complete my training, yup—teachings filled with breathtaking wisdom and insight were revealed. The brilliance and genuine grace of each Master Gowgwart was so striking. As I ascended the floors, amazement grew; the beauty of the shimmering crystals was dazzling, vibrantly captivating my view. The teachings were inspiring, profoundly uplifting and enticing."

All eyes in the room, with a glint of wonder, are on Rayïq.

"As magical as I said my training was, one emotion led me to the other; all I had to do was embrace their powers and when I was ready, I entered a new floor. Later on, after completing my training with the Master Gowgwarts, on my last day at the Gleerwoo House, I finally received my Gowgwarts' Bracelet, becoming the master of my emotions and then, I met with Master-Gowgwart-Love again on the first floor," Rayïq says.

"I definitely didn't go to Gleerwoo House. My experience in Pherrïland was quite different from yours, Rayïq," Ufaïa says.

"Really?" Rayïq asks, surprised.

"Uh-huh. You'll see when I tell you my story. Also, what was your answer to Master-Gowgwart-Love's questions?" Ufaïa asks.

"After spending a day with each Master Gowgwart, I learned the importance of widening my horizons to try new things linked to my dream. My confidence in my capabilities grew stronger, allowing me to be calmer and feel hope and optimism—demonstrating that it truly is possible to still be positive, even when you're feeling you've lost everything. I experienced compassion for my suffering and was able to delve into a part of me I didn't know I had until I met Master-Gowgwart-Freedom again," Rayïq replies.

"Me too," Ufaïa says.

"Huh?" Rayïq asks, looking confused.

"Sorry, Rayïq. Yeo got a little over excited," Ufaïa says.

With a smile, Rayïq says, "Aaah. Paccürs. Hehe."

"Go on, Rayïq. Don't mind Ufaïa," Huïumi says.

"Please Ufaïa, let him finish," Geossuth says.

"Yes, *please*," Luseïe says.

"Ouch. *Okay, guys*," Ufaïa says with silly smile.

"Where was I?" Rayïq asks, "(oh, I remember)."

"After I completed my training, I was able to think with clarity and creativity, finding wisdom in everything I had experienced since I thought I had lost my dream. In Pherrïland, I found a new dream connected to my passion for reïhng. Thanks to the positive Master Gowgwarts I met at Gleerwoo House, on my last day, I shared what I had learned from my losses with Master-Gowgwart-Freedom and Master-Gowgwart-Love—to be positive, not to give up, to focus on the opportunities that come from hardships, and to find strength in my suffering. And of course, my dream—owning a reïhng team," Rayïq replies.

"Deepïery thögh, owning a reïhng team," Ufaïa says.

"And that was my response to recreating my dream on my last day at Gleerwoo House. Then, I returned home and after graduating from high school, I moved to this kingdom. I registered in Arts and Sports Management at Brightmieda University and later on, I got involved with their Brightmieda Reïhng Varsity Team—not as a player—as an assistant coach. With them, I learned a lot. Five years later, after my graduation at Brightmieda University, I opened my own reïhng team, The Phoenïx of Bloomïeda," Rayïq says.

"Not to brag . . . but your reïhng team has already won two Quartz-Stars Reïhng Bracelets in The Six Kingdoms' Quartz-Stars Championship," Geossuth says excitedly.

Haiokïto says, "I'm a huge fan of your team, and I bet your dad is your number one."

"Mm-hmm. That's why he is no longer a fan of the Greequose Reïhng Team. I can't believe how far I've come simply by shifting my mindset to a positive one," Rayïq replies.

"A Phoenïx fan forever and ever my friend . . ." Geossuth says with enthusiasm.

"It's all thanks to the Master Gowgwarts—they saved my life. I'll never forget the path they opened for me to recreate my dream," Rayïq replies.

Maiephis says, "C'mon. Give yourself some credit for believing in Love. The Master Gowgwarts helped you become the master of your emotions, but you made it happen."

Rayïq replies, "You're right, Maie. I'm full of wisdom and can only be grateful for having the opportunity to reshape my life in a way where I can only see the bright side of what happened to me. Look at me! I am free from Guilt and every day I try to live a positive life."

Ufaïa says, "When you want something, the obstacles start to disappear, and you begin to see the path clearly . . .”

“I'm very proud of you Rayïq. It's important to keep a positive attitude even when the view is not bright,” Huïumi says.

“Thanks. The attitude we take towards what life throws at us can significantly influence the direction of our lives,” Rayïq says.

“Spot on, Rayïq,” Haiokïto says.

“Your arçaïe is the force that gives you purpose, man. That's why mine is to live a positive life,” Rayïq says.

Luseïe says, “That's what the Ūlïe people say. An arçaïɛ isn't just a statement, it reflects the values and beliefs that influence your behavior and Master-Gowgwart-Love makes sure we know it.”

Rayïq says, “That's true. A door closed and thanks to my arçaïe I'm now opening doors for others.”

“Eh, how did you receive the Gowgwarts' Bracelet?” Geossuth asks.

“I shared my new dream with Master-Gowgwart-Love, after I shared my dream with Master-Gowgwart-Freedom on my last day at Gleerwoo House,” Rayïq replies.

“You said that already,” Geossuth says, rolling his eyes.

“Let me finish, Bruh. That's why Master-Gowgwart-Freedom gave me the Gowgwarts' Bracelet and not Master-Gowgwart-Love. In the end, they are all interconnected, and Master-Gowgwart-Love is the master of all Gowgwarts,” Rayïq says.

.   .   .

Chef Glüedo enters the Clear Rock Crystal House to announce dinner. “Dinner is ready in the main dining room,” he says.

Haiokïto replies, “Thanks, Chef Glüedo.” Then, he asks Rayïq, “How did you meet Huïumi? Brightmieda University?”

Rayïq responds, “Yeah. We met in management class where we

teamed up for several assignments. Also, she likes reïhng, so I often invited her to our reïhng games, which I still do." He chuckles. "She always showed up with Ufaïa, Luseïe, and Maie, like she still does."

"It was always us, together, right girls?" Maiephis asks.

"Yes. Always together," Luseïe replies.

"Always . . . Even when we had to run from class to meet-up at the game," Huïumi says.

"I remember those were good days," Ufaïa says.

"Your story is exceptional, Rayïq," Haiokïto says.

Geossuth says, "Very touching my friend. You are very brave and optimistic."

"If we focus on the positive side of any given situation, we can always come out as champions on the other side. Having harmony between your emotions is priceless. Before I met Master-Gowgwart-Love and friends, I didn't know I could become the master of my emotions; now with the Gowgwarts' Bracelet I am," Rayïq replies.

"Well, after an uplifting story about overcoming adversity, let us enjoy a night of Greequose cuisine inside the house. We have two more days to discover how Luseïe and Ufaïa met Master-Gowgwart-Love," Huïumi says.

Meanwhile, Geossuth thinks, "I wonder what the next story would be about."

Geossuth will have to wait until the moon sets, and the light of the sun brings a brand-new day . . .

Overcoming obstacles requires a strong determination and a positive mindset.

Get ready for what's coming next.

Eight

The Game of the Mind

On the second day at Clear Rock Crystal House.

After brunch hours . . .

"Dearest forces, I need your attention please. Are you ready to hear my story?" Ufaïa asks.

Geossuth replies, "Who wouldn't be ready with an iced-cold fruity mattheïe drink? Can't complain, it's perfect."

"Mmm, while lying on the shore of Lake Flurmieda, me too. Living my best life," Maiephis says.

Luseïe replies, "You got it, Princess. Can you please pass me my hat, Huïumi?" Huïumi hands the hat to Luseïe.

"Look at this weather. It's beautiful outside. You have good taste, Haiokïto," Rayïq says.

"Uh, it was a great idea to section off part of the lake to prevent blocking the sunlight from reaching the water," Haiokïto replies.

Fully present in the surroundings, Ufaïa says, "This part of the lake—sectioned off—is just like the maze in my story. I refer to how your thoughts should flow in your mind instead of wandering."

Everyone listens attentively, nodding; except for Luseïe.

Luseïe says, "You mean ruminating . . . I am trying to visualize what you're saying."

"Paccürs. As always, you're correct, Luseïe," Ufaïa replies.

"Not surprised," Huïumi whispers to Haiokïto. He smiles.

Luseïe smiles with a glint in her eyes. "Now I can see it clearly," she says.

Ufaïa speaks, "In my story, the thoughts symbolize the water flowing into the lake from the river. The river symbolizes the mind. The lake symbolizes the flow through and outflow of our thoughts, and this section of the lake symbolizes the maze that I created in my mind ruminating, until I was able to overcome all the obstacles that wouldn't let my thoughts flow from this section of the lake, like the water that flows from the river into the lake and out freely."

Gasping, Geossuth says, "Your thoughts were trapped in your mind."

"Yes!" Ufaïa agrees, nodding.

"What exactly did you do, Ufaïa?" Geossuth asks.

"To be brief, yeo struggled with my thoughts, and therefore, I ended up playing the game of the mind . . . *And that was extremely difficult,*" Ufaïa replies.

Ufaïa is telling the truth—her destiny to find *Freedom* was up to her and no one else.

. . .

Sixteen years ago, Punta Blereuzule, Pearl Islands, Kingdom of Zūlear.

Ufaïa, then eighteen years of age, had just graduated from High School with her friends Huïumi and Luseïe. And while Huïumi and Luseïe traveled to the Kingdom of Bloomïeda, to begin a new life at Brightmieda University, Ufaïa chose to stay behind, struggling with all the noises of the people surrounding her.

Ufaïa couldn't escape all the voices in her mind. The noise was constant—it wouldn't cease, causing her great distress. She couldn't disconnect herself from all the thoughts of what others had said, and every time she walked past someone who was talking, immediately, she began thinking *it was about her*. Not only that, but every time she interacted with someone, she'd perceive it as a personal attack. She'd think that *everything others were saying to her was negative*. Thus, her light soon began to fade away. She stopped being optimistic and instead whined about everything . . . Ufaïa's negativity increased more and more every day, increasing her emotional pain to such a level that she started pushing away everyone who cared about her. Until one day, she couldn't bear it anymore and all she wanted was to escape all her thoughts, and the noises surrounding her; so, desperate for freedom to calm her mind, Ufaïa went for a walk alone in the park.

Master-Gowgwart-Love appears near Mazeïe Park.

"OH! No! She's entered Mazeïe Park, and I cannot help her there. She'll have to figure out how to exit the maze on her own and for that she will need Trust," Master-Gowgwart-Love says, worried about Ufaïa.

Master-Gowgwart-Trust appears.

"Master-Gowgwart-Love, I cannot enter Mazeïe Park either. It is restricted to us. It was established by you long ago when we saved Haeodeïe from Master-Gowgwart-Guilt," Master-Gowgwart-Trust says.

"Oh, yes! We did it so she didn't become a shimmering letter," Master-Gowgwart-Love replies.

"That pushed the negative Master Gowgwarts to request that all positive Master Gowgwarts, us, stay outside of their home. Since then, we cannot go inside," Master-Gowgwart-Trust replies.

"I know, Master-Gowgwart-Trust. That's why I am so worried about Ufaïa. I am afraid that she will get lost, and the negative Master Gowgwarts will absorb her completely. It seems she will bring to life the spirits of all seven negative Master Gowgwarts at the same time.

That's when the game of the mind truly begins . . . That's why she's entered our world. It's extremely dangerous, and she must be strong to survive all the obstacles, because there are many traps created by the negative Master Gowgwarts in Mazeïe Park," she replies.

"We can't intervene, Master-Gowgwart-Love. She has to come out Mazeïe Park on her own. Let's hope she remembers me so she can remember you, and then if she wins the game of the mind, she'll meet Freedom and us outside of Mazeïe Park . . ." he says.

"I believe she will, Master-Gowgwart-Trust, and we'll be here waiting for her until she does," Master-Gowgwart-Love says with a trustworthy voice.

.   .   .

Slowly, the daylight begins to decline. The nighttime lights set in to shine sparkling bright. Ufaïa doesn't realize that she's entered Mazeïe Park; thusly, she continues walking, wandering, unaware that she's entered Pherriland.

Ufaïa is so enchanted by all the colorful lights, that she decides to stay in Mazeïe Park.

Ufaïa thinks, "Why return home? For what? In the end, *I am the reason why, I can't have a good relationship with anyone.* I'm the problem! I'd rather stay in the park a little longer, although I don't remember being in this park. I thought I was walking to the park near home. Maybe it's a new park."

At the beginning of the park, Ufaïa sits on a peach bench—a whimsical feeling around her surrounded by peach lights—to wait for time to pass.

Suddenly, she begins to feel the bench moving up.

Ufaïa asks, "What's happening?"

"Why is this bench growing nonstop?"

"It's taller than before."

"Help!"

"Is someone listening?"

Her small eyes widened, you could finally see her green eyes. "Please someone help me!" Ufaïa cries.

Without understanding what's happening, she held on tight with one hand, covering her eyes with her other hand, being still and silent. Her heart beating faster and faster until the bench rose above the maze and she was high up feeling withdraw, and loss. Ufaïa says, "I don't wanna look. I don't know what's happening. Why doesn't it stop moving? As if I've been detached from the ground, rejected. I feel isolated, pushed out, and disconnected from everything."

Not for a second she stopped covering her eyes to look at the park—trembling until the bench had finally stopped moving and she felt that she could remove her hand off her eyes.

"No one is coming to rescue you. You are *alone* in this."

Ufaïa looks around Mazeïe Park, trying to find the voice, and surprisingly, what she thought was a peach bench turns out to be a giant peach Gowgwart, holding her in her hands . . .

"Aaaah!" Ufaïa cries out in fear.

"Who are you? Or What thing are you?" Ufaïa asks.

"Hello Ufaïa, I am a negative Gowgwart."

"My name is Sadness. I'm Master-Gowgwart-Sadness, and you have woken me up. Welcome to my home."

"Sadness! You are so peachy and bright. Unexpectedly joyful," Ufaïa replies.

"I know. I'm all that. Young lady, you have awakened all of us here," Master-Gowgwart-Sadness says.

"All of you?" Ufaïa asks with a confused voice.

"Yes," Master-Gowgwart-Sadness replies.

"How can yeo be facing, sitting on top of Sadness? Yeo don't understand, what does Sadness mean by saying all of them, in here?" A sudden thought as Master-Gowgwart-Sadness speaks.

"The negative emotions you're experiencing have brought you to our magical world, Pherriland," Master-Gowgwart-Sadness says.

"I can't believe it's happening to me," Ufaïa says, frustrated.

"It can happen to anyone. You are in Mazeïe Park. This is my home—the home to six other negative Master Gowgwarts," Master-Gowgwart-Sadness says.

"I am in your home! I thought you were joking," Ufaïa inhales and exhales. "Peaches, Master-Gowgwart-Sadness! What? There are six more . . ." Ufaïa says, feeling Master-Gowgwart-Sadness moves.

"We are seven negative Master Gowgwarts in Mazeïe Park. If you look down, you'll see that there are seven colors—peach, green, lavender, blue, brown, baby blue, and pure white—some brighter than others," Master-Gowgwart-Sadness replies.

As she looks down, Ufaïa says, "Yes, I can see the colors. They are shiny, lively, bright, and uplifting. There's nothing negative about them. Do the colors have anything to do with you?"

Master-Gowgwart-Sadness responds, "Each color you see here represents us—I with peach, Pain with green, Fear with lavender, Shame with blue, Depression with brown, Anger with baby blue, and Guilt with pure white." The seven negative Master Gowgwarts lift their voices singing, "In your mind."

Ufaïa, full of wonder, looks delighted and dismayed, shifting her emotions while all the Master Gowgwarts chanted in the maze.

Master-Gowgwart-Sadness speaks, "You must survive each of us—Master Gowgwarts—in the order I've mentioned. This is the game of the mind, and you must figure out how to move to the end of the maze, where you'll find the exit, and if you survive, you'll meet

Master-Gowgwart-Freedom outside."

"What happens if I don't?" Ufaïa asks.

Master-Gowgwart-Sadness responds, "You stay here, trapped with us. Thusly, you become a memory in your world and then your memory disappears."

"Taccgrah! I don't want that. I must find my way out of this maze, but how?" Ufaïa asks.

"The game of the mind has started. All you need to survive is in your mind. The key to win lies in the belief and attitude you adopt to approach us. I'll give you a hint, it may or may not require you to think a lot. It might be easy or difficult to win. Honestly, it takes more energy to lose than to win. Think about it. I am not as big as I look. Am I? I will leave that to you. Winning will depend on your perspective. I'm warning you; you won't be able to enter the other side of the maze until I disappear," Master-Gowgwart-Sadness says.

"But you are so big, and I am so small," Ufaïa says, looking all the way down at Master-Gowgwart-Sadness, who stands tall on the ground while she holds Ufaïa high up in her hands.

Master-Gowgwart-Sadness replies, "Think again. Try harder. I am simply an emotion. I am big because you see me as big, otherwise I am small."

Cheerfully, Ufaïa replies, "That is it! If I see you small, you will become small. You're not as big as you look. What you are trying to say is that I have power over you . . ." She smiles.

"How can yeo make Sadness small?" Ufaïa wonders.

Master-Gowgwart-Sadness replies, "The answer you seek is in your mind."

Ufaïa thinks, "Hmmm . . ."

Sitting comfortably, Ufaïa speaks, "I think I got it! I must think of a happy, optimistic memory from my past." A sudden thought,

"Oh, I know, the sparkling gold glitter sandals my mom gave me for my ninth birthday. Yeo cherished them so much and felt so happy every time I wore them, that I wore them every day."

Little by little, Master-Gowgwart-Sadness descends, becoming smaller and smaller, bringing her closer to the ground, but not closer enough for Ufaïa to move to the green side of the maze. Ufaïa needs to try harder reframing her thoughts, otherwise she will remain high-up with Sadness.

"It's not working. You are only half the size you were before descending. Why? From up here, I can't put my feet on the ground. It's not safe to jump. I won't be able to move to the green side," she says, "(not that I am excited about it, but I must)."

Master-Gowgwart-Sadness says, "It's working. Look at me, I became smaller. Progress is progress. Don't get discouraged."

"Paccürs, I can do this. I just need to focus. I can do it," Ufaïa replies. "Think. Think. Hmm. I loved . . . the books my dad read to me when I was a child. I was very happy, until he and my mom got divorced," she muffles.

Master-Gowgwart-Sadness begins to grow again and so do the glow in her ears.

"What is happening?" Ufaïa's voice trembles.

"We are going backwards," Master-Gowgwart-Sadness replies.

"Why have you grown bigger?" Ufaïa asks.

"It is you, Ufaïa," Master-Gowgwart-Sadness replies.

"Why?" Ufaïa asks.

"Your thoughts must be positive and right now they are not," Master-Gowgwart-Sadness replies.

"Aaah. I feel sad about my parents' divorce," Ufaïa says.

"You figured it out," Master-Gowgwart-Sadness replies.

Ufaïa thinks, "I love my parents, but I have to be realistic, they are happier when they're not together. Maybe if I focus on the bright side of my parents' divorce, Master-Gowgwart-Sadness will become smaller and smaller, until she disappears completely."

Ufaïa has figured out how to make Master-Gowgwart-Sadness small again—turning her back into her original form—dimming the glow in her ears, watching her entirely disappear until there is no more Sadness and her path is clear.

With excitement, Ufaïa says, "I did it! Whoo hoo! Yes! I won this one! I am stepping foot on solid ground. Now I must make sure to remember every time I am feeling sad, I must find a joyful, happy, and optimistic memory, to let go the feelings of Sadness."

Ufaïa is finally able to enter the green side of the maze where Master-Gowgwart-Pain is waiting for her.

.   .   .

"Everything is so green, this isn't bad. I don't feel Pain; instead, I feel at ease. Master-Gowgwart-Sadness was right . . . Hmm? I don't see Master-Gowgwart-Pain? Where is he?" she wonders, looking to find him. "All there is, in here, is a garden of flowers. Beautiful daisy wildflowers. I have never seen a wide assortment of hues and shades within the same garden—a stunning array of daisy wildflowers. Yeo have seen the classic white and vibrant yellow blooms, but not the pink, red, orange, purple, and blue. Wow, even a bicolored variety of pink/green," Ufaïa says, filled with wonder, looking at the daisy wildflowers.

Master-Gowgwart-Pain, watching Ufaïa looking at the garden of daisy wildflowers, says, "I am here—among the daisies. Take your time to feel me until you see me."

"Master-Gowgwart-Pain, I can't do that. I'm not going to step over the daisies. Where are you among them? I don't see you," Ufaïa says.

"Follow my voice, and you will feel me—before you see me," Master-Gowgwart-Pain says as he moves among the daisies to reach Ufaïa, enlarging his prickles to wound her.

"Paccürs. I'm following your voice looking everywhere. Yet, I still can't feel you, neither see you. You are so hard to find. I don't understand why," Ufaïa says, "(I feel numb)."

Master-Gowgwart-Pain replies, "I am not so far from you. I'm green with prickles everywhere . . . Be careful, because I can wound you. I am going to hurt you."

"Aaaah! I think, I found you. Ouch! Taccgrah! It hurts, you are painful," Ufaïa says as she limps on her right foot.

Master-Gowgwart-Pain replies, "I am Pain. What else do you expect? How else would you have acknowledged my presence?"

"At first, when I entered here, I felt relief. It felt good. But now I am feeling confused, stressed, hopeless, and discouraged. I am not winning the game of the mind. I feel in despair. I have been ignoring you, Pain," Ufaïa says, her voice muffled. She sits on a green bench across from the colorful garden of daisy wildflowers, surrounded by bright green lights. She covers her face with both hands—shedding tears from her eyes.

"I hurt you, but those wounds will heal if you grow out of it," Master-Gowgwart-Pain says, intensifying his glow.

"How? The only thing you give is pain. I am in pain . . . Am I destined to suffer? Why am I here? Look at your prickles, they are so thick, and your glow is so green. I am bleeding," Ufaïa says.

Master-Gowgwart-Pain says, "Be patient. When you're healed, your wounds will be gone, and there will be no scars. Everything will be in the past, and you will be yourself again, but stronger and better than you were." Master-Gowgwart-Pain returns to his original form with prickles everywhere—all over him.

"I need three or more bandages to cover all my wounds—big square ones," Ufaïa thinks—looking at her left ankle—as she lightly bleeds. "Is there someone out in this maze who can help me?" she wonders, desperately. "Hi! Please someone help me!" Ufaïa cries out in pain as she continues to lightly bleed from her left ankle.

"There's no one here that can hear you. No one! Mwah ha ha! Your parents are not coming to save you. You are on your own and until these prickles—all over me—have left me, I won't disappear, and you won't be able to enter the other side of the maze," Master-Gowgwart-Pain says, planted at the end of his side of the maze.

"From Pain to Fear . . . Taccgrah! But I have no choice. I don't want you to wound me again and I must get to the other side. I must think about how I can make your prickles disappear. I must think. I don't have a choice," Ufaïa says, desperately.

"If you cannot leave me behind, you will become a little daisy wildflower, like them . . . Look at them, all the little daisy wildflowers here couldn't figure out how to escape, so I became their permanent home," Master-Gowgwart-Pain says cackling, sparkling green crystal sparkles all over the daisy wildflowers.

"A little daisy wildflower!" she cries, "I can't let you do that to me. Aaaah! Help! Please! Someone out there, help!" Ufaïa cries out, frustrated, looking around the maze. Then, limping on her right leg, Ufaïa sits on the green bench to cover all her wounds with the purple satin lace she removed from her long ponytail.

"The only thing required to, poof!, make my prickles disappear, is neutralize me. If you cannot figure that out, you'll become a little daisy wildflower. You can choose the color you want, or I can create a new one," Master-Gowgwart-Pain says.

"The fact that I don't feel sad for my parents' divorce anymore has allowed me to feel better. Maybe if I think of all the good things in my life that have come with the divorce, yeo won't feel Pain when crossing to the other side of the maze. These wounds will disappear, and I will have no scars. I must regain hope. I must be hopeful that instead of Pain, I will feel comfort," Ufaïa thinks, enthusiastically, a smile on her face.

"I will trust that when I step over you, you will not wound me again," Ufaïa says, looking at Master-Gowgwart-Pain moving all his prickles.

Master-Gowgwart-Pain growls, "If you say so. Go ahead, let's see what happens."

With confidence and a firm voice, Ufaïa replies, "I am brave and strong—HMPH!"

At once, Ufaïa closes her eyes and with her left wounded foot, she confidently, steps over Master-Gowgwart-Pain.

Ufaïa walked, unapologetically, away from Master-Gowgwart-Pain; later, finding herself free of Pain on the other side of the maze.

.   .   .

Ufaïa thinks, "It worked! I didn't feel Pain. Pain didn't wound me again, instead I felt comfort when crossing over to this side. It feels good to leave Pain behind." Ufaïa checks her left ankle to see if she's still bleeding. Ufaïa says, "My wounds? My wounds are gone! I don't have a single scar. Master-Gowgwart-Pain was right, yeo feel brand new. As soon as I grew out of him, I healed. Yeo need to be more confident in my ability to control my thoughts, reframing them to be positive. It's the power of the mind, and I am in control of it. I'm confident that I'll win the game of the mind because I'm strong. I can do this."

Ufaïa screams in fear as she falls to the ground after bumping into a clear wall, "AAAAH! WHAT'S HAPPENING?"

"Hello there. You've hit yourself with your own wall. One of the walls you have built in your mind," Master-Gowgwart-Fear says, suppressed at the end of the maze.

"What? I have built walls in my mind!" Ufaïa rubs the affected area on her forehead and then gets up.

Growing bigger, Master-Gowgwart-Fear says, "Yes. Until you tear them down, you won't be able to move to the other side."

Ufaïa is sweating, touching the clear wall with the palm of her hands, leaving a mark on the glass. She's trying to see where Master-Gowgwart-Fear is, disappointed, she replies, "This is harder than I thought. Oh, my nightmare!"

Master-Gowgwart-Fear says, "You must overcome me. It's the only way to get to the other side of the maze."

"The walls allow me to see through them, but I don't see you," Ufaïa says, frustrated and tense. "This is hard!" she exclaims.

"I am here at the end, right before you enter the other side of the maze," Master-Gowgwart-Fear says, no longer suppressed and ready to act.

"The lights are blinking fast. I can't see a clear path. A blackout! No! That's the last thing that I need right now. What's happening? Where are you, Master-Gowgwart-Fear?" she asks. She begins to see Master-Gowgwart-Fear moving fast from wall to wall, confusing her with his glow.

As Master-Gowgwart-Fear moves from wall to wall, he speaks, "I am here or here. Maybe here. No, I am now here." He cackles.

"Stop! Stop! You're driving me insane. I don't know what I see anymore. I am afraid, trembling in sweat . . ." Ufaïa says with a rapid heartbeat, looking back, thinking about going back. She says, "I can't go back to Pain, yeo have to figure out how to overcome Fear. But everything is so dark. The lavender lights are gone and all I see is the reflection of the lavender glow of Fear moving from wall to wall, oh no!" Ufaïa breathe heavily, leaning forward, pushing the wall with all her strength. She's trying to tear it down to overcome Fear, but the wall doesn't disappear.

"I can see you. Your ears are . . ." Ufaïa says, staring at him.

"What's wrong with my ears?" Master-Gowgwart-Fear asks.

"Glowing a lot," Ufaïa replies.

"Oh, that! It's you," Master-Gowgwart-Fear says.

"Me! How is that?" Ufaïa asks.

"The glow you see in my shiny ears reflect how strong I am inside you right now," Master-Gowgwart-Fear replies.

"Am I feeling that much Fear right now?" Ufaïa asks.

"Yes," Master-Gowgwart-Fear responds. The lights are back and Ufaïa can see Master-Gowgwart-Fear clearly.

"The lavender hue here is so calming. How can I feel so much Fear? I should be feeling serenity. I don't want this feeling. I must find a way to make these walls disappear," Ufaïa thinks.

Ufaïa asks, "When did I build these walls?"

"After your parents got divorced, your whole life changed and you began to build walls," Master-Gowgwart-Fear answers.

"I don't even remember. I was only six years old when I moved to Punta Blereuzule from Punta Roseïey," Ufaïa replies.

"I will show you," Master-Gowgwart-Fear says.

Lavender sparkling crystals pop out from Master-Gowgwart-Fear's ears, and Ufaïa's early years appear on the walls.

Looking at the walls, Ufaïa says, "They're arguing about me in our home in Punta Roseïey. On that one, yeo was telling my dad, 'I don't play reïhng; I don't do boy stuff. I like dolls, I am not a boy.' He replied, 'Sweetie, reïhng isn't just for boys, it's a unisex game. It's also girl stuff. I love you as you are playing dolls all the time.' There, I'm hiding in a corner in the living room, covering my ears because they're arguing again. And in the last one, I see me telling my dad to please not leave . . . I remember, I cried a lot that day when he said, '*adïour sweetie.*'"

Master-Gowgwart-Fear says, "These walls have kept you from falling in love."

"In-love? No," Ufaïa says, shaking her head. "It always ends in a divorce."

"You have built an emotional barrier to protect yourself from further pain due to past traumas," Master-Gowgwart-Fear says.

"That's because I don't want to end like them. But I get it; it's only going to get worse if I don't think differently. I know I never had a boyfriend before, because I don't want that to happen to me. But perhaps, if I change my mind, I can overcome you. In the end, just because their relationship didn't work doesn't mean the same is going to happen to me. I can take my time to do things in a different way. Their divorce is an opportunity for me to learn what I want and don't want from a relationship. I admit that I haven't been positive at all. I let my parents' experiences influence my decision not to fall in love. I forgot to forge my own experiences to live my life. What have I done? Oh, no! As I speak to you, I have come to realize that I was wrong," Ufaïa says, startled.

The walls begin to collapse one by one. The path to the other side of the maze is cleared. Master-Gowgwart-Fear has disappeared. Lavender flower garlands appeared—an archway from beginning to end—blending in the space with a soothing and calming sweet smell.

"Finally! I can smell the lavender flowers!" Ufaïa says excitedly, dancing around the lavender garlands that surround her. Ufaïa walks to the other side of the maze—mused by their delicate sweet smell—

feeling relaxed and at peace with herself.

.   .   .

At the same time, while Ufaïa is celebrating her small wins after overcoming three negative Master Gowgwarts—Sadness, Pain, and Fear—outside of Mazeïe Park, Master-Gowgwart-Love and Master-Gowgwart-Trust are watching her in awe—amazed with her inner powers to overcome the obstacles she has faced so far. Meanwhile, at the end of the maze, Master-Gowgwart-Freedom waits outside.

"She's doing phenomenal. As she's advancing in the park, she's diving deep into her inner powers to overcome the negative Master Gowgwarts," Master-Gowgwart-Love speaks to Master-Gowgwart-Trust as they fly outside the maze, following Ufaïa every step of the game.

Master-Gowgwart-Trust nods, agreeing. "Yes, she's strong and confident. She's courageous and she's remembered me," he replies, expressing an intense admiration and a true sense of wonder for her exceptional nature.

Master-Gowgwart-Love sighs. She says, "We underestimated the girl. She's stronger than she looks. Her courage is a sign that she has started to remember me too."

"Yes! Look at her walking to the next side of the maze. She's confident, calm, and serene," Master-Gowgwart-Trust says.

Master-Gowgwart-Love replies, "Yes. But let us not get ahead of ourselves, Master-Gowgwart-Shame is very strong. She will need to delve into more depth within herself to find her worth."

With confidence, Master-Gowgwart-Trust says, "I believe she will do."

"If she overcomes Master-Gowgwart-Shame, she'll encounter more challenges ahead of her. It will be entirely up to her to win the game of the mind," Master-Gowgwart-Love says.

"No matter how bad it gets, I believe she will not give up. She has what it takes to overcome all the obstacles of the game," Master-Gowgwart-Trust says.

Master-Gowgwart-Love replies, "I know she does; that's why I told Master-Gowgwart-Freedom to wait for her outside."

"Look at him patiently waiting for her to come out of the white gates," Master-Gowgwart-Trust says.

Master-Gowgwart-Love looks and then says, "Let us hope she remembers me. She'll need willpower and leadership to receive the Gowgwarts' Bracelet. We cannot use our powers to help her win the game of the mind."

"I'm positive that she'll remember you completely. Then, she will meet us and Freedom outside," Master-Gowgwart-Trust replies.

"She's entered the blue side. Master-Gowgwart-Shame is ready to shame her," Master-Gowgwart-Love says.

.   .   .

Back to Ufaïa at Mazeïe Park.

Ufaïa thinks, "Oh . . . Everything is so blue here. I don't see a way out. I am only at the beginning. Hmm? How strange? . . . It is a path with a closed end."

Surprised, Ufaïa asks, "A dead end? What? I can't stay stuck here; I must overcome this challenge. Dinguï! How will I get to the next side?" Ufaïa asks, frustrated. "Wait, I am starting to see . . . it looks like my reflection. I guess . . . that is—a mirror?" She gasps.

"Oh, I understand. That's what's preventing me from seeing the other side of the maze. Brilliant, more surprises," she says with a smile, and a knowing glint in her eyes.

Blue water descends from a crystal cascade on the wall next to her. Immediately, Ufaïa sees the blue water reaching her, the floor disappearing, her feet getting wet. Ufaïa feels the cold water as she's walking in the maze towards the mirror at the end.

Tall and firm, she stands still.

Be careful, Ufaïa, you're not walking on firm ground . . .

Blue pillars are moving up and down. Frightened, not knowing what's next, Ufaïa looks down. Ufaïa stares at her reflection on the blue water that is covering the ground. Multiple blue glowing pillars surround the mirror at the end. The blue water has stopped flowing from the cascade. Ufaïa rises. She says, "I don't feel safe. I wasn't expecting this. I feel stormy. AAAHHH! I am going down again!" Ufaïa cries out madly, desperately trying to keep her balance not to fall from the sparkling blue pillar, terrified to fall.

Master-Gowgwart-Shame appears in the mirror at the end of the maze. Meanwhile, the blue glowing pillars continue to move up and down in the blue water covering the ground.

"Jump! Jump! Jump to the next glowing blue pillar; if not, you'll continue moving up and down and around on the same sparkling blue pillar that is round," Master-Gowgwart-Shame says.

"No! I'm scared! I don't want to fall into the blue water," Ufaïa says, "(how am I going to overcome this? I must jump to the next glowing blue pillar. I must! They're moving up and down. I need to be strategic and catch it when is down)."

Ufaïa jumps to the next glowing blue pillar. She jumps again to the next one, again and again, until she finally sees the mirror at the end of the maze.

"What's happened? That's not me! It's no longer me who I see in the mirror, instead, I see . . . Shame? Is that Master-Gowgwart-Shame?" Ufaïa says, unsure, staring at the mirror.

Master-Gowgwart-Shame replies, "Yes! It's me who you see in

the mirror. I am going to show you everyone who makes you feel inferior." He cackles grandiosely.

Ufaïa muttering, "I don't like you."

"What did you say? That you are feeling shameful because your parents got divorced," Master-Gowgwart-Shame says with a smile.

Ufaïa raises her voice, angrily, "Don't say more!"

"You can't stop me. You live now with a divorced mom and have two separate homes," Master-Gowgwart-Shame says.

While covering her ears with both hands, Ufaïa screams, "Yeo don't wanna be here!"

Master-Gowgwart-Shame says, aloud, "What a shame!"

Stepping out of the mirror and bending his head forward, blue sparkling crystals sprout from his ears. He begins to show images in the mirror of everyone who made fun of her since seventh grade.

Ufaïa groans. She cannot stand the noise from everyone who bullied and harassed her because thanks to her parents' divorce, she had two separate homes. As if having to live with it wasn't enough.

Frustrated and tense, Ufaïa screams, "ENOUGH!! Stop now!! Already!! Please! That is enough! I don't think I can do this! It's too much for me!"

She sits on the glowing blue pillar feeling numb, hopeless and, without strength. She then looks at the blue water and begins to feel calm and relaxed.

Suddenly, Ufaïa remembers. She thinks, "Everything I need to overcome this challenge is within me."

Ufaïa closes her eyes, staying silent—cutting the noises from everyone who bullied her before—managing to disappear all those negative memories, finding a moment of peace amid everything that disturbed her. Then, she opens her eyes and there's only the mirror. Ufaïa gazes into her reflection—full of undiluted introspection.

Calmly, Ufaïa speaks, "All those negative memories, including Master-Gowgwart-Shame, have disappeared."

While Ufaïa is lost in her reflection, the sparkling and glowing blue pillars stop moving. Dimming their lights—slowly submerging their appearance in the blue water covering the ground—fading in a magical manner—wondrously extraordinary.

Ufaïa's reflection in the mirror speaks, "I am trustworthy. All the people who bullied me will always be there. I have the power to silence the noises of their negative words. I can ignore them. Starting today, I take my power back. I won't let anyone make me feel small again. I am strong and I am brave. I am enough."

"That's what I needed to remember . . . Tagrascïe Ufaïa!" Ufaïa says to her reflection.

The blue water has drained. It evaporated from the ground as if by magic. Shiny—sparkling trails of silky—shimmering crystalline blue diamonds emerged, moving around her. The glowing blue pillar she sits on brings her back to solid ground. Ufaïa mused, filled with wonder. The mirror begins to disappear, clearing the path for Ufaïa to leave Shame behind and enter the other side.

. . .

"I did it! I overcame Master-Gowgwart-Shame! Whoo hoo!" Ufaïa shrieks. "I made it to the brown side!" Ufaïa adds, celebrating her small win.

"It's brown, earthy, not much light in it," Ufaïa thinks.

"Ugh! This side is dark and foggy, not what I expected. It is Depression . . ." Ufaïa says, walking slowly and carefully, "(a little scary with lots of short, leafless trees lining the path)."

"Ugh, it's muddy. I am glad I am wearing my green rain boots," Ufaïa says, looking at her surroundings in the maze, "(oh, I see the baby blue light, I can't wait to cross over to the next side)."

Not yet, Ufaïa . . .

Master-Gowgwart-Depression, emerging from the pond that's shortly ahead of Ufaïa, enlarges his branches grandiosely, wrapping them around her. He says, "I know you want to go to the brighter side ahead; I can see it in your eyes. Is all over your face."

He's dragging Ufaïa down the dark-murky waters.

Desperate and anxious, not knowing where he's taking her, she cries, "Nooo! Let me go! Leave me! AAAHHH!"

"You won't be able to escape from me. You are trapped! Save yourself. You want solitude, right? Well, see if you can emerge from the murky waters. You're going straight to the bottom. Later, Ufaïa," Master-Gowgwart-Depression says, cackling.

"Aaahh!" Ufaïa cries out, descending deep in the dark-murky waters, feeling the coolness and heaviness of the water enveloping her.

"Depression sent me to the bottom. Aaah!" Ufaïa feels a small fish brushing her leg. "A fish! I felt a fish!" she yells. "It's dark down here, I need to find a source of light," Ufaïa thinks.

She swims, trying to find a glint of light, encountering shadows of water lilies, submerged floating leaves, various fishes, odd plants like the water poppy, and other aquatic organisms.

Ufaïa sees various lotus rhizomes—underground stems of the lotus flower—and immediately remembers everything her mother taught her about the lotus flower. "My necklace! My mom told me that if I ever found myself in the bottom of the dark-murky waters, the lotus flower would guide me to the surface." Ufaïa touches the pink lotus flower on her gold necklace and says, "Lotus flower, guide me to the surface of the dark-murky waters."

The pink lotus flower comes to life, lighting its golden light to guide Ufaïa to the surface of the dark-murky waters.

"I cannot move my petals," Pink Lotus Flower says, reflecting pink shimmering glow in her petals as she speaks.

"Your petals glow every time you speak. Why can't you move?" Ufaïa asks.

Pink Lotus Flower replies, "First, you need to rise from your suffering."

"I did! I overcame Sadness, Pain, Fear, and Shame. Is there anything else?" Ufaïa asks.

"Uh-huh. Dive into your inner strength to find the beauty in your suffering, so you can rise from it. Like we do when we blossom in the surface, unaffected by the mud," Pink Lotus Flower replies.

"That's impossible! There's no beauty in my suffering," Ufaïa replies.

"Your growth begins here, in the bottom of the mud. As you grow and learn from your past experiences, you will emerge from your suffering, breaking through as you reach the surface to unveil the beauty of your essence, like we do when our bud slowly opens, unfolding to reveal our beauty. It's a journey from muddy depths to radiant blooms," Pink Lotus Flower says.

"It's the power of the mind. I must find meaning in my life. I need something to cling to. But what? I can't continue to live a life without purpose, otherwise, life will pass me by . . . I need an arçaïe. Yeo don't have to stop doing the things I did before because I feel down. I must find strength within me to keep going forward. My friends moved to the city of the Garden of Joy, and I stayed behind, because I am feeling depressed, paralyzed, and I don't have clarity of what I truly want. Thanks, Pink Lotus Flower. It's time to unfold all my petals to unveil my true essence," Ufaïa says with euphoria.

Pink Lotus Flower gently moves her pastel pink petals, guiding

Ufaïa to the surface of the murky waters.

"I see a gleam of light! Yeo can see the sunrise! Look at all the stems standing upward, seeking the sunlight that comes with a new day above the water's surface. This is beautiful. I am starting to see the beauty under the murky waters. I am going to college to join my friends. No more excuses. I will fall in love and won't let my parents' divorce influence my choices. I will overcome Master-Gowgwart-Depression. He underestimated me and didn't have mercy when he sent me deep down the muddy pond," Ufaïa says to the Pink Lotus Flower as she is immersed, admiring the beauty of the lotus flowers blooming on the surface.

"This is your breakthrough, you're unfolding. You're emerging to the surface. My job is complete," Pink Lotus Flower replies as she returns to her form in the gold necklace.

Ufaïa rises across the pond. The pond vanishes. She's in solid ground again, unaffected by the murky water. Dried and radiant, she begins to walk to the next side of the maze.

Master-Gowgwart-Depression is at the end of his side, waiting for her, covering the entrance to the next side with his leafless brown branches, hiding his body behind them.

"Master-Gowgwart-Depression! I thought I'd left you behind. What do you want? Tell me, what? You are not even a Gowgwart. You're just a tree without leaves. To your brutal treatment I thank, because thanks to that, I am now free of my suffering, ready to shine bright like the gold light of the pink lotus flower shines," Ufaïa says, confidently.

"I'm Master-Gowgwart-Depression. I'm just hiding inside this tree. I am not handsome. I am brutal, but I'm also good. That's why you are thanking me." He returns to his original form, clearing the path for Ufaïa to move to the next side of the maze.

"No more suffering. I will live a good life," Ufaïa says.

"A good life . . . you!?" Master-Gowgwart-Depression says, laughing sarcastically.

"I am brave and strong enough to free myself from you. Watch me use the power of the mind to leave you behind," she replies with determination, stepping out of the brown side of the maze—leaving Depression behind—not looking back.

Ufaïa is astonished; she didn't know how powerful her mind is. The beauty of her inner essence gave her willpower, leadership, optimism, positivity, and hope to live a good life.

It was Love.

.   .   .

"I did it! The new life that awaits me is good and I don't wanna miss it," Ufaïa says, happily, captivated by the bright baby blue color of the new side of the maze she is at.

"You're so cute, and you make me feel very calm. Come closer. Why are you standing so far?" Ufaïa asks, "(how can Anger be so calming? It's so contradicting. This side is empty. There's nothing. I only see Anger)."

I wouldn't be calling Anger, he's handsome but not so friendly. *Watch out, Ufaïa—you don't know where you've entered.*

Anger makes an ugly face and gnashes his teeth to scare Ufaïa.

"I am not so handsome now, huh? Huh? I have a gift for you," Master-Gowgwart-Anger grins, sarcastically.

"A gift for me?" Ufaïa asks.

"Yes, right there, exactly where you are," Master-Gowgwart-Anger says, showing his ugly smile.

"Right here? Where? I don't see anything," Ufaïa says, looking everywhere.

"Turn the page," Master-Gowgwart-Anger says in a firm voice, pointing towards the shimmering baby blue that is across from her.

"What page? I am not inside a book. That's a shimmering baby blue wall," Ufaïa says, rolling her eyes at Master-Gowgwart-Anger.

"I'll turn it for you . . ." Master-Gowgwart-Anger says, popping sparkling baby blue crystals from his ears.

His magical crystals move delicately towards her. With a gentle breeze, the sparkling crystals rush the back of the shimmering baby blue page, making a soft, soothing sighing sound in the baby photo album she has entered, when she stepped inside the bright baby blue side of the maze.

Ufaïa is silent. She's in shock processing her reality.

Ufaïa thinks, "That page went through me. That's my family. That's me as a baby. I am inside a book—a photo album. This is my early years photo album. That's our last, very last photo before my parents split in Punta Roseïey."

"Time for action. It is an open photo album. A twist of fate. You. You won't be able to overcome it. Paradoxical effect," Master-Gowgwart-Anger says, laughing sarcastically.

Ufaïa looks down, an angry glare on her face. She turns around and encounters more photos of her family. She's there, in between memories—trapped, stuck in her past, wishing she could disappear all the photos from the album. She's only getting angrier and angrier, wishing she could be out of the album.

Ufaïa yells, "Get me out of here!"

Rolling her eyes in exasperation, a heavy sigh comes out from between her lips. She sits on the firm sparkling ground, covering her face with both hands, frustrated, looking down—she doesn't want to be there. Ufaïa thinks, "I don't have a choice. I don't know how to escape from Anger."

"Feel me. Angry, right? Every time you remember how happy you were as a child—when your parents were together—your Anger grows. You get so angry, so angry, you withdraw from all," Master-Gowgwart-Anger says.

Ufaïa is numb. Ufaïa is numb. She doesn't move.

"Look at those photos. That's your family and that's you . . . Hahaha. You. Again. There you are. More of you with your parents," Master-Gowgwart-Anger laughs mischievously, sparkling baby blue crystals, turning pages against Ufaïa as if she didn't exist, showing her all her childhood photos with her family.

She's silently angry watching the pages get through her. Her gaze, fixed on the turning pages, held a simmering resentment. She thinks, "I am giving up. I am not going to win the game of the mind. My Anger is greater than me. It's only getting worse."

While Ufaïa grows angry, Master-Gowgwart-Anger begins to multiply, spiraling out of control, surrounding her. Ufaïa only sees Angers. The photo album is covered with Angers, screaming all over her, "Anger! Anger! Anger! Anger!" All the Angers cackle.

The Angers begin to sing, "Anger."

All the voices of the multiplied Angers, speaking, "We are so many thanks to you. All you can see is us, everywhere. Anger, Anger, Anger, Anger, Anger, Anger."

Ufaïa finally reacts, "What have I done?! I am surrounded by Angers. I can't see the other side! I can't give up! Not after I've come so far." She looks at the pink lotus flower on her gold necklace and says, "It's time to show the beauty of my petals. I need to control Anger; otherwise, I will be here forever, and Anger will consume me entirely. Maybe what I need to do is understand that I can't change my past, but I can embrace my present and hope for a better future. I must accept my parents' divorce and try not to get angry every time

I see a family photo. I had a wonderful childhood and that will never change. I must focus on the bright side—all the good memories with my family, and all the good things that have come with the divorce of my parents, like my new friends, oh, the double birthday gifts (my favorite), and the privilege of growing up with the tranquility of a peaceful home without arguments and all of that, 'he says,' 'she says,' that's not good for anyone. Life is better now, thanks to my parents' divorce."

Ufaïa gets up from the ground and begins to feel peace. Ufaïa looks at the photo in front of her and hugs it. Sparkling shimmering crystals all over the air and the multiplied Angers turn into Master-Gowgwart-Anger. He pops sparkling baby blue crystals to disappear the baby blue photo album. Then, he begins to disappear and finally the path to the other side of the maze becomes clear.

Ufaïa is finally able to see the baby blue side covered in bright baby blue shimmering sparkles and white cotton candy clouds.

Ufaïa smells the vanilla cotton candy and says, "Mmm, cotton candy." A spun of pure joy, sweet cloud. She teared off a whisper-thin piece from the vibrant white cotton, glued on the baby blue side with its sticky sweetness. She embraces the feeling of amusement as it touches her tongue, feeling a rush of happiness with the stickiness clung on her fingers, she takes more . . . She says, "So yummy! This is heaven." Savoring the cotton candy, delighted in the magic of edible clouds—a pure elation of serene rhythm melting away—she walks to the other side of the maze.

. . .

"I made it to the last side of the maze! The game of the mind is about to end, and I am winning! I'm so happy and proud of myself for choosing to be positive and optimistic. I must admit that without a change of mind, I wouldn't be able to be here, where everything is pure white," Ufaïa says.

Not so fast, Ufaïa . . .

"Aaaahhh!" Ufaïa cries, sliding down the path of Guilt, falling into a pool of magical letters with shimmering glow, facing up, her body submerged in them. Ufaïa watches how their shimmering glow changes to the distinct colors of the negative Gowgwarts.

"A pool of white letters with magical shimmering glow. How am I going to climb up? The exit is high up," Ufaïa says.

Master-Gowgwart-Guilt flies, emerging magically from inside the pool of magical letters.

Distracted by the shimmering glow of all the letters, Ufaïa leans back on them, closing her eyes. She's worried about how she is going to exit the maze. She feels a gentle breeze, and then an abrupt, strong gust that briefly shakes her up.

Ufaïa says, "It's Master-Gowgwart-Guilt."

Immediately she gets up. "The letters pushed me," Ufaïa says, looking up.

"Do you see me now?" Master-Gowgwart-Guilt asks.

"Master-Gowgwart-Guilt, you are like everything in here. Why did you send me down this pool of shimmering letters? What am I supposed to do in here?" Ufaïa asks.

"You must find the purple letters that spell Freedom, then the white gates to exit the maze will open, and you will meet Freedom outside," Master-Gowgwart-Guilt replies.

"The gates of the maze are wide open to enter, but I have to unlock the gates to exit the maze. Why do I have to be so trusty? I need to be more careful when choosing parks. That's why yeo ended up playing the game of the mind," she thinks, feeling responsible.

"Feeling guilty? If I were you, I take action. It's seven letters.

Freedom is waiting outside," Master-Gowgwart-Guilt says.

Ufaïa thinks, "I shouldn't have entered this park."

"You cannot stop thinking about me," he says, circling around Ufaïa. "You enjoy my company."

"I better get to finding these letters or else I will be here in the company of Guilt forever," Ufaïa thinks.

Master-Gowgwart-Guilt says, "Ever since your parents started having problems, you thought it was your fault . . . You have always blamed yourself for their divorce. Do you want me to remind you the reasons? I have all the details." White sparkling crystals pop out from his ears—a long list emerges from the pool of letters. "Here it is. Let's start with . . ."

"I don't know what you mean," Ufaïa says, unbothered, as she looks at Master-Gowgwart-Guilt holding the list. Then, she returns to search for the missing letters.

"I found the F and the D; I only need five more letters. Oh, I also found the R," she says, as she continues to look inside the pool and the letters she found float outside, above her, in correct spelling order, with their shimmering golden glow.

Master-Gowgwart-Guilt thinks, "This isn't working, I need to pivot to distract her."

"I found the M and the O; I only need two more letters. Oh, I also found the E. No, it's not. It's just a white letter with shimmering purple glow," she says, holding the letter as the letters she found join the other letters floating outside, in correct spelling order, with their shimmering golden glow.

Master-Gowgwart-Guilt uses his pure white sparkling crystals to distract Ufaïa. Letters emerge from the pool, surrounding her. He arranges the letters to create words that aim to make her feel guilty, creating a storm of words around her. Ufaïa sees the words moving fast around her with their shimmering distinct glow. "Oh, storm of words. What is happening? Was it me?" Ufaïa cries, then she begins to read the words. "Guilty. Divorce. Bad grades. I am slow. I am not good at anything. I cannot speak fluently. Guilty. I cry too much. I am boring. Guilty. Guilty. Guilty. I am not good enough. Guilty."

Desperately, Ufaïa yells, "Freeze!" The words froze. She says, "The words can hear me. They obeyed me. Your time is off Master-Gowgwart-Guilt. No more games." She sees the two missing letters and at once, grabs them and says, "Got you! I finally have the letters that I am missing." The two E letters join the other letters, forming the word, Freedom. The white gates open, but Ufaïa is still there.

"If you cannot escape, you'll become a shimmering letter. You are responsible for the divorce of your parents," Master-Gowgwart-Guilt says, from above, standing at the exit of the maze.

"No! I am not. After everything I've been through in this maze, nothing you say will make me feel guilty anymore. It's all in the past. I decided to let go, to forgive and move on with my life. I don't feel guilty anymore. I've come to understand that there are things in life that we can't control and that sometimes they must be the way they are," Ufaïa replies.

"Are you sure about that? After I read the first five reasons on my list, you'll change your mind. You're not escaping me," Master-Gowgwart-Guilt says. He begins to read the list. "I am not a boy."

"Stop! That's in the past. During all these years, what did I get from feeling Depression, Guilt, Sadness, Anger, Shame, Fear, and Pain? Absolutely nothing. It dragged me into a dark place and now I find myself playing the game of the mind, trying to survive because I was (overthinking) being negative instead of positive. All I needed was to accept things as they are and embrace what I currently have. I may have spent a lot of time with you before, but not today. I am stronger than ever, and I know what I want. I can guarantee you—that it is not you. I want to forgive myself. It's my choice and the only way to be free again," Ufaïa says.

"And how are you going to escape?" Master-Gowgwart-Guilt asks, flying closer to her.

Ufaïa thinks, "The letters can hear me. They obeyed me. I can create endless possibilities in this pool. It's time to take my power to act." Ufaïa says, "White shimmering letters, go back inside the pool. Freedom! It's time to move. Form a ladder so I can climb above the pool to exit the maze." The letters obeyed her and shortly after, she found herself outside of Mazeïe Park.

Her leadership, willpower, hope, optimism, bravery, courage, positivity I mean, everything she has learned playing the game of the mind, has healed her from all her past traumas. She has forgiven her parents and herself. That's why instead of guilty, she feels protected and safe.

Ufaïa left Master-Gowgwart-Guilt open-mouthed as she exited the maze. Master-Gowgwart-Guilt had no words left. He couldn't stop her; instead, he froze, his glow dimming as he watched her walk away from him like nothing. It was as if she had transformed into a new person, no longer afraid to face the negative Master Gowgwarts but instead embracing the goodness in them.

To her surprise, after she's finally outside of Mazeïe Park, not only is Freedom waiting for her, but she also finds Love and Trust outside of the maze.

• • •

Excitedly, Master-Gowgwart-Love says, "YOU DID IT!!"

Master-Gowgwart-Trust says, "Congratulations, Ufaïa! I knew you could do it!"

"Tagrascïe! Is Freedom among you?" Ufaïa asks in amazement.

"Yes. He is Master-Gowgwart-Freedom, Master-Gowgwart-Trust, and I am Master-Gowgwart-Love."

"You are Freedom," Ufaïa grins.

Ufaïa, you finally got your ticket to return home . . . Congratulations!

"Congratulations! All this time, we've been waiting for you to come out of the maze. I am Freedom!" Master-Gowgwart-Freedom grins.

"YOU DID IT!" Master-Gowgwart-Love says.

"𝔅𝔯𝔞𝔳𝔢 𝔤𝔦𝔯𝔩!" Master-Gowgwart-Trust says.

"You're strong and courageous," Master-Gowgwart-Freedom says.

"Whoo hoo! Tagrascïe! I feel flattered. I can't believe you were waiting for me all this time. The good thing is that I never gave up, I had hope in the unknown waiting for me at the end of the maze. I knew that if I kept going, I'd find Freedom outside. Even though there were times when I thought I couldn't go on, yeo chose to be brave and strong, and despite the setbacks, I got up again and again. Then, I discovered that everything I needed to escape the maze yeo created in my mind was within me. Not only did I find you Freedom, but I also found you, Love and Trust," Ufaïa says, her eyes brimmed with joy, a tear silently carving a path down her face.

Master-Gowgwart-Love says, "My dear, you have shown to us all that anything is possible if there is a will."

"The game was not easy, you must be very proud of yourself," Master-Gowgwart-Trust says.

"Yes . . . I am. I have been waiting to meet Freedom for a long time," Ufaïa says.

"Well, here I am, Ufaïa. You've earned it and now you are free to wear it," Master-Gowgwart-Freedom says.

"What?" Ufaïa asks, without having a clue that she's about to receive the bracelet that everyone talks about in The Six Kingdoms, but no one says the name.

"I am delighted to give you the Gowgwarts' Bracelet," Master-Gowgwart-Freedom replies.

She gasps. "Master-Gowgwart-Freedom! Yeo wasn't expecting that from you. That's the magical bracelet! The one everyone talks about!" Ufaïa says, her voice filled with surprise.

"This Gowgwarts' gift box has the Gowgwarts' Bracelet. Your emotions. You have become the master of your emotions," Master-Gowgwart-Freedom replies.

"You embraced the negative Master Gowgwarts, all of them," Master-Gowgwart-Trust says.

"The Gowgwarts' Bracelet represents, above all things, a state of calmness among your emotions. In this gift box you will also find a description of the powers of the crystal stones. After winning the game of the mind you have proven that you are ready to show your true essence—the beauty hidden in your inner self. You are stronger and better than you were when you entered the maze and you have done it all on your own. You have shown to us all that you are ready to command your emotions. You have remembered the importance of being positive when things get tough. You have regained your power," Master-Gowgwart-Love says.

"No one is more excited than me, tagrascïe," Ufaïa says, taking the Gowgwarts' gift box.

Sparkling red, purple, and starry-night-blue crystals appear and the Master Gowgwarts disappear. Ufaïa returns home, transformed.

.   .   .

Present time, in Lake Flurmieda.

"Ufaïa, I've never heard of Mazeïe Park. I was born and raised in Punta Blereuzule," Huïumi says.

"Huïumi, are you following the story?" Luseïe asks.

"Huh?" Huïumi asks, confused, looking at Luseïe.

Haiokïto whispers to Huïumi, "Babe, she was in Pherrïland."

Huïumi whispers, "Ah. Right. I remember. Sorry."

Luseïe says, "Pherrïland, Huïumi . . ."

Huïumi replies to Luseïe, "I remember. *Now. Sorry.*" She grins with wide eyes.

"When I went out for a walk alone, I became so absorbed in my thoughts—that is, my attention was entirely inward, away from all external stimuli—that I became fully immersed in my mind, and my emotions transported me to Mazeïe Park in Pherrïland. I didn't even realize it when yeo entered the magical world of the Gowgwarts and, unlike Rayïq, yeo entered the home of all the negative Master Gowgwarts. It was so sudden when it happened that when I realized I had left Punta Blereuzule in the Pearl Islands, I was sitting high up with Sadness," Ufaïa says.

Geossuth says, "You're a warrior. Defeating the seven negative Master Gowgwarts. Wow!" His voice filled with awe.

Rayïq says, "Actually, what happened to you happens to many people. It's moving to see how, by changing our mindset, things can turn around quickly."

"The way we handle our emotions has a significant impact on our daily lives," Maiephis says.

Ufaïa replies, "Mm-hmm, and I'm proof of that. I guess we all are. Somehow, our experience of meeting Master-Gowgwart-Love has changed the way we embrace our emotions, allowing us to live our lives positively."

"That's so true. Love is magical. You will understand why I say it when I share my story with everyone. For now, I'll keep it a secret until after dinner time," Luseïe says.

Geossuth thinks, "Luseïe is next. Yes! This is getting better and better."

Geossuth is keeping up. The truth is, he's right. Luseïe brings a sparkle of light. So please get comfortable, because the next story shines brightly, like the sparkles of the baby blue light.

Nine

The Blue Pearl

Dinner is over and everyone is enjoying a digestif drink at Clear Rock Crystal House.

"Attention everyone," Luseïe says, standing up, holding a drink in her hands.

"She's going to give a toast," Ufaïa whispers to Rayïq.

"Uh-huh, paccürs," Rayïq whispers back.

"Shhh, guys, Luseïe is talking," Maiephis whispers to Ufaïa and Rayïq. Huïumi and Haiokïto are listening.

Luseïe speaks, "I would like to toast to us—'forces.' Of course, Love, and friendship. May we inspire others to have the courage to be brave, to be strong, to lift each-other up, and to live a joyous and positive life even when things get tough, like Ufaïa did when playing the game of the mind. But most importantly, to encourage others to embrace the powers of the crystal stones. Oohh! I almost forget, and to never lose hope, so that we continue to live a life with purpose, lighting up the goodness in us all. Cheers because life is good!"

Everyone, cheerfully, raising their drinks says, "Cheers because life is good. Whoo hoo!"

"Now let me tell you my story," Luseïe says, after sitting down. "For me, it has been an opportunity to grow up surrounded by love; however, on the night of my fifteenth birthday everything changed. That night, I realized I no longer knew who I was. I felt completely disconnected from myself and everything I thought I knew before I came to know the truth that led me to find Love."

Maiephis says, "In some ways, I relate with you, Luseïe. Cheers to you!"

Everyone raises their drinks and says, "Cheers!"

"'You're the light that brightens our lives and makes us whole,' my mom told me every time she put me to bed. I thought she said that to me because my name is Luseïe, but then, on the night of my fifteenth birthday, after receiving a special gift from my parents, yeo realized that all those years what I believed to be true was not," she says.

. . .

Punta Blereuzule, Pearl Islands, Luseïe's room on the night of her fifteenth birthday, after the celebration.

Luseïe had just dressed for bed when her mother came into her room with a gift in her hands.

Leïeze says, "Luseïe, before you go to sleep, I want to give you one last gift for your birthday."

"Aww, one more gift. Yay," Luseïe says.

I wouldn't be so excited, Luseïe. This gift will change your life.

Leïeze says, "It's a very special gift from us and a very special person. I think . . . Tonight it's the right time to tell you about her. But first, open the gift." Luseïe opens the gift.

Excitedly, Luseïe says, "It's a necklace, and it's very—" Leïeze interrupts her, "unique? Right, darling?"

"Yes, Mom—" Leïeze interrupts her, "because of the light blue pearl that stands out among the white pearls. Am I right?"

"Yes!" Luseïe says excitedly.

Leïeze replies, "This light blue pearl once belonged to a special person who loved you very much. As much as it pains us to reveal you the truth—because we don't want to disrupt your emotions—it's time that you learn we are not your birth parents."

Angrily, as her big brown eyes widen, Luseïe replies "Are you kidding me? And you say it like that? You're ruining my birthday."

Noticing her reaction, immediately, Leïeze says, "You are right, darling. This isn't the right time. Would you rather talk about this at another time?" she asks.

Luseïe takes a deep breath and says, "Sorry. It's okay. I need to calm myself. Go on, Mom."

"Are you sure, darling? We can resume this conversation when you feel better," Leïeze says.

"Yes, Mom," Luseïe replies.

"Paccürs, Luseïe. We adopted you when you were a newborn. The light blue pearl on your necklace is a gift from your birth mom," Leïeze says.

Luseïe looks at the light blue pearl on the necklace. "What does the light blue pearl stand for?—she asks—Why a light blue pearl?"

"Hmm, the light blue pearl on your necklace is a representation of your birthplace. Blue pearls are the rarest of all pearls—a unique wonder of The Six Kingdoms, especially this light blue pearl on your necklace. I remember when Jeïemi and I met your birth mom, we heard her call you, 'My blue pearl.' I asked her why she called you blue pearl and she said, 'Blue pearls are born in winter just like her, and I am ready to share her with the world, where she will determine what she will become.' Then, she gave me a light blue pearl and said, 'The meaning of blue pearl is trust, truth, tranquility, and courage. Give my blue pearl this light blue pearl on her fifteenth birthday, she will need an extra boost of confidence and calmness when she learns about me.' That's when yeo decided to name you, Luseïe. Since, she wanted to share you with the world, I wanted your light to be seeing everywhere . . . I wanted you to be the light of the world."

Leïeze began to sing, "Be the Light."

After she finishes singing, Luseïe says, "Tagrascïe, Mom. The necklace is very . . . beautiful. Especially the light blue pearl. She's my birth mom, but you are my *real* mom. I love you."

Luseïe puts the necklace away, hugs her mother, and then goes to sleep; with a gentle smile on her face, Leïeze turns off the lights and leaves the room.

．　　　．　　　．

The sunrise brings a new day to Punta Blereuzule and Luseïe finds herself overwhelmed. In her mind, she's swimming in thoughts about the light blue pearl, her birth mother, and her birthplace.

"Now that yeo reflect on everything my mom said, yeo realize that she never mentioned my birthplace or whether my birth mom is still alive somewhere. I wonder where she is . . . Where could she be?" Luseïe thinks.

She submerged in a deep pool of questions so many questions that she doesn't know where to start looking for answers.

"I don't want my mom to feel bad because I wanna know more about my past, but I wonder if I have my birth mom's eyes or hair? Maybe . . . yeo have siblings and a dad. And if my birth mom is alive, why wasn't she present at a single special occasion, like my birthday celebrations and graduations? The only clue I have, that can lead me to find my birthplace is the light blue pearl and maybe there, I can find the answers that will unravel the questions I have," she thinks.

Immediately, Luseïe began to do research on the only thing she had that could link her to her birthplace—the light blue pearl. After the news, something inside her changed. Since then, Luseïe felt the need to return to her origins to reconnect with herself. She doesn't understand why her birth mother abandoned her when she was so young and innocent. She feels the need to do this for herself so she can find meaning in her life again.

"There it is! Yes! I found it! It's *Räïra* pearls! That's the kind of light blue pearl I have, and this kind of pearl is only farmed in Punta Blereuzule. [Gasp]. Dinguï! Here? Scientific method of the unknown hypothesis! I can't believe it! I have been living in Punta Blereuzule since I remember, and I didn't know. It makes perfect sense. We are the only producers of rare pearls in our kingdom and blue pearls are the rarest type among all. And since our kingdom was once occupied by the Ūlïe people of the Kingdom of Ūlïe, our language is strongly influenced by theirs. That's why the name of our pearls is *Räïra* and that of our Island is *Punta Blereuzule*. Before my fifteenth birthday, I wasn't curious enough about pearls; therefore, I wasn't interested in knowing the type of pearls we farm. The good news is, this means my birth mom isn't that far away from me," Luseïe says.

.   .   .

Pherrïland, Gowgwarts' Workshop.

"An alert! A new disruption. Time for action. Oh, I must notify Master-Gowgwart-Love first," Master-Gowgwart-Anger says as he begins to send a notification to Master-Gowgwart-Love.

"An alert from Master-Gowgwart-Anger!" Master-Gowgwart-Love exclaims.

"From whom?" Master-Gowgwart-Joy asks.

"It says: 'Since the news of her adoption, Luseïe has submerged into a sea of Anger, sending me an alert about the disruption in her emotions,'" Master-Gowgwart-Love reads.

"Foggy rain! You must act, Master-Gowgwart-Love, before it's too late. Look! She's in her room right now," Master-Gowgwart-Joy replies, worried.

"A greater sense of connection and harmony with herself will help her be grateful for her relationship with her family, reducing all her worries," Master-Gowgwart-Peace says, with her dulcet voice.

"Good point. That's for both of you. I will appear in her room right away," Master-Gowgwart-Love replies. Red sparkling crystals appear, and Master-Gowgwart-Love disappears.

.　.　.

Punta Blereuzule, Pearl Islands, Luseïe's room.

Master-Gowgwart-Love moves the necklace with the light blue pearl that Luseïe received the night before, to create its reflection in the mirror behind Luseïe.

As Luseïe works on her research, she notices the reflection of a bright blue light on her tablet screen. She's curious to know what's causing the reflection on the screen. Luseïe asks, "Hmm. What's this bright blue light?"

At once, out of curiosity, Luseïe looks over her right shoulder to see where the reflection on her screen is coming from.

Meanwhile, Master-Gowgwart-Love is in her room, watching her, waiting to be seen by Luseïe.

Luseïe says, "Aaah. It's the light blue pearl from my necklace. I thought I put it away last night."

Luseïe steps away from her desk and says, "Time to get back to the gift box, light blue pearl. Adïour for now."

.　.　.

Luseïe is in a sea of thoughts, "This is all so strange. I put away the light blue pearl last night. I think? Or mom was here, and moved it, because she wants me to wear it . . . I'm confused. I thought I did. Maybe, I should forget about my research and go on with my life as if nothing has changed. How can you let go of someone so precious as a baby? I can't understand it. It makes me so angry. Why me? Was I not enough for her? I don't know. I'm overthinking and it doesn't feel good anymore. I'm feeling overwhelmed by my thoughts."

"Her thoughts only increase her Anger. What if her Anger gets out of control? I cannot let that happen, I must hurry, do something to help her," Master-Gowgwart-Love thinks.

Master-Gowgwart-Love speaks, "I am here, Luseïe! I came to help you calm your Anger. It is Love! Please hear my voice. See me!" Master-Gowgwart-Love flies around Luseïe, but Luseïe cannot see her. She pops red crystals and Luseïe cannot see it.

Luseïe can't hear the voice of Love; she's too angry at her birth mother and the only voice she can hear is her own.

"I will find the address of the nearest pearl farm and probably . . . I'll find a clue there that will lead me to my birth mom. Oh, but I don't even know her name. No, no! I'll never find the answers yeo seek," Luseïe says, angrily.

Luseïe raises her arms slightly and closes her eyes to breathe deeply, then begins to think, "I'm gonna go for a walk on the beach, yeo need to clear my mind. I'll leave a note for my mom on the bed in case she gets home earlier today."

The note reads:

"*Hi Mom!*
  I went for a walk on the shoreline. I need fresh air.
  Do not worry. I am not wearing the light blue pearl.
  See you at dinner time. I love you. Xoxo.
  —Luseïe."

. . .

Luseïe passes by Master-Gowgwart-Love, sparkling crystals all over her, yet she can only see her surroundings and hear her voice.

Hoping she will notice her presence, Master-Gowgwart-Love decided to follow her.

Luseïe thinks, "The blue water on the beach isn't blue today, it's emerald green and there's no sun, instead there's a strong wind. It seems like the ocean isn't at peace or you can say it's very unhappy, angry, hurt, and even with guilt. Something is . . . eerie, inexplicable, rarely seen in Blereuzule Beach, which today is a different version of what normally is."

—Blereuzule Beach is known for its rare colored pearls, and its calm blue waters. *Luseïe is telling the truth* . . .

While Luseïe walks along the shore, she cannot calm her mind; in fact, the loud sound of the waves has given her a painful headache.

. . .

Huïumi sees Luseïe passing by her house from afar.

"Luseïe! Joureïe!" Huïumi shouts, waving at Luseïe.

"Joureïe Huïumi!" Luseïe shouts, making a stop to reply.

"Can I join you?" Huïumi asks.

"It's not a suitable time," Luseïe replies.

"Paccürs," Huïumi replies.

"Usïcs! I'm walking to get some fresh air, but the ocean sounds like if it's furious, and it's giving me a headache," Luseïe says.

"Maybe, it's better to go home, Luseïe," Huïumi replies.

"Paccürs! Usïcs!" Luseïe agrees.

"See you tomorrow at school," Huïumi says, waving goodbye.

"Adïour!" Luseïe says, waving goodbye.

"Adïour!" Huïumi replies, going back inside her room.

. . .

Luseïe returns home to find the note she left for her mother intact.

"Oh, great. Mom isn't home yet. In that case, I'm gonna watch the stars to distract myself from thinking. I guess, I'll just have jïegei-jïocs for dinner," Luseïe says.

Hoping Luseïe will see her, Master-Gowgwart-Love continues to follow her, flying around her, yet Luseïe cannot feel her presence.

Sometimes, despite what's right in front of us, we see what we want and Luseïe is too distracted thinking about her birth mother to notice the presence of Master-Gowgwart-Love.

Meanwhile, Luseïe walks to the kitchen to make jïegei-jïocs— a snack made by heating corn kernels until they pop—before sitting outside to look at the starry-night-sky until it's bedtime.

. . .

Enthusiastically, while looking at the starry-night-sky through her telescope, Luseïe says, "Oh! a big bright star surrounded by a star cluster."

"It's a beautiful night with the sky full of bright stars. Whoa, I should make a wish. I wish . . . I wish . . . Soon," Luseïe says, "(what if my mom is one of the stars in the starry sky)?"

. . .

The Big Bright Star says, "The blue pearl isn't happy. Let's give a sign to Master-Gowgwart-Love. Let's help her find her birthplace before Anger strengthens within her."

The HoneyBee Stars reply, "If she follows the light blue pearl, she will find Love." A sparkle in their dulcet voice.

The Big Bright Star replies, "That is it. You are all brilliant!"

Excitedly, the HoneyBee Stars say, "Yay! We love to help. The reward of helping is Joy and Joy is fun, like us."

"With Master-Gowgwart-Love's magical powers, the light blue pearl will lead her to find her birthplace and Master-Gowgwart-Love will be there waiting for her," The Big Bright Star says.

"Yay! We'll give Love a sign to give magical powers to the light blue pearl on Luseïe's necklace," the HoneyBee Stars say.

"You're going to form an arrow that points to the ocean, and then you're going to form a pearl; Master-Gowgwart-Love will see it and so will Luseïe. And that's how we're going to help. Then, Love will take care of the rest," The Big Bright Star replies.

Master-Gowgwart-Love looks to the sky; she sees the signs and then winks at The Big Bright Star. On the contrary, Luseïe, lost in a sea of thoughts, misses the signs.

.   .   .

Luseïe says, "I am deep in the ocean." She gasps.

Then, Luseïe looks at her body and says, "I have a blue fish tail and shimmering blue, green, pink, yellow, and purple scales . . . and long blue hair. I am a mermaid! I must be dreaming! This is a dream come true! I always wanted to be a mermaid." She shakes her head and says, "What am I saying, I must wake up. I need to find my way out of the ocean so I can be myself again."

Luseïe swims trying to find the way out of the dark ocean. She sees a glowing light blue hue among all the glowing sea animals—a glowing light blue pearl that looks like the light blue pearl on her necklace. Astonished by its resemblance, she follows the light blue pearl until she finds a pile of colored pearls and a giant white oyster with baby blue sparkles.

Excited by the baby blue hue of the giant oyster, Luseïe says, "This is so beautiful! So many colorful pearls. I wonder what makes this giant white oyster emit a sparkling baby blue light."

The giant white oyster opens, and Luseïe is surprised by what she sees. She gasps. "You're not just an oyster," Luseïe says.

"Hello Luseïe. Surprised to see me?"

"AAAH!" Luseïe cries. "You speak!"

"Yes, I do!"

"You glow like the light blue pearl I followed, but you are not," Luseïe says.

"I am not. I am . . ."

Luseïe interrupts—"I am angry. Why did I follow the glowing light blue pearl? Who are you? Why do you glow so much? Why are you hiding inside that giant oyster?" Luseïe asks.

"I bet you thought I was your birth mother hiding in this giant oyster. Or maybe . . . you thought I was Love." He cackles.

"I thought that if I followed the light blue pearl, I would find my birth mom or my birthplace. Yet here I am in the middle of the ocean—talking to . . .?" Luseïe says.

"Anger. Master-Gowgwart-Anger. I'm a reflection of how you feel inside since you've received the light blue pearl. I am a negative emotion in disguise, and you have given life to my spirit. That is why my ears glow so much."

"Master-Gowgwart-Anger?" Luseïe asks.

Master-Gowgwart-Anger responds, "You weren't supposed to be here, but you couldn't control your Anger, so your Anger came to me to let me know of the disruption in your emotions."

"No! It can't be. I never wanted for this to happen. You're not real. I'm dreaming. None of this is real," Luseïe says.

"I am real. You are too focused on your past instead of being grateful for your present. Don't you see that what you have now is greater than what you lost?" Master-Gowgwart-Anger asks.

Sadly, Luseïe says, "But . . ."

"You have lost awareness of Anger. So now that your Anger is with me, I'm in control. It was easy to bring you down here. All I did was distract you with my powers . . ." Master-Gowgwart-Anger cackles.

Meanwhile, Master-Gowgwart-Love tries to give her a sign to help her leave Master-Gowgwart-Anger behind, using her powers to control the light blue pearl to move it away from Master-Gowgwart-Anger.

"If I can calm down and focus on the brighter side, I'll be able to leave you behind. I can do it! I am strong and b—r—a—v—ę," Luseïe says, after realizing that the light blue pearl is no longer there. "Where is the light blue pearl? Oh! Dinguï! I must go. I must follow the light blue pearl. Light Blue Pearl, please wait for me. I am coming after you."

Not knowing where it would take her, Luseïe at once began to follow the glowing light blue pearl, until she lost Anger in the deep sea and had the glowing light blue pearl in her hands.

. . .

Luseïe finds herself outside the blue waters of the ocean, in a safe place.

With a cheerful voice, Luseïe says, "I made it! I'm finally myself again. Yes! We made it to the shore Light Blue Pearl. You saved me. Tagrascïe!"

Luseïe opens her right hand, where she holds the glowing light blue pearl.

"You can float!" Luseïe says.

The Light Blue Pearl circles around her.

"Hahaha. Can you talk?" Luseïe asks.

"Yes!" Light Blue Pearl responds. Her glow intensifies.

"I'm tired of being angry, Light Blue Pearl. Knowing the truth about my birth mom has changed everything . . . I feel overwhelmed by my thoughts. I'm tired, emotionally absorbed. I have awakened Master-Gowgwart-Anger and now, I must learn to be calm."

"That's a good approach. I mean the last part where you refer to being calm. Learning to be calm in stressful situations is good. It can help you maintain emotional stability and allow you to be more positive, fostering the positive emotions and reducing stress," Light Blue Pearl says.

"I will try to find ways to calm myself because I feel tense, and I don't like it. Thanks to you, I lost Anger in the deep sea, but what if Anger appears again?" Luseïe asks.

"It wasn't me; it was Master-Gowgwart-Love, she saved you," Light Blue Pearl replies.

"Master-Gowgwart-Love?" Luseïe asks.

"Yes," Light Blue Pearl responds.

"It was you I followed," Luseïe says.

"Master-Gowgwart-Love is the master of all Gowgwarts, and everything is possible with her," Light Blue Pearl replies.

"Oh. Is she, like the leader of all Gowgwarts?" Luseïe asks.

Light Blue Pearl responds, "Yes. She's the Master of all Master Gowgwarts—a Headmaster, and like her, they are superheroes with magical powers in The Six Kingdoms and Pherriland—their magical world. They are always seeking to help you find a calm state among your emotions, especially when there is a disruption by unexpected events and you are feeling helpless, overwhelmed by your emotions, ruminating, and unable to cope with the circumstances in which you are experiencing stress."

"That sounds like what I am going through right now. I need Master-Gowgwart-Love. Anger didn't feel good," Luseïe replies.

"Don't worry about Anger, you will learn about the importance of enhancing awareness to create harmony among your emotions. You will also learn the goodness in all of them. Practicing calmness can help you find Peace through challenging situations. It is a choice, your choice. You can be positive if you try," Light Blue Pearl says.

"What choice do I have? I couldn't even choose my parents," Luseïe replies.

"You can choose to live a negative life or a positive one—think through. You can focus on the bad side of the challenging situation you are facing or the good side. The way you feel can vary depending on the attitude you adopt. It's you who has the power to decide how to react to an adversity. It's your choice. You can complain about your current situation, or you can embrace the good side. Explore it and you will experience the difference in your response when faced with difficulty," Light Blue Pearl says.

"I never thought of it this way. I was complaining a lot. I chose to be angry instead of grateful for growing up surrounded by love. I was overthinking and judging my past when I don't even know the whole truth. Now I understand that how I process my emotions is my responsibility. I needed to calm myself first to process the news. You're right about something: the attitude I choose to adopt every day in my life is my choice. A choice I am free to make every day. I do have a choice," Luseïe says.

"Yes, you do! You are ready," Light Blue Pearl says.

"For what?" Luseïe asks.

"To meet Master-Gowgwart-Love," Light Blue Pearl replies.

"Are we going somewhere?" Luseïe asks.

The Light Blue Pearl begins to move in circles around Luseïe. At once Luseïe falls asleep, and they both disappear.

. . .

"Luseïe! Open your eyes, dear," Master-Gowgwart-Love says.

"It's so colorful here. Where am I?" Luseïe asks.

"Dear, we are in your room," Master-Gowgwart-Love replies.

"My room? This is a baby's room. This isn't my room. Where am I? Where is Light Blue Pearl? We were talking; she told me it was time to meet Master-Gowgwart-Love. Are you . . .?" Luseïe asks.

"Yes, I am Master-Gowgwart-Love. I gave magical powers to Light Blue Pearl. I brought you here," she responds.

"That's why Light Blue Pearl said that it was you who saved me from Anger and not her. Was I talking to you when I was talking to Light Blue Pearl?" Luseïe asks.

"I gave powers to Light Blue Pearl to save you. I was trying to help you," Master-Gowgwart-Love says.

"Thank you. I thought that Light Blue Pearl would lead me to find my birthplace, so yeo followed it," Luseïe says.

"And so it was, Light Blue Pearl brought you here. We are at your birth mother's house, your nursery room," Master-Gowgwart-Love says.

With a smile as she's walking in the room looking and touching everything, Luseïe says, "That is why there are so many baby things in here. One second. My—baby—things!"

Master-Gowgwart-Love says, "Look up, Luseïe."

"Huh?" Luseïe asks distracted looking at her baby things.

Master-Gowgwart-Love raises her voice, "Look up, Luseïe!"

Luseïe quickly looks up. Filled with amazement, she says, "This place is full of colorful pearls. They look like sparkles of lights falling straight from a magical place. I love the clouds painted on the ceiling with a baby blue hue background that resembles the color of the sky, like the wall that's right behind me. This is the most beautiful room I've ever seen in my whole life. I mean, whoa! A wall with stripes of pastel tones, a wall with circular shapes painted in vibrant colors, a sky wall, and a ceiling full of gifts. This place is truly enchanting, yeo guess . . . she wanted to give me everything she had."

"When your birth mother was a child, she loved pearls . . . She loved them so much, she became obsessed with them, and spending time on Blereuzule Beach, collecting them, became her thing. As she grew older, the number of pearls she collected increased, so much so that she began to put them in small clear boxes. Later, when she found out that she was expecting you, she decided to use the pearls to decorate this room for you. All these clear gift boxes filled with colorful pearls symbolize what you meant to her—a gift from the sky. You are the reason behind these colorful sparkles of light and that's why I brought you here," Master-Gowgwart-Love says.

"It's so magical, thoughtful, and beautiful! Does that mean she is gone forever?" Luseïe asks.

"Yes. She is, dear," Master-Gowgwart-Love replies.

Luseïe is feeling gloomy. A new Master Gowgwart appears in the room.

"Aww. Another one," Luseïe says.

"Hello Luseïe," Master-Gowgwart-Sadness says.

"Hi! You are?" Luseïe asks.

"My name is Sadness. Master-Gowgwart-Sadness," she replies.

"Don't tell me. I did it again!" Luseïe says, disappointed.

"Dear, you have awakened Master-Gowgwart-Sadness. I am starting to disappear," Master-Gowgwart-Love says, disappearing.

With a nostalgic tone, Luseïe says, "No! Love, don't go! Please! What have I done? I can't control my emotions. I'm out of control!"

Luseïe, are you feeling overwhelmed by your emotions?

. . .

After Master-Gowgwart-Love disappears, Luseïe finds herself alone with Master-Gowgwart-Sadness.

"The way you are feeling about your birth mother has brought me here. Be optimistic that I am temporary and Master-Gowgwart-Love will appear again," Master-Gowgwart-Sadness says.

"Paccürs. Tagrascïe. You're not bad. I'll try," Luseïe says.

"Find contentment in your loss. Everything you need is inside you," Master-Gowgwart-Sadness says.

"I am happy because my mom didn't abandon me. It looks like I was everything to her. I mean, look at this room. Whoa! She must have loved me a lot. It's beautiful. So bright. I hope she's in a better place," Luseïe says.

"Excellent, Luseïe. See, it's not hard to be positive. Remember to always focus on the bright side," Master-Gowgwart-Sadness says.

"Tagrascïe, Master-Gowgwart-Sadness. I'll be as positive as the positive sign," Luseïe says.

Peach sparkling crystals pop everywhere; Master-Gowgwart-Sadness disappears. Master-Gowgwart-Love appears again—bright sparkles of red crystals surrounding her.

. . .

"Well, that was fast, dear. Somehow, you were able to balance us," Master-Gowgwart-Love says.

"What do you mean, Master-Gowgwart-Love?" Luseïe asks.

"You engaged with Sadness without letting Sadness overpower

you. That's our goal, dear, to help you embrace our powers to create harmony among us, so that you can live a happier life. Terrific job!" Master-Gowgwart-Love replies.

"How did I do it?" Luseïe asks.

"Awareness and the ability to remain calm with a shift of focus to emphasize the positive side. Yet, you're still reactive. You're there, but you're not. Don't worry, my friends and I, Master Gowgwarts— Trust, Peace, Happiness, Joy, Freedom, and Care, will train you so that you understand how to embrace all our powers and your own, not to be reactive when facing unexpected circumstances that may disrupt your emotions. Once you've completed your training, you'll receive the Gowgwarts' Bracelet," she says.

With widened eyes, Luseïe gasps. "The unknown hypothesis?! The bracelet everyone talks about in school! No way!" she adds, her voice trailing off.

"Mm-hmm. The Gowgwarts' Bracelet," Love replies.

"Yes! I am getting the Gowgwarts' Bracelet!" Luseïe says.

"Only after you have completed your training with us, when your emotions are in harmony with each other, will you be ready to receive the Gowgwarts' Bracelet," Master-Gowgwart-Love replies.

"Of course. You got it! I want my emotions back!" she replies.

"Your emotions will go in the crystal stones of the Gowgwarts' Bracelet, making you their master. We will then give you the bracelet with a note describing their powers," Master-Gowgwart-Love says.

"Oohh. And after that?" Luseïe asks.

"Your responsibility is to use their powers to continue to create balance among them," Master-Gowgwart-Love says.

"Just as with Master-Gowgwart-Sadness?" Luseïe asks.

"Yes. With our help, you will soon understand your power and how you can use it to rise above difficulties," she replies.

"I can't wait to be the master of my emotions," Luseïe says.

"You will, dear. The training takes time because everything you need is within you and our job is to help you find it. Your mother believed that too," Master-Gowgwart-Love says.

"Is that why she left me the light blue pearl? To remind me of my power?" Luseïe asks.

"Mmm. Sometimes a little help doesn't hurt, that's why your mother left the light blue pearl," Master-Gowgwart-Love answers.

"Now yeo understand why she left me the light blue pearl. 'The meaning of blue pearl is trust, truth, tranquility, and courage.' That's what my mom, Leïeze, said that my birth mom said to her. That I'd need courage to accept the truth and trust to know that her decision was the right choice. She also said the light blue pearl would give me tranquility to have a good reaction to the information received. Now yeo know what she meant," Luseïe says.

"Forsooth! She is right, Luseïe," Master-Gowgwart-Love says.

"I get it now. I didn't pay attention to any of this. I focused on the fact that I'm adopted. That's why I brought the spirit of Master-Gowgwart-Anger to life," Luseïe says.

"Smart girl. I'm glad you got it," Master-Gowgwart-Love says.

"I think I do," Luseïe says.

"Remember, every time you make a choice you are using your power," Master-Gowgwart-Love says.

"I get that now," Luseïe says. "My choices reflect who I am."

"Forsooth! Sometimes you may lack knowledge, and you may make mistakes, but there's always a possibility of doing things right again," Master-Gowgwart-Love says.

"I don't even know her name. With the light blue pearl, I will always remember her . . ." Luseïe says.

"Your mother's name was Azlureis, like the color of the water of Blereuzule Beach. She was sweet, kind, and a little bit stubborn too. She loved you until her last breath . . ." Master-Gowgwart-Love replies.

"Now it's clear I was wrong thinking negatively about her. Yeo wish I could see her again. I was too young to remember her . . . At least to say goodbye," she says.

"I will give you a chance to see her again . . . She has something to share with you, which I hope answers all your questions," Master-Gowgwart-Love says.

"Really? Is she?" Luseïe asks. "My wish!! It's happening!"

"She's here with us, but not for long," Master-Gowgwart-Love says.

"Where?" Luseïe asks.

"I am right behind you, my blue pearl," Azlureis says.

Luseïe turns around and finally meets her birth mother. She realizes she looks just like her.

"Mom? Azlureis . . ." Luseïe says.

"Don't be scared, my blue pearl. I am here because I want to help you calm your Anger, and to do so, you must know the truth. I loved you since I found out yeo was expecting you. When I had you, the doctors diagnosed me with a terminal illness. They said I only had six months left and when I told your father that he will raise you without me, he got scared and abandoned us. Since then, I never knew where he went. He disappeared from our lives, and it was just you and me, except that I wasn't going to be around for long, so yeo needed to find you a home. That's when I met Leïeze and Jeïemi. They were doctors at the hospital at the time, and a nurse, who knew that yeo was looking for adoptive parents, told me that they wanted to adopt because they couldn't have children of their own. So, I said, 'I want to meet them.' And when I did, yeo realized that they were perfect to take care of you. So, I gave you up for adoption and waited for my time to leave earth. I knew you would be safe with them, and I was right. Look at you, my blue pearl, you are perfect. Never doubt that I have always loved you," Azlureis says.

Luseïe ran to hug Azlureis, but her presence dissolved—a chill in the air—as she whispered her final words . . . Luseïe's arms closed on empty air, only hugging the void.

"She's gone! No! Azlureis!" Luseïe screams with melancholy. "Love, please do something," she says.

"My dear, I cannot do anything to bring her back. She is already gone. She's been gone since you were six months old. Remember to have courage to accept the truth," Master-Gowgwart-Love says.

"You're right. Now that yeo know the truth, I feel some sort of freedom and peace. I'm grateful for Azlureis and my parents. I'm glad Light Blue Pearl led me to find you," Luseïe says.

"We will help you to develop awareness, positivity, confidence, calmness, and, most importantly, to embrace goodness in us. I know it sounds easy, but it's not. The good thing is that it's achievable, and the reward is worth it," Master-Gowgwart-Love says.

"You're really the superheroes of The Six Kingdoms," Luseïe says.

Master-Gowgwart-Love replies, "We are immensely powerful, but you have greater power over us, Luseïe. Never forget that."

.   .   .

Punta Blereuzule, Pearl Islands, Luseïe's room.

Leïeze says, "Luseïe, wake up! Darling, you're going to be late for school. Hurry! Time to shower and brush your teeth."

"I'll never forget, Love," Luseïe says, still sleeping.

"Are you dreaming about Love, darling?" Leïeze asks.

Luseïe opens her eyes and at once hugs her mother.

Excitedly, Luseïe says, "MOM! OH, MOM, I missed you!"

"Oh darling, yeo wasn't gone for that long. I love you. Get up, it's time to get ready for school. Hurry up, c'mon take a shower and brush your teeth. You have finals this week . . . Oh, I left money on your desk, so you can buy tickets to the concert you want to go to with Huïumi and Ufaïa. I packed breakfast too. It's in the kitchen. Well, I must go now. Good luck on your finals today. I Love you, darling. See you tonight. Adïour," Leïeze says.

"Thanks, Mom. You're the bestest mom in The Six Kingdoms. Love you too. *Adïour,*" Luseïe says. She gets up to look for her pearl necklace. "There you are. Today, I will wear you with pride and joy."

Luseïe is feeling calm and content about the truth her mother revealed to her on the night of her fifteenth birthday. Her negative feelings unfolded positivity and calmness in her. Luseïe understands that her mother had no choice and that her intention was to protect her, to give her the opportunity to grow up surrounded by love.

She's beginning to embrace her truth with Master Gowgwarts, Trust, Peace, and Freedom. Her healing journey has begun.

After a few months spent with the positive Master Gowgwarts, Luseïe is embracing all the positive emotions. She has gained more confidence in her powers and she's gradually developing awareness.

Master-Gowgwart-Love gave her strength, Master-Gowgwart-Care showed her compassion and patience, Master-Gowgwart-Trust gave her stability, loyalty, and confidence; Master-Gowgwart-Peace taught her to be grateful, calm, fully present, and comfortable with herself. With Master-Gowgwart-Freedom, she explored new things and understood the true meaning of joy and being positive, which brought her happiness and optimism.

. . .

Master-Gowgwart-Love appears in Luseïe's room.

"Hello dear," Master-Gowgwart-Love says.

Luseïe replies, "Aaah! It's you, Master-Gowgwart-Love! You scared me. I've been waiting for you, but yeo wasn't expecting you today. I am so busy with school projects. What a pleasant surprise."

"Oh dear, I've been here and everywhere. I was waiting for the right time to appear. And the right time is now," Master-Gowgwart-Love says.

"I've been thinking a lot about the pearls of my birthplace, and since you're here, can you tell me what happened with all the pearls Azlureis used to decorate my room?" Luseïe asks. "Only if that part of the dream was real," she says.

"Of course it was real. The pearls are no longer in that house. The house now belongs to other people, but the pearls belong to you. They're here in this house," Master-Gowgwart-Love says.

"Here? Where and how?" Luseïe asks.

"When Azlureis gave you up for adoption, she informed your parents of all the pearls she used to decorate your nursery room, and with a document signed by Azlureis, your parents removed them all. Azlureis left you all the pearls, so that when you are old enough, you can use them however you want," Master-Gowgwart-Love says.

"My mom never mentioned it. That's strange. She only gave me the light blue pearl, in a white pearl necklace, on the night of my fifteenth birthday. Why wouldn't she give me the rest?" Luseïe asks.

"She hasn't told you anything yet, but she will. She's waiting for your twenty-first birthday. On due time, you will receive all the pearls," Master-Gowgwart-Love says.

"My twenty-first birthday? Dinguï!" Luseïe snaps. "Well, yeo guess she has her reasons," she says, trying to calm down.

Master-Gowgwart-Love replies, "She does, dear. Remember to be calm and in control."

"Paccürs. What about my training?" Luseïe asks.

"Your training began months ago, and you have completed it," Master-Gowgwart-Love replies.

"I did!" Luseïe says, surprised.

Master-Gowgwart-Love nods.

"Oh, yay," Luseïe says with a smile.

"The time you have spent with us over the past three months, has helped you create a calm state among your emotions, and it has activated the golden button in the Gowgwarts' Workshop, showing your profile on our screen," Master-Gowgwart-Love says.

"My profile?" Luseïe asks.

"Yes! You are ready to wear your emotions with responsibility and confidence," Master-Gowgwart-Love says.

"Does that mean yeo can wear the bracelet right now?" Luseïe asks.

Master-Gowgwart-Love replies, "Mm-hmm. You are now the master of your emotions, and I am here to give you the Gowgwarts' Bracelet."

"Tagrascïe! I can't believe I'm ready to wear my emotions, and not only that but also becoming the master of them," Luseïe says.

"Remember, continually create balance among your emotions. The bracelet will remind you of the power you have to embrace your emotions and the importance of being positive to live a happier life. Bear in mind that at times you may lose sight of your emotions, but with the knowledge you have now, you will be able to balance them over again, awakening calmness and tranquility in yourself," Master-Gowgwart-Love says.

"I know. Like finding the equilibrium point in a circumference of a circle. Is it not?" Luseïe asks.

"Yes! That's exactly how it is. You're a very smart girl," Master-Gowgwart-Love replies.

"Well, if I understand it correctly and it's like in physics. When I refer to my emotions, the combination of the positive and negative emotions in the Gowgwarts' Bracelet, stands for the balance of the positive and negative charges around the circular object that results in a stable distribution of charges, meaning, is the stable state of my emotions. Right? Only achievable when my emotions are in perfect balance. However, unfortunate events can disrupt my emotions and therefore, they will no longer be in equilibrium. And my job is to re-create balance among them," Luseïe says.

Master-Gowgwart-Love replies, "Clever way to put it, Luseïe. The equilibrium point in the Gowgwarts' Bracelet refers to the state of harmony of your emotions when they coexist together. Achieved when your emotions hug each other in the Gowgwarts' Bracelet. Nonetheless, the state of harmony in your emotions can fluctuate if unexpected life experiences disrupt your emotions. In this case, you may lose awareness of your emotions, losing one of the Gowgwarts' Bracelets, and therefore, your emotions would be out of balance, no longer in harmony with each other."

Cheerfully, Luseïe says, "I finally got it! I solved the unknown hypothesis!"

Master-Gowgwart-Love replies, "Now it's time to put it into practice with the help of everything you have learned."

So, from that moment on, Luseïe developed more awareness of her emotions and carefully tried to keep her emotions in balance. Then, when she turned eighteen-years-old, she moved with Huïumi to Brightmieda, to study design at Brightmieda University.

. . .

Present time, in Clear Rock Crystal House.

"On my last night at home, on Pearl Islands, I received a note from Master-Gowgwart-Love. The note read:

'*Dear Luseïe,*

You're doing great. Continue to embrace awareness and remember your responsibility to keep your emotions in balance. Keep it up and never forget your power to embrace goodness.

Embrace calmness & live a positive life.

—Love and friends.'"

"You have always been the smartest among us, Luseïe," Ufaïa says.

"Oh, you are exaggerating, Ufaïa," Luseïe replies.

"*Gïocs,* she's not," Huïumi says.

"*Paccürs,* just a little bit," Luseïe replies.

"Just a little bit?" Rayïq asks.

"I mean, *Usïcs,*" Luseïe replies.

"Uh-huh. That's better," Geossuth says.

"Eventually—on my twenty-first birthday—my mom gave me over a thousand pearls, and I couldn't think of a better way to honor Azlureis, than to share them with The Six Kingdoms. I combined the skills I learned in design at Brightmieda University, and later on, with the help of my parents, yeo opened my jewelry store, Azlureis's Pearls, here in Brightmieda," Luseïe says.

"That's how it all started with your pearl jewelry designs. You named the store after your birth mom . . ." Huïumi says.

"Mm, yes," Luseïe replies.

"Luseïe, I applaud you for having the courage to share the only thing you have of Azlureis with The Six Kingdoms," Haiokïto says.

"I am proud to be one of the people in The Six Kingdoms who owns some of those beautiful, unique pearls that Azlureis collected for you," Ufaïa says.

"Ufaïa, you're a pearl. Thank you, Haiokïto," Luseïe replies.

"Tagrascïe, Luseïe," Ufaïa replies.

"I'm glad you were able to escape from Anger. Not everyone can or wants to," Maiephis says.

Luseïe says, "Tagrascïe, forces! It wasn't an easy journey, but it was worth it."

.   .   .

Rayïq asks, "Why are you so quiet, Geossuth?"

"Me? I'm fine. I was thinking, how do you get Gowgwart-Love out of the crystal stone in the Gowgwarts' Bracelet?" Geossuth asks.

With a humorous voice, Luseïe says, "Geossuth wants to meet Love."

Geossuth replies, "No. Not really."

"Anyway, it's simple. All you need to do is . . ." Luseïe replies.

Luseïe is always trying to answer everyone's questions, but that won't be enough for Geossuth to get Gowgwart-Love out of the red crystal stone in the Gowgwarts' Bracelet.

Thank you for your good intentions, Luseïe . . .

Ten

Not Your Gowgwarts' Bracelet

Geossuth, disappointed and annoyed, alone in his room, talks aloud.

"This thing is not working."

"I'm doing everything Luseïe said."

"I pressed both golden stars that seal both bracelets and then called Gowgwart-Love, but nothing happened."

"This is a joke."

"Love doesn't exist, and this bracelet doesn't work for me."

"After hearing those hopeful stories, I thought for a moment that Love is real, but hmmm, I guess . . . it only exists for everyone except me. For real, I'm starting to believe that it's just a fantasy."

Not knowing why he cannot get Gowgwart-Love out of the Gowgwarts' Bracelet, he puts away the bracelet, closes the windows, and turns off the lights in his room, before going to sleep.

.   .   .

While Geossuth sleeps, he begins to hear a voice saying, "Say the truth and it will set you free." Suddenly, he wakes-up anxious, tense, with his heart pounding with fear, and covered in cold sweat.

"Is anyone here?" Geossuth asks.

No one answers. Geossuth gets out of bed to look around the

room, only to realize he is alone.

Geossuth begins to think, "I heard a voice saying, 'Say the truth and it will set you free.' But no one knows . . . No one. Not even my friends. They think she is dead. I lied to everyone. The truth is, she . . . Yeo can't even think about it."

He shed a tear of pain and sadness; seconds later, he wiped the tear away with his right hand, while also feeling anger. Geossuth is embarrassed to reveal the truth to his friends about what happened, because he feels ashamed for what she did to him. He's carried this pain for a long time and lying about it is his way of covering it up.

"Yeo need some fresh air."

"I'm going for a walk."

"Yeo need to clear my head," Geossuth thinks.

Before leaving the room, Geossuth grabs the bracelet and puts it on.

.   .   .

"The thought of her . . . abandoning me and denying me the chance to . . . for all these years, makes me angry. I wanna get rid of the only thing yeo have left of her. It's not like she gave it to me as a gift; I found it in the trash can next to her desk the day she left the Kingdom of Bloomïeda. Forever. It seemed like, she didn't want it anymore. And there I was, picking up the only thing that reminded me of her. Not even an adïour or a letter saying that she loved me or that she was going to reunite with me. She broke my heart. I'm tired of pretending, but I'm ashamed of what she did to me, and yeo don't want to tell my friends or anyone else, especially the first-time I meet Huïumi's boyfriend. I don't think it's the right time to open-up to them and I'm glad yeo haven't met Love yet," Geossuth thinks as he walks towards Lake Flurmieda.

"Perfect! This is what yeo need to distract myself and not think . . . the dahleïea garden. Hmm, I don't remember seeing a bench on that side of the garden, but I'm glad it's there. No wonder Haiokïto never got rid of this garden; it's so beautiful at night. Maybe it's the lights and the glowing sky that turns it into a magical garden, or it's me who can see the magic in the garden. Anyway, I'm gonna sit on the bench to watch the flickering glow of the dahleïeas in the garden. It's a good distraction that can help me clear my head," he thinks.

The truth is the magic that Geossuth sees reflects Love because Love has always been there. He just needs to believe in Love again.

Geossuth feels like something is missing.

"What yeo need is classical music," he thinks before putting on his headphones to relax.

"Now what I need is to try this thing one last time," Geossuth says.

Geossuth removes the bracelet from his right wrist to summon Gowgwart-Love.

"This is the last time . . . If this bracelet doesn't work, *adïour*," he says.

As he's about to summon Gowgwart-Love, the dahlias begin to glow with different colors.

Geossuth thinks, "Hold on a sec. The glow of the dahleïeas has changed to the colors of the rainbow. Maybe . . . it's Love giving me hope. It must be a sign from Love. Perhaps I don't even need to call Gowgwart-Love or Master-Gowgwart-Love. Do I even have to call Master-Gowgwart-Love, or does she appear on her own? I don't remember. It doesn't matter. Maybe she's right here with me."

As Geossuth is removing his headphones, a calming soothing voice reaches his ears.

"Geo. Geo. Geo. Geo. Geo."

"Hmmm?" He stops and looks around, looking for the voice.

"Did I hear that right?" Geossuth asks.

"Geo. Geo. Geo. Geo."

"Oh man. These dahleïeas can talk. Why do they call me Geo?" he asks.

"Geo. Geo. Geo." The dahlias begin to sing, "Geo."

After the dahlias finish singing, Geossuth says, "Hmmm? How strange . . . She was the only one who called me, 'Geo,' and she . . . I mean, I don't even know, it has been twenty years since she left home. A lot could have happened since then."

"Oh, something changed," he says, looking at the dahlias.

Then, he says, "A sudden change in the colors of the dahleïeas to burgundy/black. That's very dark. I don't think it's good. Maybe I don't deserve love, and that's why, Love hasn't appeared in my life. Gïocs. I need to get out of my head. Really. My thoughts aren't good. I must be careful; I don't wanna end up like Ufaïa, playing the game of the mind, or like Luseïe, deep in the ocean with Anger. I need to find Peace like Maie. But it's hard, I can't stop thinking. I'm creating my own suffering. Anyway, I'll try to call Gowgwart-Love, one more time, before I let go of this thing that once belonged to her."

Geossuth presses both golden stars that seal both bracelets to call upon Gowgwart-Love. "Sparkles, sparkles, red crystal sparkles, Gowgwart-Love, I summon you!" he says.

After seeing nothing happened, Geossuth became frustrated and angry, so angry that he got up from the bench, walked towards Lake Flurmieda, and threw away the Gowgwarts' Bracelet.

.   .   .

Meanwhile, in Clear Rock Crystal House.

Master-Gowgwart-Love, Master-Gowgwart-Joy, and Master-

Gowgwart-Happiness appear.

Master-Gowgwart-Love says, "Geossuth needs help. He isn't expressing his inner suffering as he should. He's mixing emotions. He's about to bring Master-Gowgwart-Sadness to life."

"Is that why you said it was urgent to meet you here?" Master-Gowgwart-Joy asks.

Master-Gowgwart-Love says, "Yes and no. I got a notification from Master-Gowgwart-Sadness."

Gasping, Master-Gowgwart-Happiness asks, "Already?"

Master-Gowgwart-Love replies, "Geossuth was about to bring her spirit to life, so I tried to intervene. Now his Gowgwart-Sadness is with Master-Gowgwart-Sadness, so I used my powers to give him hope and then, I used my powers again to show him a reflection of his feelings in the dahlia garden. But the dahlias' new color reflects betrayal, and Geossuth's Anger went with Master-Gowgwart-Anger. So now Master-Gowgwart-Anger is in alert mode to act. If we don't intervene now, Master-Gowgwart-Anger will send me a notification. Together, Master-Gowgwart-Anger and Master-Gowgwart-Sadness (controlling his Gowgwart-Sadness and his Gowgwart-Anger) could be immensely powerful."

Promptly, with a concern tone, Master-Gowgwart-Joy replies, "Those emotions can give rise to Depression, and if that happens, his Gowgwart-Depression will send an alert. Even worse, go to—" Master-Gowgwart-Happiness interrupts, "oh! Master-Gowgwart-Depression!"

"Yes, Master-Gowgwart-Happiness. I was about to say that," Master-Gowgwart-Joy says.

"No. No. No. No! That could be catastrophic. I'm sure we can find a solution. We must do," Master-Gowgwart-Happiness replies with a serious tone.

"We cannot let that happen, Master-Gowgwart-Love, he needs optimism, positivity, and hope," Master-Gowgwart-Joy says.

"He needs us," Master-Gowgwart-Happiness says.

"Yes. That's why you are needed. We cannot let him shut down emotionally. If he becomes emotionally blind, it will not allow him to recognize his feelings," Master-Gowgwart-Love replies.

"He cannot recognize his feelings! Oh, dark clouds of heavens. No good. No good. Can we give him a sign?" Master-Gowgwart-Happiness asks.

Master-Gowgwart-Love replies, "Yes! We will use our magic to help Geossuth."

Cheerfully, Master-Gowgwart-Happiness says, "That's such a clever idea, Master-Gowgwart-Love. Such relief."

Master-Gowgwart-Joy asks, "How are we using our magic to help, Master-Gowgwart-Love?"

Master-Gowgwart-Love replies, "As I changed the color of the dahlias to the colors of the rainbow and then to burgundy/black, with our crystals, we will change the color of the dahlias again, but this time to green, to give him comfort."

Master-Gowgwart-Joy says, "So, let us use our magic then. It's time to change things around. This is thrillingly hopeful."

Master-Gowgwart-Happiness says, "Brightly promising . . ."

"Let's keep in mind that those negative emotions may come to life because he's been suffering for a long time. Hopefully, with our help, he'll be able to recognize them before they continue to increase his suffering and he becomes emotionally guarded—stoic," Master-Gowgwart-Love says.

Master-Gowgwart-Joy replies, "We bring hope, warmth, and a new beginning with a positive outlook. Let's be optimistic that he will."

Master-Gowgwart-Love says, "Wherefore, the Big Bright Star along with the HoneyBee Star Cluster will guide him to us."

Master-Gowgwart-Happiness says, "Forsooth, and he will find us."

Master-Gowgwart-Love replies, "Yes. Ready? Let us go!"

Master-Gowgwart-Happiness says, "Yay! Here we go!"

Master Gowgwarts, Love, Joy, and Happiness fly through the roof of the Clear Rock Crystal House.

They adorn all the dahlias with their magical sparkling crystals, changing their color to green.

.   .   .

While Geossuth stands in front of Lake Flurmieda, he sees a reflection of the new color of the dahlia garden in the waters of the lake.

"The color of the dahleïeas has changed again. It has given me comfort and relief. Why? Perhaps, but I just got rid of the bracelet. There's no way Gowgwart-Love could be here. Master-Gowgwart-Love? Nah. This is not Pherrïland, and I am not dreaming. Yeo feel confused—is she here or not?" Geossuth thinks.

The green color of the dahlias has neutralized his pain, but that stimulating sensation will not last long . . .

Cheer up, Geossuth.

.   .   .

As Geossuth wonders if Love has anything to do with what is happening in the dahlia garden, The Big Bright Star appears in the starry-night-sky among the HoneyBee Stars.

The HoneyBee Stars ask, "Why can't Geossuth believe in the magic of Love?"

The Big Bright Star responds, "Because of his negative past experiences. But don't worry, Master-Gowgwart-Love can make the unexpected happen. That's why she's here with her friends, Joy and Happiness, to help him free himself from what has been tormenting him for so long."

The HoneyBee Stars say, "He has lost hope."

The Big Bright Star replies, "He cannot see that all this time he has spent with his best friends at Clear Rock Crystal House, Master-Gowgwart-Love has been revealing herself through their stories."

"Ooh, no! How can he not realize Master-Gowgwart-Love has chosen his friends to reveal herself?" the HoneyBee Stars ask, not understanding why.

"That's why Master-Gowgwart-Love has given us a sign in the dahlia garden, so we can guide him to her," The Big Bright Star says.

The HoneyBee Stars say, "Joy and Happiness too."

The Big Bright Star replies, "Yes. That's what Geossuth needs right now."

"Let's help Master-Gowgwart-Love and friends so Geossuth can believe in her magic again," the HoneyBee Stars say.

The Big Bright Star says, "Yes. Let's help him be free again."

The HoneyBee Stars form a heart with a happy face.

·   ·   ·

Geossuth looks up at the sky, trying to find an answer to his question, and instead, he sees a cluster of stars moving around Clear Rock Crystal House.

Geossuth thinks, "At least something is bright tonight. Hmm." He stares at the distant glimmer. "Are the stars pointing to Clear Rock Crystal House?" he asks.

He looks at the Clear Rock Crystal House, and sees the colors red, yellow, and orange.

"I wonder who's in Clear Rock Crystal House right now?"

"Is it a sign from Master-Gowgwart-Love? Is it? I know she gives signs. Uh. She gave signs to Rayïq and Luseïe. The colors keep moving inside the house, but from this distance yeo can't clearly see who or what is inside," Geossuth says.

He begins to walk to the Clear Rock Crystal House.

Geossuth thinks, "I don't get it. This is weird. More like Mazeïe Park in Pherrïland. Why do I see these colors moving inside Clear Rock Crystal House? I must remember something of everything I learned listening to my friends' stories."

In a flash of a second, Geossuth sees the colors disappearing. "Oh, no, no, no!" he cries.

"I don't see the colors anymore, but I can see that the house isn't empty," he says.

Geossuth cannot see exactly what it is, but as he gets closer to the house, he sees . . .

.   .   .

Geossuth stops. Surprised, he says, "Balloons! What? Lots of peach balloons. The house is full of balloons. Nah." He shakes his head and says, "No way."

He's walking towards the Clear Rock Crystal House and with a playful voice, he says, "You have to be joking. Balloons! No! Peach Balloons? This must be a funny joke from my friends. I'm sure Rayïq did it. He probably teamed up with Luseïe. Those two like to play."

Geossuth arrived. He's standing outside the Clear Rock Crystal House, right in front of the door. "Come on, guys! I know it's you. Start popping those balloons [chuckles]. Silly joke that. It's not my birthday," he says.

A gloomy voice says, "I'm not just balloons, nor your friends."

Geossuth replies, "Definitely not my friends."

He thinks, "I wanna open the door, but after hearing the voice coming from inside the house, whatever is inside, it's more than just peach balloons and I don't know if it's good or bad."

"Come in and you will see who I am," the gloomy voice says.

"I changed my mind. I don't wanna know who you are. No, I am sure you're telling me the truth. You're not my friends, and nor are you Master-Gowgwart-Love," Geossuth replies.

He thinks, "From what I have learned from my friends' stories, Master-Gowgwart-Love has a gentle voice. This voice I hear sounds somber. Also, I remember I've been feeling incredibly sad lately and I'm worried that the voice yeo hears it's that of Master-Gowgwart-Sadness."

"I am keeping you from being joyful and happy," the gloomy voice says.

"I might be right. But if so, I'm not ready to face Sadness. I'd better go," Geossuth murmurs.

Geossuth turns to leave the Clear Rock Crystal House, but just then he remembers . . .

"Ufaïa met Master-Gowgwart-Sadness at Mazeïe Park, and the color of Sadness is peach. Sadness grows, and the Clear Rock Crystal House is full of peach balloons. If Ufaïa overcame Sadness, so can I. I choose to be brave; I will face my emotions. Yeo can't continue to run away from them," Geossuth thinks.

The gloomy voice says, "Allow yourself to recognize me."

Geossuth turns around. He says, "There it is again."

"Stop repressing me and instead acknowledge me," the gloomy voice says.

Geossuth thinks, "Am I sad? Perhaps, I've been sad ever since she left. I thought I was angry, but I may have been subconsciously hiding my true feelings, and it is Sadness that I feel. I must admit I haven't been at my best lately. What other possibilities are there? I must confirm that it's Sadness inside the Clear Rock Crystal House. I'm gonna ask."

"Who's inside?" Geossuth asks, bravely. "I'm not afraid to find out." He steps forward, his jaw set.

The gloomy voice responds, "Oh, you want to know. Finally. I will show you."

Immediately the balloons begin to pop one by one, sparkling a gentle breeze of peach crystals all over the house.

The gloomy voice begins to sing, "Shortly You Will See."

Meanwhile, Geossuth looks impatiently, waiting to see if he is right.

·   ·   ·

After the gloomy voice finishes singing and the balloons pop, the door opens with a creaking sound. His gaze was at once drawn to what was hiding behind the balloons, creating a surprise reaction.

Geossuth speaks, "I was right! I knew it!" He steps inside the Clear Rock Crystal House.

Geossuth, are you ready to face your emotions?

The gloomy voice asks, "Do you see me now?"

Geossuth replies, "Mm-hmm. Why are you so small?"

The gloomy voice responds, "You see me small, but the pain I have caused you is greater."

"You've caused me a lot of pain. Huh?" Geossuth asks.

The gloomy voice responds, "Each balloon that popped inside this house, represents every tear you shed after your mother passed away."

Geossuth thinks, "My. Mom. Died. That's why I never heard from her again."

"You've been so sad that you pushed Master-Gowgwart-Love and friends away, giving me life. You couldn't even see the signs," the gloomy voice says.

Geossuth thinks, "So that means the signs were from Master-Gowgwart-Love . . ."

"Even after hearing all those hopeful stories from your friends, you were not able to recognize who I am," the gloomy voice says.

Geossuth says, "Not at first, but now yeo know who you are. You are like a superhero in The Six Kingdoms. Gowgwart-Sadness. A negative emotion in disguise, with magical powers . . . A powerful one. Correction, you are Master-Gowgwart-Sadness."

"See? I remember."

"I was almost certain that it was you, but now I know it's you," Geossuth says.

Master-Gowgwart-Sadness says, "It's been twenty years since I joined you, and here we are, still together."

Geossuth replies, "Twenty years is how long it's been since I thought my mom abandoned me."

Master-Gowgwart-Sadness asks, "Don't you think that I need a break from your Gowgwart-Sadness?"

Geossuth asks, "Why do you say that? It's not like I wanna be sad. For real. Who wants to be sad?"

Master-Gowgwart-Sadness says, "You don't want to let me go. Don't you see?"

Geossuth says, "That's not true. I wanna meet Love. I wanna feel joy, happiness, and peace."

"Then, I will help you," Master-Gowgwart-Sadness says.

"I don't understand you," Geossuth replies.

Master-Gowgwart-Sadness says, "I'm not good for you when you don't know how to embrace the *goodness* in me. But as soon as you do, I become a source of optimism, warmth, contentment, and comfort for you."

"How can you be all those good things?" Geossuth asks.

Master-Gowgwart-Sadness replies, "My color is a source of my magic, a goodness that neutralizes the negativity in me and stimulate positive feelings, so you can be calmer and more relaxed."

Geossuth says, "For a long time, I thought I was angry. I even acted angry."

Master-Gowgwart-Sadness says, "It's normal to lose awareness of your emotions. Over time, you start to mix them up and can end up burying your true feelings."

"You're right. I thought I was angry. Now, I realize I am sad. I am sad. I feel sad. It feels good to say it. Sad," Geossuth says.

"That's why I am here," Master-Gowgwart-Sadness says.

Geossuth replies, "I know after twenty years I must let you go, Sadness."

Master-Gowgwart-Sadness says, "Thanks. It's time to embrace the goodness in me so you can have Gowgwart-Sadness back and are able to welcome the positive emotions."

"It doesn't sound easy, but it's the right thing to do," he says.

"There are things you cannot control in your life, but you can control how you react to those things. Remember that you're writing your own destiny and that amid adversity it's important to stay calm and be optimistic," Master-Gowgwart-Sadness says.

"I need to remember all the good times I spent with my mom as a child. In the end, the ten years we spent together were the best of my life. She was a good mom, and she wouldn't want me to be sad. I will always hold her close to my heart," Geossuth smiles, sadly.

"I am starting to fade away," Master-Gowgwart-Sadness says.

"It's working, Master-Gowgwart-Sadness! Soon, I will set you free and there will be no more Sadness," Geossuth says excitedly.

"You must reflect to find meaning in your suffering," Master-Gowgwart-Sadness says.

"It's not that easy," Geossuth replies.

"Find contentment in your reality. Your music. Through your music, you bring comfort and warmth to people. And it's all thanks to your suffering," Master-Gowgwart-Sadness says.

Geossuth says, "There's goodness in my suffering. Everyone in The Six Kingdoms loves my music. Without suffering, I wouldn't have been able to play the way I do."

Master-Gowgwart-Sadness says, "Embrace your suffering and you will let me go . . ."

Geossuth replies, "You lift me up, Master-Gowgwart-Sadness. For real."

"I told you I'm good too," Master-Gowgwart-Sadness says.

"It's time to let you go, Master-Gowgwart-Sadness," Geossuth replies.

Master-Gowgwart-Sadness replies, "I know. I am fading away. Soon you will be in control of your Gowgwart-Sadness."

"Adïour, Master-Gowgwart-Sadness," Geossuth says.

"Farewell, Geossuth," Master-Gowgwart-Sadness says fading.

.   .   .

Geossuth sits on the floor and, while shedding tears, begins to reflect on the past twenty years. He cries, not because he's sad but because he cannot understand how he remained in the company of Sadness for so many years.

Geossuth thinks, "It only took the spirit of Master-Gowgwart-

Sadness to appear in my life for me to recognize her, and to accept that it was time to face life differently, so that I could embrace my suffering in a positive way. Otherwise, I wouldn't have been able to be free from Sadness by embracing the goodness in her."

.   .   .

Geossuth begins to feel calm, and positive emotions begin to bloom again. The Clear Rock Crystal House is illuminated with the colors red, yellow, and orange sparkling in the air. He is in awe. He cannot believe what his eyes can see.

Master-Gowgwart-Love speaks, "Oh dear. We are back!"

"You?" Geossuth asks.

She replies, "I am Master-Gowgwart-Love, and these are my friends Master-Gowgwart-Joy and Master-Gowgwart-Happiness."

"The colors, red, yellow, and orange," Geossuth says.

"It's all of us! . . . A sparkle of me will help you smile," Master-Gowgwart-Happiness says as sparkling orange crystals pop out from her ears. Geossuth, instantly smiles.

"Love, Joy, and Happiness! It was you, here, earlier today. You disappeared so fast," Geossuth says.

"Forsooth! We're so very glad you can see our colors," Master-Gowgwart-Joy says in a cheerful voice.

Geossuth says, "Things have changed. I can finally see you as you are. Before, I imagined you through my friends' stories, but now I can see you through mine. It was you! You were here before I met Master-Gowgwart-Sadness."

"We came earlier to help you recognize your feelings, so you could let go of Sadness to balance your emotions. But after you met Master-Gowgwart-Sadness, your ability to embrace your suffering in a positive way has freed you from her and has calmed your Anger, enabling our powers," Master-Gowgwart-Love says.

"That's why we're back," Master-Gowgwart-Joy says.

With enthusiasm, gleefully, Master-Gowgwart-Happiness says, "We bring a sparkle of positivity. Grin, grin, grin, grin with delight!" Geossuth grinned with delight at Master-Gowgwart-Happiness.

Master-Gowgwart-Joy says, "That's right. What you have done tonight has made you stronger."

Master-Gowgwart-Love says, "Be proud of yourself for being brave enough to embrace Sadness."

Geossuth replies, "It wasn't easy to face my emotions, but yeo finally let go of Sadness, and I'm now in control of it."

"You are a brave young man. You did the right thing," Master-Gowgwart-Happiness says.

Geossuth says, "I hope my mom is proud of me."

Master-Gowgwart-Joy replies, "Be certain that she is."

"I don't understand why my dad said she left us. Why did he lie to me?" Geossuth asks.

Master-Gowgwart-Love responds, "Oh, I can answer that! The night before you found the Gowgwarts' Bracelet in your mother's room, she died in a terrible car accident. The car she drove exploded with her trapped inside, and the only thing left of her—found at the scene—was the Gowgwarts' Bracelet, later returned to your father upon receiving news of the accident."

"That must have been the hardest night of his life," he says.

"Your father was devastated; that night he cried a river of tears until he fell asleep," Master-Gowgwart-Love replies.

He says, "That's probably why I heard him crying angrily from my room." Geossuth is shocked by the facts revealed.

Master-Gowgwart-Love replies, "The next day when he woke-up, he didn't know how to tell you the news, but he knew he needed to be strong for you. So, since your father wasn't strong enough to come forward with the truth, he told you a different story."

"That she left us," Geossuth replies.

"Your father thought it was better for you to think she was still alive somewhere in The Six Kingdoms rather than knowing she had passed away," Master-Gowgwart-Love says.

"My dad was my role model," Geossuth says.

"I know it sounds awful but, your father was in a lot of pain at the time, and he did what he thought it was best for you and him," Master-Gowgwart-Love replies.

"He cared for me, loved me. But I get it, he wanted to protect me. He always did what he thought was best for me," Geossuth says.

Master-Gowgwart-Happiness replies, "You must be proud of your father for showing strength in the face of pain."

Master-Gowgwart-Joy says, "Love is harmony and that's what you received from him."

"I just needed to know the truth and that's why I needed you," Geossuth says.

"What matters is that you now know your mother always loved you. She didn't abandon you," Master-Gowgwart-Love replies.

"My bad. Yeo made a mistake. A terrible mistake. My emotions pushed me. And look at me now, I just threw the only thing I had left of my mom into the waters of Lake Flurmieda," Geossuth says.

Master-Gowgwart-Love says, "Oh dear, about that, I meant to say earlier that you found the Gowgwarts' Bracelet in the trash can by accident."

"By accident?" Geossuth asks.

Master-Gowgwart-Love replies, "Forsooth! The bracelet fell in the trash can by accident. In fact, your father was planning to give you the bracelet the next day, but when he returned to his room to get it, the bracelet was gone. Later, after he saw you wearing it, he decided not to say a word."

Geossuth replies, "All this time I thought it was my mom who threw it away. It turned out to be an accident."

"The truth is, it's our fault," Master-Gowgwart-Love replies.

"Why is it your fault?" Geossuth asks.

"We were supposed to retrieve the Gowgwarts' Bracelet after your mother passed away. In the end, those were her emotions, not yours. Unfortunately, you found it before we brought it back to our workshop," Master-Gowgwart-Love responds.

"That explains a lot," Geossuth replies.

"You can only summon your emotions from your Gowgwarts' Bracelet, and for that, you need to complete your training to receive it. That's when we're notified in our workshop that you are ready to carry your emotions. Then, the emotions go inside the crystal stones of your Gowgwarts' Bracelet, and that's when we deliver it to you in the Gowgwarts' gift box with a personalized note from us, and the description of the powers of the crystal stones," Master-Gowgwart-Love says.

"That makes sense. Now I understand why I couldn't summon them when I was pressing the stars on the Gowgwarts' Bracelet that belonged to my mom. Since you never appeared in my life before, I thought you weren't real and that you only existed for everyone but me," Geossuth says.

"Not your Gowgwarts' Bracelet," Master-Gowgwart-Joy says.

"Yes. Now I get it. I was wrong. It was an accident," Geossuth replies.

"Oh dear, that was a terrible accident, but after you threw the Gowgwarts' Bracelet into the waters of Lake Flurmieda, we brought it back to our workshop," Master-Gowgwart-Love says.

"From now on, you will carry your own emotions in the crystal stones of your Gowgwarts' Bracelet," Master-Gowgwart-Joy says.

"You mean, like, right now?" Geossuth asks.

"Soon enough, Geossuth," Master-Gowgwart-Joy replies.

"Really? Geossuth asks excitedly.

"You already know everything about us . . . Luseïe even taught you how to use the Gowgwarts' Bracelet. And through your friends' stories, you've learned everything about the powers of all fourteen Gowgwarts," Master-Gowgwart-Love responds.

Master-Gowgwart-Joy asks, "Art thou ready to embrace thy emotions?"

Geossuth smiles feeling happy. "Forsooth!" he replies.

Master-Gowgwart-Happiness says, "He is ready for a thrilling new beginning."

"I feel primed!" Geossuth replies.

"Take the Gowgwarts' Bracelet and wear it with pride. You've earned it," Master-Gowgwart-Joy says, giving him the Gowgwarts' gift box.

"Oh, *tagrascïe!*" Geossuth replies.

"Soon you'll know what my final gift is for everyone," Master-Gowgwart-Love says.

Geossuth replies, "Mmm. There's a final gift . . ."

.   .   .

It's 7:00 a.m. and it's the last breakfast at Clear Rock Crystal House.

The alarm is ringing on Geossuth's phone. Geossuth hears the alarm. He wakes up, and the first thing he does is to smile.

Geossuth says, "Love did it again. Yeo was dreaming."

Geossuth is trying to turn off the alarm, when suddenly he sees a crystal gold sparkle not too far from him. "That's the Gowgwarts' gift box Master-Gowgwart-Joy gave me!" He sighs. "It is real and there's a note just like they said. I mastered my emotions."

The Gowgwarts' gift box sitting there, right next to his phone, with the note.

He turns off the alarm and at last, reads the note:

"Dear Geossuth,
Continue to foster harmony among your emotions to embrace their powers.
Remember, all emotions are good if you see the goodness in them.
The powers of the crystal stones are inside the gift box—use them wisely.
You are now the master of your emotions.
—Love and friends!"

Geossuth says, "Well, in the end, it wasn't just a dream—and they also sent me a reminder of the powers of each of them."

Geossuth smiles, puts on the Gowgwarts' Bracelet, and then puts away the Gowgwarts' gift box in his silver Ūmieda suitcase—filled with all his belongings.

He feels at peace, free, happy, and joyful. He is excited to know what the final gift is.

Eleven

The Final Gift

Chef Glüedo wakes up with the sunrise at 5:28 a.m.

"Hello, Chef Glüedo," Master-Gowgwart-Love says.

"Gowgwart-Love? I didn't summon you," he says.

"Dear, it's me—the master of all Gowgwarts," she replies.

"What are you doing there standing by the window next to my bed?" Chef Glüedo asks.

"I suppose what you mean is, '*good morning, Love.*'" Sparkling crystals pop out from her ears.

"It's lovely to see you," Master-Gowgwart-Love says.

"Sorry, Master-Gowgwart-Love, I'm not wearing my glasses," he says, putting his glasses on.

"Now, I can see you clearly . . . It's lovely to see you, Master-Gowgwart-Love. Is everything okay? Why this sudden visit?" Chef Glüedo asks.

"Oh, yes. I need your help this morning, Chef Glüedo. I have an assignment for you," Master-Gowgwart-Love replies.

"Always ready and available to help," Chef Glüedo replies.

"I'd like to share my final gift with everyone during breakfast at Clear Rock Crystal House today," Master-Gowgwart-Love says.

"Ooh, does that mean, they are . . . All of them, huh?" Chef Glüedo asks.

Master-Gowgwart-Love responds, "Yes! They are ready now,

just like you once were."

Chef Glüedo asks, "Will all the Master Gowgwarts be with you this morning?"

"Now that everyone joining us for breakfast this morning at the Clear Rock Crystal House has received the Gowgwarts' Bracelet, all Master Gowgwarts will gather to share words of wisdom with them," Master-Gowgwart-Love responds.

"Mmm. That's good news. Very, so so very good news," Chef Glüedo says. "All Gowgwarts are good, but only to those who have completed their training with you and your friends."

"I want you to get creative. Please, help me give them a hint," Master-Gowgwart-Love says.

Chef Glüedo replies, "Noodle-noodle-dough! Count on me, Master-Gowgwart-Love."

"Thank you, Chef Glüedo," Master-Gowgwart-Love replies.

Chef Glüedo says, "You're welcome, Master-Gowgwart-Love. Adïour."

.   .   .

"Master-Gowgwart-Love gave me a tricky task."

"What kind of breakfast I'm gonna prepare for everyone?"

"Should yeo use fruits, or vegetables?"

"Maybe turn it into an Ūlïe feast."

"Think Glüedo-do. Uh, a traditional Bloomïeda breakfast with cceïebbu, üossant, yëorh-eggs, berry jammeïe, eh. Perhaps, combine all the cuisines of The Six Kingdoms. Oh! Oh! Oh! Noodle-noodle-dough! Yeo got it! Tagrascïe imagination . . . I will create a unique experience that will at the same time give everyone a clue about the *final* gift of Master-Gowgwart-Love. In the end, their last breakfast at Clear Rock Crystal House certainly isn't going to be just an *adïour*, but a celebration with all the Master Gowgwarts."

Chef Glüedo says, "I hope everyone is ready for a breakfast with wisdom."

.   .   .

And while everyone is packing to go home . . .

"It's a beautiful, bright, sunny morning; perfect weather with fresh air, no clouds, and plenty of sunshine," Chef Glüedo says as he's working his magic with the meat, eggs, and bread in the kitchen, outside the Clear Rock Crystal House, to give everyone a clue about Master-Gowgwart-Love's final gift.

Chef Glüedo thinks, "I want a fun, creative, and unexpected breakfast—a delicious magical breakfast full of emotions and gifts."

While Chef Glüedo is preparing breakfast, he says, "Today we have—" Geossuth interrupts. "A beautiful morning," he laughs.

"Run-sun-run!" Chef Glüedo says, dropping the jïegy batter ladle from his right hand.

"Heïjour! Chef Glüedo! It's Geossuth," he says with a pleasant voice.

"Aah, paccürs. You scared me, Sir. Heïjour or good morning, it's all the same," Chef Glüedo replies.

"Sorry, chef. Let me help you clean that up," Geossuth says, a puzzled look on his face as he glances around, searching for a rag to help clean up the mess.

"Gïocs. You're early today," Chef Glüedo replies.

"Usïcs! That's because Master-Gowgwart-Love will join us for breakfast," Geossuth replies.

Chef Glüedo replies, "Aaahh, I heard you finally met Master-Gowgwart-Love."

"Uh-huh, last night. It was magical and unexpected. But that's how Master-Gowgwart-Love is; out of the whoop whoop, but with sparkles," Geossuth replies.

"Mm-hmmm. That's a clever way to put it, Sir. She's Sprinkle-sprinkle-sparkles! Shimmer-glitter-dust!" Chef Glüedo chuckles.

"That's funny! Sugar-candy-honey!" Geossuth chuckles.

Chef Glüedo giggles. He says "Good one, Sir! I'm gonna add it to my list."

· · ·

"I'm very hungry and a little overexcited to know what it is that she . . ." Geossuth says.

"Excuse me, Sir? Did she tell you about the final gift?" Chef Glüedo asks.

"Well, not exactly, but yeo know she'll share it soon, and today is our last breakfast here. You seem to know about the final gift, chef. Do you know anything?" Geossuth asks, curiously.

"Oh, oh, oh, usïcs!" Chef Glüedo says, nodding.

"In that case, can you give me a hint about the final gift? . . ." Geossuth asks.

"It's a surprise, Sir," Chef Glüedo replies.

"Please . . . chef," Geossuth begs.

"Paccürs. I'll give you a piece of candy," Chef Glüedo replies.

"Tagrascïe!" Geossuth replies, a smile on his face.

"The theme is 'The Gift,'" Chef Glüedo replies.

Gasping, Geossuth replies, "Aaah . . . wow. Sprinkle-sprinkle-sparkles! Can I help you set the table?"

"Honey-butter-jïegy! Gïocs, Sir. That's my job," Chef Glüedo responds.

"Oh, please, Chef Glüedo, let me help you. I don't think there's anything wrong with a little help setting up the table. Please, please,

please, let me be useful," Geossuth replies, begging to help.

"Paccürs, Sir. You can start with the honey-butter-jïegy," Chef Glüedo replies.

"Haha. Paccürs. Gïocs kidding. You are funny, Chef Glüedo," Geossuth says.

.   .   .

"Good morning, Geossuth! Am I late?" Haiokïto asks.

Geossuth responds, "Heïjour, Haiokïto!" he shakes his head.

"Sorry, I had a long night last night. Packing and everything," Haiokïto says.

"Sure. I follow. Is Huïumi on her way?" Geossuth asks.

"Usïcs. She should be here shortly. You know how it is. Must make sure everything is in place before returning to the city of the Garden of Joy," Haiokïto responds.

"Cool. I'm just so excited for our last breakfast, that, you know. Up with the sun this morning. Yeo arrived a little earlier," Geossuth says.

With delight, Haiokïto replies, "That's great, my friend! Let us see what Chef Glüedo has prepared for breakfast. Come!"

.   .   .

They head to the dining room.

Haiokïto asks, "Good morning, Chef Glüedo, what do we have for breakfast today?"

"Good morning, Sir. Well, today everyone will have a very special breakfast. The theme is 'The Gift,'" Chef Glüedo responds.

Gasping, Haiokïto says, "Oh, wow. I'm in awe. You definitely got creative with breakfast today. Everything looks so much fun and colorful. This is quite unexpected and unique. It looks so delicious and full of gifts."

"Tagrascïe, Sir," Chef Glüedo replies.

.　.　.

"Heïjour! Morning!" Huïumi says.

"She's here, Haiokïto," Geossuth says.

"Heïjour, Huïumi! We're coming," Geossuth yells.

"Morning, dear. How are you? Tired?" Haiokïto asks.

"Ugh. So tired from packing, but glad to see you. Mmm. Smells good," Huïumi responds.

"Hey! Look who's here," Geossuth says.

"Good morning!" Maiephis says. "Am I a little late?" she asks.

"Gïocs. Right on time for breakfast," Huïumi replies.

"Oh, great! This is it. Our last breakfast before heading back to the city of the Garden of Joy," Maiephis says.

"Heïjour! Is there still breakfast? Yeo overslept," Ufaïa says.

Rayïq whispers to Ufaïa, "Sure, there is silly . . . I can smell the yëorh-eggs."

"Oops, I can smell it too," Ufaïa replies, "(be present Ufaïa, not now please)."

"Good morning, 'forces!'" Rayïq says.

"Joureïe! Yeo woke-up with the sun," Geossuth replies.

"Ɖawn-dustɛr. The sun rose before me . . ." Ufaïa says, "(like always, that's me)."

"The inseparable 'forces' are here," Huïumi says.

"Heïjour, 'forces!' Mmm. Yeo can smell a delicious breakfast," Luseïe says.

"Heï-good-jour, 'forces!' You're glowing. This place suits you," Geossuth replies.

Everyone says, "Tagrascïe! Tagrascïe! Tagrascïe! Thanks!"

"Right on time for our last breakfast here, at Clear Rock Crystal House," Haiokïto says.

Rayïq replies, "We are excited, but not that excited because we don't wanna leave."

Everyone says, "Yes. Usïcs. Usïcs."

"It looks like everyone enjoyed their time here, and that makes me very happy. You can always come back. The doors are open for everyone," Haiokïto says.

Everyone says, "Tagrascïe. Tagrascïe, Haiokïto. Usïcs. Paccürs. Tagrascïe. Thanks. Sure."

. . .

Haiokïto says, "Chef Glüedo has gone an extra mile preparing our last breakfast today. Come and see, I have a surprise."

Ufaïa gasps. "Awe. Look at the table," she says.

"The breakfast is serendipitous," Rayïq says.

"It seems like breakfast is all about gifts today," Luseïe says.

"Mm-hmmm. You're spot on. The theme of breakfast is, 'The Gift,'" Geossuth replies.

"I'm gonna take photos of the breakfast," Ufaïa says.

"Huïumi, let's take a selfie," Luseïe says.

"Usïcs! With breakfast. Come, Maie and Rayïq," Ufaïa says.

"Geossuth, there's room for you and you Haiokïto. Come take a selfie with us," Ufaïa says.

Chef Glüedo asks, "How about a photo of everyone together to remember this breakfast?"

Everyone says, "Paccürs. Sure. Usïcs. Usïcs. Yes!"

Hïuramïur says, "Don't forget about me!"

Huïumi yells, "Hïuramïur!"

Hïuramïur grinding, says, "Heïjour, everyone!"

Everyone smiles, eyes on Hïuramïur, surprised by his sudden appearance.

Huïumi asks, "How did you get here? You promised to behave this weekend."

Geossuth says, "He certainly behaved."

Ufaïa says, "I don't think he listened."

Maiephis says, "Pleasant surprise."

Luseïe says, "Brainy-genius. Well done."

Rayïq waves his hands dramatically. "Magic! Poof!" he says.

Hïuramïur replies, "I had to do it. I wanted to meet the owner of thy heart. So, I packed myself in the extra bag you didn't pack. I have been hiding all this time. I even learned from all of your stories about harmony, love, and not giving up. And including Hïuramïur in your trip. Not leave Hïuramïur behind."

Huïumi replies, "That's *cookūn*, Hïuramïur! The things you do. You don't stop surprising me. Come here and meet Haiokïto."

Haiokïto says, "Welcome Hïuramïur, so nice to meet you."

Hïuramïur replies, "I am her protector, take good care of her heart, or else this isn't a nice to meet you." Hïuramïur raises his right eyebrow.

Haiokïto replies, "Deepïery thögh. You got it!" his voice had a tremble to it.

Huïumi asks, "Are you happy now, Hïuramïur?"

Hïuramïur replies, "Yes. I'm glad I finally met the owner of thy heart." His voice had a confident tone.

Haiokïto says, "Alright, let's take a group photo now."

Haiokïto gives his phone to Chef Glüedo to take the photo.

As everyone gathers around to take the group photo, Master-Gowgwart-Love magically appears.

Chef Glüedo takes the photo, he says, "Look behind you."

Red crystal sparkles everywhere, Master-Gowgwart-Love flies inside the Clear Rock Crystal House.

Chef Glüedo says, "Enjoy the sparkles."

Everyone surprised to see Master-Gowgwart-Love in the Clear Rock Crystal House, with emotion says, "Love! Love!" Except for Ufaïa, who, after everyone else, says, "M-G-Ło!"

Master-Gowgwart-Love says, "Oh, hello! Are you ready for a breakfast with emotions?"

Everyone replies, "Yes! Yes! Paccürs! Usïcs! Usïcs!"

"Great! The Master Gowgwarts will join. Let's have breakfast, shall we?" Master-Gowgwart-Love asks.

Luseïe says, "Wait! Did Geossuth meet you? Geossuth?" she asks.

Geossuth responds, "Ooh. Me? Yes! I met Master-Gowgwart-Love last night. Here, in this house, it's where it all happened with balloons and all that thing that you already know."

"Really? Like, really? Balloons, really?" Luseïe asks.

Master-Gowgwart-Love replies, "We had a wonderful time last night, right Geossuth?"

Geossuth responds, "Yes! I met Master Gowgwarts: Love, Joy, and Happiness. Oh, and Sadness. I have to say that sometimes we think we're ready to face unexpected challenges; however, no matter how prepared we may think we are, there are things/events we can't avoid and that perhaps . . . are even necessary for our own personal growth. And thanks to all of you and everything I learned from your stories; I faced Sadness and embraced the goodness in her."

Master-Gowgwart-Love says, "That's right, Geossuth now has his own Gowgwarts' Bracelet."

Geossuth shows his Gowgwarts' Bracelet to everyone.

· · ·

With sparkling crystals shining in the color of each Gowgwart, all Master Gowgwarts appear inside the Clear Rock Crystal House.

All Master Gowgwarts say, "Together, we stand for . . ."

"Strength, willpower," Master-Gowgwart-Love says.

"Compassion, friendship," Master-Gowgwart-Care says.

"Stability, loyalty," Master-Gowgwart-Trust says.

"Calmness, safety," Master-Gowgwart-Peace says.

"Creativity, wisdom," Master-Gowgwart-Freedom says.

"Positivity, hope," Master-Gowgwart-Joy says.

"Optimism, enthusiasm," Master-Gowgwart-Happiness says.

"Growth, renewal," Master-Gowgwart-Pain says.

"Serenity, uplifting," Master-Gowgwart-Fear says.

"Trustworthiness, relaxation," Master-Gowgwart-Shame says.

"Contentment, comfort," Master-Gowgwart-Sadness says.

"Forgiveness, honesty," Master-Gowgwart-Guilt says.

"Patience, weightlessness," Master-Gowgwart-Anger says.

"Safety, resilience," Master-Gowgwart-Depression says.

"In here, we are the masters of all emotions—a genuine open life development opportunity, available to everyone willing to create harmony among their emotions," Master-Gowgwart-Love says.

Geossuth says, "You're the superheroes of The Six Kingdoms . . ."

"In our world, Pherriland, your emotions receive our wisdom through our master classes or better said, Gowgwart classes, until they're ready to return to you in your Gowgwarts' Bracelet. The time difference between our worlds gives us an advantage with time . . ." Master-Gowgwart-Love says.

"That means time runs slow here compared to your world. Am I right?" Huïumi asks with doubt.

"Yes! That's correct!" Master-Gowgwart-Freedom replies.

"I remember, Rayïq. You said it in your story," Geossuth says.

Huïumi rolls her eyes. She says, "Ugh, yeo forgot. I must have been distracted when you were saying that." Huïumi sighs, looking disappointed for not remembering the time difference in Pherrïland.

"Your emotions have enough time to be trained, just like you to become the master of them," Master-Gowgwart-Depression says.

Maiephis interrupts him. She asks, "What if we don't want to become the masters of our emotions?"

Ufaïa responds, "Don't you think you're a little late to ask that question?"

"Taccgrah! You don't know why she asks," Luseïe says.

"Gee! Luseïe is right," Maiephis says.

"My bad. Back to the emotions please," Ufaïa says.

"If you're not willing to accept our help, your emotions will be all over the place. Like, really, all over the place," Master-Gowgwart-Joy replies.

Master-Gowgwart-Pain adds, "Also, it can lead to challenging everyday situations where you might experience stress and anxiety, affecting your daily performance in different tasks and even in your physical health. To sum up, emotional instability isn't good for you."

"That's why I send you signs hoping you will hear my voice on time," Master-Gowgwart-Love says.

"We want you to see the goodness in us," Master-Gowgwart-Fear says.

Master-Gowgwart-Trust says, "Our goal is to bring stability to your life."

"We also want you to remain positive and optimistic," Master-Gowgwart-Happiness says.

"So that you have serenity and a glimmer of happiness thanks to the goodness you see in your suffering through the opportunities we bring in our teachings," Master-Gowgwart-Sadness says.

Master-Gowgwart-Anger says, "So that your emotions can be locked within the crystal stones in the Gowgwarts' Bracelet crafted in our workshop."

Master-Gowgwart-Shame says, "That we present to you in the Gowgwarts' gift box after you have completed your training."

Master-Gowgwart-Care says, "That also includes a description of our powers, so you don't forget them."

Master-Gowgwart-Freedom says, "And so that you continually create harmony among your emotions."

Master-Gowgwart-Peace says, "And you be calm and therefore have a better life."

Master-Gowgwart-Love says, "We want you to be the masters of your emotions."

Geossuth says, "Maie, I don't think you'll get a better answer than that."

Maiephis replies, "I only asked because of my mama. But not everyone is brave and strong to face their emotions like us."

Huïumi says, "Be strong and brave for them. Become the one person they look-up to. Do it for you and do it for those that didn't do it for them. Do it for future generations."

Maiephis replies, "You're right, Huïumi. Hear, hear, for future generations."

All, including the Master Gowgwarts, say, "Hear, hear!"

.　.　.

Luseïe asks, "So, like, in your workshop you oversee everyone's emotions."

"Forsooth! In our workshop we oversee everything related to your emotions. Like, when your emotions are in danger of becoming unknown to you and also, when they're about to become a threat to your well-being. Depending on the emotion affecting you the most, we receive alerts and since I am the master of all Gowgwarts, the masters warn me of the disruption in your emotions and that's when I begin to send you signs so that you hear my voice and I can appear in your life, to help you embrace the positive side of your emotions," Master-Gowgwart-Love replies.

Luseïe replies, "Oh, so the master of each emotion receives an alert from our emotions. I get it. That's why my Anger went to you, Master-Gowgwart-Anger, to let you know of the disruption in my emotions, and then you appeared in the darkness of the deep sea, except that I didn't know how to see the goodness in you back then, until I met you, Master-Gowgwart-Love."

Haiokïto says, "Once emotions become unknown to us, they go to the Gowgwarts' Mountïs. I mean the Gowgwarts' Workshop, where their Master Gowgwarts welcomes them in their mountïs to give them training in master classes until they are ready to go inside their crystal stones in the Gowgwarts' Bracelet."

"You've been to the Gowgwarts' Workshop!?" Luseïe gasps.

Haiokïto responds, "Mm, yes." He nods. "That's where I met Master-Gowgwart-Love."

Rayïq says, "So you've been to Pherrïland!?"

Haiokïto agrees, "Mm-hmm. Master-Gowgwart-Love gave me a map to visit the fourteen mountïs in Pherrïland—you know, the workshop where I learned about the different powers of the crystal stones. And then, through its portal, I returned to the Kingdom of Gemmïes."

Ufaïa asks, "Why didn't you say anything?"

Haiokïto says, "Hmmm. I didn't wanna get the spotlight from you."

Huïumi says, "I knew this was gonna happen."

Geossuth says, "Give him a break. We can catch up on that later. All Master Gowgwarts are here to reveal the final gift."

Huïumi says, "There is a final gift . . ."

"Is that why the theme for breakfast is 'The Gift?'" Maiephis asks.

Geossuth responds, "*Usïcs!* I mean, yes."

Maiephis says, "*Paccürs.* Haha."

Geossuth asks, "Did you just say 'paccürs?'" He smiles.

Maiephis responds, "I know what *paccürs* is. It means okay. I'm friends with you, though."

Geossuth replies, "I mean, I know you understand, but I didn't know you can speak Ūlïe. *Paccürs.*"

Maiephis says, "I don't speak Ūlïe, but I can defend myself."

Master-Gowgwart-Love says, *"Paccürs!"*

Everyone laughs.

Master-Gowgwart-Love says, "There's one last gift I want to share with you that will remind you of your inner strength to bounce back from difficult times. It is a choice you made, and it has shaped you in ways you never imagined."

Impatiently, Geossuth asks, "What's that supposed to be?"

Ufaïa asks, "Yes, what is it? Is it tangible? Edible? Cute? Cool? Sweet? Shiny? Is it in this room?"

"I don't think it's any of that. It's a choice we made. *Capïcsh?*" Luseïe replies.

"Aaah. *Capïcsh,*" Ufaïa replies, "(a choice we made)."

Master-Gowgwart-Depression says, "It's a key component of well-being to thrive in the face of adversity. It helps you have a more positive and fulfilling life experience. This is emotional resilience."

"Emotional resilience isn't something easily recognized when you see someone; rather, their strength in overcoming setbacks will reflect it in the Gowgwarts' Bracelet," Master-Gowgwart-Love says.

Master-Gowgwart-Freedom says, "No matter what form your suffering might take in your life, everyone accumulates experiences that reflect their emotions. Whether good or bad, those experiences can shape your life, and it's you who has the power to choose how those experiences can change you."

Master-Gowgwart-Trust says, "What's most important is that everyone in The Six Kingdoms can, if they want, rebuild themselves. But there's one thing I do know: if you choose to fight and believe in yourself, you can come out better on the other side."

Master-Gowgwart-Care says, "All of you have been through great suffering, but with my help and the help of my friends, you've been transformed and are now stronger than you were before."

Master-Gowgwart-Joy says, "And those who gave up on the process of rebuilding themselves to develop resilience didn't get to embrace positivity, change, and the reward of Love that comes with the light of the sun."

Master-Gowgwart-Happiness says, "If only they had just given themselves an opportunity to be hopeful and optimistic about the future, the light of the sun would have hugged them, bringing a new day full of possibilities to them."

"That's why it's important to stay calm to develop patience in your transformation process to resilience," Master-Gowgwart-Peace says.

Huïumi adds, "And to grow so as not to lose hope, because if you believe, there will be endless possibilities to find Love again."

"Never give up, and you'll receive my reward, the Gowgwarts' Bracelet. More like winning a Quartz-Stars Reïhng Bracelet in the Quartz-Stars Reïhng Championship. If you know, you know what I mean. Right, Rayïq?" Master-Gowgwart-Love says.

Rayïq responds, "*Deepïery thögh!* If you know what I mean. Of course!" He grins.

"The Quartz-Stars Reïhng Bracelet is proof that your team is the best at reïhng in The Six Kingdoms when they win the Quartz-Stars Reïhng Championship, and when the players wear the bracelet, everyone sees that they are the best reïhng athletes in their kingdom. Similarly, the two stars that click the Gowgwarts' Bracelet show that you have the strength to spring back from adverse circumstances in your life," Master-Gowgwart-Love says.

Luseïe asks, "So, does that mean the stars on the Gowgwarts' Bracelet stand for emotional resilience?"

Master-Gowgwart-Love nods. "Forsooth, dear," she says.

Ufaïa asks, "What if you decide to switch them around from time to time?"

Master-Gowgwart-Love responds, "That's fine as long as you have both bracelets and neither of them is missing."

"What if others don't recognize I have developed emotional resilience when I don't wear both bracelets as one?" Luseïe asks.

"That will be at your discretion based on how you choose to wear your emotions. In the end, my reward is not just emotional resilience, but resilience itself," Master-Gowgwart-Love replies.

Rayïq says, "We couldn't have asked for more. You have taught us that with the right attitude and a positive mindset, accompanied by emotional balance, it's possible to develop resilience no matter what the circumstances. For example, for me it was to recreate my dream. So, having the positive and negative emotions here today, it's proof that if we acknowledge our power to master our emotions, we can always be proud to wear them as we please."

Master-Gowgwart-Pain says, "When you see me, you will feel

warmth and comfort in knowing that I no longer have power over you, and it is you who now have power over me."

Master-Gowgwart-Guilt says, "When you see me, you will feel a serene forgiveness as a reminder that you were able to overcome me and are now free."

Master-Gowgwart-Anger says, "When you see me, you will feel relaxed because my color brings a calm serenity to your life, making me temporary, inspiring in you soothing peace, a sense of tranquility, and positive light."

"When you see me, you will remember you are trustworthy, and I will no longer make you feel inferior because I will remind you of your sense of self-confidence, and that will make you feel secure, respected, accepted, and confident," Master-Gowgwart-Shame says.

"When you see me, you will feel optimistic and happy because you'll remember you've become my master and know my powers," Master-Gowgwart-Sadness says.

"When you see me, you will remember everything you need is healthy boundaries, and that will uplift your mood, empowering you to be positive in everything you do," Master-Gowgwart-Fear says.

Master-Gowgwart-Depression says, "And when you see me, I will remind you of your power to bounce back from adversity. And that is resilience, the final gift of Love."

All the Master Gowgwarts sing, "Resilience."

That morning, after the Master Gowgwarts shared words of wisdom with everyone, Huïumi and her friends learned that all the suffering they went through turned into strength, allowing them to rebuild themselves and learn that suffering can also be good. After all, suffering brought Love, a new beginning full of hope, positivity, and resilience to all.

It was then, in the Clear Rock Crystal House, after the Master

Gowgwarts disappeared, that Huïumi and her friends agreed to open up to share their story with all in The Six Kingdoms, to remind them to be courageous, truthful, fearless, hopeful, and not to forget the power in them, to choose to embrace change in a positive way. They wanted to help others who, like them, at some point in their lives, found themselves suffering in a dark place, wishing to escape their emotions because they didn't know that through Love, they had the power to transform their suffering into something great. In the end, the greatest satisfaction in life one has is being able to help those in need. So, they devised a plan to organize 'The Six Forces'—a tour to share how the power of Love transformed their lives in positive ways, allowing them to rebuild themselves and to give hope to those out there looking for Love. Also, to remind the people of The Six Kingdoms that Love is within themselves and that all they need to do is to keep hope and a positive mindset.

.   .   .

Five years later, in the study room of the Clear Rock Crystal House.

Huïumi sits at her desk watching the video of her first speech in 'The Six Forces.'

"Transformation can happen in the most unexpected ways . . . Sometimes, you don't look for change when it comes to you. And that's exactly what happened to me."

"When Neephoos said in the Neephis Library that the answer to finding Love was within me and not there, I couldn't understand it until I met Love and realized that love begins with me. Besides, what I wanted then is not what I needed. What I needed was to work on my inner self to learn to love myself again. I needed to start over so I could rebuild myself. What I needed was time. I needed time to travel back, to remember my inner child, my dreams, all the simple things that gave my life meaning when life meant everything to me, before I was immersed in Pain and, and all I could see was me with Depression, alone on a dark night beneath that old leafless tree, just because I wanted to escape my life."

"For a long time, I felt unloved, rejected, and ignored by those around me, until I realized I was wrong and that I was creating my own suffering. All I needed was to shift my focus to being positive to create my own happiness. Understanding that no one is obligated to love me because Love is free, has taught me that Love is a choice I am free to make every day—a choice we are all free to make every day. If others don't choose to love me, then I'll choose myself and love myself. Because my happiness depends on me and no one else."

"It took me time to understand this and that's why it wasn't an easy journey, but with courage and strength I continued to spend time with myself until I learned the true meaning of love."

"I remember when I heard the voice of Love for the first time; it was like the sound of a flame and it felt as if the light of that flame burned in my heart. Just then, something in me changed forever."

"I started letting go, and that's when I discovered who I was. It was always there inside me, even if I didn't remember it, but with Love and her friends, I realized that to be myself, I needed to leave everyone behind, and that's when I blossomed into who I am."

"Over time I understood what Neephoos was saying and in the end, Love brought healing to my life and gave me back my identity."

"My process of healing took time, but it was worth it."

"Love is worth it!"

"I didn't understand it then; I understand it now. I am not the same anymore. Now I have Trust and learned how to embrace the negative emotions. I no longer remember Pain. I feel Freedom, Joy, and Happiness. And in the end, not only have I improved my ability to manage my emotions, but this time, I'm embracing the goodness of all emotions."

"I've developed emotional resilience, and with the Gowgwarts' Bracelet, I am proud to show you, I am resilient too."

"I've become the master of my emotions."

"Together we join forces to support one another."

"We don't know where you are in your healing journey or if you haven't met Love, but we do know that Love is watching you from where you are. Sometimes, all you need to do to welcome Love is open your heart. Love is waiting. And 'the forces' here are ready to share their wisdom with everyone. Let Love be the center of your life. And remember, Love is worth it, and you deserve it. Love is patient, gentle, compassionate, and most importantly, Love is peace. You can turn your suffering into your greatest gift, the final gift of Love—resilience."

.   .   .

Haiokïto enters the study room. Huïumi pauses the video.

"Hey honey!" Huïumi says.

"Babe, did I interrupt you? Are you watching the video of your first conference, again?" Haiokïto asks.

Smiling, Huïumi replies, "Usïcs, remembering how it all started five years ago. The clouds opened so the sun could hide its bright light, making a hole in the sky. Finally, I was able to see it clearly. As the sun moved away, the moon began to arrive, but before the moon arrived, the sun took its time and that's when everything happened, and they finally met in the sky."

Haiokïto says, "The greatest second chance given to me in my entire life."

Huïumi replies, "You are my sun."

Haiokïto replies, "And you are my moon. Thanks to Love, we are whole."

Huïumi says, "I love us."

Haiokïto kisses her and says, "You're my greatest gift. Oh, and I made dinner tonight. See you in a bit."

Huïumi smiles and Haiokïto leaves the room.

Huïumi plays the video again.

Huïumi speaking, "And this is what I wanted to share with all of you. I am brave enough to put my emotions out there for you. In the end, what I needed turned out to be everything . . . and so much more than what I wanted. Now I have it all. Now I have true love."

.   .   .

"After Huïumi finished watching her first speech, she paused the video and drank the magical sparkles drink . . . Sparkling purple amethyst crystals appeared in the room and Huïumi disappeared, transporting herself to Pherrïland, where Master-Gowgwart-Love and I are waiting for her, here at Gleerwoo House."

"You may be wondering who is narrating these stories. It's me, The Star of the Universe, and with my powers, while Huïumi was talking with Haiokïto, I switched her peach pearl tea for the magical sparkles drink. And here she is." The Star of the Universe giggles.

Surprised, Huïumi asks, "Where in heaven? Where am I? Why is everything so red?"

The Star of the Universe says, "Hello, Huïumi."

Huïumi gasps. "Oh, oh, oh, whoa," she says.

Master-Gowgwart-Love says, "Welcome to Gleerwoo House, the home of the positive Master Gowgwarts. You're on my floor."

"Oh, whoa. This is my first time here. I cannot believe it. It's even more beautiful in person than how Rayïq described it," Huïumi says as she looks around the room. "Why am I here?" she asks.

The Star of the Universe replies, "You are expecting a baby."

"I am having a baby!? You are kidding, right?" Huïumi says, laughing nervously.

The Star of the Universe shakes her head. "No kidding. The baby you're carrying isn't any baby; she will be born with the light of the Big Bright Star," she says.

"She? I'm having a baby girl! *Taccgrah!* How is she going to carry such big light?" Huïumi asks.

The Star of the Universe replies, "With our help, she will figure it out."

Huïumi asks, "How?"

"She needs to discover the mysterious secret . . . to receive the reward hidden in the petals of the Ūmieda flower in the Garden of Joy," The Star of the Universe replies.

Huïumi gasps. "The secret from the Garden of Joy!" she says.

"Her name is Velazürei," Master-Gowgwart-Love says.

"Velazürei, a beautiful name, but it also means guarded light," Huïumi replies.

The Star of the Universe says, "The light of The Big Bright Star will glow in her in the dark, after the sunsets and until the sunrises."

Master-Gowgwart-Love says, "She will bring light to The Six Kingdoms."

The Star of the Universe says, "Her light is not just any light. Her light can only glow in her because it is a different kind of light."

"But she will be different," Huïumi says.

Master-Gowgwart-Love says, "Being different is a gift to those who are not."

"To be continued."

Glossary

Ūlïe Language

Ūlïe language is the official language spoken in the Kingdom of Ūlïe by their people, who, once upon a time conquered Kingdom of Bloomïeda, Kingdom of Zūlear, and Kingdom of Gemmïes—created as part of the fictional setting by the author.

Constructed with Latin, French, and Spanish words (with a minor twist for authenticity), the Ūlïe language pronunciation is in English. The pronunciation and definition of key terms, names, and phrases (used within the narrative) are included to help understand the fantasy world of the emotions created by the author, M.R. Livly.

Glossary:

- Adïour: (Ūlïe interjection) – Bye bye, goodbye, see you later, (pronounced "Ah-dee-oor").
- Arçaïe: (Ūlïe noun) – Motto, a guiding principle. A secret force that gives purpose to the Ūlïe people in the Kingdom of Ūlïe (pronounced "Ahr-sai").
- Azlureis: (Ūlïe proper noun) – Blue (pronounced "Ah-zlu-re-is").
- Cceïebbu: (Ūlïe dish) – Sunny side-up eggs over Bree cheese with sprinkles of honey on toasted bread (pronounced "See-ceeb-boo").
- Capïcsh: (Ūlïe verb) – To understand. Do you understand?

(Pronounced "kap-keesh").

- Cookūn: (Ūlïe adjective) – Cuckoo, loco, silly (pronounced "kuh-koon").

- Deepïery thögh: (Ūlïe adverb) – Of course. For agreement, emphasis, permission, and obviousness (pronounced "deep-airy-thoo").

- Dinguï: (Ūlïe interjection) – Oh no. Oh well (pronounced "DING-ee").

- Gemmïe: (Ūlïe noun) – Precious stone, gem, jewel. In occasions used to describe a person (pronounced "jem-ee").

- Gïocs: (Ūlïe adverb and interjection) – No. At times used as not or instead of do not (pronounced "ghee-awks").

- Gowgwart: (Proper noun) – Emotions in disguise with magical powers (pronounced "goug-wart").

- Hameïeo: (Ūlïe noun) – Means, Hanami, flower viewing in springtime—specifically cherry blossoms when they are in full bloom (pronounced "Ha-mee-oh").

- Heï-good-jour: (Ūlïe greeting) – Good morning (pronounced "hey-gud-jur").

- Heïjour: (Ūlïe greeting) – Hello. (pronounced "hey-jur").

- Jammeïe: (Ūlïe noun) – Fruit spread (pronounced "jam-mai").

- Jïegei-jïocs: (Ūlïe noun) – Popcorn, snack made by heating corn kernels until they pop (pronounced "jee-gee-jy-awks").

- Jïocs: (Ūlïe noun) – Corn (pronounced "jy-awks").

- Jïegy: (Bloomïeda dish) – Pancake—flat, round cake made of batter—fried on both sides (pronounced "jee-eg-ee").

- Joureïe: (Ūlïe expressions) – Hi. Hey. Day. Night. Is a short casual form of greeting (pronounced "jur-ee").

- Kosmïes: (Ūlïe proper noun) – Name of a band that means

Cosmos—referring to the universe ("kawz-mee-es").

- Lūneïe: (Ūlïe proper noun) – Moon. Name of hotel in Punta Ablanc, Lūneïe Hotel (pronounced "loo-nay-ee").
- Lïanda: (Zūlear drink) – Frozen Coconut Cookūn drink (pronounce "lee-ahn-da").
- Luseïe: (Ūlïe proper noun) – Light (pronounced "loo-see-ee").
- Macceïe: (Greequose dish) – A bread type inspired by Pizza (pronounced "mack-key").
- Mattheïe: (Noun) – Matcha drink (pronounced "ma-thee-ee").
- Mountïs: (Ūlïe noun) – Mountain or mountains (pronounced "mown-tis").
- Neephoos: (Proper noun) – Wisdom (pronounced "neef-oos").
- Paccürs: (Ūlïe interjection) – Okay. Sure. Show agreement; affirmation of acceptance (pronounced "pah-kurz").
- Pherrï: (Proper noun) – Wander—magical stroll (pronounced "feh-ree").
- Pherrïland: (Proper noun) – Wanderland—world of emotions. Fantastical place holding the mysteries of emotions—through and through—vividly.
- Ppucceïe: (Ūlïe noun) – Cappuccino, coffee drink—made with espresso, steamed milk, and a layer of foam (pronounced "put-cheya").
- Punta Ablanc: (Ūlïe noun) – White Point, island in Kingdom of Zūlear, Pearl Islands (pronounced "poon-tuh" "ah-blahn").
- Punta Blereuzule: (Ūlïe noun) – Aquamarine Point, island in Kingdom of Zūlear, Pearl Islands (pronounced "poon-tuh" "blur-oo-zool").
- Qomïen: (Ūlïe verb) – Go. (pronounced "ko-mee-uhn").

- Quozereis: (Proper noun) – Is a beach in the Kingdom of Greequose, known for its calm, clear waters, and white sandy beach. Perfect for long walks, with a fishing village atmosphere (pronounced "kwoh-zuh-rays").
- Räïra: (Ūlïe adjective) – Rare (pronounced "ra-ee-ra").
- Rei: (Ūlïe noun) – King (pronounced "ray-ee"). The ruler of the realm and the highest ranking noble.
- Reïhng: (Ūlïe common noun) – Ring, is a type of game or sport in The Six Kingdoms (pronounced "ray-ing").
- Roseïey: (Ūlïe noun) – Rose (pronounced "roh-zee-e").
- Rooqūo: (Greequose dessert) – Made with a variety of nuts: walnuts, pecans, raisings, and a touch of maple syrup. Served with lime Greequose yogurt and a sprinkle of toasted maple oats (pronounced "roo-koo-oh").
- Spïeral: (Ūlïe noun) – Spiral (pronounced "spee-ruhl").
- Taccgrah: (Interjection) – Gee (pronounced "takph-grah").
- Tagrascïe: (Ūlïe noun) – Thank you (pronounced "tag-ra-see").
- Ūlïe: (Ūlïe noun) – Official language of Kingdom of Ūlïe, the smallest kingdom of The Six Kingdoms. Also known as the little ones or Ūlïe people (pronounced "oo-lee").
- Üossant: (Ūlïe noun) – Croissant (pronounced "oo-sant").
- Usïcs: (Ūlïe interjection) – Yes (pronounced "u-seeks").
- Yeo: (Ūlïe pronoun) – I (pronounced "yo").
- Yëorh: (Greequose dish) – Soft creamy scrambled eggs (pronounced "ye-or").
- Yïecs: (Ūlïe noun) – Rice-belts, Ūlïe dish made with rice (pronounced "yee-ecs").
- Zūlear: (Ūlïe noun) – Archipelago (pronounced "zoo-ler").

About M.R. Livly

A new author rises from the dark-murky waters of the pond.
M.R. Livly is born, growing up with a strong passion for the arts,
exploring almost everything from theater to singing. She was part
of the performing arts writing crew in high school. She developed
characters whom she personified through performing arts. Did I
say that it was in the Dominican Republic, before she moved to
New York? No? I didn't? Well, that's where it was . . . Set on the
Caribbean, on a dreamy island, is where she was born. Later, after
moving to New York, inspired by the simple question—"Where
is love?" and an idea to bring the emotions to life in a fantastical
world—M.R. Livly wrote her first fantasy book, *Gowgwarts and the
Powers of the Crystal Stones*. Set within The Six Kingdoms and
Pherriland, her fantasy novel takes you on a powerful emotional
journey, portraying emotions vividly with full intensity and depth.

GOWGWARTS

and the Powers of the Crystal Stones

The Gowgwarts' Workshop is in motion.

The Six Kingdoms brings new adventures.

The Master Gowgwarts await thee.

It's The World of the Emotions and thou art in it.

See thee in Pherrïland . . . ☆

GOWGWARTS

GOWGWARTS

www.ingramcontent.com/pod-product-compliance
Lightning Source LLC
Chambersburg PA
CBHW021957130726
47903CB00014B/1562